LOVELY RITA

The Education of Clark Westfield
BOOK ONE

A NOVEL

RANDALL BLAIR

In memory of Dad

Claude M Blair 1913-2010

"I believe that what we become depends on what our fathers
teach us at odd moments,
when they aren't trying to teach us. We are formed by little
scraps of wisdom."

— Umberto Eco, *Foucault's Pendulum*

CHAPTER ONE

Denver, Colorado, 1963

It was a warm, spring day, the kind that holds within it the promise of summer. Lazy clouds hung over the Rocky Mountains to the west, offering no hint of any trouble that might be lurking just out of sight.

Clark Westfield sat cross-legged and quiet on the grass. He was alone on the shallow hillside that ran along the left field side of the Harrison High School baseball field. He liked to watch the Harrison High Cougars baseball team practice. They were a good team, but not an exceptional one. As they approached the end of what had been so far an uninspiring season, the team still had a slim chance to qualify for the Denver Regional High School Baseball Tournament. Over the past twenty-five years they had often been in the tournament. They had won it numerous times, but not for several years now.

Across the field from Clark, Julie Wells practiced her cheers with the rest of the Harrison High cheerleaders. Julie was a junior like Clark and one of the most popular girls in the school. Clark had had a crush on her ever since they had met the previous August at the Harrison High Welcome Day for new students. But he had barely spoken to her in the past eight months.

Today, however, neither his desire to play baseball nor his interest in Julie could override his preoccupation with The Question. It was early May, just a few days after Clark's seventeenth birthday, and any day now his father would arrive home from another business trip, and then The Question would be asked and answered. The Question meant that his father had received another work promotion, and the Westfield family would be moving to a new city over the summer. The Question always came sometime between March and early June, before the end of the school year when most kids daydreamed of swimming pools, summer camps and little league baseball. For Clark, summers only promised packing boxes, moving vans, and long, uncomfortable, car trips to new places that he would only temporarily call home.

So it had been every year since Clark was four years old.

A foul ball bounced near Clark and rolled right up to his feet. The player in left field looked over at Clark and called, "A little help?"

At first Clark didn't realize that the boy, Miguel, who was in his sixth period social studies class, had called to him. But when Miguel repeated it louder, Clark shrugged to his feet and retrieved the ball. He eyed Miguel, who held his mitt up in anticipation. Clark considered his throw. Should he throw ten yards to Miguel or should he show off and throw to the third baseman, standing some twenty yards further away? It wasn't that he couldn't make the longer throw. His decision centered solely on whether or not to call attention to himself. And that was very much complicated by the presence of Julie Wells across the field.

Hung up on his indecision, Clark threw and totally mistimed the release. The ball bounced eight feet in front of him and rolled slowly halfway to Miguel, who trotted over to retrieve it. "Uh, thanks," he mumbled, and shook his head at the astonishing display of Clark's athletic ineptitude.

Clark grabbed his black backpack and walked away quickly toward home, which was just through the woods that bordered the athletic fields.

What a spaz. Oh God, I hope she wasn't watching.

Such was Clark's life during the time of The Question.

Julie Wells had noticed Clark and his pathetic throw. She watched him hurry from the field.

What a strange boy.

She really didn't know him, yet she had felt this odd interest in him ever since meeting him the previous August. She thought he was decent looking, but he was deathly quiet. They had English together first period, and he never spoke unless the teacher made him. But then what he had to say was always interesting, intelligent, thoughtful.

She appreciated it that his short haircut, his clothes and everything about him seemed to be calculated to never call attention to himself. But that definitely wasn't her style. She had a high standard to meet as the only junior who had ever been elected captain of the Harrison High cheerleaders. She certainly looked the part of the quintessential cheerleader: long blond hair pulled into a ponytail; bright blue eyes; and a trim but full figure. Her positive personality was legendary. But it was a skin that she wasn't totally comfortable living in.

She wondered why Clark sat out there almost every day and watched practice. And he hadn't missed a single home game. But he never sat in the stands. He was always out there on the hillside, by himself.

Does he want to play?

He was tall, a little over six feet, which was three or four inches taller than Julie. And except for that throw, she thought he seemed pretty coordinated, or at least when he walked he didn't trip over his own feet.

Maybe he just likes boys.

She giggled to herself, but her instincts told her that he probably wasn't a queer.

Dad would like him, but Bea would call him a total loser.

As the thought of her mother flashed through her head, Julie panicked and looked at her watch. Julie knew that there would be hell to pay if she didn't get to the grocery store to buy her mother's cigarettes before the store closed. She looked around to tell Dwight Dunn, her boyfriend, that she was leaving, but he was on the pitcher's mound, talking to the baseball coach, Mr. Duncan. She gave Dwight a little wave, which she didn't expect him to return, then retrieved her bicycle from the bike rack next to the backstop and sped off.

* * *

At home, Clark lay on his bed and stared blankly at the ceiling. He didn't turn his head when he heard someone at his door.

"Dreaming of Julie again?" Sarah Westfield mocked in a syrupy tone. She had sensed Clark's fascination with Julie Wells and had spent the past eight months teasing him mercilessly.

"No. Why would you think that?" Clark sputtered.

"Just the goofy smile and the little bit of drool coming out of your mouth."

He impulsively wiped the corner of his mouth as he sat up. She hopped on his bed next to him, and they sat quietly for a moment.

Sarah was Clark's fraternal twin sister, but few students in their school had made that connection, partly because they looked different. She had their mother's haunting dark blue eyes and chestnut brown hair with natural blond highlights, while Clark's hazel, mostly green, eyes and dark brown hair came from their father. The biggest difference between them, however, was their personalities. Sarah's self-assured, dramatic nature had gotten her the role of Maria in the school's spring theatrical production of *West Side Story*. Whereas Clark's persona, if people noticed him at all, would be described as shadowy, ghost-like.

"Any news?" she asked. She was as curious about The Question as he was. Most of the time it was their only point of common interest.

"No. But he's coming home next weekend, so next Saturday will probably be the day."

"You really think it's coming?"

"Of course, it always does."

"Well, sure it's coming at some point, but now?"

"All the signs are there."

"But it's only the beginning of May."

"Does it really matter? You know they won't pull us out of school early. Last year it was late, mid-June, but the year before remember, early March. So it should be any time now."

She stood up and started to move slowly out of his room.

"Are you okay?" he asked. She wasn't normally this pensive.

She replied, unconvincingly, "Oh, yeah, I guess."

"What is it?"

"I don't know. I guess I kind of like it here."

"You like it everywhere."

"I suppose. But why don't you?"

"I don't dislike it. I just don't make friends, fit in, like you do."

"But you could if you tried." She wasn't sure she believed that, but she did feel some empathy for her brother and his loner, James Dean like ways.

"I have," he replied defensively.

"One time."

"That was enough."

"Well, make friends but just don't, you know, get all super serious."

"Good advice, sis."

His sarcastic tone wasn't lost on her. She stuck her tongue out at him and bounced out the door and into her bedroom while singing *Gee Officer Krupke* from *West Side Story*.

Clark felt the energy in the room disappear along with Sarah, and his thoughts went racing back to the previous spring and his budding relationship with Margaret and the awful feelings that had consumed him when they moved. They always moved, and he had vowed then to never again get close to anyone, especially a girl.

Clark worked on his math homework while he waited for dinner. He really didn't like math and seemed to have little aptitude for it. And he resented the extra work required to make up for some of the big curriculum gaps that had occurred because of their constant moves and the different sequences of courses used by the various school systems.

Clark heard the doorbell ring, and then his mother called to him from the kitchen.

"Clark, can you please get that? I'm working on dinner."

Clark headed downstairs. It was almost dark so he switched on the hall light and then the front porch light before he opened the front door. He went completely still as he stared at the person who stood on the front porch.

It was a young woman, probably early twenties, and dressed in a way that Clark had only seen in a magazine. She wore a British Life Guards red-coats jacket that covered a black halter-top tucked into her blue denim bellbottom pants. She looked exhausted, as if she had carried her old suitcase for miles. A taxi idled on the street in front of the house.

A quizzical grimace crossed her pale face and tightened around her striking green eyes. And with the first words she uttered, Clark knew she wasn't from his world.

"Hey love, I'm looking for a John Westfield. Is he about?"

Clark heard more than a hint of desperation in her voice. "Um, yeah, that's my father, but he's not home now, today, this week," he stammered and knew that he sounded and looked like a total idiot.

"Oh, bollocks!" she cursed, and looked like she was going to cry as her body began to lose its stability. She stretched a hand out to the doorframe to steady herself.

In a panic, Clark yelled, "Mom! There's someone here to see Dad." He turned back to her and asked cautiously, "Are, are you all right?"

As Clark's mother, Coleen Westfield, arrived at the front door, the young woman seemed even paler than before and looked like she was about to collapse. Alarmed, Coleen pushed past Clark and took the young woman by the arms and steadied her.

"Oh my, here, come in and sit. I'll get you some water. Clark, help me."

She had to nudge Clark because he stood stone still, staring, mouth wide open. They guided the young woman into the kitchen and helped her sit at the table. Her head promptly fell forward on her crossed arms and the only sound she made was a series of low groans.

"Clark, get her a glass of water," his mother said, as she went to deal with the taxi.

All Clark could do was stand and stare.

Rita MacDonald was seized by the fear that she had really screwed things up.

What the bloody hell am I doing?

She was too exhausted to raise her head and look at them, maybe too afraid to do so. She could sense that Clark stood nearby after he had put a glass of water on the table next to her. Then he cautiously sat across from her. She heard Clark's mother come back.

"Fifteen dollars from Stapleton, that's outrageous." Coleen checked her pan of pasta sauce but kept a cautious eye on the young woman.

Why in the world did I let her into my house?

Coleen felt that there was something very familiar about her, and she was obviously in distress, and she had asked for her husband. Several vague and mostly unpleasant scenarios raced through her head.

Rita raised her eyes, and when she looked over at Clark, he quickly looked down and stared at his hands. Finally, she gathered some strength, pulled her head up off her arms, and took a drink of water.

"Thank you so much. I'm so sorry to be such a bother."

Clark thought it was an English accent for sure, while Coleen correctly assumed there was some Irish in it. Coleen suddenly remembered a photograph, an old picture that her husband had. It was a black and white photo of his grandmother as a young woman, just off the boat from Ireland.

Strong resemblance.

"You're looking for my husband?" Coleen asked cautiously. She didn't look up from the tomato sauce, which was her mother's recipe, and she always worked diligently to make it correctly.

Rita looked around, not exactly feeling trapped, but not comfortable either. She gulped down the rest of the water.

"I'm looking for a John Westfield who served in the United States army in London, England, from 1941 to 1942. He was a leftenant and a telly man, as we call it. Did telephones and communications stuff."

Coleen processed this as she turned the heat way down under the sauce and then came over and sat next to Clark.

"Well, John does fit that description. May I ask why you're looking for him?"

Rita had envisioned this moment for a long time. Now it was here, and it seemed so anticlimactic and so wrong - it was supposed to be him, not his wife and son.

Best thing to just get it out.

"I believe that he's my father."

She reached into her beaded handbag and pulled out a black-and-white photo, which she put on the table facing Clark and Coleen. It pictured a young man, who wore a U.S. Army uniform, and smiled at the camera. His arm was around a very pretty young woman, who bore a striking resemblance to Rita. They stood in front of the Nelson Monument in Trafalgar Square, London.

"My mum gave me this right before . . . a while ago, and said it was my father."

Coleen's face had turned ashen, and she turned to Clark. "Clark, please go to your room so I can talk to . . ." She turned back to address Rita. "I'm sorry I don't know your name."

"Rita, Rita MacDonald."

"To Rita."

Coleen looked at Clark, pleading more than demanding. He could tell his mother was upset, but he really didn't want to leave. "Sure, Mom. I've got a little homework to finish up." He very reluctantly left the two women as they sat quietly at the table.

Coleen had had a few big surprises in her life, but none quite like this. She stared at this odd but pretty young woman, who she guessed was twenty, twenty-one. It was clearly her husband in the picture, and she ran the math through her head. She knew that John had been in England briefly during the war until sometime in 1942. So a baby could have been born around then. So maybe.

But no, he would have told me.

"Excuse me, can I use your loo?"

Coleen looked confused. "Sorry, what?"

"Oh, your bathroom, we call it a loo," Rita explained, and she tried to smile but was too exhausted and sick to her stomach.

"Oh, of course, it's just down the hall that way." Coleen noticed the pained expression on Rita's face. "Are you okay?"

"I'm really tired, and I think I might have eaten something at the airport this morning that didn't agree with me."

With that she rushed off to the bathroom. Coleen went to the stove to try to save her dinner, but her heart wasn't in it anymore. She leaned against the counter and stared into space.

When Rita came back into the kitchen, Coleen noticed that she was still very pale and red around the eyes. Rita had pulled her dark red hair back into a ponytail. Then Coleen acknowledged that Rita's eyes were the same brilliant green as her husband's. She took in a deep breath. "Can I get you something? Maybe some tea?"

"Oh, tea would be lovely, ta," Rita answered, as she collapsed back down on the chair.

A silence then ensued that was understandably uncomfortable for both of them.

Sarah had been singing in her room and hadn't heard the doorbell or the commotion downstairs. Now she was hungry and went to the kitchen to see what was happening with dinner. The last thing Sarah expected to find was her mother standing and staring silently into space while a strange young woman sat at the table drinking a cup of tea. There was no evidence of any dinner except a pan of spaghetti sauce that sat unattended on the stove.

"Hi Mom," she said cautiously.

Coleen just gave her a weary little smile. "Oh, hi dear. Ah, dinner will be . . . later I guess."

"No problem, I'm not that hungry."

Sarah noticed that the young woman looked quickly at her and then away. The tension in the room was palpable, and

Sarah rushed off to find Clark. She knew something big had happened.

Clark sat on his bed in his room, unsuccessfully trying to concentrate on his homework.

"Clark, what the hell is going on? Mom looks like someone has died, and there's a girl in the kitchen who looks like a fucking zombie."

"She says she's Dad's daughter."

"What? No fucking way!"

"Yeah, way."

"What's her name? Where's she from?"

Clark realized, "I don't remember her name. But she's from England. Accent and all."

"But that hair, that's not Dad," Sarah offered.

"No, but she sure has Dad's eyes. And she has this picture of Dad and her mother, and they look like a happy couple."

Sarah plopped down on the bed next to Clark. She sat very close, touching him, and he instinctively moved over a little.

"I just don't believe it though." Clark tried hard to convince himself. "We would have known, Mom would have known, if he had been married before."

"What's married got to do with it?"

"Well, you know, you have to be married to have kids."

She looked at him like he was an alien from another planet, planet Naive. "Clark, this is the twentieth century, not the fucking dark ages. And that was wartime. Everyone was getting laid. They didn't know if they would live through the night, let alone long enough to get married. I'll bet there are millions of bastards running around Europe."

"But Dad, he's so, so straight. I can't imagine . . ."

"Imagine him fucking some cute English girl? You probably can't imagine him fucking Mom either." She loved to tease him, and she knew that he didn't share or like her fondness for swearing.

"Sarah! That's awful. That's . . ." This conversation had gone so far off the tracks that Clark was speechless.

"When did you get so prudish?" After a moment of reflection, she continued, "Didn't you and Margaret do anything? You must have gotten a feel. She had very nice breasts."

Clark jumped up and moved over to the door to the hall, listened to the silence downstairs. "None of your business," he replied, as he recalled the feeling of Margaret's firm breasts under her shirt.

"Not judging brother. It would be natural. That's what people do when they like each other. It doesn't even have to be love." She mocked with an air-quote. "I've seen you looking at mine, and we don't even like each other."

Clark grimaced - it was true, the looking part. He tried to change the subject. "It's so quiet down there. I wonder what's going on?"

"So she's from England?"

"She talks like it, that's for sure." He came back and sat on the bed, but with a little more distance between them.

"Oh, I love that accent. What's she like?"

"I don't know. Very tired and she looked like she might be sick. But . . ."

"What?"

"I've just never seen green eyes like that except with Dad. And if you look at the two people in that picture you can definitely see that she could be their daughter."

* * *

Julie Wells played her guitar as loudly as she dared. She had hung a thick blanket over the door to her bedroom to muffle the sound. She was never sure what condition her mother would be in and how sensitive to sounds she would be at any moment. Julie had already lost one guitar to her mother's drunken temper. And this used six-string acoustic instrument wasn't any more valuable than the last one, but she had grown fond of its sound and didn't want to see it smashed to pieces like its predecessor.

Julie fancied herself a folk musician in the mold of her idol, Pete Seeger. For three years she had struggled to teach herself how to read music and how to play the guitar. Now she could play with real confidence and had begun to compose her own melodies. She was working on a new song now, but she felt frustrated because she couldn't create the lyrics to fit her music.

Through her open window, she heard her father's car pull up in the driveway. It had that unmistakable roar of a big V8 engine, standard in the Plymouth sedans used by the Denver County Sheriff's department. Her father, Frank Wells, was a captain on the force and the head of the southern division.

Julie paused her playing to listen to the front door open and close. Then she waited to hear the initial interaction between her mother and father. That would tell her whether it was safe to come downstairs. She was hungry but hadn't dared to venture downstairs until she knew what condition her mother was in. Her father normally served as a safety buffer between Julie and her mother, but that didn't always work if Bea was really drunk.

The absence of loud shouts, slammed doors, or crashing dishes gave her hope that this would be a better evening than the past five or six or more. She'd lost track.

Julie cautiously approached the kitchen, and she heard her mother and father talking, not shouting. She stopped at the doorway, took a deep breath and walked in.

Her parents were a major study in contrasts. Her father looked as trim and fit as he had in high school. The only signs of age were a few touches of gray in his hair, mostly around his ears. On the other hand, Bea Wells, her mother, had the slouch and sickly pallor of a drunk. Once a real looker, she had let her former cheerleader-body collapse from lack of exercise and too much alcohol.

Frank stood facing Bea, who had her back to the door, and when he saw Julie, he smiled. Bea noticed and spun around.

"Oh, it's you. When did you get home?"

"A little while ago. You were . . . resting." Julie tried to be very casual as she looked around the kitchen for any signs of dinner. Not that she really expected to find anything. Bea had long ago stopped performing that domestic chore. Julie went to the refrigerator and began to rummage for something to eat. Nothing. She checked the cupboards. Nothing. "Jesus, Bea, there's nothing here to eat."

Bea swung her attention to Julie like a sword poised to take her head off with one mighty swing. "You were just at the God damn store, why didn't you buy something?"

"Because . . ." Angry but realistic, Julie stopped herself and backed up near her father. "Never mind, I'm not hungry anyway." She slid out of the kitchen, leaving her father to stare angrily at his wife. She didn't go back into her room, however.

Somethings going on with those two.

She had felt an unusual vibe in the kitchen, so she stopped at the top of the stairs and listened quietly. She heard them go into the living room.

"George and some people have been talking to me about running for sheriff now that George has decided to retire. They think I could win," her father said.

"Are you sure that's what you want?"

"Yes," he replied quickly. "How about you? Would you be okay with it?"

"Cut the bull-shit Frank and say what you really mean. Am I willing to be a good girl while you run for office? No naughty wife embarrassing the candidate."

"Okay, you're right, that's the question. Marvin says that it would be easier to get elected with a divorce than a drunk."

"Fuck you Frank!" Bea screamed, and stormed out of the room.

Julie barely made it into her room before Bea reached the top of the stairs, stormed into her bedroom, and slammed the door behind her.

CHAPTER TWO

After a fitful night, Clark woke Friday morning and hurried to get dressed and go downstairs. The kitchen was empty and hadn't been cleaned up. The spaghetti sauce sat cold in the pan on the stove, and an empty teacup lingered on the table. He then remembered that there had been no dinner the night before. That was all extremely out of character for his mother.

No wonder I'm starving.

Clark had almost finished a bowl of cereal when his mother entered. She still wore her robe over her nightgown, also very unusual for her. She looked like she had slept very little.

"Good morning," Clark offered.

"I don't want to talk about it," she replied, obviously not referring to the condition of the morning.

They were silent while Clark finished and Coleen fixed herself a cup of coffee. When she took out a cigarette, Clark knew that things were really off. His mother never smoked during the day, only occasionally at night, and only when his father was home, and they were having a cocktail or an argument. Then his curiosity got the better of him.

"Did she leave?"

"No, she's in the guest room." Coleen took a deep drag on her cigarette. It brought her a calming sense of being back home in Georgia with her family, all of them big smokers.

"She's staying until your father gets home tonight."

"I thought he was gone for another week."

"Well, he's coming back to, to deal with . . . with this." Another deep drag on the cigarette. "Aren't you going to be late for school? Where's Sarah?"

"She left a while ago. I'm going now. See you later." He gave his mother a quick semi-hug and a kiss on the cheek. That was definitely not his normal routine, but it felt like the thing to do. If she noticed, she didn't acknowledge it.

As Clark walked on the path through the woods toward school, he thought that he would much rather stay at home and not miss any of the potential drama. He didn't like to be a part of any drama, but he really enjoyed watching it.

Clark normally liked Fridays at school because it meant that the jocks would pay attention to their plans for the weekend and forget their normal impulses to bully, tease, mock, and play mean tricks on the nerds, greasers, and other unpopular or different kids. While he wouldn't be classified as a nerd or a greaser, and no one knew him well enough for him to be considered unpopular, Clark was definitely in the different category.

Aided by his size, facial hair (he had started to shave when he was twelve), and body hair (most of his body was covered in brown hair), Clark had perfected a scowl that quickly dissuaded anyone who might think to torment him. The boxing lessons, that his father had bought him for his fifteenth birthday, had given him confidence that he could handle any high school bully. But he felt sorry for all those others who couldn't fight back. If he saw some nerd being bullied, he would go stand next to them and just stare at the aggressor until they backed off. Any attempts by the nerd to express their gratitude were stoically rebuffed by his casual silence, as Clark would just walk away. As a result, and completely unbeknownst to Clark, an almost super-hero image of him had grown among the nerds in the school. They had nicknamed him The Bear - clearly inspired by his body hair.

This particular Friday, Clark felt the strong influence of The Question as he sat in his first period English classroom. The finality provided by The Question gave him a heady sense of certainty that his approach to life this past school year had been the right one. He had made no friends to have to say good-bye to. And this time there wouldn't be a special friend like Margaret to shed tears over. He had sworn to himself that that wouldn't happen again, and he had been true to his word. He was feeling confident and pretty proud of himself until Julie Wells sat down next to him.

They had been in the same English class all year, but they had had few interactions. An occasional smile from her had always been met by his carefully designed grin - not welcoming but not being a jerk. He knew how to straddle that fine line of social interaction.

Clark sat very still and focused on his hands, which rested on his desktop. He could sense her staring at him, almost daring him to look at her. Finally, he had to.

"Hi, Clark." She smiled.

"Hi."

"I saw you at the field yesterday."

Oh shit. Is she teasing me?

"Yeah?" A weak reply but all that he could manage.

"I was wondering . . ." She paused as another student came between them, and then she leaned across the aisle, closer to him. "I was wondering if you played and ever thought of going out for the team. Dwight says they could use some extra players."

Relief spread through him but it was then quickly replaced by fear. He could never tell her that it was his dream to play but that he had never done so because of all his moves. Boys learn to play baseball during the summer on little league teams.

That had never been an option for Clark because he had spent every summer moving. All of that, however, was much too much personal information to share with Julie Wells, or with anyone else.

He looked cautiously at her as she sat there eager to engage. His first impulse was to flee. That would be awkward and rude, and he knew that he'd probably embarrass himself by tripping over his chair. He was saved by the entrance of their teacher, Mr. Smith, who always expected full attention when he entered the classroom.

Julie gave him another smile. "Talk to you later." And she moved quickly to her normal seat, two rows over and close to the front.

Clark exhaled. But he knew that this wasn't over. A girl like Julie Wells wouldn't let it drop so easily.

Mr. Smith called the class to order, reminded them that their poems were due, and announced that he was going to have some of them read their poems to the class. A collective groan filled the room, loud enough to be heard halfway down the hall.

The first half of the class was devoted to one of the books they were currently reading, *Death Comes to the Archbishop* by Willa Cather. Mr. Smith asked several questions about the plot and its depiction of the failings of some of the priests. Even though it was an advance placement class, it was a Friday, and Mr. Smith wasn't surprised that it seemed like half the class hadn't done the reading. Clark had, and he knew the answers to Mr. Smith's questions. But as was his practice, he didn't volunteer.

Mr. Smith called on Chrissy Webber to read her poem. It was a safe choice because Chrissy always had her work done and seemed to have a fair imagination. The rest of the class let out a partial sign of relief, but they couldn't completely relax because there was still enough time for several more students to have to read.

As it turned out, Chrissy went all Homer with a very long poem about a mythical continent and a tall, strong, woman hero. The class held its collective breath - was it now safe to relax? No one dared to look up as Chrissy finished.

"Clark. Can you please read for the class?"

As soon as he heard his name, Clark knew he was doomed. He had inexplicably decided to hand in a very personal poem that he had written about leaving Margaret last year in Boston and his confusion over his feelings for her and for Julie. He thanked God that he hadn't mentioned any names, but the sentiments were raw and unfiltered.

He searched for an excuse, any excuse. He knew that Mr. Smith would never believe that he didn't have one. He then considered making a run for the door, or maybe he could fall to the floor, curl up in a ball and die. But he was quiet, not a coward. Slowly he took his paper, and without looking at anyone, quietly began to read.

> "Always Leaving New
> I wonder what you're doing tonight
> Catching fireflies in the moonlight
> Speaking softly to the full moon
> Humming a sweet mournful tune
> I was just passing through invisible
> Sheltered secure barely livable
> No one saw me but you did
> Even when I ran and hid
> On our last night together we walked
> On our last night together we talked
> Our last night I held you tight
> Our last night it felt so right"

Clark read in what started as a monotone, but as he got into it, his voice flowed with the rhythm of his words and began to reflect a little of the intensity of his feelings.

> "It wasn't what I wanted
> It wasn't up to me
> It wasn't what I wanted
> It wasn't up to me"

He felt himself begin to turn red. The warm blush rose from his neck, over his cheeks, and up to cover his scalp. Unable to stop, he carried on to the end.

> "Dreams flash, images fly
> Is that you I see go by?
> Or another, someone new
> But will she love me too?
> Mountains high, valleys low
> Is she, isn't she, I need to know
> It isn't what I wanted
> Wishes, dreams undaunted"

If he had thought to look up, Clark would have seen a room full of students mesmerized by the spectacle of someone, especially a boy, exposing his feelings. In their experience, that was unprecedented. It just didn't happen in the eleventh, or any other grade. As Clark finished, they didn't know whether to applaud, laugh, or cry. So they all sat stone still and stared at him.

Julie was particularly transfixed. As she listened to the words she had heard the melody that she had composed, and they began to work together. It seemed as if Clark had heard her music and had written these words to go with it.

Moments later, the bell rang. Clark bolted for the door, shot from a cannon, and was far down the hall before Julie or any of the other students had left their seats. He ducked into the boys bathroom and hid in a stall. The only thing that finally got him off to his next class, besides the terrible smell, was the fact that no one from his English class, most importantly Julie, would be there.

Later, he almost didn't go to lunch, but was glad he did because he was hungry, and Julie wasn't there. He noticed that some of the students from his English class looked at him as if seeing him for the first time. He tried not to focus on that.

* * *

Rita woke and slowly pulled herself upright in bed. She didn't remember getting out of her clothes, but here she was in her sleeping shirt. Her brain felt like it was shrouded in one of the famous London fogs. She tried to concentrate on where she was and fought off the beginning of a panic attack.

Christ, what the bloody hell am I doing?

She thought it must be late morning as indicated by the flood of sunlight that poured in through the lacy curtains on the large window. Last night she had fallen asleep immediately, so that meant maybe twelve hours of sleep. She really needed that, and a lot more, to begin to alleviate her debilitating fatigue.

She looked around the room. She had only focused on the bed last night as she collapsed onto it. The room seemed to be almost as large as her entire flat in London. It was tastefully furnished in a style that was contemporary but not too modern. Sturdy and functional.

Handsome, that's the word.

She had not spent much time imagining where her father would live. Her personal frame of reference was the series of small flats that had been home for her, except when she and her mother were on tour with one of her mother's bands. And then it had been hotel rooms, most of them okay but some awful. Many of the nicer hotels wouldn't let bands stay there, even if they could afford it. It took a big name to have enough clout to overcome the objections of those hotels, and her mother had never had that kind of success.

Rita's stomach started doing something unpleasant, and she couldn't decide if it was hunger or another bout of morning sickness. She remembered that the day before all she had eaten had been a ham sandwich in a little coffee shop in Chicago's O'Hare airport during her layover between flights. And even that she'd left it half uneaten because it hadn't tasted right. So she decided, hoped, it was hunger, quickly put on some clothes and went to wash up.

When Rita later entered the kitchen it was empty, but there was the faint aroma of cigarette smoke and a note from Coleen that she had gone to the grocery store and for Rita to make herself at home. Rita liked the handwriting - it was clear and precise.

Cautiously she peeked into the refrigerator. She wasn't a big breakfast person. Normally just a cup of instant coffee and a roll with some butter and jam before she ran off to work.

She saw the box of tea bags on the counter and put the kettle on the stove. She found a plastic bag of bread and the toaster. No jam, but a jar of peanut butter, which she had heard was an American favorite. She opened the jar and the smell, combined with the cigarette odor, almost overwhelmed her sensitive stomach.

As she sat and ate her breakfast of buttered toast, she wondered where the children were. She remembered that the boy was Clark, but she didn't remember if she had heard Coleen say the girl's name.

So they would be my half-brother and half-sister.

She recalled the many nights when she had sat alone and waited for her mother to finish a show, thinking that it would be nice to have a brother or sister to talk to, to share her frustrations about their lifestyle. She would have wanted to be the eldest, of course, but not too much age difference.

How are those two going to react to me?

Rita liked the way that Clark had seemed protective of his mother. The girl had come and gone so fast that Rita didn't really have a solid impression, except that she was pretty and probably sixteen, maybe seventeen. She did have a spark in her eye that Rita had seen in plenty of musicians and artists over the years.

A self-assured arrogance that can be endearing or bloody annoying.

When Coleen came in about an hour later, Rita was on her second cup of tea and had cleaned up after herself.

"Hi, you're up." Coleen tried to be upbeat as she began to put away the groceries.

"Yes, good morning." Rita wondered if she should offer to help, but that felt a little strange. There was a very tentative dynamic developing between them that could go either way.

Coleen finished with the groceries and sat down across from Rita. "John's coming home tonight."

"Really? That's grand, but I thought . . ."

"I talked to him last night after you went to bed, and he agreed that he needed to come home and . . ."

"Check out the crazy girl?" Rita finished Coleen's sentence, trying to keep things light.

"No, meet you. Try to sort this out. He remembers dating Patricia MacDonald, your mother, but he said there was no pregnancy."

"My mum never told him she was pregnant. She only found out right after he got his orders to leave."

Coleen nodded her head. She couldn't imagine such a thing and wondered whether it had been a very good relationship. The photo of her husband and Patricia certainly indicated a relationship that was probably more than just friends, but was it proof of their having a child, this child?

"Does she say why she didn't tell him?"

"Only that she knew he had to go, you know, army orders, wartime. And that if he came back, she wanted it to be for her and not a feeling of guilt over some obligation, like a child. Me." Rita smiled as she faux-mocked the obvious.

"That's a very mature decision for someone her age, in her condition."

"Yeah, right. But that was my mum, very mature."

The casual sarcasm was not lost on Coleen but before she could respond, she noticed that Rita was looking a bit green. "Are you okay? You look like you could-"

Before she finished, Rita jumped up and raced out of the room toward the bathroom.

After listening to Rita throw-up several times over the next ten or so minutes, Coleen went to the bathroom door. "Are you sure you're okay? Can I get you something?"

As she sat on the floor next to the toilet, Rita replied weakly, "No thanks. I'll be all right."

Later when Rita finally emerged, she still looked sick. Coleen suggested that she lie down and rest. Rita readily agreed, and she stayed in the guest room for the rest of the day.

* * *

Clark left school quickly after his last class. Almost immediately, Sarah caught up with him.

"Clark. Clark!" she repeated, as he refused to slow down. "Wait. You've got to tell me what you did."

"What do you mean?" Of course he knew.

"Idiot brother. The whole school is talking about what this weird guy - no one knows your name of course - and what he did in English class."

"Oh, that." He tried to continue walking, but she grabbed his arm and spun him to a stop.

"Not so fast. I don't know if you care, but I've got a rep to protect, and it won't do, my not knowing what my spazo brother did."

"I read a poem in class. No big deal, okay?" But he knew it was a big deal. So big that he wanted to run away.

"Oh, not just any poem I heard, but a pour your soul out on the desk and let everyone gawk over it, that kind of poem." She was now enjoying this, probably way too much.

A love poem from mister I-don't-give-a-shit.

"Unbelievable," she mocked.

"Yeah, unbelievable."

"Well, all your careful work to remain anonymous just got blown to hell. Now everyone knows who you are, even if they couldn't pick you out of a police lineup." She couldn't help laughing, but then she felt sorry when she finally noticed his miserable expression.

"Thanks Sarah, I really needed that." He pulled away and headed for home. He needed to release a lot of tension and pent-up energy.

When he arrived home, Clark searched for his mother and Rita, but the house seemed empty. The door to the guest room was closed, as was the door to his parent's bedroom. In his bedroom, he quickly changed into some old baseball pants and a well-worn t-shirt that he had gotten at a Yankees baseball game he had gone to with his father when they lived in New York. He retrieved his baseball glove and a cardboard box full of baseballs from the floor of his closet and headed outside.

In the backyard, a large fishing net hung on a wire strung between two pine trees that stood at the edge of the woods that ran along the rear and the east side of their backyard. The net served as a workable backstop. An old home plate, liberated in the sixth grade from the school baseball field in Chicago, sat on the ground between the trees. His father had never questioned where it had come from. On another wire that stretched between the trees hung a rectangular piece of canvas that represented the strike zone for Mickey Mantle who was 5 feet 11 inches tall. Periodically he would change the height of the strike zone for different imaginary batters.

After ten minutes of warm up and strengthening exercises for his arm, Clark moved to the pitcher's mound that he had built 60 feet 6 inches from home plate and started throwing baseballs at the canvas strike zone. Starting slowly, he gradually built up the velocity on his fastball.

Clark had started this routine five years ago, after he had finally realized that he would never learn to catch, throw, or hit a baseball with his father. His father liked baseball, but to watch, not to play. He would occasionally play catch with Clark, normally right after he got home from a business trip and felt guilty about not spending time with him. But that sentiment would quickly subside as his father would feel compelled to tackle the chores that had piled up in his absence. So Clark had rigged up a pitching area in every place they had lived and concentrated on the one thing he could do alone - pitch.

The hard thwack of the ball into the canvas told him that his fastball had gotten pretty good. But without a real batter trying to hit his pitches, he would never really know how good he was. He tried to imagine Roger Maris standing there, unable to catch up to his fastball.

He pitched the twenty or so balls in the box. Then he went to retrieve them from the backstop and started again. After almost an hour, he began working on his curve, then a slider, and finally a changeup, which he was still developing.

It was spring, he was pitching, and he felt content, almost happy.

* * *

When Rita woke it was dark. She still wore her clothes and remembered going to sleep on the top of the blanket, but now there was another blanket covering her.

Coleen?

She finally felt rested and almost human but still wary.

God, what an image I've made for myself.

She sat up in bed and listened to the quiet house. It was such a contrast to her noisy flat in Earls Court, a working class neighborhood of London. That area was slowly transitioning with the influx of a predominantly immigrant population, and she loved all the different languages and styles of dress, music, and food.

She now heard the faint sounds of people talking downstairs. There were two female voices and two male voices. She assumed it was Coleen and the two kids, so the other must be John, her father.

He's here.

She felt paralyzed, suddenly unsure after years of imagining this moment.

Now what should I do? Rush down there and throw my arms around him? Wait for him to come up and check on me? Climb out the window and run back to London?

Finally, she pulled herself together and did the logical thing - the thing she had traveled over four thousand miles to do. She went down to meet him.

Rita's first sight of John Westfield, her father, was as he stood in the living room and looked at the photo. He looked good in his tailored suit and freshly barbered hair that was still dark brown with no traces of gray. His body hair seemed to be even denser than Clark's. Despite having shaved that morning, his five-o'clock shadow was noticeable, dark. But his dominant feature was the same as hers. His brilliant green eyes reflected their shared Irish ancestry.

As she stood and stared at him, John realized that she was in the doorway. He looked at her and a wide range of emotions swept over him. Wave after wave, too fast to process. She looked a lot like her mother: the dark red hair, long arms and legs, modest chest and hips. And suddenly John was back in the winter of 1942. A kaleidoscope of images of Patricia MacDonald, his first love, flooded through his mind and ended with her standing in his living room, twenty-one years later.

He didn't know what to do. If it were Patricia, he would embrace her. But he saw Rita, so he cautiously stepped toward her to get a closer look.

She tensed a little, not knowing what to expect or what to do. The emotions that she had seen him experience had been really intense. His eyes were moist, and his lips quivered. He looked sad. Her emotions grabbed at the back of her throat, stole her voice.

Why had he never come back? Had he forgotten all about her mum? Had he met Coleen?

She bravely stuck out her hand to him. "Rita, the daughter."

Her father broke down and cried.

Coleen immediately grabbed Clark and Sarah, and quickly ushered them out of the living room and upstairs. Then she went into her bedroom and closed the door behind her.

"What the fuck was that?" Sarah exclaimed, so loudly that Clark pushed her into her room and closed the door. "Did you see that? When have you ever seen dad react like that. And fucking cry? Never!"

Clark couldn't argue with that. He couldn't recall ever seeing his father cry, not even when his own mother had died a few years ago.

"You know what this means?" she asked.

He nodded his head, but hadn't really fully processed it.

"She really is his daughter, and he knows it."

"But he didn't know she existed until yesterday," Clark offered, confused.

"She looks just like the woman in the picture, and he must have really loved her."

Clark considered that. "But he moved, just like he does all the time. Only now he pulls us along with him." Clark tried not to let any bitterness invade his thoughts, but he felt conflicted. It had also begun to bubble in his subconscious that he, like his father, maybe used moving as a crutch.

Sarah asked, "What the hell are we going to do about it?"

"What do you mean?"

"Well, get her out of here for one thing. Send her back to England with her accent and weird ass clothes."

"Oh, sure, we just box her up and ship her off. Return to sender."

"But if we don't, you know what's next."

He shook his head, not following her train of thought.

"Her mother. His God damn first love. She'll be here and then, then the shit will really hit the fan with Mom." She took a deep, dramatic breath. "I don't want to be from a broken home, Clark. I won't let this fucking hussy break-up our family."

"That's a bit dramatic don't you think?" Clark asked, but he wasn't totally convinced that his sister was wrong.

Meanwhile, the fucking-hussy sat uneasily on an over-stuffed armchair and watched as her father paced the floor and tried to gather in his emotions, collect himself. Never in her wildest flights of imagination had she foreseen that reaction. Sure she had wanted an emotional bonding, but not like that, and not in front of his wife and kids. She was really thankful that Coleen had taken the kids and left. Now she hoped that Coleen wouldn't come back right away.

She assumed that he had reacted to the fact that she looked so much like her mother. She occasionally met people on the street who would stop her and think she was the singer they had seen and heard in some club. She didn't know if he was an emotional person by nature. Some men were okay with big shows of emotion, but most of those men, in her experience, were homosexuals. However, it did make her feel good. It showed that he had really cared about her mother.

Though not enough to come back after the war.

She knew that she had to try to sort that part out. She noticed that he had stopped pacing and now looked at her.

"I'm so sorry for that. It's just that it was like, like seeing a ghost."

Then Rita started to cry. And it was his turn to be confused.

The day that she had found out that her mother had cancer, Rita had been at the local school working on a musical production of *The King and I*. She had come home to find her mother already deep into a bottle of scotch. That hadn't been too unusual of late, but what had been different was that it had been a very expensive bottle of scotch.

Always direct and to the point, Patricia had calmly told Rita of the doctor's diagnosis and estimate that she had approximately six months. They had held each other while they cried, and then together they had finished off the bottle of scotch.

The next months had been a blur of activity as her mother planned her wake and had many pre-wake parties so she could enjoy them. Her stamina had been strong almost to the end. And then it had been over. One morning she just hadn't woken up. Rita had marveled at her mother's control and ability to go out in her own style. The fact that she had later found the large empty bottle of sleeping pills hadn't ruined the image.

It's better than a dive off Tower Bridge.

Rita had already done her mourning, as well as made adjustments to her life. She had been almost seventeen and very self-reliant. She had lived on the road with her mother for most of her life and knew her way around. Her mother had left her with some money, but Rita had known that she would have to find a job and forgo university.

But there had always been a sadness in her mother beneath her carefree exterior. It hadn't been until almost at the end, when she had told Rita about her father, that Rita had begun to see him as possibly the cause of that sadness. She had thought that maybe he was her mother's one true love. She had so casually professed many loves over the years, but there had definitely been something different about the way she had talked about John the American. She would get a far-away look and fall silent for long periods between stories of how they had been together every minute they could in wartime London. How frantic they had felt with each Nazi bombing, only relaxing when sure that the other was safe. It had been borrowed time, and they had known it. He had been her first lover, and she had been pretty sure that she was his first also.

And then there had been the pregnancy. Her mother had always been so careful about contraception that it was hard for Rita to believe that she had once been careless and gotten pregnant. Maybe it had been a residual of her strict Catholic upbringing in Ireland? Rita had always thought of herself as an unwanted accident, but now she wasn't so sure. But why hadn't she told him? Unfortunately, the answer to that mystery had gone with her mother.

Now, Rita was here with that man - her mother's first love - her father.

They were both emotionally exhausted. She readily agreed to his suggestion that they get some sleep and talk in the morning. Rita didn't envy him as he went off to his bedroom to face his undoubtedly confused and upset wife.

* * *

Julie sat on her bed and merged the words of Clark's poem into her melody. She had immediately tried to write out the poem during and after English class and felt pretty sure that she had most of it correct.

There were some minor adjustments, but for the most part his words fit like they had been written specifically for the music. She paused and reflected on the meaning behind that. She had always considered herself a rational person, a survivor, but this was beyond her comfort level. She didn't know how to deal with this strange, strong connection. It made her uncomfortable, but it also excited her. His words mourned a lost love and yearned for a new one.

Is that me?

She had absolutely no rational basis for it, but she thought it might be. And she wondered if that was something she would like to see happen. All of that was crazy and exciting.

Emotionally exhausted, she put down the guitar, got undressed, and slid into bed. Under the covers she reached down and touched herself and began to move her fingers in the way she knew would bring her quickly to a climax. All the while her song, now complete with melody and lyrics, played in her head.

CHAPTER THREE

Clark awoke with a start the next morning. It was close to nine o'clock. He listened to the almost absolute quiet of the house and wondered if he had heard something that woke him?

Nothing. That's odd, very odd.

Normally on a Saturday morning his father would have called him by now to get started on the list of chores. He debated about whether to take advantage of the situation and go back to sleep. But then he leapt out of bed when he remembered Rita, standing in the living room fighting back tears, and his father crying.

I've got to see what's going on.

He came out of his bedroom and looked around the upstairs. All the doors were shut. Downstairs it was quiet and deserted. No evidence of anyone. Then he saw the note on the kitchen table from his mother that she had gone to the grocery store. While he fixed himself some cereal and toast, he debated whether or not to make some noise, wake people up. Normally he would have relished this quiet alone-time, but not today. There was too much going on, too many unanswered questions.

Clark lingered after he finished his breakfast. No sounds came from anyone upstairs, and his mother wasn't home yet. He looked at the chore list. Not very long. His father had only been gone a week this time. He thought about starting on the list but quickly dismissed it. Clark wasn't reluctant to do the chores, but it bothered him that that was the only time that his father spent with him. And it wasn't a nice casual time with plenty of opportunity to talk and bond. His father pushed to get the list completed as quickly as possible so he could go to the golf course for an early afternoon tee time.

Clark knew that he needed to change the oil in his red Vespa motor scooter. Clark loved his scooter because it was the one positive thing about their move to Denver. In Colorado he could get a license to drive a scooter at 16, a full year before getting a license to drive a car. He had turned sixteen last May in Boston, and as soon as they arrived in Denver, he had played on his father's guilt until he bought him the scooter. It had held a promise of instant freedom, but that promise had been mostly unfulfilled because he didn't have anywhere to go. School was close enough to walk, and his mother wouldn't let him explore outside the city limits or cruise up into the mountains.

Maybe this summer. Oh wait, we won't be here. Damn.

He decided that he needed to pitch, not change oil. After he stretched and pitched about twenty balls with only a few hitting his target, he stopped, frustrated. He couldn't concentrate or get his mind to relax so he could feel the pitch. When one ball completely missed his backstop net and disappeared into the woods, he gave up.

He plopped down to sit on the mound and stared at the house. The curtains in the guest room window, which looked out over the back yard, fluttered closed. He noticed and wondered if she had been watching him.

Rita had come back from getting sick in the bathroom and decided to see if some meditation would help her system settle down. She sat on the carpet and crossed her legs. Stretching her arms out and making the eternity circle with her thumb and forefinger, she tried to relax.

"Om." She breathed out the all-knowing sound and pulled her conscious mind in on itself.

She was almost in a state of peaceful nothingness when a sound came from outside that she couldn't identify or ignore. It kept repeating every twenty or thirty seconds. The meditation moment was lost, so she got up and went to the window to investigate. She pulled back the curtain to see Clark pitching. She had seen newsreels in the cinema of American baseball so she thought she knew what he was doing. And it was clear to her from his body language that he was not happy with the results. She saw him start to look up at the house toward her, and she quickly pulled back and closed the curtains.

She crawled back into bed. There was still some nausea, and she desperately wanted to go back to sleep and wake up in her flat in London. She closed her eyes and tried to remember the feeling of Keith's body next to her, maybe after the time they made love and created this thing growing inside her. She hadn't told him that she was leaving to try to find her father, and she now felt guilty about that. She could picture him trying to get information from Eva, her flat-mate, who tolerated Keith, which was more than she did for most men.

Coleen was putting the groceries away when Sarah stumbled into the kitchen around ten-thirty.

"Mom," Sarah whined, "why'd you let me sleep so late? I'm going to be late for rehearsal."

"You're old enough to get yourself up Sarah. Anyway, you didn't mention that last night."

"I have rehearsal every Saturday from now 'til the performance. I told you that," she added, but was only half convinced that she actually had.

"I think this play is too much. That's all you do."

"I like it, and there's nothing else to do anyway."

Sarah finally tuned in on her mother's tense and abrupt movements. She took some of the groceries and helped put them away. "Where's Dad?" she asked.

"He's fixing the garage door with Clark."

Sarah thought to ask about Rita, but it was clear that her mother was on edge and that was probably why.

"We're having dinner at seven. You have to be home. No excuses, young lady. Understood?"

Sarah knew better than to question or argue when her mother was in such a state. "Seven it is," she answered, as she grabbed a banana from the bowl of fruit and escaped out the back door.

A little while later Rita crept cautiously into the kitchen. Coleen stood at the counter working on potatoes to go with the pot roast that she had bought for dinner.

"Good morning," Rita said quietly. "Mind if I make myself a spot of tea?"

"No, that's fine. I can do it for you."

"Oh, please, you're busy, let me." Rita grabbed the teakettle and put water in it. She began to open cabinets looking for a cup.

"Over there." Coleen pointed to a side cupboard. "And the tea is in there."

"Ta, very much."

An uneasy silence settled over the kitchen, broken only by the whistle of the teakettle. Rita made her tea and sat at the table, indirectly watching Coleen. "I'm so sorry to be such a bother. Barging in here and dropping this, you know, father-bomb on all of you." She fought back the emotions that were leading her toward more tears.

Coleen paused and considered. "Well it is a shock, that's for sure." She turned to face Rita. "But I understand your need to find out, to find him. It must be hard not knowing."

Rita smiled, an acknowledgement. "It actually was easier not knowing; not knowing that there was any way I would ever know." She took a sip of tea. "But once, once it became a possibility, then I guess it became sort of an obsession. And well, here I am." Rita tried to laugh, but it came out more of a choking sound as her stomach lurched. "Excuse me," she said, as she quickly put the teacup in the sink and headed for the bathroom.

* * *

Sarah smelled the pot roast as soon as she opened the door. She knew then that her mother was going all out. Pot roasts were for Sunday dinner on the big Sundays, like Easter, or on a Saturday night when The Question was coming. She was pretty sure that that wasn't happening tonight with all the rest that was going on. She looked at the kitchen clock.

Six forty-five, not late, thank God.

Sarah went upstairs and found Clark in his bedroom. He was reading *Catcher in The Rye* for English class, for the second time. He tried to hide it under his pillow as she entered.

"Don't even try. I know you're reading it again. Won't you please give me the Cliffs Notes summary? I just don't have time to read."

He sighed because he knew he would resist and then eventually cave and help her.

"So what's been going on here? Any more unknown relatives show up? Or ex-lovers? Wives?"

"Very quiet," Clark answered. "She stayed in her room most of the day. Dad tried to get her out to have lunch, but she said she wasn't hungry."

"How about Dad?"

"Pretty normal, chores, but he kept dropping things. Then he hit his thumb with a hammer." Clark involuntary flinched as he remembered the sound and the swearing that followed. "After that he just sat and watched TV."

Sarah raised her eyebrows. That was certainly not normal for their father who disliked most television.

"Dinner in five minutes," their mother called from downstairs.

"Is she coming to dinner?" Sarah asked, looking across the hall at the closed guest room door.

In answer to the question, the door opened and Rita stepped out. She wore a puffy blouse that didn't accentuate her figure the way the tank tops had. She looked better, more rested than she had the past forty-eight hours. She gave them a cautious smile and headed down the stairs. Clark and Sarah gave each other a guarded look before they followed.

The table was set for one of the big occasions like Thanksgiving or Christmas, with the good dishes and silverware that they had inherited from John's mother. Coleen found them a bit ostentatious, but they were perfect for this dinner, which was meant to make a statement.

"Oh, my God, what a beautiful table." Rita's reaction was exactly what Coleen had been going for.

Sarah couldn't help interjecting, "Oh yeah, this is how we eat every night." She ignored the negative look from her mother.

"Rita, you sit here please." Coleen motioned to the side of the table with one place setting. Across from her were places for Sarah and Clark. Coleen and John were at the ends of the table, with Coleen closest to the kitchen. All was in its proper place, sort of.

Rita sat, and as she did, she noticed the pot roast on the table in front of Coleen. It put her in another awkward position, and she considered how to handle it.

Take some on your plate but don't eat it, move it around a bit. Or, tell them straight out.

Coleen took a plate from the stack in front of her and looked to Rita. "Pot roast, Rita?"

Candor won, as it normally did with Rita. "Ah, thank you no, Coleen. I'm a bit of a vegetarian actually."

"Oh." Coleen caught her breath, controlled it, and moved on. "Well, there are plenty of potatoes and carrots and salad."

"Yes, that will be marvelous. Thanks so much."

Coleen handed the plate to Rita and turned to Sarah. "You still eat meat don't you Sarah?" It would have been truly fitting, that kind of day, for her daughter to tell her no.

"Yes, please, Mom, it looks great."

Clark and John sat absolutely still and quiet while all this went on.

Coleen finished serving, and everyone ate in silence. Clark and Sarah stared at Rita's use of her utensils. She held her fork in her left hand and used the knife in her right hand to push food onto the fork. Then the fork went to her mouth without changing hands. Clark remembered seeing that in a foreign film that he had watched last year with Margaret.

Clark surprised everyone when he was the one to break the awkward silence. "Rita, do you go to school, college in England?" he asked, while only partially looking at her. He wasn't exactly sure how old she was, but she looked like she would be in college.

"No, Clark, I work. I have a job at the EMI Abby Road Studio in London."

"Is that a movie studio?" he asked.

"No, we record music, mostly popular, some classical."

John now jumped in. "What do you do there?"

"I'm an AP, associate producer. I work with the talent to select and record their music."

"That's neat," Sarah said, despite herself. "Anyone famous? Do you do musicals?"

"I worked with Gerry and the Pacemakers on *How Do You Do It* earlier this year. And Elvis was there to record last fall, and I worked on one of his tracks. We do have a group that works with musicals from the West End theaters. But rock-n-roll is my area."

"That's so groovy," Sarah gushed, before she caught herself. She still thought Rita was hiding something that was going to explode in all their faces.

"I read that there might be an election for parliament soon," Clark offered after another period of silence.

Sarah laughed. "What do you know about parliament Clark?"

"Sarah!" Coleen scolded.

"We read a news summary from the *New York Times* every week in social studies. A little while ago it said that the Conservative party was about to lose to the Labor party. But it was confusing as to when or how that would happen."

Rita looked perplexed. "You've got me there Clark. All I know is that Harold Wilson is the new head of Labor, but he seems a twit like the rest of them."

"It's called a vote of no confidence," John interjected. "And if the ruling party loses the vote then they have to call national elections. The party with the most delegates then gets to name the Prime Minister."

John then recalled when and how he had learned that and went quiet.

Finally, Sarah could no longer contain herself and blurted out, "So, Rita, is your mother coming over too? Are you like the advance party?"

While Sarah fixed Rita in a challenging gaze, Coleen and Clark looked down at their plates. John was stunned to hear his daughter ask the very question that had been on his mind all day.

Rita hadn't expected that question, but she now realized that they didn't know. She gathered up her composure. "No, actually my mum died of cancer four years ago this August."

All the air went out of the room. It was hard to breathe. Sarah jumped up and ran out. Coleen went to see about Sarah while John, Clark, and Rita sat in silence - strained and awkward silence.

"Clark, don't you have something to do in your room?" John asked with very little tact.

It took Clark a moment to get his father's intent, but then he left, not very successfully hiding his unhappiness at being dismissed.

John and Rita sat quietly. Coleen returned, cleared the table, and then stayed in the kitchen. Upstairs Clark's record player started to play *The Sloop John B.*

"He likes folk music it seems," Rita mentioned to John.

"Who? Oh Clark, yeah I guess so." But John really had no idea what Clark liked. "Do you recognize this group?

"The Kingston Trio, yes we have them in England, they're quite popular. I prefer Joan Baez myself."

John wasn't really listening. The news about Patricia's death hit him hard, harder than he would have thought because it was so unexpected. He had assumed that she was alive and had even had a small fantasy about going see her at some point. It wasn't a leave-Coleen type of fantasy but merely the possibility for a small thrill in an otherwise mundane existence.

"I'm so sorry to hear about Patricia, your mom. You were 16, 17?"

"It was three months before my seventeenth birthday."

"Who took care of you?"

Rita had grown proficient at answering that question as she had moved from place to place, staying first with different people from her mother's band, and then just on her own.

"Oh, I had a good support system my mum set up before she died. She was actually a pretty good planner."

"Really? I remember her as being a bit scatter-brained. Except for her music, of course." He wanted to smile, make it light, but it didn't feel totally appropriate.

But then Rita laughed. "Her personal life? Forget it! A mess, constantly. But she sure knew how to manage her bands."

"When I first saw her she was singing *Alexander's Ragtime Band* in a pub near Trafalgar Square. It was my twentieth birthday."

"She loved that big band, 1930s and 1940s stuff."

John nodded. He did also. "When did you find out about, about me?"

"It was right before she died. She had never talked about a father, and I had stopped asking after I was about five or six years old. But then one day she pulls out that photo and says, 'Here's your father, I want you to know'. But she made me promise that I wouldn't try to find him, you."

"Really? Why not?"

"I'm not totally sure, and I actually don't think she was serious. I think it was more that she didn't want me to do it until she was, you know, gone."

John looked away, lost in thought.

"I'm pretty sure she knew me well enough to know that I would eventually have to track you down and try to meet you."

"That could have gone much differently."

"That's for sure. You could have been rich and famous."

The laughter was therapeutic for both of them.

"I remember as a child thinking that my father must be so rich and famous that he didn't have time for us. Or that he was exploring dark continents, or ruling a country like India. I had never imagined an American."

"Why not?"

"Mostly because she never seemed to have much use for them. We had a number of Americans try out for the band over the years, and she turned all of them down because she said they would soon be going home. She used to say that a lot of people think they want to live in other places, other countries, but in the end what they chose is what they're familiar with, comfortable with."

John thought about whether that was what had happened to him. Over the years he had just thought less and less about her, and now here was her child, maybe their child. From her looks and her personality there was absolutely no doubt in his mind that Rita was Patricia's child.

"So, when were you born?"

"November 14, 1942. Seven months after you left England." She had made the same calculation.

So unless Patricia had been seeing someone else, which he didn't believe at all, John accepted it that Rita was his daughter.

CHAPTER FOUR

Clark woke the next morning still upset at having been dismissed from the room just when things were getting interesting.

Sarah, as usual, messed things up.

But then he had to admit that she had only asked what was on all of their minds.

She's fearless like that.

It was Sunday, and Clark was determined avoid going to church. He decided to try his sleep ruse, which had worked in the past. He heard the sounds of his parents getting ready, then his mother in the kitchen. He ignored her calls for them to get up. Then Sarah swore in the bathroom that he had taken all the hot water, which was so unfair - he hadn't been in the bathroom. And then Sarah yelled to their mother, "Clark's awake. He's just faking so he doesn't have to go."

His mother's footsteps echoed in the hall, and she knocked on his door. "Clark, I know you're awake. Get up now and get ready for church."

"I'm tired and someone should stay with Rita." That excuse had been developed as his backup plan.

"I'm staying here while you go with your father and Sarah."

His mother's tone left no doubt that this was a final decision, not to be overturned by solid argument, logic, or outright begging. So he slid out of bed and headed for the bathroom and what promised to be a cold shower.

Rita had listened and had waited for the others to leave before she came out of her room and went down to the kitchen.

Coleen stood at the stove preparing lunch. She planned to have fried chicken and biscuits and had plenty of vegetables for Rita. Her mother was a great cook and had a wonderful recipe for collard greens, which Coleen imagined would be new for Rita. She didn't mind another mouth to feed. She had grown up helping her mother who always had to feed seven at a meal.

"I didn't know whether to wake you for church or not."

"That's okay. I'm not much of a church person really. My mum escaped the Catholic Church, and we both became Buddhists some years ago. It gave her a lot of comfort when she was sick."

"John was raised Catholic also."

"Not like my mum I'll wager. Not in rural Ireland with ultra conservative parents and three older brothers - all of them priests. It was so bad she ran away from home when she was sixteen."

"Really? Did she ever go back?"

"Never. I had never met any of them until one brother came to the dharma and demanded her ashes."

"What?"

"Yeah, cheeky bugger marched right in and made this big scene, which of course the monks wouldn't engage in. They just kept nodding and sort of smiling while this pompous arsehole ranted on about the sanctity of the church and that my mum had been baptized and therefore had to be buried in a proper fashion." Rita laughed at the memory. "Truly bizarre."

"Did you give him the ashes?"

"Hell no. She would have killed me. Reached right through the ether from the beyond and strangled me. Anyway, I had already scattered them as she wanted."

"Where was that?"

"She had a list of five, no six, clubs and venues where she loved to sing and always had a good crowd. So that's where most of it went."

"Where? On the floors?"

"Right. I snuck in after the cleaning crews had done the best they could with the ciggy butts, spilled beer and such. And scattered the ashes so they were a fine layer on the stage."

Coleen paused before she said, "That's unusual."

It's also totally bizarre, wacko.

"I only disobeyed on one part."

"What was that?"

"She told me not to keep any. Didn't want me to obsess over her that way. But I did, I kept a small amount in a little pill bottle. One of her prescriptions for the pain."

That ended the discussion on a down note, and the room went quiet as Rita watched Coleen cook.

"Can I ask you where you're from? I don't recognize the accent."

Coleen prided herself on having lost all trace of the heavy southern accent she had had when she married John. She was surprised that Rita had heard something. "I used to have a southern accent, but it's gone now."

"Mostly yes, but I've a good ear for accents. I think it's very nice actually."

Coleen took it as positive. "So you're like Rex Harrison in *My Fair Lady*."

"I guess, except he was a total shit."

The laughter triggered Rita's stomach. "Sorry, gotta use the loo." She bolted for the bathroom.

Rita returned as Coleen pulled the biscuits from the oven.

47

"Are you sure you're okay?" she asked.

Rita hesitated, trying to anticipate the effects of the disclosure that she knew she had to make. "Well, truth be told Coleen, I'm what we call preggers."

Coleen wasn't surprised. That had crossed her mind as a likely reason for the sickness and for the visit. "How far along are you?"

"According to the doctors, eight to nine weeks by now. I'm just beginning to expand, but my boobs hurt like hell, and I seem to live in the bloody toilet."

Coleen weighed her words carefully. "I know it may look like we live pretty well, but we're really not, you know, terribly well off. Just making it through, but I guess a bit showy, appearances for John's work." She paused to gauge the reaction, but there was none so far. "What I mean to say is that we don't have a lot of extra money, and I know that John will want to help you out, but . . ." She lost heart and couldn't finish because it sounded so callous, so wrong, as she heard herself say it.

Rita processed the words and the sentiment and then realized what Coleen was getting at. "Oh, no Coleen, no, no, I'm not interested in your money. Is that what you think? Oh, my, that's . . ."

Relief washed over Coleen. She believed Rita and sat down and put her hand on Rita's arm. "Oh, I'm so sorry, I didn't . . . well I guess I did fear that was why you were here."

"I understand completely. This woman shows up unannounced and says, Hi, I'm your long lost daughter, and I'm pregnant with your grandchild. Surprise! And oh by-the-by, I'm broke." Rita couldn't help but laugh at the look of chagrin and distress on Coleen's face. "No, Coleen, believe me, I don't need money. I have a very good job and national health care is the best. I really just wanted to meet my father and maybe get a better sense of who I am, by knowing him."

Coleen, now completely relaxed, nodded and then focused on the other thing that had been bothering her. "I just find it hard to believe that John didn't know your mother was pregnant. And that makes me angry."

"Well, I don't know him that well yet, but most men wouldn't recognize a pregnant belly if it hit them in the face. They would just tell us to exercise. Believe me, my mum would have been very good at keeping that to herself. She did say that it would've been too much of a complication because he had to go. She knew that. She accepted that."

Coleen nodded and tried to understand.

* * *

Clark spent his time in church thinking of Rita and how disruptive she might be to their family. His mother certainly appeared to be nervous and upset because the situation was wreaking havoc with her carefully crafted family routines. Sarah was the easiest to read, she just wanted Rita gone. But so far he couldn't tell whether his father was going to be any more interested in getting involved with Rita than he was with Sarah or with him.

Clark also found himself thinking of ways that he could spend some time with her. He had never known anyone from another country, and he had a fantasy about living as a writer in Europe, preferably Paris, but maybe Rome or London. He imagined a life patterned on Ernest Hemingway or F. Scott Fitzgerald and the Lost Generation in Paris in the 1920s. It was a romantic vision of intellectual curiosity and artistic talent, but without the alcoholism and drug use. He vividly remembered his feeling of loss when he had learned of Hemingway's suicide in the summer of 1961. They had been moving from New York to Boston when he read the news while they ate lunch in a Friendly's Coffee Shop in Connecticut.

While he mostly identified with the beat writers and poets, he saw no reason that he had to be confined to the coffeehouses of San Francisco or New York City. London and Dublin were both ideal because he could speak the language. And unfortunately he seemingly had no aptitude to learn another language, which had been confirmed by his solid C- in introductory French in seventh grade.

Clark didn't know what to expect when they got home from church. An image of Rita and his mother wrestling on the kitchen floor had flashed through his mind during a sermon that had seemed like it would never end. His father seemed similarly nervous. But as they entered the kitchen, they were both surprised to find Rita and Coleen chatting amiably while they finished preparations for lunch.

Lunch proved to be enjoyably free from any stress and tension as they all ate and exchanged small pleasantries. Rita profusely complimented Coleen on the biscuits and collard greens. Even Sarah kept a civil tongue despite the dark cloud that seemed to hover over her. Clark struggled to find another topic of conversation. This was especially difficult for him because it was way outside of his comfort level, which hovered just slightly above that of a social hermit. He noticed that Rita didn't eat any of the fried chicken.

"So, being a vegetarian means no chicken?" he asked, and immediately regretted it.

What a lame thing to say.

Rita smiled and responded, "Normally. Some do it and just don't eat red meat and others go the whole way, don't eat anything that can look you in the eye as you're killing it."

"But it's just, you know, a dumb animal," Clark said and then felt like smacking himself on the head.

"It's surely a living thing same as us, but I don't know about dumb. I've never been one, have you?" Rita responded with a challenge, but she also smiled as she said it.

"No, but they aren't smart enough to not get slaughtered for food." Clark stood knee deep in it now and couldn't let it go.

"Seems to me we have plenty of wars where people go and get slaughtered without much reason."

Sarah couldn't help but smile as she thought that a vegetarian pacifist half-sister was a lot more interesting than a potential home wrecker.

Coleen interjected, "Interesting, but your father and I have a tee-time soon. Sarah, would you and Clark please clean up? We'll be home around six."

Clark and Sarah groaned in unison.

But Rita jumped up and cheerfully grabbed some plates. "I'll help."

Clark always hated doing the dishes with Sarah, but today it was different with Rita. They didn't talk a lot, but it felt oddly comfortable.

Later, Clark sat in his room and listened to the new album by the Kingston Trio. It was titled *#16*, which he thought showed a surprising lack of imagination on their part. Suddenly he sensed someone at his door, and he turned around to see Rita.

"Kingston Trio. You play them a lot."

"Yeah." Nothing else found its way into his head.

"I like them too. Their voices work really well together even though none of them alone has a great voice." She came into the room and picked up the album cover off his bed and started to read the credits on the back cover. "Have you heard of a new folk singer named Bob Dylan?"

Clark shook his head, as he answered, "No. Is he British? Like Dylan Thomas?"

She appreciated his intelligent literary reference. "Actually I believe his last name is a tribute to Dylan Thomas, who was Welsh. This Bob Dylan's American, and I heard him a few months ago at the Troubadour. That's this groovy jazz/folk club in London. And then he came by our studios. He has an album coming out soon, and I think he's really gonna be big. He sang this song of his, *Blowing in the Wind*, which was incredible. He has this strange voice, not very good actually, but he writes incredible lyrics, and it all comes together, very powerfully. "

"No, I haven't heard of him. Are you a musician?"

"Not really, not like my mum. Oh, I can play and sing a little, but mostly I have a good ear for music and accents. I help the musicians find their best sound when they're in the recording studio."

"That's so cool."

She smiled at his enthusiasm. "Yeah, it's pretty groovy. What about you? Do you play anything?"

He laughed, slightly embarrassed. "I tried the trumpet in fourth grade, but I was so bad that my mother had to wear ear plugs. I have a hard time telling the notes apart. Sarah's the musical one. She's a very good singer. She's in a play, *West Side Story*, the lead, and it's in a few weeks. You should come if . . ."

"If I'm still here? Who knows, maybe."

Thinking about her future, she forced a little smile and grew quiet.

* * *

While Clark got acquainted with a new sibling, Julie was stuck at home and would have given anything for a sibling to help deflect some of her mother's ire. She desperately wanted to go somewhere, but all her friends were busy with their families on Sunday.

Her father was at work, which was where he spent more and more time. And now, in addition to his regular shift times, he was spending many hours with his campaign group to get ready for his upcoming run for Sheriff. He knew that one incident with Bea could derail the entire thing. So the best thing, he had figured, was to avoid her and any potential confrontation.

The avoidance technique worked for her father, but it left Julie on the front-line when her mother emerged from her bedroom with a titanic hangover, as she did today.

Julie sat on her bed reading *On the Road*. It was on Mr. Smith's suggested reading list, and she was fascinated with Ken Kesey. And she had seen Clark reading it the month before.

Bea thrust her head in the doorway. Her bloodshot eyes scanned the room and finally settled on Julie and then her book. "Another piece of crap book. How many God damn times have I told you I don't want trash like that in my house?"

Julie processed the possible responses and their probably consequences while she avoided looking at her mother. But she took too long, and her mother reacted.

"Don't ignore me, God damn it." Bea moved surprisingly quickly into the room and snatched the book from Julie's hands. Her face reddened with exertion as she tried to rip the book apart. "Think you're better'n me, just like your God damn father. Well, you're not different 'en me and you'll end up knocked up and no-wheres to go."

Julie tried to grab the book back. "That's a library book. We'll have to pay for it." She had no hope that reasoning would work with her mother when she was in this state. She knew she had to be careful. Julie was no longer really afraid of her mother because she knew how to protect herself. Not only was she bigger and stronger than her mother, but she had also been to many self-defense classes at the police academy. She had gotten pretty good with karate and had done dozens of rounds in the boxing ring. Annabelle, the boxing instructor, had complimented her on her strong left hook. But the memories of past years of physical abuse from her mother still caused her to keep her distance.

Bea was seldom too drunk or so hung-over that she forgot that Julie was no longer a defenseless child. But not today. Bea lashed out with her hand to slap Julie's face when she tried to retrieve the book.

Julie instinctively blocked the slap and jabbed her left fist at her mother's face. It connected to the side of her nose, below her eye. It was not a very hard blow but hard enough to drop Bea to the floor and bring blood gushing from her nose.

"You God damn bitch!" Bea cried. She put her hand to her face and then saw the blood on it. "Look at what the fuck you did! I'll teach you, you can't . . ." Bea struggled to get up, but only managed to get to her knees. A strong wave of nausea kept her there.

"Stop Bea. Calm down. I'll get you a cloth for your nose." Julie carefully maneuvered around her mother, not too close, and went to the bathroom.

Bea collapsed back to sit on the floor with her back against the side of the bed. She closed her eyes and tried to control the nausea. Julie returned with a damp washcloth and went to put it on her mother's face. Bea grabbed it away from her. "I'll do it." Her mother wiped some blood from her face and then puked into the now bloody washcloth.

"Oh, gross," Julie exclaimed, and went to get another cloth. When she returned, her mother had slumped to the floor, passed out. Julie got a pillow and blanket from her mother's bed and tried to make her comfortable. She picked up the book from the floor and inspected the damage, which wasn't too bad. Looking back at her mother, she shook her head sadly and went downstairs.

Several hours later Bea came into the family room where Julie sat strumming quietly on her guitar. Neither of them said anything, and Bea left for the kitchen. Julie heard her banging around. "The coffee in the pot is pretty fresh."

The banging stopped. Then, coffee cup in hand, Bea returned and plopped down on the couch. She stared at the dark television but didn't have the strength to get up and turn it on. Julie kept playing, determined to not give in to her mother's mood. She noticed traces of blood still on her mother's face.

"I thought I was pretty god damn special at your age too," Bea spoke, but didn't look at her daughter. "I was a cheerleader and dating the big jock, with the big cock." A shudder went through her, maybe a laugh, maybe a cry.

"Oh, I love you my beautiful Bea, just let me put this in there and you'll see, you'll like it. We'll be together forever. Fuck'n horseshit. Oh yeah, your daddy was quite the stud, but once he had it, he lost interest. It's the challenge, the conquest that turns 'em on. Gets 'em hard. But once they fuck us, there's no more challenge to get them excited. And then they move on to another conquest. Well, no, Frank didn't do that, not him, he just lost interest in any conquest." She laid her head back against the couch and closed her eyes.

Julie wanted to flee but knew that would be a mistake. As upset as her mother was, she had never seemed this vulnerable. Julie desperately wanted this pathetic thing to not be her mother.

"Yeah, I was just like you - determined not to be like my mother. Not get knocked up at seventeen and have my life spiral down and out of control. No, I was better than that. Yeah, I didn't get knocked up until eighteen." A bitter laugh turned into a coughing fit that racked her body.

Sad, depressed, Julie contemplated what passed for a mother-daughter talk in her life. She recalled the very clinical manner her mother had used years ago to describe the differences between men and women, and then she had explained the sex act in very graphic detail. Julie had been twelve and swore that she would never let that happen to her.

He mother called it the birds and bees, but Julie never understood that phrase. She always thought her mother was using it as a reference to her own name, Bea. But she didn't equate men with birds when, in fact, she knew that birds was British slang for girls. She had chalked it up to another nonsensical thing coming from her mother.

She noticed Bea looking at her. Resisting the urge to look away, she tried to look calm and non-judgmental. She even tried to find a small smile, but it wouldn't come.

"I was so excited when I was pregnant with you," Bea said, as she looked far away beyond Julie. "Frank was happy to get married. He was off to a fabulous baseball career. Fame and fortune. I happily shoved it all in my mother's face - see, I can be better. I wasn't some loser with an illegitimate kid, no job, no money, no hope. HA!"

The final exclamation was so loud and unexpected that Julie jumped in her chair and fought off a moment of pure panic. Bea stared at her, and Julie couldn't tell if her mother's expression was one of anger or pity or indigestion.

"You think your life's gonna be so thrilling, so exciting, but then one day you realize that the excitement, the thrill, is gone. But you know what? Life goes on whether you fuckin' want it to or not." Her gestures became more exaggerated and flamboyant. "Some get out like your boyfriend's mother. They say fuck it, I'm not doing this anymore. But I'm not that brave."

Julie was shocked by the intensity, the vulnerability that Bea exposed. They sat in silence for a while. Julie wondered if her mother had maybe passed out with her eyes half open.

"Are you still a virgin?" Bea suddenly demanded.

Julie couldn't answer and wouldn't have even if she could have found her voice. The silence was oppressive.

"Don't matter a fuckin' bit whether you are or aren't. Just take my one piece of motherly advice and don't get knocked up. Keep your little cheerleader panties on and keep them wantin' it. Once you give it to 'em you're screwed, literally."

Bea burst into laughter at her inadvertent pun, and the laughing quickly turned to coughing, and she had to rush off to the bathroom.

Julie sat, unable to move until she heard her mother get sick, and then she leapt up and fled from the house.

* * *

The Westfield's normal Sunday supper of grilled cheese sandwiches and Campbell's chicken noodle soup was usually casual and quiet, but this evening it proved more subdued than usual.

Clark had overheard his father tell his mother that he would likely be gone for at least two weeks; that there was critical stuff going on with work. That had led Clark to anticipate that his father might ask The Question after supper. Sarah hoped that Clark was wrong.

John was frustrated at his short game, particularly from the sand traps that he had found himself in all afternoon. Coleen thought about the possibility that her husband might be interested in some quiet sex. And Rita had gone to bed early.

As Coleen cleared away the supper plates, Clark and Sarah nervously watched their father for signs that The Question was coming. Clark thought he seemed particularly calm for someone who was about to once again disrupt the life of his family. The waited for their father's nervous laugh that always preceded The Question.

But no laugh came, and then suddenly John rose from the table. "Don't want to miss the start of Jackie Gleeson, that's the best part," he said over his shoulder, as he headed off toward the den.

Sarah felt relieved because she had worried that they might, for the first time, have to move during the school year, and she didn't want to miss out on being the star in the play. Clark was upset because he just wanted to get it over with. He had no doubt that they would move, but now he had more time to have to keep up his lone-wolf routine without having the solid, verified, justification that came with The Question.

Later, as Clark lay on his bed, he thought of Julie and her question in English class. No way could he go out for the team. But he knew from watching her all school year that Julie Wells would probably not let this drop, and his go-to excuse was on shaky ground.

I wonder if I could even make the stupid team.

CHAPTER FIVE

Monday morning. Clark was surprised and relieved when he found that his father had already left for the airport by the time he got downstairs for breakfast. Surprised, because he had thought that Rita being there might keep his father around. Relieved, because Rita being there hadn't been enough to keep him around. She evidently didn't hold any greater interest for his father than he or Sarah did. That meant that Clark didn't have to resent her. Well, he did a little because she got to sleep in while he had to get up and go to school.

At least his mother seemed to be getting back to her normal self, using her velvet hammer approach, which meant more positive encouragement than threats to motivate them to get up, have breakfast, and get off to school on time.

It was a glorious Denver day - the air crisp and cool with the promise of dry heat, and it offered a spectacular view of the Rockies to the west. As he walked to school, Clark watched the early morning sun reflecting off the snow-covered peaks.

Fame is fleeting, and Clark and his poem were mostly forgotten. But he was not quite as invisible as he had been before. Surprisingly, he found that he wasn't totally unhappy about that. As he walked down the hall to first period English class, he made eye contact with a cute, curly haired, tenth grade girl and got a nice smile in return.

As he entered the classroom, he glanced toward where Julie always sat. She was there, but she looked tired and bereft of her usual aura of energy. Before he could look away, she noticed him and reacted with a small, weak smile.

When class started, Mr. Smith passed back the poems and said to him, "Wonderful poem, Clark. I'd like to submit it to the school's literary magazine if you don't mind."

Clark mumbled a weak, "Okay," while he avoided looking at anyone.

The rest of the school day passed uneventfully. After school the sun was still out, and he felt emboldened to head for the baseball field to watch practice. He arrived at the field before anyone else and sat on the hillside, enjoying the peace and quiet. He allowed himself his normal daydream about pitching from the mound in a real game, a professional game, with tens of thousands of fans in the stands. He imagined pitching in Yankee Stadium as he remembered it from a few years earlier when his father had taken him to a game between the Yankees and the Baltimore Orioles. The Yankees' pitcher, Ralph Terry, had struggled that day, but he had made an impression on Clark with his stoic demeanor, even as the Orioles kept hitting his best stuff.

Lost in this daydream, Clark didn't notice Julie until she plopped down on the grass beside him.

"Hi." She smiled, as she asked, "What are you thinking about?"

Oddly he was not as nervous as he would have expected to be. "Going to a Yankees' game with my father a few years ago."

"That's so neat. I've never been to a real game like that. I'll bet it was great."

"Yeah. We've lived in a lot of places with teams. St. Louis, Washington, LA, Chicago, New York, Boston. My dad would always take me to at least one game each place."

"You're so lucky. I'm a Denver lifer, and we'll never have a real team." She smiled and then they sat quietly for a moment.

He tried to look at her without turning his head in her direction. Clark noticed that she seemed comfortable with silence, which surprised him. Most people weren't, especially girls. In an odd twist, he became the one who felt compelled to talk, but he didn't know what to say.

She finally broke the silence. "I really liked your poem the other day."

He could feel the heat of his blush as it began to creep up his neck. He took a deep breath. "Thanks."

"I don't know how you did that; it was really brave. I would have been terrified."

"You? You're in front of people all the time, cheering."

"Oh that, that's easy, I'm part of a group and the real focus for everyone is on the team."

"Not everyone," he said tentatively.

She smiled at him and wondered if he was trying to flirt with her.

Just then the team arrived and started to warm up. Clark could sense that her body stiffened a little when she saw Dwight look over at them. It looked like he started over toward them, but was called back by the coach.

"What position do you play?" she asked.

"Oh, I don't really, I mostly watch," he stammered, suddenly very nervous.

She noticed his discomfort and changed subjects. "Don't you think Holden Caulfield a self-indulgent, whinny little fag? I'm almost sorry that the school board took that book off the banned list last year."

Clark had read *Cather in the Rye* before they had to read it for class this year, and he identified in many ways with Holden's angst and feeling of isolation, alienation. "Why do you think he's a fag?"

"Primarily because he had the chance to screw Sunny, and he didn't, or couldn't. I think what he really needed was to get laid and get over himself."

Clark would have fallen over if he hadn't already been sitting on the ground. He couldn't tell if she was kidding him or serious, but her expression was somber behind a thin forced smile. A response was far beyond his capacity for engaging with a girl, or anyone else for that matter. He tried to think of what witty thing Sarah might say, but nothing came to mind, so he changed the subject again. "I've noticed that Dwight balks a lot."

She graciously accepted the change. "You know, that's one rule that I've never understood. What's the point?"

Clark was back on safe ground. He knew the major league baseball rulebook almost word for word. And he had been thinking about balks because umpires had recently begun to enforce the rule. Just the day before he had read in the newspaper that there had been seven balks called in a Pittsburgh Pirates game against the Cincinnati Reds. "It's kinda subjective on the part of the umpire. Mostly it's when they think a pitcher is pretending to start to pitch, but he's not really going to. He's, you know, trying to fake out the runner on first base so he can pick 'em off."

"What's wrong with that? There're fake-outs in lots of other sports. Football. Basketball."

"True. I don't know, it's just the way it is, and they're starting to call it more. At least in the majors, I don't know about high school or college." He kept watching the practice as he spoke. "Wait, there did you see that, how he started to pitch, then stopped? That would be a balk."

"No, I wasn't watching." She had been watching him. Now she turned and noticed that the rest of the cheerleaders had arrived, and several were looking over at them. "Gotta go practice. You really should think about trying out, you know a lot. See ya."

She bounced off, and he sat there and stared at her. A strong, indefinable emotion washed over him - warm, thrilling, and more than a little frightening.

What the hell just happened?

* * *

Rita had begun to learn the rhythms of the Westfield household, which were very regular when John was gone. She didn't hide, but she did manage to schedule her appearances to coincide with times when they were mostly all together, which helped to maintain conversation that wasn't too intrusive.

Rita had overheard Clark and Sarah moan about going to school. She laughed to herself as she recalled the oft-expressed fear her mother had had that Rita wasn't getting a very good education as she bounced around from school to school. And then finally, beginning at age fifteen, not going to school much at all. Rita had looked older and was physically very developed by then, so no one paid any attention to why she wasn't in school.

In the middle of the afternoon, Rita heard that same sound coming from the backyard. She went to the window and saw Clark, throwing pitch after pitch, most of which smacked loudly into the leather strike zone. She knew nothing about baseball, but she was a pretty keen observer of human anatomy and was impressed with Clark's strength and coordination. There were a lot of footballers and ruggers who had hung around the clubs and often tried to show off their great bodies on the dance floor. Many of them had tried to hit on her, but none had succeeded. She went more for brains and character than muscles. But in Clark she thought that she maybe saw both.

He must have to fight the girls off with a stick.

Little did she know.

The only stick that Clark thought about was a bat held by an imaginary batter standing next to home plate. He had never thrown to a real batter, and it frustrated and frightened him. It had always been easier to avoid putting himself in that position, a position in which he assumed that he would probably fail. But more and more he felt like a coward, that he needed to prove something to himself and, truth be told, to Julie. He had really enjoyed talking to her, and he couldn't get her question out of his mind. So he had hurried home and begun to take out his frustrations on the imaginary hitters in his batter's box. He imagined Julie watching him, and then he realized that someone was watching. He spun around to see Rita sitting quietly on a nearby lawn chair.

"Hi," he ventured, with a small wave of his glove.

"This is baseball that you're doing?"

"Well, it's pitching, which is part of baseball. Probably the most important part." He hoped that he wasn't bragging too much, but he believed it, and it felt good to say it.

"We call it bowling in cricket, which is sort of like your baseball I think."

"I really don't know. I've heard of it, but that's all."

He shifted restlessly on the mound, not sure what to do next, go back to pitching or talk to her. The prospect of talking to this woman was surprisingly less intimidating than he would have expected.

"Are you on a team?" She was pretty sure that it was a team sport and had already expended her very limited knowledge of cricket.

"No. Not at the moment. Not ever, actually." Without consciously deciding to do it, he came over and sat on the chair next to her. "It's mostly a summertime game and I've, well we've always moved in the summer, so I never had the opportunity."

"Well that sucks, don't it?"

He laughed, "Yes, it does suck."

She had moved a lot also, but her image of Americans was that they tended to stay in one place. They seemed to define themselves by what part of the country they were from. And they had different accents to go along with it.

"So you move every summer?"

Clark nodded as mixed emotions, mostly sadness, spread across his face. They sat in silence, and both realized and appreciated it that neither of them was uncomfortable. After a few minutes, Clark began to massage his arm. If he didn't get back to throwing soon, he would tighten up and it would be over for today. But he could always pitch again tomorrow.

"You looked happy out there, pitching you call it? I didn't want to stop you."

"Oh, it's okay. I was almost done. I set a limit of a hundred and fifty pitches, including warm up. That's what Whitey Ford does."

She looked quizzically at him.

"He's a great pitcher for the New York Yankees. They're the best team in the world."

"Is that what you want to do?"

"Oh yeah, that would be awesome, but not likely."

"Why not?"

He considered the question for a moment. "For starters, I've never pitched in a real game. And I'd probably choke under the pressure."

"Why do you say that?"

Now he began to feel uncomfortable. "Oh, I don't know. Just a feeling I guess. This is a game that gets into your soul; it's much more than a game really." Her open expression encouraged him to continue. "When I stand there and get ready to pitch, I don't see anything but the plate, and I see the ball cross where I want it to, even before I throw it. That probably sounds a little crazy." He stared off into the woods, a little embarrassed by his openness.

She felt his struggle and reached over and gently touched his arm. She could feel the immediate tensing of his muscles, which then quickly relaxed. "Sounds very Zen," she commented.

"What? Like the meditation thing?"

"Meditation is part of it, but the philosophy of Zen comes from Buddhism and revolves around seeking an inner peace with yourself and the world around you."

He nodded. That did resonate with how he often felt out there on the pitcher's mound when the rest of the world dropped away. "My school has a game tomorrow afternoon on the field right over there." He pointed toward the woods and the school beyond. "We could go if you want to see a game."

"Why don't you play for them?" Rita asked. "It's not summer yet."

His silent reaction made it clear that this was a very sensitive question, so she didn't press for an answer. She liked the connection that they had begun to establish and didn't want to ruin it by being too pushy. He was certainly not like the boys she had known when she was sixteen or seventeen.

CHAPTER SIX

It was the top of the second inning and Sebastian Grimm pitched for the Harrison High Cougars against the Stapleton High Aviators. He had already walked two batters and now faced a third with a count of three balls and one strike. The next pitch came in right over the middle of the plate and was met with a solid swing that sent the ball sailing over the head of Billy Barnes, the Harrison right fielder, and over the outfield fence. The Aviators batter slowed down around third and then sauntered home, mocking the opponents and their fans. It looked like it was going to be a long afternoon for the Cougars.

The afternoon had begun on a high note as the Harrison cheerleaders, led by Julie, got the small but eager home crowd into what was not quite a frenzy but an energetic display of enthusiasm for their team. But the cheerleaders had to struggle to regain that spirit when the Cougars had come to bat in the bottom of the first inning, and were already losing by two runs.

Now it was five to nothing and only one out in the top of the second inning, and many people in the home crowd wondered whether homework was more important than a lame team. A trickle of fans exited the stands, and it threatened to become a flood.

Clark never sat in the stands. He had his usual spot on the hillside along the left field side of the field. He felt sorry for Sebastian. Pitching wasn't easy, and it had to be so much harder with real batters. A slight involuntary shudder went through him as he imagined himself out there.

"How's it going? Which team is yours?" Rita asked as she sat down next to him.

"They're the ones in white with green numbers, out in the field, the Harrison Cougars."

When she had asked him at breakfast what time and where the game was, he hadn't seriously expected that she might actually come. And then Sarah had made her comments about lame-jocks, which Rita had laughed at and seemed to agree with. But here she was, and he sat up a little straighter.

They watched as Sebastian gave up another hit. It had been a pitch that was maybe meant to be a curveball but just sat out over the plate, begging to be hit. The Cougars had a pretty good infield, and they kept that batter on first. The next Stapleton batter grounded into a nicely turned double play, but only because he miss-hit another easy pitch from Sebastian.

"He doesn't seem to be able to pitch very well, not like you were doing." Rita didn't look at him, gave him some space.

"That's Sebastian Grimm. He's the number two starting pitcher, but they only have one good one. School teams are really lucky if they have two good starting pitchers because they play two games a week."

"Why doesn't the best one pitch all the time?"

"It's too hard on their arm. Major League starters pitch every four or five days. But amateur school rules only allow a starter to pitch in a game once every seven days and only so many pitches per game. So most high school pitchers only last five, maybe six innings."

"What's an inning? I think cricket has that also."

"I don't know about cricket, but in baseball an inning is when both teams have a chance to bat and keep batting until they have three outs. First the visiting team bats until they get three outs; and then the home team bats until they get three outs; and then that inning is over. There are seven innings in our games, nine innings in the majors. Doesn't look like Sebastian is going to last even two innings today."

"Does that mean the game is over?"

"No, although today it would be merciful to end it. They have relief pitchers who come in and pitch for an inning or two or sometimes just for one batter. It's up to the coach. That's Coach Duncan going out there now to try to get Sebastian to settle down, get one more out and get out of this inning."

"He doesn't look too upset."

"No, he seems like a pretty laid back guy."

They watched in silence as Sebastian concentrated on the next batter. It wasn't a great pitch, but the ball popped up to the center fielder for the third out. A round of mild, almost sarcastic, applause rang from the now much smaller home crowd. Fortunately, the visiting team, in typical fashion for an away-game, didn't have many supporters other than their cheerleaders.

The Cougars gave their crowd something to cheer about as they scored three runs in the bottom of the second inning. Sebastian then settled down and escaped the third and fourth innings with lots of hits but only one more run. The Cougar defense proved to be very effective.

Rita kept peppering Clark with questions about everything that went on in the game. She was amazed at his command of all the rules and strategy. He anticipated almost every move the coach made, including an intentional walk with only one out and a man on third in the fifth inning. She had assumed that it would be very boring, like the one time she went to a cricket game with some mates from the studio. But it wasn't because Clark was so into it.

"Do they normally lose like this?"

"Their record is eight and eight, and they have to have a winning record to get into the high school tournament for the county. It's possible, but not likely I guess."

Just then he noticed that the Cougars had pulled Sebastian from the game and put in Rory Coleman, a relief pitcher.

"There, they've finally taken Sebastian out and put in their best relief pitcher."

They watched as Rory easily retired the first Aviators' batter he faced.

"Oh, he seems better," Rita offered.

"That's Rory, he's a good pitcher but a huge asshole."

Rita laughed, but Clark just couldn't.

Several times Rita noticed him staring at the cheerleaders, and she noticed how his eyes widened when the one who looked like the leader jumped out in front and did a very graceful acrobatic series of cartwheels.

He seems to fancy her. Can't blame him, she's very pretty and quite a body.

As the Cougars came up to bat in the bottom of the sixth inning, down by two runs, she leaned back and rested on her elbows on the grass.

"So, Clark, why don't you?"

"What?"

"You know, pitch for the team. You could be their second good pitcher. Get them a winning record."

"It's too late in the season. The team's set."

"Is that a rule?"

"No, not that I know of. It's tradition."

"Then it's time for a new tradition. Groovy new pitcher takes them to the tournament kind of thing."

Clark tried to be cool, but that was almost exactly the dream scenario that had gone through his head the last few days. He wasn't yet ready to admit that the dream came up every time he looked at Julie.

"Nah, I've never thrown to a live batter. And I've never batted. Pitchers have to do that in this league."

"Bullshit excuse mate, you'll never know unless you try. Just imagine having all those cheers be for you." She couldn't help but smile as his head swiveled immediately toward Julie.

Then just as quickly it swung back around to Rita. "You don't know anything about me."

"No, I don't know you except that I see a person with a skill and an incredible interest in a sport, who's too afraid for some reason to try it. What have you got to lose?"

Just then the Cougars' batter hit a soft grounder to the Stapleton pitcher who threw to first for the final out of the game. The Cougars' record slid to a losing season.

The coach brought the players together for a talk while the cheerleaders quietly dispersed along with the few fans that were left. It took a moment for Clark to realize that Julie was not headed for the school but straight for them.

Julie had wondered whom it was sitting with Clark. She knew Sarah, his sister, and that wasn't her. The girl looked to Julie like a college girl, and they obviously knew each other. She had looked whenever she could and hadn't seen any outward signs of affection. Then she had caught herself.

Why the hell should I care?

But funnily enough, she did care, and as soon as the game was over, without hesitating, she headed over to them.

"Julie, where are you going? We're all going back to school," called Suzie, another cheerleader.

Julie yelled over her shoulder, not breaking her stride toward the hillside where Clark and Rita sat, "Go ahead Suzie, I've gotta do something and then a ton of homework. I'll see you tomorrow."

Julie got close to them and now got a good look at Rita.

Oh, she's very pretty.

Julie loved Rita's dark red hair. And as she got even closer, Rita's bright green eyes were visible and very impressive.

Clark and Rita watched Julie approach. Clark looked concerned, and Rita smiled coyly. As Julie got closer, Rita could sense some tension run through Clark.

"Clark, hi. Bad game huh, thanks for coming out," Julie said brightly.

Clark had a moment of panic because he didn't know whether to stand up and talk to Julie or continue to sit with Rita and talk up at her. This put him way out of his comfort zone with girls. Fortunately, Rita solved the problem by getting up and extending her hand to Julie.

"Hi, I'm Rita, Clark's half-sister."

"Julie Wells, a friend of Clark's. We have first period together. I love your accent."

"All you former colonists say that," Rita teased, having taken an immediate liking to this friendly girl. Rita had a sixth sense for women who were dealing with lots of shit. Some were about to succumb to it and others, like Julie, were fighters. And she immediately had a strong feeling that Julie might like to be more than friends with Clark.

Julie also felt a connection with Rita, and she felt herself relax for the first time in days. She had been on edge ever since leaving her mother in the house on Sunday. She had crept home that night, after she was sure Bea was asleep, and then raced out the next morning before her mother was up. The next couple of nights her father had been home, and things were quiet but very tense. She had lived with a lot of stress for years, but this was far beyond that, and she didn't know what to do about it.

Julie almost laughed as she noticed the look on Clark's face.

He's so clueless it's sweet.

Unable to resist, she grabbed his arm and squeezed. "Well, we former colonists whupped your British accents right proper, didn't we?" she boasted and puffed herself up very patriotic-like.

Rita and Julie laughed, but Clark was too stunned by the powerful shock that Julie's touch had sent through his body. Both women noticed and laughed some more.

"This is bloody brilliant. Julie, you can help me convince Clark to go out for this team."

"Rita no," he warbled.

"I asked him the same thing last week. That's so groovy."

Clark sighed. He should have known that he was beaten, but he didn't.

"I do not want to go out for this stupid team. Drop it, will ya!"

Julie held up her hands in a mock surrender gesture. "Okay, okay, relax big boy." She didn't want to tell him that Dwight had been very mean and negative when she had suggested that they ask Clark to try out.

Rita smiled at Julie and thought she would like to know her better. So far she had met some interesting and very different Americans. Her trip was going pretty good after all. She almost forgot about her condition as they stood in the warm sun and said their goodbyes. She didn't try to penetrate Clark's silence as they walked through the woods toward the Westfield house. She almost bumped into him because he had stopped suddenly.

"Do you want to see something cool?"

"Sure," she replied, as she glanced around but didn't see anything unusual, just some trees and some thick vines.

He grabbed one of the vines and pulled himself up a tree trunk to the first branch. Once there he paused to stand on the branch and looked back down. "Up here," he said. "Can you make it?"

It wasn't said as a challenge, but she took it that way and immediately grabbed the vine and pulled. She didn't spend a lot of time exercising, but she wasn't weak. So she managed fairly easily to join him on the branch, but he had already climbed to the next one. She followed him up and watched him disappear through a hole in what looked like a canopy of matted vines and leaves.

Rita poked her head through the opening where he had gone and looked around. It was like being on top of a tent or a carpet made of vines. Clark was stretched out on his back, looking up at the brilliant blue sky and the mountains in the distance. They appeared so sharp in the clear crisp air that she thought she should be able to reach out and touch them. She could almost feel the cold radiating from the snow that topped the highest peaks.

"Wow, Clark, this is brilliant." She lay down next to him and relaxed as she felt the strength of the vines that intertwined beneath her. "How'd you find this?"

"Did some exploring when we moved here. I have a lot of time to myself."

"Do you come up here a lot?" She nudged around to avoid a vine that was poking into her kidney. "I'd bloody well come up here every day."

He smiled and nodded agreement. Then they lay there quietly for almost ten minutes, each lost in their own thoughts.

"Julie seems nice. A lot of energy. I'd never met a, what do you call them, a cheer girl?"

"Cheerleader. Yeah, she's okay, I guess."

"I think she fancies you." She could feel his body stiffen against the vines, and then he sat up and wrapped his arms around his knees.

"Nah, she acts that way with everyone. Besides she's got a boyfriend. He's on the team."

"Is that the reason you aren't on the team?" she asked, but didn't look directly at him.

He hadn't thought of that, but maybe. It did bother him to see them together, although he hadn't seen them together as much lately. Like today, she normally would have waited around and gone back to the school with Dwight, but she had come over to them. He tried to stop thinking like that, but didn't completely succeed.

"Most girls like a bit of competition for them. Makes them feel special. Sometimes they act like daft cows about it, but not always. She doesn't seem at all like a tosser."

"A what?"

"A tosser, an idiot, a wanker, daft cow, planker, knob head. We Brits have many names for the same thing, particularly when it's derogatory."

He smiled and replied, "No, she's definitely not a tosser, but I don't know much about her really. She's smart and . . ."

"And pretty."

"Yeah, and way out of my league."

"Well, I think you should try for it, both of them, Julie and the team. Even if you completely cock-it-up, at least you'll have tried."

They heard Sarah shout from below them. "Clark if you're up there, Mom says it's time to come in for dinner."

Sarah looked up at Clark as he emerged from the canopy of vines. "Do you know where Rita is, Mom wanted-" she stopped as she saw Rita come down right behind Clark.

Interesting.

"Where have you guys been?" Coleen asked Clark and Rita, as they came into the kitchen.

"Clark took me to see an American baseball game. It was wicked cool."

Rita's eager smile and Clark's sheepish grin made Coleen happy, despite the frown on Sarah's face.

"Well, we all know Clark loves baseball," Sarah interjected, with more than a hint of sarcasm. She didn't like any sports and particularly didn't like the sports jocks at school. She found all of them to be loud and gross.

CHAPTER SEVEN

Clark was tired the next morning as he and Sarah walked to school. His dreams during the night had been about Julie and baseball and had swung wildly between erotic and nightmarish. He had been on the vine canopy with Julie next to him, and they were kissing and then tentatively feeling around each other's bodies. All of a sudden they were in the middle of the baseball diamond near the pitcher's mound and the team and the cheerleaders surrounded them, laughing and pointing. Then he stood on the mound trying to pitch to Dwight and realized that he was naked. He tried to pitch, and the ball wouldn't come out of his hand. He couldn't pry his fingers open. Then Julie was there in front of him, laughing at him and calling him a loser.

As they neared the school, he tried to suppress the anxiety that arose when he remembered the decision that he had made right before going to bed.

Clark enjoyed getting a smile from Julie as he walked into the first period classroom. He tried, of course, to be cool with his response, a small smile and slight nod of his head.

When Mr. Smith announced that his poem that had been accepted for the annual Harrison Literary magazine, Clark felt less embarrassed then he would have a week ago. And he felt good when Julie past him in the hall after class and said sweetly, "Congrats, Clark." But that hadn't prepared him for the real shock during lunch in the cafeteria when Julie plopped down on the empty chair next to him. Clark always sat at the nerds' table, and he could see the stunned looks on the faces of her cheerleader friends as Julie broke the unspoken high school rule that the cool kids would never be seen anywhere near a nerd and certainly not at their table, which was the high school equivalent of a gulag in Siberia or a leper colony in India.

"I liked your sister Rita," she opened directly. "It must be groovy to have an interesting sibling."

"I guess, but we didn't know she even existed until last week."

"Really? Far out."

"Yeah, she just dropped in out of the blue. Even my dad, her dad, didn't know about her."

"Oh my God, that's so cool. A mysterious woman with a wonderful accent. How did your dad react? Or your mom? That must have been really interesting. My mom would have grabbed a large knife and stabbed her." She forced a smile to cover the fact that she wasn't kidding about her mother.

"Well, it's been okay, they've both been pretty cool about it after, you know, the initial shock."

The bell rang to end the lunch period, and everyone responded like Pavlov's dogs. They only had five minutes to make it to their next class.

"I'd love to hear more about that," she said, as she jumped up leave. "Maybe after school?"

He felt confused and conflicted as he replied to respond, "I'd like to, but I have to do this thing first and then maybe."

"Well, I'll be in the music room. Come by if you want to, or have time."

"Sure," he said, as she bounced off. He stood there, mesmerized by her amazing body. It took a moment before he realized that he was the last one in the cafeteria and that he would be late to class unless he ran, which he did.

Clark floated through the rest of the day, like riding a raft on the highs and lows of a rough sea. The highs were his thoughts of Julie, and the lows were when he thought of what he had planned to do after school. When the last bell finally rang, he slowly went to his locker, took a couple of deep breaths and then strode purposefully to the athletic department offices, which were next to the gym and connected to the locker rooms. As he approached the door to Coach Duncan's office, he kept images of Rita and Julie in his head for motivation and courage.

Coach Duncan sat behind a desk that barely fit in his small, cramped, office. There was no practice on Thursdays after a Wednesday game. That wasn't the coach's idea. He would have them practice every day and for twice as long as he was allowed, but the school district had its rules. They didn't want sports to interfere too much with their children's precious education. During the season, he was allowed only three practices a week and never more than two and a half hours each. When they were winning that was okay, but in a tough season like this one, it was killing him. He had several good players and one very good pitcher, Dwight, who drove him crazy because he was eighteen and already un-coachable.

Clark stood at the coach's door, hesitated, and then said quietly, "Excuse me, Coach Duncan."

The coach looked up and stared at Clark. He vaguely knew him from gym classes and had pegged him as quiet and athletic, with no interest in any team sports. But he had also seen him lurking around the baseball field. He struggled to recall his name.

"Yes."

"Well, I was wondering if it was possible to try out for the team?"

"The baseball team?"

Clark nodded, "Yes sir."

"We're almost done with the season. Only a couple more games, and then maybe the tournament if we're lucky. What do you play?"

"I'm a pitcher, sir."

He liked the kid's manners, and he sure could use another good pitcher. "Are you any good?"

"I think I'm okay."

"Why didn't you try out before - when the season started?"

"My family always moves this time of year, and I assumed that would be the case again this year, but it hasn't been."

"So where have you played before?"

Clark shuffled his feet. He had anticipated that this would be the hardest question to answer. "To be honest sir, I haven't."

Coach Duncan felt the air rush out of his balloon of hope.

"Is this some sort of joke, son?"

Clark stood tall as he responded, "Oh, no sir, not at all. I pitch every day, almost every day, and I study pitching. I've just never played on a team before, we're always moving."

"What're your pitches?"

"Fastball, a pretty good curve and slider, and I'm working on a change-up."

The coach had to admit that at this level just a good fastball and a decent curve were all most of them had. Someone with other pitches was a find.

Probably a big old time-suck, but what the hell.

"Tell you what Clark." He now remembered his name. "You come out before practice tomorrow, and I'll see what you've got. We could always use a little pitching help."

"Yes sir, thank you sir, I'll be there," Clark said quickly, then turned and left before the coach could change his mind. As he walked away, he couldn't believe it had worked. He especially couldn't believe that he was mostly happy about it. It was enough positive energy that it propelled him toward the music room.

* * *

Julie mentally kicked herself that she had never thought to ask the music teacher if she could bring her guitar to school and practice there. No more hiding in her bedroom with the blanket draped over the door. And Mrs. Rimaldi, the music teacher, turned out to be a guitar player and had already given her several great tips. She had loved Julie's song and wanted to put her into the spring concert. Julie knew it was crazy, but as comfortable as she felt standing in front of people as a cheerleader, she was terrified to think of playing and singing in front of an audience.

Julie tried to practice her song, but she kept getting distracted thinking of Clark and wondering whether he would show up. She played the melody of her song again, not looking at her fingers as they found the right chords and then the notes, lead guitar style. As she played, she sang the lyrics, Clark's poem, very softly to herself. Then, sensing that someone was watching, she turned and saw Clark standing in the doorway. She kept her composure and finished the song.

"That's really nice. What song is that?" Clark asked, as he tentatively entered the room and came close, but not too close.

"Thanks. It's my own actually. No big deal, I just like goofing around with it." She knew she had to tell him about the lyrics, but she didn't, struggling for the right approach.

"I think it's great. You should play it for Rita, she's a music producer in London."

Her interest in Clark's sister jumped five hundred percent. "Does she do folk music?"

"I don't really know, although she was telling me about this new guy, Bob Dylan. I think he's folk."

Her nervous energy caused her fingers to softly strum the chords to *If I Had a Hammer*.

"Hey, Peter Paul and Mary, I like that."

"Actually it was written by Pete Seeger. He's my favorite. But Peter, Paul and Mary do sing it very nicely."

"Oh yeah, didn't Seeger write the Kingston Trio song, *Where Have All the Flowers Gone?* Great song." He barely paused to catch his breath. "Have you played the guitar a long time? You're very good."

She felt like she blushed a little, which surprised her. She tried to hide it with a laugh. "So you're a Kingston Trio guy, figures."

He thought it was meant as a joke, but he didn't know her well enough to be sure. "I guess. What do you mean?"

"Oh, they seem like a guy group - they are a guy group obviously. But their hits are all written by other people."

"Well I guess they're not as talented as you are."

She couldn't tell whether he was teasing her or not, but she decided that he was and made a small bow from her waist. "Thank you oh exalted music critic."

He laughed. "I'm no critic, but I know what I like."

"And what's that?"

"A lot of things actually. I do like folk. I also like rock and roll, especially the bluesy stuff, but not much of the bubble gum. I even like classical." He threw the last bit out there tentatively. He knew that it would make him seem weird to the high school crowd, but he did sit at the nerd table.

"Really?" She stared at him and considered just how much she wanted to reveal to this unusual boy. "Bach or Beethoven?" she asked.

"Beethoven definitely. The angst of the tormented artist really appeals to me, and I hear it in everything he wrote. Although it's not always performed that way. Jack Kerouac calls him the first beat artist." He stopped, convinced that he had gone too far out there and probably ruined whatever this was that he seemed to want so much.

Julie just continued to stare at him. She was amazed at the range of interests he had and how much they aligned with hers.

Things that she had never admitted to anyone. She had never met a boy like this before. "So what do you play?"

He paused for a moment. He first thought about baseball, but then he remembered that they were in a music room and talking about music. "Oh, I don't play anything. My music teacher in fourth grade said I was tone deaf and that she'd give me an A for the whole year if I promised to never again attempt to play anything in her class."

"Oh that's so uncool. You must have felt terrible."

"No, actually I was very happy and relieved, and so was my mother who had to stuff cotton in her ears when I practiced at home."

"But your sister is so musical, such a wonderful voice."

"She gets her talent from my father, and I get my no-talent from my mother, who can't sing, and I've never heard of her playing an instrument."

They were both silent for a moment, but it didn't bother either of them.

Clark's feet were the first to start shuffling. "I've got to go pra—do something at home before it gets too late." He didn't want to tell her, or anyone, about his tryout the next day.

"Oh, sure, I've got more to do here." She didn't add that she planned to go home as late as she could. She would stay until the janitor told her that he was locking up the building. "See you tomorrow."

After Clark left she wondered where this was going.

Or is it going anywhere? Do I want it to go somewhere?

She went to the window and watched him cross the parking lot and head toward the fields. She had never had a relationship, or even a friendship, with any boy other than a pure jock. Dwight certainly didn't know she was a musician, nor would he care unless he thought it would get him into her pants. Clark just didn't seem like that at all. She was sure he could be a jock, but he didn't have the same narrow mindset of a typical jock.

Fucking Beethoven.

She smiled to herself. She hated Beethoven because he seemed so depressing, and she had enough of that in her life as it was. She turned back, picked up her guitar, and prepared to start in on her song again. This time with the lyrics, his poem. But she hesitated.

Why the hell didn't I just tell him about the lyrics?

She realized that she didn't really have a good sense for his potential reaction, and she was afraid that he might say no.

* * *

Clark pitched ball after ball into the strike zone. He was on fire. He continued to pitch, but easier now. He didn't want to overtax his arm before his tryout. He knew that he probably shouldn't be throwing at all, but it was what he did when he felt stressed or tense or just confused. This afternoon, in a period of less than thirty minutes, he had done two things that were contrary to everything he believed he had to do to maintain his sense of equilibrium, his very sanity. He tried to compare his feelings for Julie to what he had felt for Margaret, and he quickly realized that this was a whole new experience. Last year with Margaret, they had found common ground in their shyness and sense of being different. Neither had been the leader in the relationship. And while that had been sufficient for the short time it lasted, it probably would have led them to crash into an emotional wall at some point. But Julie was so different. The potential impact was not comparable. And then there was Rita. He wasn't sure what to think about her. She made him feel more like a man than a seventeen-year-old boy. Clark was a creature of habit, and he didn't feel comfortable having so many unknowns in his life. He feared that he was beginning to expose himself, and while that was exciting, it also scared the hell out of him.

Later during dinner, he was torn whether or not to tell anyone about his tryout the next day. His instinct was to keep quiet. He assumed that he wouldn't make the team and that he would feel bad, or at least disappointed, about it. But if no one else knew about it, he wouldn't also feel embarrassed. So he followed his instinct.

* * *

The house was dark and quiet, but Rita couldn't sleep and just lay in bed. She had taken a long nap that afternoon and wasn't tired. She marveled at the changes that were happening to her body. There was the obvious rise on her abdomen, but the changes inside were more astonishing. All her normal physical rhythms were off, way off. Her job in the music business had its own peculiar flow of time. Because most musicians worked late and slept in the mornings, she would seldom get to bed before 2 AM. Her life with her mother had been much the same, and she had loved it. But now something else had taken control of her body, and she had yet to reconcile with that.

Then she heard the faint sound of music playing - it sounded like Mahler - so she got up and went downstairs to investigate. A light was on in the living room, and Coleen sat on the couch, drinking a glass of wine. She didn't look unhappy to see Rita.

"Want a glass of wine?" Then she remembered. "Oh no, you shouldn't."

"I'd love to get bloody pissed," Rita said, as she plopped down on the other end of the couch. "I just can't get over what a daft cow I was to get up the duff." She noticed the confusion on Coleen's face. "Oh, pregnant I mean."

Coleen smiled, aided by her second glass of wine. "Right, two people separated by a common language."

They sat quietly for a few minutes.

"You do seem to be feeling better."

"The morning sickness is much less, thank God. But my whole schedule is so wonky. It's driving me nutters."

"You get used to it. At least I did, but it took some time. All in all, I really loved it, most of it . . . "

Rita waited for her to continue, but she didn't. Another period of silence ensued.

"Coleen, I really appreciate how, how nice you've been to me. I know it's got to be hard to have a bloomin' stranger drop in like this."

"Well, I wasn't thrilled to start with, I admit," Coleen laughed. "But now, well it's nice to have someone else around. It gets a bit lonely sometimes." She sipped her wine. "Your . . ." Coleen fumbled for the right word. "Your boyfriend, man, what's he like?"

Rita laughed as she replied, "Keith? He's an ace I guess. He's a singer with a band that's pretty good."

"What does he think about . . .?" She pointed at Rita's stomach.

"Bloody hell, I haven't told him, and he's totally clueless, like most men."

They laughed loudly, then stopped and listened to whether they had woken Clark or Sarah. There was no sound of anyone else stirring.

"Have you thought about what you're going to do with it?" The question had been on Coleen's mind, but without the aid of the wine she never would have asked.

Rita had thought a lot about it. She'd been unable to sleep many nights worrying about it. He flat mate Eva argued to get rid of it. Eva had gotten pregnant once, before she realized she really liked women more than men. She had quickly arranged an abortion with a doctor in Paris, where it was perfectly legal.

Rita couldn't ignore her mother's decision to keep her. It hadn't been a religious thing because Patricia had already ditched her Catholic beliefs. And now Rita considered herself a

Buddhist, if she was anything religious. While it didn't have a specific anti-abortion edict like Catholicism, Buddhism did stress the value of all life and that you reap what you sow, in this life and the next.

"Oh, I'm keeping it," she replied, with as much conviction as she could muster.

"Do you think you'll marry him?"

Rita laughed and she shook her head. "Marry Keith? I don't know." She didn't want to dwell on it because it seemed so unlikely, so perilous. Raising a child as a single mom was tough. She had experienced that first-hand. But raising one in a bad marriage reached a much higher magnitude of awful. And very few marriages worked for people in the music business. It was especially problematic if both people were in the business.

"You're so young. Are you sure you're ready for the responsibilities? It really changes your life. Mostly for the better, but . . ."

"I've thought about having it and then giving it up, you know, for adoption. There are umpteen women in England who can't have babies."

Coleen considered that for a moment. She couldn't imagine doing that. "Is Keith someone you've been seeing for a while?"

"Almost a year. He's on the road a lot with his band, and if he makes it, which I think he will, then he's . . . Well it's not a life that makes for good parents."

Coleen certainly related to that. "Well, if you got in this state, there must be some strong attraction there."

Rita nodded. She felt good talking to someone who was more rational about it than Eva. "Yeah, he's fun and has these little boy qualities that I like, but he's also very mature. And it doesn't come out often with his bandmates, but he's wicked smart."

Coleen got very quiet, and Rita waited for a while to see if she was okay. "John seems to be gone a lot," Rita stated tentatively. She had picked up some negative vibrations from Clark, and now a few from Coleen.

"Oh, he has to for his career, and we manage just fine." Strong face, weak smile. "When John got out of the Army again after Korea, the telephone company wanted him back. But they wanted him in Dallas, not in Atlanta, where we had lived for four years before he got called back. The kids were born there." Coleen paused, reflected - she had been happy in Atlanta. "So we moved to Dallas, and then the next year to Los Angeles, and the next year to St. Louis, then New Orleans, and so on, every year."

"That must have been, must be, really hard on you and the kids."

Coleen nodded. "Yes, but the real problem is that, sometimes only a few months after we move, John gets another promotion, another new job in another city. And then he travels there every week until the school year is over. We never want to pull the kids out of school during the school year. And then we move again."

"Like now?"

"Yes, like now. We know the move will come, but we don't yet know where to."

Rita had led a very nomadic life and knew the problems, but she couldn't imagine it with two kids and an absentee husband. Not even the financial rewards would make that terribly attractive over anything but the short term. Rita also sensed, however, that there was something else at the core of Coleen's frustrations. She sat quietly, sipped her water, and waited to see if Coleen wanted to talk more.

Coleen had hoped that the wine would help her relax, and it had. She was surprised, however, at how comfortable she felt around Rita. She smiled when she realized that she was her stepmother. She would have been about seventeen when Rita was born. They were of very different generations - hers of the Depression and Rita's of the frantic post war boom. Yet there was something about her, a maturity, which made them seem more like contemporaries than mother and daughter.

"It's a real strain on our relationship, and sometimes I even fear that he's, well that he's . . ." she just couldn't say it.

Rita, however, got the inference loud and clear. "You think he might be on the pull?" She caught herself before Coleen could react. "I mean having an affair?"

Coleen nodded slowly, carefully. "He just doesn't seem interested in me anymore. Years ago he would come home from these trips and couldn't wait to get into bed, and sometimes we didn't, ending up right here on this couch." Coleen smiled at the memory. She didn't need sex to feel like a woman, but it had been a strong part of their connection as husband and wife. It seemed to be slipping away and that worried her.

"Have you," Rita began tentatively, "ever tried meeting him before he gets home?"

"What do you mean?"

"I guess I mean, I wonder if getting home to a house, to kids, responsibilities, might be distracting, consuming. What if you were to meet him at the airport or maybe a hotel for the night? No house. No kids. Just the two of you. Romantic."

"You mean like a date?"

Rita nodded.

Coleen's first reaction was that it was far too frivolous and shouldn't be necessary for a married couple. But the more she thought about it, the more it intrigued her.

We can afford a night at the Brown Palace Hotel, and maybe can't afford not to.

She decided to try it the very next night. She was decisive that way.

CHAPTER EIGHT

Clark was nervous, more nervous than he had ever been in his life. He looked toward the school as he stretched, and he prayed that the coach would get there soon and see him throw before anyone else on the team came out.

So far it had felt like the longest, slowest day of his life. Everything had dragged by in slow motion like some strange cartoon movie. He had constantly watched the clock and once, in fourth period, he had sworn that the second hand had actually moved backward. He had even raised his hand to answer a question in science, hoping that such an uncharacteristic move would reset the universe and make time run normally again. Nothing had worked.

He had had a moment of panic at his locker after lunch, when his baseball mitt fell out on the hallway floor. He had scooped it up as fast as he could, and then quickly looked around to see if anyone had noticed. Finally, the last bell of the day had rung, and he had sprinted to his locker and to the field.

Now he breathed a slight sigh of relief as he saw the coach approach with the team managers, who pushed the equipment carts that looked like big, cumbersome wheelbarrows.

"Okay, Clark Westfield, let's see what you got," Coach Duncan said, as he pulled a catcher's mitt from one of the equipment carts and headed for home plate.

The equipment managers stood and stared, not sure what was going on, knowing only that this seemed very unusual.

Clark walked slowly to the mound and stood for a moment with his back to home plate.

Just relax and throw.

He kept repeating that to himself as he then turned to face the coach, who squatted behind home plate. He put his foot on the rubber and went into his stretch. As he propelled his body and arm forward, he momentarily lost sight of the plate and miss-timed his release. The ball flew four feet over the coach's head. Clark couldn't read the coach's expression, and he didn't want to think about it. He caught the ball coming back and settled in. He brought up the image of his pitching background at home and focused on that.

Just like at home.

He went into his stretch. This time his delivery was perfect, and the fastball smacked hard into the coach's glove. Clark thought that he could see the beginning of a smile appear on the coach's face. It almost made him smile, but he managed to maintain his composure and focus. He fired five more fastballs and then watched the coach pull his hand from his glove and massage it to alleviate some of the sting.

"All right son, you got some heat, what else do you have?"

Clark nodded and decided to go with the curve. He shifted his grip on the ball as it rested in his glove. But then he noticed that there were spectators. Some players on the team had arrived and stood behind the backstop, staring at him.

Clark took a couple of deep breaths and tried to regain his focus.

Just like the backyard. Just like the backyard.

The curve broke hard and away, eluding the glove of the coach. Clark sensed some reaction from the team, but he was determined not to look at them. He threw two more big curves that the coach caught. Clark was going to try his slider next, but the coach got up and walked toward him. Coach Duncan tried to contain his excitement behind his normal gruff exterior.

"Nice movement on that curve. Let's get some boys up there to bat."

The coach turned to the players who stood behind the backstop. "What're you all standing around for? Get warmed up. Miguel, get a bat and take some swings at what Clark here is throwing."

Clark groaned. Miguel was the team's best hitter. Clark had never thrown to a real batter before and now his first was Miguel, who was also one of Dwight's best friends. Miguel's body language screamed that he thought this was a waste of time. His smirk indicated that he couldn't wait to clobber the ball.

To make matters worse, Clark caught sight of Julie as she and the other cheerleaders began to warmup along the first base side. He didn't want to look at them, but he couldn't help notice that Julie had stopped and now watched him.

He had to wait for what seemed like forever while Joey Benton, the catcher, pulled on his equipment and finally stepped behind the plate. All that time, Clark felt his concentration slip away. His hands became damp with nervous perspiration, and he aggressively rubbed them on his pants.

"Do you know any signs?" Joey asked, and Clark nodded.

Joey signaled for a fastball inside.

Miguel crowded the plate, taunting Clark.

Clark went into his stretch, paused, and made the fatal mistake of mentally acknowledging that people, especially Julie, were watching. His throw was fast and hard and smack into the side of Miguel's arm. It was too fast for him to get out of the way.

"Son of a bitch!" Miguel swore, as he dropped his bat and started to run at Clark.

"Stop!" The coach's voice boomed across the field and stopped Miguel in mid-stride. "Anything broken?"

Miguel shook his head slowly, no.

"Okay. Then get back in there."

Miguel returned to the batter's box but didn't crowd the plate as he had before. He glared and snarled at Clark, who looked down at his feet.

Clark struggled to regain his focus, to see his backstop and not the catcher or the very angry Miguel.

Joey called for a curve, down and away. Clark felt like his head was going to explode.

What the hell am I doing? This is crazy.

He knew that he would never live this down.

"Any time now," the coach yelled, concerned now that this had been a cruel tease and a big waste of time.

Clark went into his motion. But he knew, as soon as he released the ball, that it was a disaster. The ball curved wildly away from the catcher and bounced back to the backstop. As the laughter from the team rang in his ears, Clark turned and walked off the mound. He strode quickly across the infield, desperately trying not to panic and break into a full run. He headed into center field, toward the woods and home. He heard the coach's voice but couldn't tell what he said, and he didn't care. He'd made a fool of himself, and he wanted to disappear.

As he entered the woods, anger took over. Anger at Rita for pushing him and at Julie for . . . well, for being Julie. But mostly anger at himself for thinking he could do it, for exposing himself like that.

Julie had been shocked at how nervous she felt for Clark as she watched him stand out there on the mound. She had felt more than a little responsible because she had been the one who had suggested he try out. She realized that she hadn't really thought he would do it. But there he was, and he looked absolutely terrified.

When he hit Miguel, she had to cover her mouth to hide her smile.

Serves that big bully right.

She knew that Miguel was the one teasing Dwight that he should just make her have sex with him. Dwight wasn't up for rape, but she thought that Miguel would be. She had been sorry that Clark's pitch hadn't hit him in the balls.

She hadn't been prepared for the depth of feelings that hit her when Clark's next pitch went wild, and he turned and stormed away. She desperately wanted to give him a hug and tell him it would be all right. But she knew that it probably wouldn't be all right, and she couldn't expose herself like that in front of the girls and the team. She felt trapped, which was becoming a much more frequent feeling, and she hated it.

* * *

Clark listened to his mother call up the stairs to tell them that she was leaving. When he had arrived home from the ball field, Clark had immediately gone to his room. He had told his mother that he wasn't feeling good and didn't want any dinner. That's when she had told him that she was going downtown to meet their father for dinner and that they were spending the night in a hotel, just the two of them. If he hadn't been in such turmoil from the tryout, he would have reacted to, been curious about, that unusual news. His parents were occasionally gone on short trips for a convention or some business thing; a couple of nights max. But never had they just gone out and gotten a hotel room. As it was, he had shrugged it off, fled to his bedroom, and closed the door.

He tried to quell the rage of emotions and fears that surged through him. He couldn't get the image of Julie out of this mind, as she stood there and watched him make fool of himself.

Did she laugh with the others?

He wasn't sure, but he wouldn't be surprised if she had. He undoubtedly would have laughed himself if he'd seen someone put on that kind of a pathetic performance.

No way I want to play on a team with such morons.

Later he heard Rita come up the stairs and go into her room, and he was glad that he hadn't told her or anyone what he was doing. He knew it wasn't her fault. She had just encouraged him to do what he had always wanted to do. And in large part, he had to admit to himself, he had done it because of Julie. He did care what she thought of him, and he wanted to be on the team, because he assumed it would impress her. Just as his performance today must have really turned her off completely. She was the essence of what bothered him. He knew he could pitch, and he was pretty sure that he could get over the nerves he had felt as he pitched to a real batter.

But if I'm not on the stupid team, no big deal.

He rolled off the bed and turned on his record player, but he was tired of his albums. He turned the radio on but couldn't find anything he liked there either. Finally, he decided that he'd check out what his mother had left for their dinner and try the television. He hadn't heard Sarah come home yet, so he assumed that it would be quiet downstairs.

He emerged from his room and noticed that the door to the hall bathroom was open, and the light was on. As he walked by, he glanced in, then froze. Rita was in there, standing naked in front of the mirror.

Rita rubbed her hand over the bulge on her lower abdomen and seemed to be lost in thought. Her hair was wet from a shower and her skin glistened. She pulled her towel off the sink and started to dry her shoulders and breasts. She then realized that Clark stood there, staring at her. She turned toward him and smiled.

Clark was absolutely mesmerized. He had seen Sarah naked once but that had been years ago, before she had any hint of breasts or a figure. Rita was a cosmic revelation to him. He knew he shouldn't look, but he couldn't help it.

Rita had to stifle a laugh as she saw the look on his face.

Could it be that he's never seen a naked woman before?

Part of her wanted to do a little show for him to see his reaction, but most of her felt sorry for him.

Clark felt a stirring in his pants. He was uncomfortable in so many ways. His instinct was to run, but his feet were pinned to the floor. His eyes fixed on the breathtaking curves of Rita's body and—

"Clark!" Sarah screamed, as she reached the top of the stairs and saw him staring at Rita. "You pervert. I'm gonna tell Mom."

Clark bolted past his sister and down the stairs.

Rita giggled quietly and resumed drying herself off, but then realized that Sarah had taken Clark's place and now stared at her.

Sarah noticed that the sensual smile that Rita had given Clark was now tuned to her. She felt her body shiver slightly as Rita's green eyes sucked the breath right out of her. She shook her head and forced herself to break eye contact by looking down at Rita's naked body. Her breasts were full, and her nipples were firm. Rita didn't dress to accentuate them, but they were really beautiful. Sarah's gaze moved further down and she noticed the bump, but it didn't register with her at first because she was mesmerized by the soft red hair that formed a perfect wedge at the juncture of Rita's long legs.

Rita noticed where Sarah was looking and began to towel her pubic hair, extending her hand between her legs in a very sensual motion. After she met Eva, she had learned that she did love the attention of another woman almost as much as that of a man.

They stood like that for almost a minute before Sarah finally realized what she had seen. The bump. She had never seen a pregnant woman before, but she knew immediately what it was. It was definitely not too much rich American food. She looked up and found the green eyes, so full of life.

"You're pregnant?" Her voice was barely more than a whisper.

Rita nodded slowly and rubbed her bump. The mood and moment had passed, so she grabbed the robe that Coleen had lent her and put it on.

"How much, how long?"

"Oh almost eleven weeks now. Won't be able to hide it much longer."

"Does my dad know?"

"No, but your mum does."

"Figures. She doesn't miss much. And Dad's clueless about girl stuff. You should see him panic if he comes into my room while I'm getting dressed."

They shared a laugh as Sarah continued to stare at Rita's abdomen. Rita thought she knew what Sarah wanted.

"Do you want to feel it?"

Sarah tried at first to act nonchalant, to hide her excitement, but then she gave in and nodded. Rita opened her robe and took a step toward her. Sarah gently put her hand on Rita's baby bump and began to caress it. Then her hand began to move lower toward Rita's pubic hair. Rita watched, interested and surprised.

Evidently I've got a lot to learn about Sarah.

Suddenly Sarah realized what she was doing. She jerked her hand away and stuffed it in the small pocket of the skirt she wore. She stared at the floor and Rita's feet.

Rita gave Sarah a quick kiss on the cheek before she went to the guestroom and closed the door behind her.

Clark had raced out to the back yard to get away from Rita and Sarah. He didn't want them to see his erection. He tried to sit on a lawn chair, but it was too uncomfortable. He plopped on the ground and semi-reclined to reduce the pressure as it pressed against his pants. He felt like such a loser because he didn't know what to do. His only experience with erections had been with Margaret when she had let him feel her breasts. He had been very embarrassed and struggled to hide it from her. He didn't know that Margaret had only pretended not to notice. She had liked it that he was very naive and never tried to do anything more than what she allowed him to do. She had decided to go further with him, but that was right before she had found out about the move. After that, she had decided to let some girl in Denver have the fun.

He didn't know how long he was there before his erection subsided, and he realized that everything seemed very quiet in the house. He knew that Sarah would have followed him by now if she intended to torment him. His hunger finally got the best of him, and he ventured into the kitchen. Coleen had left a pot with spaghetti and meatballs in the refrigerator; and he warmed it up on the stove. All the while he nervously listened for movement upstairs or coming downstairs. He didn't know what he would do if he heard one of them coming, but he knew that he didn't want to interact with them.

* * *

Julie was home alone with all the lights off. Actually, she was hiding from Dwight who had been a real jerk after practice. He wouldn't stop mocking Clark, and when she had told him to stop, his reaction had been to become even more aggressive.

Finally, she had told him that she had a headache and couldn't go out with him.

Since it had gotten dark, the phone had rung several times, and then she had seen his car drive slowly by the house. She realized that she was maybe a little afraid of him. She thought about calling her dad, but she didn't want to bother him. It wasn't like she didn't spend many nights alone, which her dad knew about but just didn't want to acknowledge. She knew that she could go to Suzie's where she had a standing initiation to stay anytime she wanted to.

Her thoughts kept drifting back to Clark. She tried to imagine what it must have taken for him to try out for the team. He had looked so sad and vulnerable as he walked away from the field. Her urge to comfort him had been partly a friendly instinct but mostly a woman and man thing. It was then that she realized she might see herself being with him, and that was a real revelation.

And totally insane.

Suddenly the house seemed very hot and claustrophobic. In her bedroom, she quickly packed a bag. As she finished, she noticed a flyer that she had found in the grocery store. It announced tryouts for a new women's amateur fast-pitch softball team that was being formed by the Denver Cowgirls, the local semi-pro team. The tryout was Sunday morning.

Julie was desperate for an athletic outlet where she could be a player and not a cheerleader, but there were very few opportunities for women other than gymnastics or basketball, neither of which she liked. She had originally dismissed the idea of the softball team as unrealistic, but now she felt motivated to take a chance, put herself out there like Clark had done. She laughed at herself.

Hell, it certainly can't be any worse than it was for him.

She added some workout clothes and shoes to her bag. After checking the street to make sure that Dwight was gone, she left her house and started for Suzie's.

* * *

Rita was tired, but she hadn't been able to fall asleep as she thought of what an unusual family this was, herself included. She wondered how it was going with Coleen and John. They hadn't come home, and she thought that must be a good sign. She knew that she probably should have kept her mouth shut, but Coleen had seemed so unhappy. And it had seemed like a pretty sensible idea. She thought back to what her mother had always said, "If you're bored, it's probably because you're boring".

She had heard that Americans were sexually repressed, but this family was a real fun-fair of weird. She understood that most couples reached a plateau in their sexual lives, especially after children. Her mother had often pointed that out with the couples they encountered. It didn't apply to most people in the bands because they were never in a relationship long enough. But Rita had noticed it with several people at the studio; Terry, her boss, in particular. At least he wasn't one of those blokes who tried to shag every woman he met.

And these two kids. Bloody hell.

She laughed to herself.

One so repressed he's gonna explode, and the other's possibly a carpet muncher.

All of a sudden she was famished, so she got up, put on her robe and went down to the kitchen. She found a pot of spaghetti and meatballs still warm on the stove. And she heard the sound of the television coming from the den. After making a plate for herself, she ventured into the den and found Clark on the couch, watching a film on the television. He acknowledged her with a nod of his head and a half-smile. She sat at the far end of the couch, and they both watched in a comfortable silence.

CHAPTER NINE

Sarah had fixed her lunch and sat in the kitchen eating, when Rita appeared.

"Good morning," Rita said.

Sarah nodded agreement and added, "Just getting up?"

When Rita smiled, Sarah continued, "Me too. I slept through a rehearsal, but it felt good."

"Have you seen Clark?"

"You know my brother. He's either out there pitching or up in that stupid tree thing of his."

"I like his lair up there. It's peaceful and private."

Just then they heard the front door open, and Coleen called out, "Hi, we're home."

Then it went silent. Curious, they went to the front hall and found Coleen and John in a tight embrace, lost in a passionate kiss. Sarah was taken aback. She had never seen them display affection in that way, ever. They finally noticed that the girls were there and turned to them, but didn't let go of each other.

"Hi pumpkin, how are you?" her mother asked Sarah.

"Good," Sarah mumbled a reply, while thinking that her mother hadn't called her that since she was four or five.

John stepped over to Sarah and gave her an awkward hug and a quick kiss on the top of her head. More very unusual behavior.

Coleen then went to Rita and gave her a big hug.

Sarah could hear her mother whisper in Rita's ear, "Thank you, it was a great idea." She was curious and a little perplexed about what this idea had been. Did Rita have something to do with her parents' night out and this surprising transformation?

"Where's Clark?" Coleen asked, looking around.

Sarah shrugged her shoulders as she answered, "We don't know. We both just got up a little while ago."

"He'll turn up soon, I'm sure. I need to get changed and start on that chores list," her father said, almost like he was looking forward to it.

"Not today honey, let's just relax." Coleen smiled as she took his arm and guided him toward the stairs. Rita and Sarah stared after them for a moment before they went back into the kitchen to finish their lunches.

"That must have been some night," Sarah offered.

"Righto, looks like they've been properly shagged."

"Shagged?"

"British for having sex."

"Shagged, shagging," Sarah tried the word. "I like that. It sounds much better than fucking."

"Too right," Rita agreed.

* * *

Clark could hear the sounds of the Saturday afternoon baseball game from the top of his arbor. It sounded mostly like cheering, and he assumed that meant the Cougars were winning. He knew that if they won this game and then the one on Wednesday that they would squeak into the county tournament. He tried to shut baseball and Julie out of his mind by returning his attention to the book he had been reading, *Portrait of the Artist as a Young Man*, by James Joyce. He was successful enough that he didn't hear Rita climbing up the vine.

"Mind if I join you?" Rita asked, as she emerged through the layer of vines and looked over at him.

"No," he replied.

"Your parents are home."

He nodded.

"Your dad is looking for you."

"Great. I don't feel like being his lackey today."

"No, he's not doing chores. Your mom told him not to."

"Really?" Clark pondered that for a moment. He couldn't remember a Saturday without his father doing the chores on his list.

"Is something buggering you, Clark?"

"What?"

"Oh, blimey, translation, are you upset? You seem very cranky."

He wanted to tell her, but it was hard. Openness was not his strong suit. It certainly didn't help that she was now sort-of family. He could never talk about personal stuff to his father or his sister or mother. Actually, sometimes he could to his mother, but only if it had to do with schoolwork.

Rita sat quietly and didn't press, which was exactly the right thing to do with Clark. Sarah and John were big pressers, naggers, dogs-on-a-bone kind of people. In the face of that, he normally clammed up even tighter and stubbornly refused to respond.

"I tried out for the baseball team yesterday," he finally offered quietly.

"That's great," she responded, but then she considered his mood and continued tentatively. "How'd it go?"

He struggled to keep his emotions under control. He felt like he could lose it at any moment. What surprised him was that it didn't seem to bother him so much with Rita. She had already seen him at his worst last night, and she still seemed to like him. He had really enjoyed just sitting with her and watching *The African Queen* on late night television. Neither had spoken, and it had been cool.

"It was a complete disaster. I hit Miguel on the arm. And they all laughed at me." He paused. "And Julie was there."

"She didn't laugh, did she?"

"I don't know. I don't think so."

"And this Miguel, is he a friend, a good bloke?"

"No, he's a jerk."

"Well, it seems like they're all a bunch of prats, and this Miguel is a bloody tosser. Setbacks happen. Doesn't mean you pack it in. You need to get right back in there. Hit him on the other arm or better yet in the goolies."

He almost laughed but looked confused too.

"Goolies, translation, balls, testicles." She pointed toward his, and he involuntarily flinched.

Now they both laughed, and he felt much better.

"Maybe your dad will have time to play baseball with you?"

The laughter drained out of Clark. "Nah, he doesn't like to play."

"But he built that pitching thing for you."

"No, he didn't actually, I did that by myself. His only reaction was that I had ruined the backyard, so he made me agree to do all the yard work. All he cares about is golf, and work, of course."

"Do you ever play golf together?"

"Twice. I really sucked, and he got super frustrated that he couldn't teach me. And he's not that good himself. My mom's the great golfer."

Rita didn't have any experience with fathers, but she did know that it was a critically important relationship for a boy. She wondered if she could somehow help them improve theirs. She decided that she would have a talk with John about Clark.

* * *

Julie stood in line with almost fifty other girls who looked about her age, a few a little older. At first she had been surprised that there were so many. But after thinking about it, she realized that there would, of course, be other girls like her who wanted to play sports and not be confined to being cheerleaders or spectators.

Julie was almost the last one in line, and she hoped that the dark overcast sky wasn't going to let loose the rain that was predicted. She had had to take two buses and then walk over half a mile to get there. All of the others had been dropped off by parents or had driven themselves. She tried to look as calm as the others seemed to be. It couldn't be that they had more experience than she did, which was none. Maybe some of them had older brothers who taught them. She knew that Dwight used to play catch with his younger sister.

She reviewed the mimeographed information sheet that they had all been given to read while they stood in line to register. No cost to try out, but $25 to play for the summer, which included practices and games. Evidently there were other teams forming in Denver, Colorado Springs and Boulder, and they would travel there and other places for games. That would mean additional money for travel expenses. She knew that Bea would never pay, but she hoped that her father would support her.

Finally, she was at the head of the line and took a registration form from the Cowgirl manager, who looked to be about the same age as her parents. The cowgirl glanced at the form as Julie filled in her name and address.

"Wells. Are you any relation to Frank Wells?"

"Yeah, he's my father," Julie replied cautiously, hoping that her father hadn't arrested the cowgirl for something.

"Oh wow, I knew your father in high school. He was a year ahead of me. He was such a great pitcher. I had a terrible crush on him."

"Oh, that's far out." What else do you say to such a statement? But she couldn't help but think that it was too bad he hadn't hooked up with this pleasant woman instead of her mom.

"I'm Becky, Becky Arnson. I'm a Cowgirl player and the coach. Frank Wells with a daughter in high school. Hard to believe." Becky again glanced at Julie's form. "No experience, well that's okay. I'm sure that Frank's daughter will pick it up very quickly. No glove?" she then asked, as she looked at Julie who stood there empty-handed.

"No, the flyer said we didn't need them," Julie replied, suddenly nervous.

"Oh, no, that's alright, we have some extras. You can buy one if you make the team. Just go hang with the others over there, and we'll get started in a minute."

Julie joined the others. Some talked like they knew each other, and a couple of other girls played catch. But most of them stood around on nervously shifting feet. Julie knew from cheerleading that she had to warm-up and stretch, so she proceeded to do so. She noticed that several of the other girls then followed her example.

The rest of the morning proved to be the most fun that Julie had had in a long time. Becky and the other Cowgirl players were pleasant and very excited to have so many girls interested in their sport. They worked basic drills and discussed rules and some strategy. Julie felt very comfortable with the physical part. And she knew many of the rules for the same reason she knew so much about baseball in general. It had been her main point of connection with her father since she was young. She tried to pitch and found that the unusual underhand motion was very awkward, difficult.

"It's all in the timing of the release point," explained Becky, who worked with the pitchers. "Even the best players will sometimes bury it in the dirt."

That comment immediately brought up a memory of Clark and his awful throw.

God, he just keeps popping up.

As she continued to pitch, it very quickly began to feel almost natural, like she had been born to do it. At the end of the day, Julie sat with the others on the bleacher seats and watched Becky and the other Cowgirl players conferred on whom to invite to return to practice. After some intense debates, they made their decisions and approached the group.

"If I call your name you are free to go. Thanks so much for coming, and I hope you will come back next year and try again. We were really impressed with everyone and these were very hard decisions, but we can only manage twenty-five for the initial practices, and then we'll have to cut to a final roster of maybe eighteen or nineteen."

Julie sat and tried to control her anxiety as Becky began to call names. One by one, girls were called and expressed varying degrees of surprise and disappointment. It was then down to about thirty girls left and all of them struggled to keep calm. Then it was done, and Julie was one of the twenty-five remaining.

"Congratulations and welcome to the Junior Cowgirls practice squad. I know that's a lame name for the team, and we're working on something better, suggestions are welcome. Here's a form that your parents have to sign to allow you to play if you're under eighteen. Get it signed and bring it to our first practice in two weeks. Oh, and be sure you have a glove and cleats."

Becky smiled, and Julie was sure that she looked right at her. "Once we have our final roster, we'll provide uniforms for games, but you'll need to wear your own stuff for practice."

Julie's excitement was tempered by the fact that she had to get the permission form signed. She would have to make sure that she approached her father at the right time.

But never Bea, oh, what a . . .

She shuddered and couldn't complete the thought. Then, with a bounce in her step, she headed off to get the first bus.

* * *

Rita didn't get an opportunity to talk to John until Sunday evening. Everyone had slept in on Sunday morning, and no one mentioned church. When John and Coleen had finally emerged from their bedroom, they had been dressed for golf and left after a quick breakfast. It had been late afternoon before they returned, and it was after dinner before Rita had a chance to approach John in his room as he packed for another trip.

"Off again?"

"Oh, hi, yes." For the first time in ages, John felt reluctant to leave. His mind drifted off to an image of Coleen's smiling face after a climax, one of many that weekend.

Rita brought him back to the moment. "Why do you do it? All this travel, not being here, so many moves."

"Well, my company, AT&T, known affectionately as Ma Bell, has operating companies all over the country and likes to have executives, some of us, work in many, if not all of them. It's their way to handle development and promotions for fast-rising executives, and I be one of them." He tried to mock himself to lighten the mood and not appear to be bragging too much.

"And they don't think of the toll on you, on the families?" Rita had now seen the evidence of that first hand.

"No, not really. It's only a handful of us that it's happening to, and I guess none of us ever complain. The new challenges and competition are exciting. There's always so much to learn. And the compensation is very good." He couldn't tell if she understood, but he could see that she looked upset, unhappy. "I'm so sorry that I haven't, we haven't, had a chance to spend some time together, talk."

"That's all groovy. Are you gone all week again?"

He nodded as he replied, "Yeah, afraid so. New York mostly, then a day in Miami. I'll be home Friday night and Coleen and I . . . Well, I'll be home Sunday and we can talk, I promise."

"Righto, that's cool. But . . ." she paused, not sure how to begin.

He noticed and stopped packing. "Is everything okay? We can talk now, of course."

"I'm fine, but I'm worried about Clark."

"Clark?" John realized that he had barely seen either of the kids all weekend. "Is something wrong?"

"He's a boy turning into a man, and he needs a role-model around." She regretted being so blunt but that was her nature, and she believed it was important.

John felt a bit like he'd been slapped by this daughter. He sat down heavily on the bed, not noticing the neat stack of clothes that Coleen had put there for him to pack. He tried to remember when he had last spent time with Clark, and all that came to him were memories of Clark's reluctance to help him with chores. Gradually he remembered his own feelings at that age when he had had to do chores with his father. He then realized that he had been doing the same thing with Clark. Guiltily, he looked up at Rita. "Do you know the expression about the sins of the father?"

"No."

"The sins of the father are visited on the son, is how it goes, I think. Anyway, it means that we tend to repeat the mistakes that our fathers, our parents, made with us . . . probably because we don't know any better. That was our model."

"Your father traveled a lot?"

"Some, but he worked all the time. He was a federal court judge and was never home. And when he was, he didn't have much time for me."

"So why would you do the same thing? That's daft."

He nodded as he replied, "I don't know. Maybe I was afraid subconsciously that I'd screw it up."

"Pure rubbish. No action is far worse than trying something even if you muck it up. It's a bloody poor excuse if you ask me."

He grinned. He hadn't asked her, but she sure had told him. It was clear that Rita was a formidable woman, just like her mother. Patricia had made him very uncomfortable at first because she had just spoken her mind and her heart.

"I'd like it if you would call me Dad," he offered softly.

She nodded, but it wasn't a commitment. She would like that also, but she wasn't ready yet. Unlike with Clark and Coleen, John and Sarah still felt more like strangers than family.

CHAPTER TEN

Clark arrived at school Monday morning with a plan, a survival plan, which he had developed after deciding Sunday evening that he couldn't play hooky for the next month. He knew he would get a rough time from Dwight, Miguel, and the other players who were in Dwight's little gang. That would be during lunch and sixth period Social Studies class. He brought a lunch from home and would eat it outside. For sixth period class he would show up just as the bell rang, and Mr. Keller would demand quiet. After school he would race out and go home.

I have to go but this can work.

At about the same time, Rita came to a decision about Clark and his problem with the baseball team. She decided not to sit on the sideline but to get involved, and she knew that Julie was the key to it all.

Her sensitivity to body language was well developed from her years traveling with her mother's bands and watching the super-sensitive, and often surprisingly inarticulate, musicians. Many of them would use their music and not their words to communicate their feelings. She found Clark to be a similar type of creature. And his body language screamed a deep interest in Julie and real concern about what she thought of him. Rita realized that his vocabulary didn't contain enough words to communicate with or about girls.

Her conviction that she was right about the Julie-factor brought Rita to the front of Harrison High that afternoon. She found what she thought was a strategic spot next to a large oak tree, where she could hopefully avoid Clark but find Julie as school let out for the day. She was pretty sure that Sarah had play practice and wouldn't be a problem.

Rita was surprised when Clark was almost the first one out of the school, and she barely managed to duck behind the tree so he didn't see her. After that, she had a long wait until she finally saw Julie emerge from the school. But Julie was with her cheerleading team, and they all headed for the athletic fields next to the school and began to practice.

Fascinated with the whole cheerleading thing, Rita watched the girls as they loosened up. Most of them were in great shape and moved with the grace and fluidity of gymnasts or athletes. Julie was clearly the leader and pushed them hard from the first stretches, to the exercises, and then the routines, which demanded strength, timing, and trust in each other. Before Rita realized it, almost an hour passed, and the practice was over. As the cheerleaders walked back toward the school, Rita stepped forward so she could easily be seen.

Julie saw her and came right over. "Hi, Clark's sister."

"Righto, Rita, half-sister. Nice to see you, Julie."

"If you're looking for Clark, I haven't seen him."

"No, actually I'm here to talk to you. Do you have a moment?"

"Oh, why sure." Julie then called to Suzie, who had waited for her at the door to the school, "Suzie, I'll be along in a bit. You go ahead." She then turned back to Rita. "We can sit over there." She pointed to a bench in a little landscaped area along the front of the school.

They sat in silence for a minute. Julie waited patiently but anxiously for Rita to talk. She was fascinated by this young

"Clark, have you been pitching this afternoon?" Rita interjected, coming right to the point.

Immediately on guard, he shook his head no. That was not the topic of conversation that he wanted with anyone, especially Julie.

Rita sensed his anguish and pushed ahead by touching his arm and taking a conspiratorial tone, like they were plotting a big bank heist or a revolution. "Julie wants to see you pitch again."

Clark was too flabbergasted to respond, but he finally managed a weak, awkward, reply. "Why? She saw me last Friday."

Julie responded, "I don't think you got a fair shot, all the people, the jerks on the team."

"Maybe, but there are always people there if you pitch, and some try to distract you. It's just not usually your own team."

"Sure," interjected Rita, "but I have a strong belief that if you have someone there who knows how good you are, then you don't have to try so hard to prove it to everyone."

"Yeah, but I do have to prove it to someone - the coach."

"Him too, but I'm thinking of a special person, two actually." She indicated Julie and herself. Julie wanted to look away but couldn't. She wasn't sure about this, but Rita was very convincing and determined.

"Just give it a try. What do you have to lose?" Rita argued.

"The same thing I lost Friday."

Julie looked around and tried to change the tone and the approach. "Where do you pitch? Not up here I imagine." Her laugh was forced, but it did the trick with Clark.

"No, I'd break both legs, for sure." He sighed, and Rita knew he was going to do it before he did. "It's in my backyard. I'll show you." He pointed to the way down and let Rita and Julie go first.

Julie was jealous that Clark had such a special place where he could escape the world and be alone. She felt bad that they had barged in. She knew that she wouldn't have liked it. But Rita had been persuasive. And Julie also wanted to help Clark because, in a way, he had helped her take the first step with the Cowgirls. As she climbed down from the arbor, she hoped that she would be back, that he would invite her back.

As Julie watched Clark stretch, she noticed his strong yet graceful movements. There were no wasted motions. She found herself imagining what it would feel like if his arms were wrapped around her, and his body pressed up against hers. Suddenly unsure of herself, she tried to dismiss those thoughts. The loud smack of a baseball hitting a tree brought her back to the moment.

Wow, that was really fast and hard.

She had watched Dwight and the other pitchers enough to know that this seemed different. But then she realized that it had hit the tree, not the canvas strike zone over the plate.

Fast and hard but wild just like at the try-out.

Julie didn't look at him as he threw and missed the canvas again.

Rita went up to Clark, put her hands on his arms, and looked into his eyes. She squeezed his arms as he looked at her. "I've seen you throw hundreds of these and never miss. We're here and that's a distraction but make it a point of focus. Don't hide from it. Acknowledge it. Embrace it. We're here for you. Stand on that and just throw."

Julie had never heard a better pep-talk from any coach, and she admired Rita's positive aura as she stepped away from Clark. She watched, almost mesmerized, as he then threw six perfect pitches, each one maybe harder than the one before. Then she realized that he had purposefully hit all the corners of the rectangle and then several struck squarely in the center.

Rita grab Julie's arm as she whispered, "Didn't I tell you?" Then she called to Clark, "How about the swively one?"

Clark couldn't help but smile, "The curve ball?"

"Don't make fun of the girl who speaks the foreign language, it's not polite."

Julie marveled at their friendly, almost intimate banter. She felt like she was on the outside, but she wanted in. "That's really good, Clark," she offered.

The change in his body was subtle, but immediately noticeable as he threw the curve ball into the grass, ten feet in front of the plate. He tried to shake it off, but he couldn't, and the next pitch sailed wide right. His body language now screamed defeat.

Julie was certainly aware of her impact on boys. She often used it to her benefit and enjoyed seeing their reactions, so clumsy and foolish. This felt different. It felt good that he reacted to her, but at the same time she felt guilty that it caused him to lose his concentration and perform so poorly. On an impulse, she stepped over to him, put her hands on his arms as Rita had done, and gave him a quick but meaningful kiss on the mouth. She almost laughed at his reaction. His eyes went very wide and his whole body seemed to vibrate. But then she realized that some of the vibration originated in her body also. She had to force herself to step back and not kiss him again. The kiss had been purely instinctual, and she stood there terrified that maybe she had made things worse.

It seemed like forever before he slowly began to go into his pitching motion. The ball sped toward the plate and then curved sharply to the left and hit the side of the backstop. Perfect. She tried to keep her relief and excitement under control as she watched him throw several more curve balls, all breaking perfectly.

"Jolly good!" Rita yelled. She thought her plan seemed to be working. She hadn't seen the kiss coming, but that was clearly a bonus.

"You're ready mate."

"Ready for what?"

"To try again. Make the team."

"Oh, no. I was just doing this for you. I'm not trying out again. No way." He left the mound and started to pick up the balls near the backstop.

As Julie watched him, she felt an uncontrollable anger surge up inside her and make her yell, "That's bullshit!"

He stopped and looked back toward her. "What?"

She struggled to explain. She had to sneak off to play softball. "It's bullshit that you won't even try to use the talent you have when there are others who, who just never have, aren't allowed the opportunity."

"I don't care about others."

"Well you should, and maybe they would care about you." As tears welled up in her eyes, Julie turned and stomped off into the woods.

Clark was dumbfounded. He had been totally surprised by the kiss. Then floored by her anger. And now he was devastated by her tears. He regretted his thoughtless statement about not caring. He did care, at least about her. A part of him wanted to run after her, but most of him stayed rooted in place.

"Well, that didn't go exactly as I expected," Rita offered, trying to lighten the moment.

"What the hell did you expect? Just stay out of my . . . I don't need your help."

"I'm really sorry. I thought it could, that it would help you if you saw that people believed in you," Rita confessed, as she sat heavily on the lawn chair and stared off into the distance.

Had he been able to think rationally at that moment, this would have made sense to him, and he probably would have agreed. But he couldn't, and it didn't, so instead he walked into the house without saying another word.

Later, Clark reluctantly came to dinner when his mother insisted, and he was relieved to find that Rita was in her room with a headache and Sarah had stayed late at rehearsal. He only pretended to listen to Coleen describe her encounter at the grocery store with some strange old woman who had been convinced that Coleen was her granddaughter. That sort of thing happened to her all the time, and normally Clark would have been interested. But tonight all he could think of was the feeling of Julie's kiss and her stormy, tearful departure.

As he struggled to concentrate on his homework, Clark again dreaded having to go to school - this time because of Julie. His dread grew as the evening went on. He gave up on homework and instead wrote a new poem that reflected the turmoil inside him. Teenage angst was in full spring bloom.

* * *

It was late when Sarah arrived home with Paul, who was her costar in the play and ostensible boyfriend, although his primary interest in her seemed to be purely sexual. As his car pulled up in front of the house, the porch light was on, and Sarah saw Rita sitting on the front steps. Her red hair bloomed in the light.

Paul was immediately mesmerized. "Who's that on your porch?"

"That's Rita my half-sister, I told you about her."

"Wow, she's . . . , uh great hair." He jumped out of the car and was halfway up the walk before he remembered Sarah and came back for her. He didn't normally open her door or do anything else very gentlemanly, but now he did because she just sat there, glaring at him. He practically dragged her up the walk.

Rita watched them approach. She knew a lot of actors who hung out in the clubs in London. Paul seemed to fit the type, good looking but with something missing behind his dull brown eyes. His sexual hunger poured from every pore, and she hoped that Sarah had enough sense to resist him.

"Hi Rita, I'm Paul. Sarah has told me so much about you, and it's great to meet you." He struggled unsuccessfully to keep his eyes on her face and off her breasts. She sat up straighter to minimize her cleavage. She nodded a silent response to him as she spoke to Sarah. "Hi Sarah, how was rehearsal?"

"It sucked."

"Oh, it wasn't so bad, you'll get it soon," Paul crooned, never taking his eyes off Rita.

Rita almost laughed at the hungry look on his face. She could see that it wasn't lost on Sarah either. Rita didn't want this silly boy to mess up the very tenuous relationship they had, so she stood up to leave. "Nice to meet you, Paul." A natural toucher, Rita gently touched his arm as she spoke. Immediately she knew that that was a mistake because his body did a little shudder and his knees seemed to buckle slightly. Not wanting to make things worse by laughing, she quickly turned and went into the house.

Sarah stood and stared at Paul until he realized she was still there. Sheepishly, he smiled at her. "Well, she's, she's nice." Reflexively he tried to kiss her, but she turned quickly, went inside, and slammed the door behind her.

In her dark bedroom, Sarah looked out the window to see that Paul's car was still parked in front of the house. She didn't notice Rita come up behind her.

"He's probably wanking off," Rita said quietly, startling her.

Sarah spun around, "What do you want?" It came out sounding angry, but she was mostly confused. She felt what she thought might be jealousy. But she had a hard time figuring out whom or what she was jealous of.

"It seemed like you were upset about something," Rita offered.

"I'm fine," Sarah countered defensively and turned from the window.

"I hope it's not about that wanker."

Sarah couldn't help but laugh. She had studied up on British slang two years before in preparation for the fall play, *The Importance of Being Ernest.* "No, it's not about that tosser."

Rita smiled. "Finally, someone I can talk to without a dictionary." She sat on Sarah's bed, not eager to leave until she knew what was bothering her.

Sarah puttered around a bit. She put the clean clothes that Coleen had left on her bed into the proper drawers of her dresser. Finished, she sat on the other side of the bed. The silence wasn't too awkward, and after a while Sarah felt more comfortable. Finally, it poured out of her. "It's the fucking play. I keep screwing up my lines. I just can't remember them. I'm so stupid."

"Well, stupid you're very definitely not, so there must be something else going on. Is it this Paul? You have a lot of lines with him if I remember the play."

"Yeah, but he isn't the problem. It's always this way for me."

"But I hear you singing all the time, and you know all those lyrics."

"It's different with lyrics. I learn those super easy. But the dialogue, I just can't get it."

Both of them had now swung around and sat cross-legged on the bed so they almost faced each other.

"This might be a bonkers idea, but maybe you should just put it all to music."

"What do you mean?"

"If you remember lyrics easily, maybe it's because your brain focuses on the music or the music helps with the memorization. So just think of the lines along with a tune or maybe just a rhythm in your head."

"Oh, I don't know, I can't create music."

"Sure you can. You have a wonderful voice and can read and hear that music."

"Well, I can't actually read music," Sarah confessed quietly. "But if I listen to it, I can do follow it."

"Okay, fair enough, I can try to make some up for you. Do you have a script handy?"

Sarah nodded and went to her bag to retrieve her script. She placed it on the bed between them as she sat back down. Rita picked it up and began to read, almost immediately humming a tune to accompany the lines.

Sarah watched her carefully. "Does it hurt?" she asked quietly.

Rita instinctively reached down and touched the baby bump on her belly. "No, not hurts, but it does make you wicked sick. It's better now, but when I first got here, I couldn't stay out of the bloody loo."

Sarah shifted, a little uncomfortable, before she responded, "No, actually I meant the, the sex. The first time."

Rita couldn't help but smile, glad that Sarah was still a virgin. Then she was perplexed.

Don't these parents ever talk to their kids?

She vividly remembered that first discussion with her mother. She had just gotten her first period. They were on tour on the continent at bigger clubs than they had ever done. Her mother had already given her the basic description of the parts and their functions, very proper and academic, which was no big deal for a child who lived in backstage dressing rooms where clothes came off regularly, and penises and vaginas were a common sight.

"My mother warned me that it would hurt like bloody hell itself, and it did." She studied the reaction on Sarah's face.

There was a flash of recognition as if it confirmed what she feared.

"But the first time for many of us is a quick boff with a boy who doesn't know fuck-all either. He's scared that he'll shoot his off before he gets inside and embarrass himself. So he jams it into us, not thinking, not knowing, that we need some prep time."

Rita flashed back to Barry the drummer laying on top of her, grunting as he had tried to force his stiff thing into her. She had screamed as it tore her skin and crammed down her tight passage. She had tried to push him off, but he had hung on with amazing strength for someone so skinny. And then he had come quickly and collapsed on her. She had immediately rolled out from under him and run to the bathroom.

"It's a wonder that we ever do it again," she mused, and noticed the horrified look on Sarah's face.

"It's just that it seems so, so gross," Sarah offered cautiously.

"You sound like Eva."

"Who's that?"

"She's my flat-mate, and she's not into boys at all. She thinks they're all grotty."

"So she's homosexual?"

"She prefers women, but she's had bit of experience with men as well. Many people aren't only one thing or the other thing."

"Have you ever, you know, with her?" Sarah asked cautiously.

Rita laughed. "Oh, Eva and me, we've had some moments for sure. Mind you, I do prefer men and don't find them too gross, not most of them anyway." Rita paused and considered before she continued, "Have you thought of a girl like that?"

Sarah's eyes immediately expanded then she quickly turned her gaze away from Rita. "Oh, no. Not exactly . . ."

Rita clearly felt the unspoken message. She recalled the level of intensity that she had felt when she explored Eva, a type of connection that she had never felt with a man. "In some ways being with another woman is like caressing yourself, you both have breasts and vaginas, you both respond to similar stimulus, and are sensitive in the same areas. A guy's body is totally foreign and reacts very differently. Now that's what makes it fun, but it's not the same kind of intimacy as with a woman."

Sarah sat quietly as she tried to process all that.

Rita then felt a need to change the subject, so she picked up the script and started to flip through it. She could sense some of the tension begin to seep out of Sarah. "Okay, here's scene three with Maria and Anita in the bridal shop. What's your first line?"

"Por favor, Anita. Make the neck lower." Sarah used her Puerto Rican accent.

"Wow, that's really a very good accent," Rita complimented her. "Stop it Maria."

"One inch. How much can one little inch mean, or do. Shit, see, it's hopeless."

"No it's not. We'll take this whole scene and put it to some music, and I guarantee you'll know it in no time and never forget it. You still remember lyrics years later, don't you?"

Sarah nodded and smiled.

Holy shit, could it really be that easy?

She really wanted to hug Rita but didn't want to return to the awkward feeling.

* * *

For the next few days Clark managed to avoid any contact with Julie. And it felt to him like she was doing the same. It didn't feel hostile, but it didn't feel good either. On Wednesday, he stared straight ahead in homeroom as the PA announcement mentioned the game that afternoon. It wasn't a home game, and Clark was glad for that.

"If our Cougars win today and Saturday they will be in the city tournament for the tenth year in a row," Julie spoke over the PA system, and finished by encouraging everyone to come to the last home game on Saturday.

During lunch, Clark tried not to look over at the cheerleader table, so he didn't notice Julie eat quickly and leave. The jeers from the baseball team table had quieted down, mostly because he'd refused to react, and they all had short attention spans.

Clark left the lunchroom and wandered down the hall to the art and music rooms. He liked it down there. He felt comfortable around the artists and nerds. And Julie might be there. The sound of a guitar drew him to the open door to the music room. Inside, Julie sat with her back to him, singing and strumming that same catchy tune on her guitar. Gradually he began to realize that he knew the lyrics to the song.

Hey, it's my poem!

His shock manifested itself as a loud, half-formed sound, but not really a word.

Julie heard something behind her and turned around to see an empty doorway. She shrugged her shoulders and went back to the song.

Clark stood with his back pressed flat against some lockers and slowly exhaled. He prayed that he'd reacted quickly enough and that she hadn't seen him. He heard her start to play again. He had never thought of his poems as lyrics but it really sounded good. And it made sense, he realized, because he always listened to music as he wrote. Julie's pacing and inflection were not exactly what he had intended for the poem. He noticed a few minor word differences, but they seemed to work perfectly with the music and didn't change the intended meaning of the poem. It had the same mix of heartache and longing.

Just then, he saw some students he knew coming down the hall. Afraid that they might say something to him, he quickly turned and hurried away.

* * *

Julie sat with the other cheerleaders in the front of the bus on the way to the game. The coaches and players sat in the middle and back. The team liked to have the girls go out first and form a little gauntlet that they could run through as they came off the bus. That would be the only cheering they would hear all afternoon. No other supporters went to these away games, not even the parents.

She listened to Coach Duncan tell the team that this game against Cherry Hill High was a must-win game. They had to win to have a chance to get into the state tournament, which Harrison High had been in almost every year for as long as he had been coach. He said that he would take it as a real personal failure if that streak was broken, and he wanted them to feel the same. Julie wondered if that was really an effective motivational technique; but they were boys and the strangest stuff got them worked up.

The coach's message seemed to work because after four innings they were ahead by one run. The teams exchanged runs in the fifth inning. And after not scoring in the top of the seventh and final inning, the Cougars brought in Rory as a relief pitcher to close it out and win the game. Almost immediately it was apparent that something was wrong with him. After Rory threw four straight balls into the dirt and walked the first batter, Joey went to the mound to see what was wrong. Rory curtly said that he was okay and turned his back on his catcher.

At that point Suzie whispered in Julie's ear, "I guess maybe it's true what Maggie said."

"Maggie?"

"You know Maggie, the weird chick with the blue streaks in her hair, senior who looks like a thirty-year-old slut."

Julie nodded as she watched Rory walk the second batter. "Oh yeah, tall, skinny, but really stacked."

"That's her. I overheard her telling one of the greaser boys that she had a date with Rory last weekend, and that he tried to rape her, and she sent him to the hospital with some Kung-Foo type thing."

The next Cherry Hill batter hit a single to tie the game with no outs. Now Coach Duncan headed to the mound. After a brief conference the coach left Rory in and was rewarded with another walk to load the bases.

Suzy continued, "I wouldn't put the rape thing past Rory, but how would Maggie know Kung-Foo. That's just a movie thing, isn't it?"

Julie wondered why the coach let Rory stay in the game when he was pitching so poorly. She watched as Rory grimaced and tried to throw a fastball. But it went wild and hit the batter, scoring the winning run for Cherry Hill. Rory stomped off the mound holding his hand and seemingly in a lot of pain. Julie felt bad for the team, but not for Rory.

Serves you right you big asshole. Maybe I should get to know this Maggie.

The bus ride home was deadly quiet. Rory sat in the last row with only Dwight near him, but not next to him.

Julie hated to see the season end that way, but now the game on Saturdays didn't mean anything, and she would probably skip it to practice her softball pitching. Maybe that would end her cheerleading career, but she was sick of it anyway. She wanted to play and not prance around being perky for a bunch of jerks who didn't appreciate it. That brought her back to Clark and her outburst the other day. He had this talent, and he didn't want to use it. She would kill for it.

Julie sighed as she realized that it wasn't all his fault, but he was being a jerk for no good reason. He said he didn't care what others thought, but that seemed to be exactly what kept him from trying again. Well, it didn't matter now because the season was effectively over. She would find some way to reconnect with him - she had to talk to him about the song. She also wanted a chance to get to know more about Rita.

When the bus arrived back at Harrison High, she bolted away quickly with Suzie to avoid Dwight. She knew he would be in a piss-poor mood, and she wanted no part of that. She didn't want to have to show off her own martial arts moves on him.

* * *

Clark tried to concentrate on his English homework, but he couldn't get Julie's song out of his head. He didn't know what to do about it, about her.

It seemed like everyone was distracted at dinner. His mother informed them that she and their father were going away for the weekend, but she wasn't sure where - John had planned a surprise. She seemed like a different person, a happier one, as she moved around the kitchen humming a song from some old movie.

Rita and Sarah had this odd girly-girl thing going on as they whispered to each other and kept looking at Sarah's script for her play. Rita pointed at some musical notes that had been written about the lines. But Clark knew that Sarah didn't know how to read music. After dinner they rushed off to Sarah's room and closed the door.

Clark finished his English homework - abandoned it really. He knew it wasn't going to get much better without a lot more work, and he already had a solid A in the course.

The house was very quiet as he came downstairs and then out to the back lawn. He lay down on the grass and stared up at the brilliant display of stars. There was very little light pollution in this part of town, and the high altitude of Denver afforded an awesome view of the constellations. He had just started to get chilly when he heard the door open. He glanced over and saw Rita plop down on one of the lawn chairs. He started to sit up, and it startled her.

"Blimey, Clark, you scared the shite out of me."

He didn't need a translation for that. "Sorry, I thought you saw me."

"Not laying about on the pitch I didn't. What are you doing out here?"

"I was going to ask you the same," he replied, as he sat on the chair next to her.

"Fair enough. I often come out here to look at the stars. There's nothing like this in London. Do you know any of the things up there?"

"You mean the constellations?"

"Yeah the horoscope things - I'm a Scorpio evidently. We had a back-up singer in the band when I was around ten who fancied herself an astrologer and wanted to do everyone's fortunes. She always had very dark visions for people, and I never let her do mine. She did my mother's, but mum would never tell me about it." She paused with her memories. "What sign are you?"

"Taurus, I guess. My friend Margaret last year was into that a little bit. She said that I was born in the right sign, that I'm definitely a Taurus. Whatever that means."

They sat quietly and enjoyed the view until Rita asked tentatively, "So, have you seen Julie since the other day?"

"Well, you know, I see her in school but not to talk to." He paused and looked down at his hands. "Although I did hear her today."

"Oh, what did she say?"

"It wasn't what she said, she was singing, singing this song, that . . ."

She waited patiently for him to continue.

"She's taken a poem that I wrote and put it to music, made this song that she was singing."

"Oh, that's cool."

"Yeah, I guess."

"I didn't know that you wrote songs."

"I don't. I write some poems, and then I had to read this one in class a few weeks ago, and Julie's in the class. She said that she liked it, but she never said anything about taking it for her song."

Rita got the sense that Clark didn't know, or didn't want to acknowledge, how he felt about it. "Oh, I can see how that would be confusing."

He nodded.

"Did you like the song?"

"Yeah."

"Did you tell her?"

"No, she didn't notice me."

"You were hiding?"

"No, not really. Yeah, I guess I was. I've wanted to talk to her about, you know, the other day, but I can't seem to find the right time, right way. I get so damn nervous."

"Have you tried meditating?"

"Like the Zen stuff you mentioned?"

"Bang on. My mother and I got into it the last year she was alive. It helped her relax, and it gave me a way to calm myself in the chaos that always swirled around us. I've rediscovered it the past month with the baby thing. It might help you also."

Clark nodded and then realized. "Whoa, back up a minute, baby thing? What baby thing?"

Rita realized that they all knew except for Clark. She assumed that Coleen had told John. "Yeah, I'm pregnant. Bun in the oven as we Brits say."

"Wow."

Clark leaned back on his chair and looked up at the stars. This would take a little processing time. After a while he asked, "Are you happy about it?"

"Being pregnant?"

He nodded as he continued cautiously, "I mean was it something you planned even though you aren't, you know . . ."

It took her a moment to realize where he was going with that. "Married?" She shook her head after he nodded. "Well, no, Clark, sometimes shite happens that we don't plan. But now that it's happened, I'm pretty happy with it. And you don't have to be married to get knocked-up, you do know that don't you?"

"Oh, sure," he replied quickly, to cover the fact that he had, in fact, assumed that marriage was somehow necessary. He knew that his father was supposed to have a talk with him about that stuff, but it hadn't happened yet. And while Clark knew it was important stuff to learn, he certainly wasn't going to initiate that conversation.

CHAPTER ELEVEN

When Clark got to school the next morning it was abuzz with the news that the baseball team from Mesa High had inexplicably lost their game. That left the door open for Harrison to make the playoff if, but only if, they could win their last game on Saturday against Aurora High.

Clark wasn't sure how he felt about it, but he was surprised to see that Julie didn't seem to be as excited as he expected her to be. She actually seemed unhappy. He briefly thought about asking her, but that didn't seem like a good topic to break the ice. So he kept quiet and went about the morning as he normally did - staying to himself.

Clark saw Coach Duncan enter the lunchroom but didn't think much of it. He assumed that he was there to talk to the players at the baseball team table. It surprised him when the coach approached him.

"Clark, can you come see me right after school?"

"Uh, sure. In your office?" Clark stammered.

"Yes," the coach replied, quickly turned and left.

Clark glanced around the room and tried to ignore the curious looks and the hostile glares from the guys at the baseball table.

For the next few hours Clark puzzled over that strange request. During Social Studies, the negative vibrations were more intense than usual coming from Dwight and his cronies. He also noticed that Rory had a cast on his hand.

When the last bell rang, Clark made his way to the coach's office. Coach Duncan was on the telephone, but his door was open and Clark could hear him.

"So, as long as he's been a student for six months, I can add him, right? Charlie, I don't want to get screwed later on this. Okay, okay, thanks." He hung up and noticed Clark standing at his door. "Come in, Clark, sit down."

Clark sat, and forced himself to maintain eye contact with the coach.

"So, let me get straight to it. You know about our big game on Saturday?" He didn't wait for Clark to answer. "And you know about Rory? Broke his hand. Out for six weeks. Our best reliever."

Clark processed this and nodded.

"Okay. So I need a new reliever, and I think that you're it."

Clark was glad that he was sitting down. His stomach tightened. "Me?"

"I saw you throw some good stuff the other day. Got a bit flustered, but I think, I hope, you can keep it together for a couple of batters, an inning. Can you do that?"

Clark struggled to find his voice. "I guess so."

"No guesses, son. I need to know. I want you to come out tomorrow during lunch and throw some to Joey, our catcher. Just him. Can you do that?"

Clark didn't know Joey that well, except that he was also a junior. And Clark was pretty sure that he wasn't part of Dwight's gang.

"Sure coach, lunch time."

"Tomorrow."

"Tomorrow," Clark confirmed, and then he realized that the coach was done. He got up and headed out the door. "See you tomorrow," he added nervously.

The coach just nodded, already engrossed in the stat sheet from their opponent's last game. He had thought that the season was dead. Mesa had been a lock to win, but didn't. His team wasn't great, but it was solid. Pitching was their Achilles' heel, and then Rory goes down doing some asshole stunt. He had enough experience with these kids that he knew all about the temptations they faced. Raging hormones combined with big growth spurts and more than healthy appetites for food, booze, and sex.

Now he had to put some faith in this strange kid with the potentially good arm, but who knew what upstairs. Clark seemed bright enough, but it was hard to know with the quiet ones what the hell lurked around in there. If Clark pitched okay at lunch with no one there, he'd have him available on Saturday in case of an emergency. He needed an insurance policy, and maybe this kid was it.

Damn crazy luck.

* * *

Rita heard Clark start pitching in the back yard. The consistent thwack sound of the balls hitting the canvas was soothing in its familiarity. She needed that. She had had a restless night. Thoughts and dreams of Keith had constantly interrupted her sleep. She knew that she missed him, but she didn't want to admit that she needed him. That would mean making a decision about their relationship, and she wasn't ready to do that.

The past weeks had been the first time that Rita had ever experienced a normal family life from the inside. She felt comfortable, and even though she was occasionally bored, she was oddly content. And she had the baby to think of. Would she consider raising a child as she had been raised? Would it make a difference to do it with a husband, father? Could she be a suburban mom? Then she thought of her attraction to Eva.

Was she capable of a normal heterosexual relationship with Keith? And then work. What was happening while she was away? She had a lot of unused sick days, but she couldn't stay away long term, she had to work. It gave her a headache just thinking about all of it.

She noticed that the sound of the baseballs had stopped. She went to the window and saw Clark slumped on the chair. He looked stressed. She considered leaving him to his troubles, but then she decided to go down to talk to him.

Better than stewing in my own problems.

As she went, she pulled her t-shirt down. The baby bump was now hard to hide, but she hadn't gotten to the point of being comfortable enough to just let it show. She would soon need some different clothes.

Clark realized that Rita had joined him, but he didn't react right away. He struggled to sort out his emotions, which bounced around between anger and fear and hope. One moment he was angry that the coach had caught him off guard and really hadn't given him a chance to say no. Then hope slid in like a runner to second base and told him that maybe he could do it and impress Julie. Fear then bashed hope with a baseball bat as memories of last week's disaster stormed through his psyche. Underneath all of it lingered the feeling of Julie's kiss on his lips. It had definitely not been a throwaway thing as he had tried to convince himself over the past days.

And what the hell is going on with her using my words in her song?

Rita watched him. She could sense that he was in turmoil. When his body shuddered, a chill despite the warm afternoon air, she finally asked, "Are you okay, mate?"

Even though he knew she was there, it still startled him to hear her speak. He appreciated it that she could feel as comfortable with silence as he did. And then he wondered how Julie would handle that. After a moment, when Rita didn't press, he answered, "You'll be happy to know that I'm going to try again. Tomorrow. The coach asked me."

Instinctively she grabbed his arm. "Clark, that's so grand."

He nodded with a weak smile. Fear then pushed the smile off his face. "Tomorrow is only with the coach and a catcher, but if that goes well, then . . ." His voice trailed off as fear chased it away.

She understood immediately and squeezed his arm. She had known plenty of quiet and shy performers who had a completely different personality on stage. She didn't know where they found it, but she knew it could happen, and that was what Clark needed. "I'd like to tell you about this one mate of mine, Sean, Sean O'Neil. A brilliant singer, but he was terrified of being on stage in front of people. But he overcame it."

"Really? How?"

"Well, it was my mum actually. She told him one day that she had developed this thing to help overcome stage fright. She said that when she first started singing on stage she always felt exposed out there, like she was naked. So she tried to turn that around and imagine everyone in the audience being naked."

Clark laughed nervously, any mention of naked did that to him. "Did that work?"

"I guess it did because he went out there and performed brilliantly and afterward thanked my mother." She leaned back on the chair and thought of her mother's good soul. Then she enjoyed the memory of Sean as he had followed Patricia around like a puppy for the rest of the tour. Rita had expected to find them in bed one day, but she had realized later that her mother had probably already begun to feel the effects of her cancer.

Clark saw the change come over Rita, and he sat back and stared up at the sky. They sat there quietly for a while.

Rita finally broke the silence. "We need to come up with something for you. Do you think the naked thing will work?"

Clark certainly related to the part about feeling naked out there; he had dreamt just such a thing. He tried to imagine the other people naked. He had seen guys in the locker room, and that made him uncomfortable. Then he imagined the cheerleaders and Julie. The memory of seeing Rita naked was also strong. His imagination bounced back and forth between the two - the reality of Rita's nakedness and the fantasy of Julie's. Then he remembered the tight tank top that Julie had worn to school the day before and her firm round breasts. Suddenly, he realized that he was becoming erect, and he shifted in his chair to take the pressure off as it thrust up against his pants.

Rita noticed his discomfort and quickly saw the cause.

Well, I guess we need another image.

She turned her gaze to the house and waited for Clark to either relax or go inside to take care of that. He continued to squirm.

"Clark, do you want to go inside and take care of that?"

"What do you mean?" he replied weakly, embarrassed.

She laughed. "Your pan handle. You're going to hurt yourself keeping it caught up in there." Then she began to realize. "You do beat the bishop, don't you?"

His bewildered look answered her.

"Oh, bloody hell. Masturbate. You do it, right?

He looked down, then around, anywhere but at her.

"My God, Clark don't you . . ." She paused as she realized that indeed he really didn't know anything about anything.

Now completely embarrassed, he got up and fled into the house. Rita noticed that his erection was almost gone. She felt sorry for him, so clueless and uncomfortable. Her instinct was to help him, tell him what to do. But she knew that that was his father's job, and she didn't want to overstep her role, whatever it was, in the family.

* * *

Julie was worried. Her first practice for the Junior Cowgirls was on Sunday, and she didn't have her permission slip signed. Her father was seldom home anymore, and she didn't want to ask her mother. But tonight Bea seemed quiet, with an almost sober demeanor, so Julie took a chance and asked her. The cruel smile that appeared on her mother's face caused Julie to take a step away from her.

"Now why on earth would I do that?" Bea oozed with phony concern. "I have to protect you, you stupid girl. You'll never hook a man acting like a big dyke, and that's what they all are, you know, they're all big queers." She spat the last part out with a vehemence that bordered on pathological. She tried to grab the permission slip but missed, and Julie turned and ran from the room. "You can run but you can't hide, little girl," Bea mocked. "You're nothing but trash just like me, and you'll wind up just like me." She pulled a pint of bourbon from her purse and took a big swig.

CHAPTER TWELVE

Clark woke after a fitful night of little sleep and weird sexual dreams that mostly involved Julie. In one of them, Julie had laughed as he struggled to get his erect penis out of his pants. Then he had found himself walking naked down the hallway of the school. No one seemed to notice until he had come to Dwight and Rory who had locker room towels that they had used to snap at him.

As he got dressed, his humiliation from the interaction with Rita fought with his growing sense of dread about the lunch appointment with the coach. He was relieved when he entered the kitchen for breakfast and found that Rita wasn't up. On his walk to school, he mostly managed to keep thoughts of her or of Julie at bay. He did, however, allow himself to enjoy a moment with the memory of Julie kissing him, but he quickly pushed it away when he began to think of her being naked while doing it. He considered skipping first period to avoid seeing her. But he didn't, and he was glad because she gave him a wonderful smile that lifted his spirits for the entire morning and carried him out to the field at lunchtime.

There were a couple of seventh graders from the nearby middle school throwing a Frisbee in the field, but otherwise no one was around as Clark sat on the bench, put on his cleats and began to stretch. After about five minutes he began to worry that the coach wasn't coming. Then worry turned to hope as his small amount of confidence began to fade.

"Hi, Clark."

Clark hadn't noticed Joey approach and was pleased that he knew his name.

"Hey, Joey."

"Coach is on his way," Joey reported, as he grabbed his mitt. "Want to loosen up?" he asked, as if he did it every day with Clark.

It immediately put Clark at ease, and he replied, "Sure," as he headed for the mound.

Joey had a bag of baseballs, and he threw one to Clark.

Clark took a moment to try to calm down and not throw too hard to start. Then he threw a series of about five or six pitches, each one a little faster as his arm loosened up, each one directly into Joey's mitt as he crouched behind home plate. Then Clark stopped and looked around for the coach. He didn't see him, but he did see Rita sitting on the hillside along left field. She didn't look right at him, but he knew she was watching and it made him happy.

"Sorry I'm late," the coach yelled, as he rounded the backstop and came up next to Joey.

Clark pulled his attention back from Rita. "No problem, sir."

"If you're warm, let's see some stuff. You know the standard signs from the catcher?"

"Yes, sir." Clark looked to Joey for a sign. Joey signaled for a fastball inside as the coach took the place of a batter. Clark had worked on a concentration sequence, which included seeing the sign, a glance to first base even if no one was on, a stare into his glove where his hand found the right grip on the ball, then a flash memory of Julie's kiss before he started his windup and threw. He now added a quick look up to the hillside for Rita.

It took about six or seven seconds, which seemed long to him, but wasn't unusual in the world of baseball where idiosyncrasies and behavior ticks were very common. Ball players were creatures of habits that were born of superstition and their understanding that skill accounted for only a part of their success. Something intangible, luck mostly, made the difference between average and great.

Clark's first fastball caught Joey by surprise as it smacked into his glove and almost caused him to lose his balance.

"Whoa! Nice pitch!"

As Clark threw several more impressive fastballs, all hitting Joey's target, the coach had to struggle to maintain his excitement. "Call for some curves," he said to Joey, who then flashed the curveball sign to Clark.

Clark glanced over to see Rita still there, and then he responded with a big breaking curve that kissed the outside corner of the plate.

After two more of those, Joey glanced up at the coach and said quietly, "This is the best stuff on the team."

The coach nodded slightly, noncommittal. There was still the big unknown of how Clark would do in a game with the crowd and a real batter. The last time hadn't been pretty.

"Do you have any other pitches?" the coach asked Clark after another great curveball.

"A slider," Clark responded.

Joey called for it and then, after a few good pitches, the coach finally had seen enough and he walked out to the mound. "The slider is good, but your fastball and curve are very good. I'd like to add you to the team as a reliever. What do you say?"

Clark paused and quickly weighed his decision. He really wanted to play, but he was terrified of what might happen in a real game situation. He glanced over to see Rita still sitting there.

But what the hell, I can't hide forever.

He looked the coach square in the eye as he responded, "Yes sir, I'd like to do that."

Joey smiled as he put his mitt in his bag.

The coach maintained his stoic demeanor, which belied real excitement mixed with dread.

Dumb crazy luck.

"See me after school, and we'll get you a uniform. Game is tomorrow at one o'clock, here against Aurora. You know it's a big game, right?" He purposefully added the last comment to gauge Clark's reaction. He noted that Clark seemed calm as he nodded and went to the bench to take off his cleats.

The school bell rang across the field, and they all rushed off.

Joey ran up alongside Clark. "Great job. See you this afternoon at practice."

Clark nodded and smiled, but now he was confused. Coach hadn't mentioned coming to practice. He looked around, but the coach was already involved with his sixth period gym class that was about to play soccer on the football field.

* * *

Rita had read the body language of the coach, and it had clearly said that he was happy with Clark and had asked him to be on the team. She would, of course, act surprised when he told her, but she had felt extremely positive and happy as she walked back to the house.

Coleen wasn't home. She'd left early for a golf game and then planned to go to the grocery store. Rita had offered to help, but Coleen said that she liked to do it. She noticed the dirty breakfast dishes in the sink and spent the next fifteen minutes cleaning up. She was on her way upstairs to rest when she noticed that the mail had come through the mail slot in the front door and was lying on the floor. She bent down to retrieve it and put it on the small table in the hall. Stamps with an engraving of Queen Elizabeth caught her eye. The letter was addressed to her.

In her room, Rita opened the envelope and found a letter from Eva plus another sealed envelope. She sat on the bed and read the letter from Eva.

> Dear Rita, Very relieved to find that you are okay and getting to know your American family. Must be totally weird. On a map Denver looks like it's in the middle of nowhere. He could have had the sense to live in New York or Los Angeles or San Francisco. But he left you and your mum, so what sense does he have? Keith is driving me absolutely bonkers. He's practically camped out in our hall. The neighbors are getting steamed. I finally told him that if he wrote you a letter, I'd mail it to you. So here it is. Stay you, and come home soon. Pamela went back to Barcelona, and I'm horny. Love Eva

Rita smiled and then hesitantly opened Keith's letter.

> My Dearest Rita, Eva has been a bloody vault with information about where you are and what you're doing. America. I can't bloody well believe it. Did you really find your father? I've missed you, and I love you. I realize it now that you've been gone and I'm sorry I've been a wanker to not realize it while you were here. I know you probably think I'm on the road boffin every bird I see. But that's not true. There hasn't been anyone else since you, and I don't want anyone but you. So please come home soon. Love, Keith.

Rita flopped back on the bed. She felt bad that she hadn't said goodbye or even told him she was going away. And about the baby? If she were there he would know by now unless she refused to see him, and she knew that she wouldn't do that.

143

Now her short meet-and-greet trip had extended to well over a fortnight, with no end in sight. She missed both Eva and Keith, but she was also really happy and knew that it wasn't time to leave this family yet. She had this fear that after she left she would never see any of them again.

She heard the back door open and Coleen come in. After a moment Coleen came up the stairs and knocked on the door. "Rita, are you there? Thanks for doing the dishes."

Rita pulled herself together and opened the door.

She must have looked tired because Coleen immediately reacted. "Oh, I'm so sorry were you taking a nap?"

"No, just resting, cooling off. I was over at the school watching Clark try out for the baseball team, and it was bloody hot in the sun."

"Clark did what?"

"He tried out, and I think he got on the team to pitch."

"He's never done that before. He always said he didn't want to."

"Now he does, and he did it. I believe they have a game on Saturday. You and John should go."

"Oh, Saturday we can't, we're going to Las Vegas. I thought I told everyone." Coleen was now conflicted between the excitement of the trip and the stunning news about Clark. "John's already paid for everything. I don't think we can cancel. He's coming home tonight so we can leave early in the morning."

Rita shrugged, not knowing what to say.

"But they have lots of games, right?" Coleen offered hopefully.

"I don't know, but according to Julie this might be the end of the season."

"Julie? Who's that?"

"She's a cheerleader who likes Clark, and he likes her, but hasn't done anything about it. Well, except for trying out."

Coleen was stunned and stammered, "Clark has a girl-friend?"

"Well not officially, but she did write a song using his lyrics."

"No, no stop right there! You're talking about some other boy, not my Clark."

Rita could only smile knowingly.

"Since when does he write lyrics? Oh my God, I need a cup of tea or something stronger." Coleen turned and rushed down the stairs.

Rita watched her go.

One strange family.

* * *

After school Clark made his way to the coach's office. The team was in the locker room getting ready for practice while the coach talked to his assistant, Mr. Jackson, the tenth grade science teacher. Dwight and his pals gave Clark some hard looks, but didn't say anything with the coaches around. Coach Jackson hurried them all out to the field, leaving Clark with Coach Duncan.

"Okay Clark. Let's go see what we have for a uniform. We'll wear the whites tomorrow at home."

He went into his office, and from a closet he pulled out a couple of big cardboard boxes and dug around inside. He pulled out a uniform shirt, held it up and looked at Clark. "No, too small, you can't pitch in that." He held up another shirt that was obviously too large and quickly discarded. There followed maybe a half dozen shirts, and none seemed to be right. The coach was getting frustrated, and Clark suddenly felt nervous that the lack of a uniform would derail his big chance.

"Damnation," the coach swore, as he pushed the boxes aside and then moved into the closet and rooted around. "Ah ha," he exclaimed, as he pulled out a crumpled uniform shirt with the number seven. "Buddy Swain's shirt, he was your size. And our best pitcher two years ago."

As he handed the shirt to Clark, they both noticed a large rip in the seam under the armpit.

"I'm sure you must have someone at home who can sew that up."

Clark nodded and took the shirt, followed by a pair of pants that looked the right size but needed to be washed. There were three hats and fortunately one fit.

"Team meeting at noon sharp, dressed and ready to go. You got a cup don't ya? For protection." He didn't wait for Clark to answer. "I can't promise you'll play, but you gotta be ready. Okay?" He started to head off.

"Coach, should I go out to the practice?"

Coach paused and replied carefully, "I, uh, didn't think you'd be prepared, and besides, you've thrown already today. Go on and get a good night's sleep tonight. See you at noon tomorrow." The coach then rushed out of the office to put an end to the conversation. He didn't want to spook things by having the others get on Clark's case at practice. He hoped that the boy would prove himself on the field. That was the best way to gain acceptance on a team. Finding Swain's uniform was another bit of luck - now he wouldn't stand out like a rube in a brand new uniform.

Dumb crazy luck.

Clark skirted around the baseball field on his way home. He had the uniform tucked under his arm, hidden from the team as they practiced. He had also carefully avoided the cheerleaders, who were practicing near the school. He tried to keep his excitement in check and was doing okay until he saw Rita sitting in the back yard. Then he couldn't keep the big grin from taking over his face.

"Well, look at you. Let me guess, mate. I'd say you made the team."

"Yeah, there's a game tomorrow." The grin got bigger. "I hope you can come. I'm gonna ask Mom and Dad also."

"You know Clark, I think I heard your mum say something about them going away for the weekend."

"Oh yeah right." His curiosity overcame his disappointment. "You know it's so odd, he's just been gone a week, and they were acting really strange last weekend."

What Rita considered strange was that it seemed like American kids were not aware of, or exposed to, their parents as sexual beings. Her experience had been so different. For her mother, sex had been right out there, as normal as eating or sleeping. She realized that maybe Clark's and Sarah's experience was normal for most kids, and that her mum had been unique.

Clark's nervous energy got the best of him, and he went over to pitch. He wouldn't throw hard. Just enough to release some of the tension that had already begun to build as he anticipated the game the next day.

* * *

It was late and she was tired, but Rita finally succeeded in catching John alone. The evening had been hectic and a bit unsettling for everyone, as John had come home and then immediately got ready to leave with Coleen for their weekend in Las Vegas.

His parents' reaction to his news about the team had been almost adequate, but not exactly what Clark had hoped for, as evidenced by his strained smile. He had laughed at Sarah's reaction, which had been strong, even though caustically negative. She couldn't believe that he would put himself out there like that. Sarah had rehearsal and Colleen and John were leaving early, so that left just Rita available to go to the game. Clark had put up a good front, but Rita could tell that he had been disappointed. That had made her even more determined to talk to John.

John sat alone in the living room with a half-empty glass of scotch. He smiled when he saw Rita. He stared at her growing baby bump as she sat on the chair across from him.

"You're up late," he offered.

"I rested some this afternoon."

The ensuing silence hung heavy in the room.

"You know Clark really put himself out there for this team. It's a very big deal for him."

John fought the defensive reaction that threatened to overtake him. "I know."

She didn't think that he really did, and she couldn't resist the urge to challenge him, "I'm not sure that you do."

He really wanted to avoid a confrontation with her. He was in a good mood anticipating the weekend, and he didn't want to ruin it. "I'll make the next game."

"As I understand it, if they don't win tomorrow the season is over."

"Oh, I sure hope they win then," he responded, with a forced laugh that fell flat and led to another awkward silence.

"I have to go back home pretty soon. I only had a little holiday time from work."

Now he felt guilty as he remembered that he still hadn't spent any time with her.

She sensed his anguish and debated whether to press ahead. In the end she accepted it that he needed more time, and that he was limited in his ability to connect to other people on intimate personal stuff.

I'll give him some more time, and try to help Clark if I can.

CHAPTER THIRTEEN

Clark woke up on Saturday morning surprised that he had slept so well. Even the disappointment that his parents weren't going to be at the game couldn't temper his excitement. A strong thread of fear also worked through him, but he found that he could make the fear a stronger motivator than inhibitor. At least he could then, still three hours before he had to report for the game.

He ate breakfast alone. His parents had already left. Sarah had gone to her rehearsal. And Rita was still in her room, probably asleep. Minute by minute he felt the fear become a bigger presence, and he knew he had to address it head-on.

What's the worst that can happen?

He knew that he could be an utter disaster and would never be able to go to school again.

I can deal with that. The school year is almost over anyway. The Question is coming and we'll be moving soon.

Then he realized that he probably wouldn't even get into the game. There were two other relievers. Benji and Jason weren't nearly as good as Rory, but if Dwight was starting, he could possibly pitch all seven innings. If it was Sebastian, then four or five innings were as many as he usually lasted.

Clark retreated to his room and tried to read. They had just started reading *To Kill a Mockingbird* for English class. He had learned that the author, Harper Lee, based the story on her own life, and he worried whether he could be a writer without having such interesting and formative things happen to him.

He heard Rita come out of her room, and he looked at the clock. Almost two hours had passed, and it was eleven o'clock. He would have to get ready soon. He looked over at the uniform on his bed. His mother had washed it last night, but . . .

Shit, I forgot about the rip!

He rushed into the kitchen as Rita drank her tea and ate a boiled egg and a slice of toast, which was more breakfast than she normally had, but she knew that she needed to eat more in her condition.

"Ready for the game?" she asked, as she tried to decipher the look on his face.

"Mostly, except for this." He put the uniform shirt on the table and lifted the arm to expose the rip in the seam.

She looked at it and immediately knew what he wanted. "So I guess you're looking for a bit of thread and a needle to sew that up," she teased him, but quickly backed off when she saw his horrified expression. "Oh, I'm just windin' you up. I'll do it. Does your mum have a mending kit?"

Clark flew from the room and was back in less than a minute with Coleen's sewing box. He carefully placed it in front of Rita. "Thank you so much."

"No worries, I was stitching up my mum's costumes before I could even read. She was a very energetic performer and tough on her wardrobe. Although I think sometimes she liked to have things rip just to show off her strawberry creams." She noticed his bewildered look. "Oh right, translation, her breasts." She gestured to hers, and he began to turn red and shuffled his feet. She tried not to laugh as she began to work on the rip.

As Clark approached the entrance to the team locker room, he felt his stomach tighten in a knot, and he stopped. Anticipation of the negative comments from Dwight and his cronies almost made him stop and turn around. But he took a deep breath and entered.

It wasn't as bad in the locker room as he had anticipated. Coach Duncan introduced him and made it very clear that he would not tolerate any negative reaction to adding a new teammate at this late date. "This is possibly the biggest game of your young lives as baseball players, and there can be no distractions. With Rory down, we needed help, and Clark is going to give it. End of story."

Joey took Clark to an empty locker near his and tried to make him feel welcome.

Clark kept his back to the room as he undressed and changed. He did hear a couple of players take sharp intakes of breath as they saw him. A few indistinguishable whispers came from the area where Dwight sat with Ed and Miguel and the other seniors.

"He's got more hair than me," some boy said.

"He's got more than your dog." He thought that was Miguel.

"Pussy." That was definitely Dwight.

Clark had heard it all before when people saw his body hair for the first time. If he went to a pool or the beach, he always kept his t-shirt on. He noticed that Ralph, the shortstop and only black boy on the team, stood next to him and stared. Ralph smiled as he realized he wasn't the only odd man in the room anymore. Ralph whispered, "Man you're a beast." His tone was positive, not insulting, and Clark forced a small smile of acknowledgement.

Julie was tired as she walked to the ballfield and tried to soak in some energy from the midday sun. She had been home alone the night before when Dwight pounded on the front door, yelling that he knew she was in there. She had yelled back at him, through the closed door, that he had to be quiet or he'd wake her mother.

"No, I won't," he had snickered. "She's at the Lizard Lounge, completely wasted. I saw her."

It had been obvious that he had been drinking, and she had this terrible image of her mother and Dwight together in a bar. She knew that she had to be careful of his increasingly aggressive drive to get her to have sex. "I'm not feeling well, it's that time of the month for me."

"Hell it is. You said that two weeks ago. I wrote it down, just so I'd know. Laurie says the curse only gets girls a few days once a month."

Why doesn't he just go fuck her?

"You should be home. You've got a big game tomorrow."

He hadn't answered, and she had begun to worry. Then she had heard him at the back door. She had raced to it, praying that it was locked - it had been. For the first time she could remember, she had been glad to hear her mother's car pull into the driveway and run over the same garbage can that she always hit when she came home drunk. She knew that Dwight wanted no part of Bea when she was drunk. Hell, he didn't want to be around her when she was sober. But of course no one did, including Julie. She had heard him curse and run off through the side yard as Bea burst through the front door.

"Julie! That boy had better not be in here. I seen his car. I told you no fucking around in my house." Bea had staggered to the living room where Julie waited. "There you are. Where is he?"

"He came over, but I wouldn't let him in. He said he'd seen you at the Lizard."

"Yeah, and I seen him too, that's why I'm here. He lit out like his dick was on fire, and I knew where he was going."

"I can take care of myself."

"Shit you can. Nothing stops a drunk horny man. Certainly not your little martial arts, karate shit. Your daddy's a fool thinking that'll keep you safe." With that she had collapsed on the couch and immediately passed out.

Julie had then finally been able to breathe a sigh of relief.

Julie reached the baseball field, and that gradually lifted her spirits. She hoped the good weather would continue the next day when she had Junior Cowgirl practice. She waved at Suzie as her friend got out of her car, and then they joined the other girls who were already there and stretching. Julie really did love the games and the energy that they were able to pull from the crowd. It wasn't as good as playing, but it was better than sitting in the stands like a lump. She looked around and saw the Aurora High team warming up along the third base side and in left field.

Is it my imagination or do they look older, bigger? Where are our guys?

Then she saw the Cougars team jog over from the school. Dwight and Joey led the way. The others followed with one player hanging back by himself. Someone she didn't immediately recognize. Then she did.

Oh my God, Clark?

Clark was so pumped up that he could barely hold himself back at the end of the group. He wanted to sprint ahead and circle around the field a couple of times to burn off some of his excess energy. As they reached the field, the first person he noticed was Julie. She stood there and stared at him. He tried to avoid eye contact while he deciphered the look on her face. It was definitely shock, but was it good or bad? He hoped it was good.

As the team stretched and warmed up, he cautiously glanced around at the crowd. There were a lot of students and quite a few parents in the home team stands along first base. There was even a pretty good crowd in the visitors' third base stands. He looked out toward the hillside along left field and was relieved to see Rita sitting on a blanket.

As the portable speaker system blared the national anthem and everyone stood facing the flag that hung from the backstop, Clark felt a completely new sensation. He felt at home, like he belonged. He knew the crowd wasn't cheering for him specifically but for the team, but now he was a part of it. It didn't sync with his entrenched lone wolf persona, but it felt good, natural, something he could get used to. A moment of intense fear whipped through him as he imagined being called on to go out there and pitch. But he quickly suppressed it. Dwight was pitching and he prided himself on being a horse who could go the full seven innings of a game, especially a game this important. The chance that all three relievers would be called upon was extremely small.

Harrison High was the home team, so they took to the field to start the game. They all seemed tense, but Dwight looked terrible, tired, hung-over. And he was. After fleeing Julie's house, Dwight had gone to see Laurie, and she had been all too happy to let him take out his sexual frustration on her. Then they had raided her parents' amply stocked liquor cabinet. He had felt invincible then, but now he felt like crap.

Coach Duncan noticed that Dwight looked pale and lacked his normal swagger as he warmed up. He attributed it to nerves, acknowledging that anyone would have them starting a big game like this.

Biggest game of the boy's life.

Nerves, exacerbated by a queasy stomach and bleary eyes, resulted in a very shaky start. Dwight walked the first batter on four straight pitches in the dirt. Joey managed to catch the first three, and then the fourth one blew past him and hit the backstop. He'd known that Dwight was fucked up when he saw him in the locker room. It had happened before but not this bad. He knew he should call time and go out to try to settle him down, but he also knew that Dwight was a prick and would deny that anything was wrong.

Dwight's first pitch to the second batter hit him squarely on the shoulder, and he took first base, glaring at Dwight all the way down the baseline.

The coach called time and went out to try to calm Dwight down. Clark watched the exchange - an intense, but short, conversation. Dwight seemed to gain some control as he threw a low fastball to the next batter, which he hit as a weak ground ball to Ed, the second baseman. Ed tossed the ball to Ralph, the shortstop, who had moved to cover second base, and who then got the ball to Bill at first for a nice double play. Two out and a man on third presented Dwight with a golden opportunity to get out of this first inning okay. But he didn't, as the next batter hit a solid base hit into the gap in right field, easily scoring the man from third. The Aurora crowd cheered loudly as their team went ahead, one to nothing. A pop-up to Billy, the right fielder, ended the inning with no further damage.

Clark noticed that no one spoke to Dwight as he sat on the bench and hung his head. Then almost immediately, Dwight jumped up, ran behind the stands, and got a few steps into the grass before he bent over and violently threw up. Everyone noticed, but few looked directly as their star pitcher continued to heave. Unfortunately for Dwight, by the time he returned to the bench, the first three Cougar batters had struck out, and it was time to take the field again. The coach spoke briefly and quietly to Dwight, who slowly stood and walked out to the mound.

Rita knew very little about what was going on with the game, but she was thrilled to see the pitcher for Clark's team get sick behind the stands. Not that she wanted anyone to feel bad, but she knew that, compared to that level of embarrassment, it would take a lot for Clark to look bad.

Julie was conflicted - glad to see Dwight suffer the consequences of his behavior but upset for the team. She looked at Clark, who seemed surprisingly calm, and she was thankful that he didn't appear to gloat over Dwight's discomfort. Noticing how quiet it had become in the Harrison stands, she quickly gathered her team and began a routine of cheers. The crowd's response was forced but still hopeful. Certainly an inauspicious start, but it was still early.

For the next two innings Dwight seemed to gain some strength. He gave up some hits, but no one else scored. Julie kept an eye on Clark who appeared to be very intensely focused on the game. She didn't see him look over at her even once, and she felt a little disappointed at that.

Normally when he watched a game Clark studied the pitcher's moves and every batter's tendencies. Most players had certain tendencies, habits that could be used to predict what they were going to do. What pitch were they likely to throw. Were they going to try to pick-off a runner at first base? Were they eager to swing away at the next pitch? What pitch were they likely to miss? It was what Las Vegas gamblers called a player's tells. Clark had seen it in a Humphrey Bogart gangster film. He knew Dwight cold and could easily predict almost every pitch. The Aurora pitcher was a little harder, but by the end of the second inning Clark was getting it right more than eighty percent of the time. After their second time at bat, he had ascertained the tells of more than half of their batters.

"How's it going Clark?" Joey sat down next to him as the team came up to bat in the bottom of the third inning. He began to loosen some of his gear because he was up fourth in the inning. If someone got a hit, he had to be ready to bat.

"Good," Clark responded, never taking his eyes off the action.

Joey smiled, "Man, you're really into this aren't you?"

"Did you see how their pitcher always looks into his glove before a fast ball?"

The Aurora pitcher looked up from his glove and proceeded to throw a fastball that blew by the Harrison batter.

"There. See?"

"Yeah, cool. Anything else?"

"He looks like he has to take a dump before a curveball, like it's hard for him to get it out."

Joey broke up laughing, which caused the others on the bench, including the coach, to look over at them.

Just then, Ira, the centerfielder, laid down a surprise bunt and beat it out for a base hit. He stole second before the next batter struck out. That brought Joey up to the plate with a runner in scoring position. Joey was a decent hitter, but prone to streaks, and he had been on a cold streak of late. He watched as the pitcher grimaced before throwing a good curve ball. He looked over at Clark, who nodded to him. Another grimace brought another curve that Joey was ready for but only managed to foul off. The pitcher looked down into his glove, and Joey dug in waiting for a fastball. He was ready and swung hard, sending the ball screaming into the gap in left center for a double and an RBI, as Ira scored easily from second base. Joey was pumped up as he stood on second base and pointed excitedly at Clark. The coach noticed and was curious.

The next batter struck out and the inning was over, but the Cougars had tied the score.

The coach came up to Joey as he put on his gear. "Great anticipation on that fastball, it seemed like you knew it was coming."

"I did, Coach, thanks to Clark."

"Clark? What do you mean?"

"He's been over there analyzing everything and picked up some little things the pitcher does before different pitches. We need to tell the other guys."

Clark knew at the beginning of the top of the fourth inning that Dwight was done. He was very lucky to get out of the inning without further scoring by Aurora - saved by some very good defensive play by the Cougars. Clark wasn't surprised to see the coach ask Tommy, the backup catcher, to warm up Benji to go in for the fifth inning.

The coach had Joey talk to every batter in the bottom of the fourth, and they managed to get two more runs before the Aurora coach pulled their pitcher. Their relief pitcher got the final out, but the damage was done, and Harrison now led three to one.

Julie could feel the crowd come alive as Harrison surged ahead, and she urged her cheerleaders into action as the team headed to the field for the top of the fifth inning. She had watched the players' interactions on the bench, which had increasingly involved Clark - first with Joey, then with several others, and eventually the coach. She had been worried about him at first, but less so as he maintained this very intense but seemingly calm demeanor. He really studied the game and didn't engage in the typical clowning around on the bench. Mature or scared, she wasn't sure which he was, but she assumed that it was a bit of both.

She could soon tell, as could everyone else, that this wasn't Benji's best day. The crowd let out a collective groan as the first

Aurora batter sent Benji's fastball over the head of Billy in right field and came around to score on an inside-the-park home run.

Benji struggled to keep his composure. She knew that being a pitcher was extremely stressful. Pitchers were constantly the focal point of the team and the action.

All eyes are on you. There's nowhere to hide.

After Benji walked the next two batters, she realized that Clark might get into the game, and she'd have to watch.

Clark had the same thoughts as Julie as he realized that Benji probably wouldn't last much longer. If Jason went in for Benji, that left him as the last relief pitcher if Jason didn't perform.

He focused even more intensely than before on each batter and his tendencies, strengths and weaknesses. Normally this just helped Clark pass the time, but now it also kept him from thinking about what he might be called upon to do. He watched the Aurora pitcher lay down a great bunt, which moved the runners to second and third. The next Aurora batter was a big left-handed hitter who Clark had watched eat up curve balls down and inside to him. He swung his bat almost like a golf club and crushed the ball. They had been fortunate so far that he had gotten under them just enough to send them high but not so far that Miguel hadn't been able to catch them in deep left field.

Don't throw the curve inside.

Joey and Benji didn't hear Clark's telepathic message, and the Aurora batter sent the next pitch hard to the gap between left and center. That scored the two men on base. A great throw from Ira in center field surprised the hitter as he rounded third, trying to score. Too late, he realized his mistake and tried to dive back to third base, but was tagged out by Andy. It was now four to three in favor of Aurora, and Benji fought for control.

Joey joined the coach at the mound as he tried to settle Benji down. "Don't try to be perfect," Coach Duncan said. "Rely on your defense. Just one more out."

Benji nodded but he was too nervous to process anything the coach said.

Clark watched and felt terrible for Benji even though he was part of Dwight's gang. He felt his own sense of dread rise and looked away from the field. He immediately saw Julie, who stood with her group near the end of the bench. They tried to get the crowd back into a positive mindset, but it wasn't working very well. Clark felt a surge of positive emotion as he soaked in Julie's intensity and spirit. He was mesmerized and didn't notice that she had turned in his direction and was looking right at him. Her sympathetic smile dove deep into him, and he felt like they were the only two people in the entire world. He didn't know whether or not he smiled back, but he couldn't stop staring at her.

The crack of a bat on a ball brought them both rudely and suddenly back to the game. They turned to see Ralph, the shortstop, make a great grab of a hard line drive. The inning was over, but the damage was done.

As the Harrison players trotted off the field, the coach implored them to keep their focus. "All right guys, we'll get it back. Look for your pitch. Don't get too aggressive. Make him pitch to you."

The coach went to Benji and had a few quiet words with him, and then he went over to Tommy and told him to get Jason warmed up to go in at the top of the next inning, the sixth.

Clark thought he saw the coach glance over at him, but he wasn't sure. He turned to Joey, who sat next to him on the bench.

"Hey, see anything with this pitcher yet?" Joey asked.

Clark shook his head as he responded, "Not yet, but I'm watching."

Clark watched Jason warm up. He was definitely a step below Benji in ability. But if he couldn't last the next two innings, that meant Clark would have to go in. He turned back to Joey. "Hey, I don't want to, you know, get into your stuff. You're calling a good game . . ." he said hesitantly, then paused.

"Clark, we're a team. If you've seen something, tell me."

Clark nodded and proceeded to tell Joey what he had noticed about the three Aurora batters that were due up next inning. Some of it Joey had picked up also, but Clark had been able to watch more carefully from the bench and had some great insights. A couple of times Joey questioned Clark and then felt comfortable that what Clark had seen was more accurate than his own observations.

Coach Duncan noticed the intense conversation between Clark and Joey. Jason had never gone more than an inning and a third, and the coach knew it was very possible that the entire season could come to rest on the arm of this strange, intense kid. He saw Joey go over and bring Jason to join the conversation with Clark, and then he had to go over and see what was going on.

Clark explained that the weakness of the second batter was clearly the curve ball away but stopped when he noticed that the coach stood there, listening. He was unsure if he was somehow doing something wrong.

Joey followed Clark's look to see the coach. He stood up and they all followed suit. "Coach, Clark's helping with some great info on the next few batters. He's seen some things that I didn't notice."

The coach stared at Clark and couldn't believe that anyone who saw a pitcher's tells and analyzed batters, had never played before. Then he remembered seeing him out there on the hillside for all the home games, and even most practices. He looked at Jason and saw a more confident stance and expression than he'd ever seen on the kid before.

Dumb Crazy Luck.

The coach turned to watch his number eight batter strike out. Benji was up next, but he only had one more person on the bench, and he was a better fielder than hitter, so he let Benji bat even though he hadn't had a hit all season. Predictably, Benji struck out looking, and the inning was over.

Rita was incredibly bored, and she had to pee in the worst way. But she was determined to stay and be there for Clark. She had been able to follow a little of what was going on. She could see on the little scoreboard that it was Home 3 and Visitor 4, and she knew that wasn't good. She could read the body language from the team and particularly from Julie and the cheerleaders. When she saw Julie's shoulders slump, she knew it was bad.

It made her happy to see what appeared to be the gradual acceptance of Clark by the team or at least several of the boys, particularly the one who Clark called the catcher. He had started out sitting all alone, and now he had several of them crowding around him. When she saw the coach go over to Clark, she held her breath, wondered if he going to put him in? She wanted him to but also dreaded it.

If I feel this nervous, what must Clark be feeling?

She relaxed a little when someone else went in to pitch. Then her bladder couldn't wait, and she hurried off toward the woods and home. She hoped that if she ran she wouldn't miss much.

Clark noticed Rita leave and had a moment of panic. He knew that she was there for him. It was easy to see her out there next to left field because she was in his line of sight as he watched the game. He hoped she was all right. He knew that she would be there, if she could.

Jason's first pitch brought Clark's attention back to the game. Low and away, just like they'd discussed. The batter swung violently and twisted around on his heels, almost toppling over. Next pitch, same one, same result.

Will he chase another one?

No. "Ball," The umpire called.

Joey called for a fastball away, and the batter fouled it off. Then Jason finished him off with a fastball inside.

"Strike!"

Jason pounded his fist into his glove. He didn't strike out many people.

Julie and the crowd cheered. She couldn't believe the difference in Jason. She wondered what had been going on in that intense huddle, with Clark seemingly at the center of it.

As the next batter dug in around home plate, Jason shook off the pitch signal from Joey. Joey again called for a fastball inside as they had discussed. Jason had a curveball in his head, just like the last batter. He glanced over at Clark, who was caught off guard. He couldn't see what Joey had called for, but he was confident that he knew what he was doing. Now Jason stared at him, and he got very uncomfortable. Finally, Joey called time and went out to talk to Jason. The coach joined them for an intense discussion. At some point they all looked over at Clark, who shifted uneasily on the hard bench. He could feel the eyes of everyone on the team, everyone in the stands, turn toward him.

The umpire broke up the meeting, and they all took their places. Jason finally threw the fastball inside, and the batter swung too late and missed. After that he followed Joey's calls and struck out his second batter. The home crowd, urged on by

Julie and the other cheerleaders, was now re-energized and getting louder. A couple of them chanted Jason's name.

Clark hadn't been able to get a good read on the next Aurora batter because he hadn't swung at many pitches. He'd struck out looking once, and the second time had made a partial swing that hit the ball and popped it up to third. Clark noticed that he took a stronger stance this time, and that worried him. The batter held off from swinging at Jason's curve ball, which was too far off the plate. Then he watched two fastballs for strikes, one of which was hotly questioned by the Aurora coach. Behind in the count one to two, the batter swung defensively at the next pitch, and the grounder went toward Bill who played off first. Jason broke a little late to cover first base and had to accelerate to beat the batter. Bill led him perfectly with his underhanded toss, and Jason stretched out to just beat the batter to the bag.

The Harrison crowd went crazy, and Bill pounded on Jason's back. Clark noticed, however, that Jason favored his right leg, and it seemed to get worse as he approached the bench. As his adrenalin quickly wore off, Jason grabbed his right leg and stumbled the rest of the way to the bench.

Coach Duncan watched Jason and knew immediately that it was a hamstring pull, and that he was going to have to put Clark in for the seventh and final inning. He hoped that they would score a bunch of runs and take some of the pressure off the kid.

Dumb Crazy Luck.

Clark didn't need to hear it from the coach to know what was happening. Jason was in real pain. There was no one else to put in. This was why the coach had asked him to join the team. But what was surprisingly his biggest point of concern resolved itself when he looked over and saw that Rita had come back. Not only that, but Sarah had joined her and gave him a little wave. And without looking over at her, he sensed total support from Julie.

He walked over to the practice field where Tommy waited to catch his warm-up pitches. Tommy was part of Dwight's gang and looked at Clark with a challenging stare. He seemed about to say something when Joey came up beside Clark and stood with him on the mound. As Clark threw some easy pitches to begin warming up, he and Joey discussed the first two Aurora batters that were due up at the top of the seventh and last inning. The third batter was the pitcher and they knew that they would undoubtedly face a pinch hitter. By now Clark had almost reached his regular velocity, and Tommy was visibly surprised.

The coach watched them and tried not to think about the fact that this game, unlike most regular season games, could go to extra innings if tied at the end of the seventh. How many innings could this kid pitch, if he could pitch at all?

Dumb Crazy Luck.

Quietly Andy drew a walk. Then Ralph singled to right and stayed on first while Andy aggressively went to third, just beating a good throw from the Aurora right fielder. As Ed took the first pitch for a ball, Ralph tried to steal second and was easily thrown out. The coach was furious because he hadn't called for a steal. Ralph wisely avoided him as he trotted over and sat on the end of the bench. That was quickly forgotten, however, as Ed lifted a fly ball deep to center. Plenty deep for Andy to tag up and score from third. The game was tied at four runs each.

The coach and the team held their collective breath as Ira walked to the plate. The center fielder had been in a season-long slump, batting just .155. Clark had watched him all season and was reminded of Joe Pepitone, the rookie first baseman for the Yankees the previous year, who had developed a bad habit of letting his hands drop before he swung.

Without thinking, he yelled out, "Ira, keep your hands up."

Ira and the rest of the team stopped and stared at him.

Dwight, who had been very quiet on the bench since coming out, yelled mockingly, "Oh yeah, thanks coach."

Some of the team, his gang, laughed. But the others reacted uneasily because they knew how Clark had helped Joey with his pitch calls and a lot of them when they were batting.

Ira swung at a fastball down the middle for the first strike. He then concentrated on keeping his hands up before the next swing. He connected solidly with the next fastball, and it went deep, but foul. Suddenly energized and more confident, he waited for the next pitch and saw a curve down and away for a ball. Then he anticipated another fastball, and when it came, he connected perfectly and watched it sail over the head of the Aurora right fielder and over the fence for a home run.

When Rita had told her what was going on, Sarah had to see for herself.

Clark fitting in on a team? No way.

She had seen him waste hundreds of hours out in the backyard throwing balls at the target, but she never equated that with the actual sport of baseball. Not that she knew anything about baseball, or any other sport for that matter. Now as she and Rita watched Ira race around the bases, they could feel the excitement from the Harrison team and the fans. It was infectious. The scoreboard showed the new score: Home 5 Visitor 4.

"Is that it? Is it over?" Sarah asked Rita.

"I have no idea, I'm British remember. I hoped you would know."

"Not a clue. They do seem to be celebrating over there. And look, that boy who ran around is almost hugging Clark! Oh, my God. They're all so queer."

It was meant as a joke, but the reaction on Rita's face clearly said she didn't find it that funny.

"Oh, I'm kidding. I've just never seen Clark hug anyone."

Sarah scanned the crowd, then the team. She did know this one boy from chorus class who she thought was on the team. Then she saw him as he sat next to Clark and put on all this padding stuff and then a huge mask. It wasn't exactly a crush that she had on Joey, but he seemed to be a nice guy and had a very nice singing voice. She had asked him to try out for the play, but he had said he was on the baseball team. That had surprised her, and she certainly hadn't understood it at the time. But this was kind of exciting.

Rita suddenly stiffened and exclaimed, "Oh blimey look, Clark's going out to pitch." Now very nervous, she instinctively grabbed Sarah's hand and squeezed.

Sarah wasn't sure which had more impact on her, Clark actually going into a game or Rita holding her hand. She tried to concentrate on Clark. Then she noticed that the home team crowd had gone very quiet.

Julie felt her knees go a little weak as she watched Clark head for the pitcher's mound. Her brain couldn't function enough to call for a cheer, so instead she and most of the crowd went totally silent as this new kid went to the mound to try to close out the biggest game of the year.

Oh, my God. Did I do this?

She didn't know what else motivated Clark, but she knew she had been a factor. She was thrilled and terrified all at once. She wanted to cheer his name, and she wanted to hide. So she wound up doing what everyone else did - watched nervously as he threw his final warm-up pitches to Joey.

Clark knew what the coach was going to say before he said it.

"Okay Clark, show them what you got. Just relax and you'll be fine."

Clark nodded. He didn't really notice the home crowd and their sudden silence. He tried not to listen to the noise from the Aurora team. However, he did hear Dwight's comment, "Oh shit, there goes the game." But he used it for motivation. He knew he could pitch. Now he had to do it in this setting. He had imagined this for so long. He had pitched so many times in his backyard while he imagined himself in Yankee Stadium. He wasn't there, but it was a start.

He focused on Joey as the first Aurora batter stepped into the batter's box. As they had planned, Joey called for the fastball to the outside, and he set up to catch it. Clark stared at Joey's glove and then went into his windup and threw. Joey had to react quickly and was barely able to catch the pitch, which was fast but much too far outside.

Clark blocked out both the cheers from the Aurora team and the collective groan that arose from the Harrison crowd.

Julie made a silent little prayer to a god she didn't really believe in.

Sarah squeezed Rita's hand a little tighter.

Joey called for the same pitch and gave Clark an encouraging nod of his head.

Clark glanced quickly toward the field and saw Rita and Sarah. Then he relived the memory of Julie's kiss. He took a deep breath and pulled his focus inside his body and out of his head. He then let his body go automatically through the motions that he had practiced so many times. Pure muscle memory. The ball crushed into Joey's glove while the batter watched.

The umpire called, "Strike!"

Julie did a little jump for joy.

Clark tried not to react as he caught the ball from Joey and waited for the sign. As he expected, Joey called for another fastball but inside this time. Another quick glance toward Rita and Sarah, kiss, and then a good fastball that the batter swung at, but too late.

He could see the batter suddenly get serious and dig his cleats in the dirt for a better stance.

Joey flashed his sign for a curveball. Clark felt like another fastball, but trusted Joey's instincts. The only thing Clark did that was different for this pitch was to carefully change his grip in his glove. No one was going to pick up any tells from him.

The curveball had good, but not spectacular, movement on it, but it was enough to fool the batter, who had anticipated another fastball from a new pitcher that the Aurora coach had told his team had to be a one-pitch guy.

Clark felt more than heard the sound of the cheers that now came from the Harrison side. The visitors side had gone quiet, unsure of what was happening.

The batter guessed right on the next pitch, a curveball again, but he only managed to get a piece of it and sent it on the ground toward the Harrison bench. Foul ball. The count was now two balls and two strikes. Joey called for another curve, but Clark shook him off. He really wanted to blow a fastball by this guy. Joey didn't argue and changed the sign.

Clark had now established his pattern. He sent the pitch screaming toward the plate. The Aurora batter had anticipated a fastball and swung as hard as he could, but had no chance to catch up to the pitch, which hit Joey's glove with a resounding thwack. First out. Two more to go.

The Harrison team now stood and yelled. Even Dwight got to his feet, but he didn't say anything as the conflict raged inside him between wanting to win and not liking Clark. Tommy stood next to Dwight and started to say, "He can pitch-" but he stopped when he saw the look on Dwight's face.

The Aurora coach made a mental note to check with the district office about this new guy. Pitchers like this didn't just drop from heaven for the last game of the season. Transfer students had to wait six months to play a varsity sport, and he would hate to have to use a rules violation to win the game. But he would if he had to.

The next Aurora batter was hyper-alert as he tried to anticipate Clark's first pitch, fastball or curve. Clark had seen this batter chase curve balls all game, so why not give him some more? But he would try it inside and give him something new to think about. Rita there? Check. Julie's kiss? Check. The ball started coming right at the batter, and he instinctively leaned back to avoid getting hit. But the ball suddenly curved sharply to the left and crossed right over the plate. Strike one.

Coach Duncan struggled to keep from pumping his fist and yelling.

Dumb Crazy Luck. This kid can really pitch.

He forced himself to calm down. It wasn't over yet.

The Aurora batter shook his head. He wasn't going to embarrass himself again. He didn't react as much to the next pitch, but he did flinch a little as it came straight at him before curving away. His defensive swing missed the ball by a foot. Now the batter was completely unnerved and steeled himself for the curveball that never came. Instead he watched a fastball whiz over the outside corner of the plate. Out number two.

The Aurora coach selected a left-handed pinch hitter for his pitcher. In response, Joey called time and came out to the mound to confer with Clark.

"How do you want to do this guy?"

Clark quickly responded, "Fastball in, curve, slider."

The Aurora batter guessed right on the fastball and made solid contact. The ball popped up along the left field line. It drifted foul, but Miguel had a chance to catch it for the out. As he approached the ball, he caught a glimpse of Rita and Sarah. They weren't close to the ball, but it distracted him enough that he missed the catch. He glared at them as if it was their fault. Sarah stuck out her tongue at him. She had always thought he was a jerk.

Now Clark thought that the batter might anticipate the curve, and he smiled when Joey made the sign for another fastball. They were thinking the same way. The Aurora batter had anticipated a curve and came nowhere close to catching up to the fastball. Strike two.

That's when Clark started to think about what was happening. Suddenly he noticed the cheers and his name being called from the Harrison team and fans. He noticed the complete silence that had overtaken the Aurora faithful. He noticed that Rita and Sarah now stood and clapped.

"Clark!" Joey shouted to be heard over the fans.

No response.

"Clark!" Louder.

Clark struggled to pull his attention back to Joey. He saw his sign for the slider and nodded. No glance at Rita. No control. He threw the ball into the dirt two feet in front of the plate.

"No problem, you got this," Joey shouted, as he tossed a new ball out to Clark.

Clark desperately tried to clear his head, to regain his focus, but he couldn't. The next pitch, a fastball inside, went too far inside and hit the batter on his right side. The batter swore a choice profanity and glared at Clark as he jogged down to first base.

That brought up their leadoff hitter, who Clark had watched all game and had decided was the best hitter on the field, either team. He was patient, and he had very quick hands when he saw something he liked.

Clark agreed with Joey's sign for a fastball - they should go right after this guy. The batter calmly watched the fastball miss the outside corner. Ball one. Then he didn't flinch at the curve as it headed at him and then broke over the plate - but too high. Ball two.

The Harrison crowd grew restless, nervous, while the Aurora crowd had new energy and volume.

Clark stepped off the pitching rubber and used his sleeve to wipe the sweat from his forehead. He desperately wanted to look over at Rita but was afraid he'd lose it entirely.

The coach stood and glared at Clark, trying to somehow send him the strength to finish.

Damn Crazy Luck. To be this close and . . .

Clark got set to throw the curve that Joey asked for. He glanced over to first where the Aurora base runner had taken a big lead off the bag. A steal would set them up to score on a single. Clark groaned with a fatalistic acceptance. He had never practiced a pickoff move to first. He would just have to concentrate on getting the batter out. He threw the curve, and this time the batter swung. But he was early and fouled it off behind the Aurora stands. Two balls and one strike. The base runner had to go back to first.

The positive reaction from the home crowd washed over him but didn't help his struggle to regain his focus. The next pitch, a fastball was outside. But the batter couldn't hold back his swing, and the umpire called a strike. The Aurora base runner had stolen second as Joey made no attempt to pick him off. Two balls and two strikes.

Clark knew he had to finish this off now, or he was going to lose it completely. Joey felt the same way and called for the slider. Clark stood rigid, as things seemed to slow down. Time stopped. He then did what he had been avoiding - he looked over to Julie. She was the only thing he saw. She smiled at him, and then she puckered her lips and blew him a kiss.

His visceral memory of her real kiss slammed him back to the moment, and he turned to face the batter. His focus went completely to the sensation of that kiss on his lips, and then he threw the ball. The slider looked exactly like his fastball but completely fooled the batter as it moved sharply down toward the lower left corner of the plate. The batter had a perfect swing for the fastball, but missed the slider by a foot. Strike three. Game over.

The excitement of the win overcame everyone. Joey rushed out to congratulate Clark. Only Dwight and Miguel hung back while the rest of the team charged the field from the bench. Dwight had noticed the little kiss that Julie had blown Clark before the last pitch.

On the hillside, Rita and Sarah jumped up and down and yelled. Then Sarah hugged Rita, and neither one wanted to let go.

Clark struggled to keep the emotions of the moment from overwhelming him. The feeling was better than he had ever imagined. Through the barrage of handshakes and chest bumps he tried to find Julie. He saw her with Dwight and hesitated, which gave the coach time to reach him.

"Hell of a game. Nice work, Clark."

"Thanks Coach for giving me the chance."

"Take care of that arm, and we'll see you at practice on Tuesday."

Damn Crazy Luck.

Clark turned back from the coach and was immediately swamped again by teammates. It was several minutes before he could search for Julie. She wasn't with the other cheerleaders, who mingled with the team and the fans. Then he saw her walking away from the field. He started in that direction but stopped when he realized that Dwight walked next to her with his arm around her waist. He stared at them for a moment and then turned away, dejected. He didn't see her briskly push Dwight's arm off her.

Clark entered the locker room on a wave of positive emotion. He undressed slowly, and by the time he walked into the large communal shower room it was almost full. There were five showerheads along each of two walls, and the steam from all that hot water was thick. He kept his eyes from wandering and quickly washed off and left. He didn't feel completely comfortable, but he no longer felt that he didn't belong there.

If they don't like my hair, then the hell with 'em.

Joey came up to Clark as he finished dressing. "Hey man, if you're not doing anything tonight you should come to the party at Andy's. His parents will be there, but they're very groovy and even provide brewskies."

Two questions influenced Clark's decision: would Dwight be there and would Julie be there? "Oh, thanks, I don't know."

"That's okay, I'm sure you've got other things to do."

"No, no that's not it. I'd like to but . . ."

"Yeah?" Joey was sensitive enough to pick up his hesitancy but also aggressive enough to push him.

"Well, there are some guys on the team that I don't get along with too well."

"Not after this there aren't," Joey said laughing, and then thought it through. "And if you mean Dwight, I know he won't be there. I heard that his old man reamed him a new one after the game. He'll be grounded for a month."

Clark couldn't stop the grin that spread across his face.

If he's grounded that means Julie might be there, and alone.

"I'll check with my sister. My parents are out of town."

"Sarah?" Joey couldn't believe that Clark would have to get permission from his sister.

"Oh, no not Sarah. I've an older half-sister who's staying with us."

"Oh, you mean the red-head who was sitting out there with Sarah during the game?"

Then it struck Clark, so he asked, "How do you know Sarah?"

Joey would have blushed if he weren't already hot and red-faced. "Oh, I'm in chorus this year with her. Anyway, you could invite them both."

Clark laughed at the concept. "Sarah wouldn't be caught dead at a party with ballplayers and other jocks. And Rita, well she's pregnant." Clark then started to tie his shoe and didn't notice the crestfallen look from Joey.

* * *

Rita wasn't sure how to react to Clark when he got home, so she did what seemed natural. She threw her arms around him gave him a big hug. "Clark, I'm so proud of you." She loved the huge grin that dominated his face, and if he hadn't been her brother, she would have given him a big kiss on the lips. Actually it wasn't the brother thing that stopped her as much as it was this particular boy and his obvious hang-ups and inexperience with women.

I've got to get John to talk to him.

"Is Sarah here?" Clark asked. He had promised Joey that he would tell her about the party even though he knew it would be more likely to find little green men from Mars at the party than Sarah.

"In her room, going to take a nap she said. Your mum left a casserole in the fridge that I was going to warm up for dinner. Does that sound okay?"

Later at dinner, Clark told Sarah about the party and got the reaction he anticipated.

"Some lame-oh jock-fest? I don't think so. But now that you're the number one jocko you're suddenly into that?"

"I'm not, but it might be fun," he countered defensively.

"Well, don't have too much fun. You get some cheerleader knocked up, and Mom will have a cow." She immediately looked at Rita and was afraid she had said something terribly inappropriate. "Oh, I'm so . . ."

Rita just laughed. "No worries love, getting knocked-up is an occupational hazard for women who want to live life with spontaneity." She then looked at Clark with a twinkle in her eye and continued, "But just in case Julie's there, be sure to use a johnny." She didn't need to see the quizzical look to know that required a translation. "A condom."

Clark blushed three shades of red as he looked down at his food and kept quiet.

Sarah squealed, "I knew it. I knew you had a crush on her. But isn't she going steady with that jerk Dwight?"

"Let's just drop it, okay," he mumbled, without looking up.

"So where's this party, and I guess since your parents kind of asked me to look after things, I should ask if it's an empty rage."

Both Sarah and Clark looked up at her.

"Oh, for Christ's sake. An empty, as in house with no parents, rage, party."

They all laughed.

"Joey said that Andy's parents would be home."

Sarah's ears perked up, and Clark noticed. "Actually it was Joey who asked me if you'd want to come. Do you know him?" he teased her, loving some payback.

She shifted ever so slightly on her chair. "He's in my chorus class. He has a very nice voice, but . . . he just seems afraid to really use it. I tried to get him to try out for the play, but he said he had baseball." Her inflection on the word baseball clearly indicated that she didn't consider any sport to be an acceptable choice over the theater.

Rita sat there and smiled. That afternoon she'd had the distinct feeling that Sarah wanted Rita to join her in her nap. And now she was obviously intrigued by this Joey boy.

CHAPTER FOURTEEN

"Call me when you want to come home," Rita called to Clark, as he shut the door to Coleen's car.

He knees were a little shaky. Twice he'd had to remind her that cars drove on the right side of the road in America. Fortunately, the streets in their neighborhood were not very busy. She assured him that she had driven in Europe where they also drove on the right, and that her British license was accepted there, so it should be okay in America.

Clark had originally planned to ride his scooter, but he had made the mistake of telling his mother about the party when she called to find out how the game went. She forbade him to ride his scooter because she knew that alcohol was occasionally served at these high school parties.

"Hey, Clark, great game, man," said some random boy that Clark didn't know.

Clark mumbled, "Thanks," as he turned to go into the house. He wasn't sure he could face that all night.

Andy's father stood at the front door and directed people downstairs to a recreation room that opened out onto a large patio and a swimming pool. It was a great party house, already crowded and loud. It seemed to Clark like the whole school was there. As he moved through the crowd it became crystal clear that his shield of invisibility had now fallen away completely. Everyone knew his name and was his best friend. A real trip, but a scary high for someone so used to anonymity.

He searched for Julie, the reason why he had come, but she didn't appear to be there. He did find Joey, standing by the pool with Bill and Andy and a small keg of beer. As Clark approached them, Andy immediately thrust a paper cup of beer into his hands. Clark hesitated, and they misread his reluctance.

"Don't worry man, its near beer. My dad gets it for us, very low alcoholic content, like half of regular. You can legally drink it at eighteen." Andy raced through this explanation, aided by the several beers he had already consumed.

Clark wasn't eighteen, but he knew that Andy and many of the other seniors probably were. He hesitated mostly because he had never had a beer before. He gamely took a big sip and found the strange taste not too bad. It was cold and carbonated, and he quickly drank the rest.

"All right Clark, my man," Joey shouted and laughed as he held up his cup to toast Clark.

"Great party, hombre," shouted Bill, who had also had a few beers. "I see Mary, and I'm gonna ask her."

"Are you sure that's a good idea?" Joey cautioned. "Remember what happened at the last party."

"It was something I ate, some bad cheese dip. And anyway, she forgave me for that," Bill said, as he headed off toward the house, a little wobble in his step.

"Poor Bill," Andy confided to Clark. "He thinks that if he gets her to go to prom with him that he'll get laid."

Joey chuckled knowingly, and Clark joined in to cover his nervousness. Andy then left to go find his dad for something. Clark tried to work the keg tap but didn't know how, so Joey showed him.

"Did Sarah come?" Joey asked cautiously.

"Eh, no, she had this thing with the play, those people. She said to say hello to you."

"Really? That's cool."

Joey's enthusiastic reaction made Clark immediately sorry that he'd lied.

"You were amazing today man. I just can't understand why you didn't come out for the team before. You must have been killing it in your other school."

The near beer had enough alcohol to begin to loosen Clark's reluctance to talk about himself. "No, actually that was the first game I ever played."

"First high school game?"

"No high school, no junior high, no little league."

"No way!" Joey exclaimed.

"Way."

"No, you're shitting me, right? No one just steps out on the mound and does what you did having never played."

"I watch a lot and pick up things."

"Come on, what's the big secret? You can tell me," Joey demanded, getting upset.

"No secret. That was my first game."

"Fuckin' A man, I try to be a friend and you can't even tell me something that simple," Joey almost yelled.

Clarks level of frustration had grown with Joey's anger, and he couldn't keep it from his voice, "It is that simple. I. Had. Never. Played. Before."

Joey controlled himself enough that he stormed away rather than push Clark into the pool. "Asswipe," he muttered, loudly enough that several people heard him and wondered what was going on.

Clark felt bad about the interaction, and his first instinct was to leave. But he still hoped that Julie might be there or would show up, and he didn't want to give up so easily. Then Ira and Tommy came over and the subsequent dissection of every play from the game took his mind off the encounter with Joey.

* * *

Julie sat with Suzie on the couch in Suzie's recreation room and had no intention of going to the party. She was perfectly content to watch the color television that Suzie's parents had gotten the family as a Christmas present. Most families now had one, except for hers. They munched from a bowl of popcorn that Suzie's mother had popped for them.

"Isn't she beautiful?" Suzie asked, as they watched Marilyn Monroe in the movie, *The Seven Year Itch*, on NBC Saturday Night Movies.

"Yeah, but I really don't like her voice. It sounds so fake. Who would want to talk that way?"

"Well, if you don't want to watch, it's not too late to go to Andy's party," Suzie said hopefully. "My parents are asleep, and they wouldn't mind anyway."

Julie just sat and stared at the television.

"Oh, come on, it'll be fun." Suzie still didn't get a response, so she tried another tactic. "Is it because Dwight's grounded? You can still have fun, you know that, right?"

Julie cringed at the mention of Dwight. He had been a total jerk after the game. He swore that he was just sick and not hung-over. But he had never apologized for trying to break into her house. She had wanted to stay at the field and celebrate the win, but he had insisted that they go to his house, where she had spent several hours resisting his attempts to have sex.

"No, actually I'm glad he's grounded. It's about time his dad and stepmom did something. Teach him a lesson."

"Why do you still do it?" Suzie asked.

"Do what?"

"Keep going with Dwight. It doesn't seem to make you very happy anymore."

"I don't know. Habit maybe."

Suzie paused. She knew she had to say this the right way. "I know you know about him, don't you?"

Julie considered acting confused, but she wasn't. She knew that Suzie was just being a good friend. "That he's fucking Laurie? Yeah, I know."

"And it doesn't bother you?"

"Sure it pisses me off, but I'm also happy about it." She noticed the incredulous look from Suzie. "I like him and we've had a lot of fun but . . . but he wants to do it, and I'm not ready. So when he's feeling that, that need, Laurie performs a useful public service being the school slut."

"Well that's certainly a unique attitude. Not many girls would feel comfortable with that arrangement. I know I wouldn't."

They both turned their attention back to the television and the movie as Tom Ewell continued to fantasize about having an affair with Marilyn Monroe.

"I wonder if it has something to do with Clark," Suzie then asked, very tentatively.

Julie tried to hide her reaction to Clark's name. "Why do you say that?"

"Maybe because the only time I see you smile anymore is when he's around."

"That's not true," Julie replied defensively, but knew that it probably was true.

"Well, if not, then do you mind if I go after him? I think he's kinda hot."

Julie struggled to control her feelings. She knew Suzie was just trying to tease her into talking. "I don't think he's your type."

"Oh yeah, so what is my type?"

"Have you ever seen him at a party, let alone drunk out of his gourd at a party? Can you see him making goofy puppy dog faces whenever you walk by?"

"Hey, don't talk about Henry that way. Those were adorable faces. But don't worry, you're right, he's probably not my type, too quiet, too serious." Then she added with a dramatic flourish, "And too much hair."

Julie laughed so hard that she barely got her words out, "I'm not worried."

"Sure, sure. But you do like him, right?"

"He's nice."

"And hot?"

"I guess. Oh, did you see that, that's the scene, her dress blows up and you could see her panties"

"No. Shit! I missed it!" Suzie pouted for a moment, then quickly recovered. "So now can we please go to the party?"

* * *

Clark had moved around the party a couple of times, carefully avoiding Joey, but hadn't seen Julie. He saw a couple of the other cheerleaders, but not Suzie, the one who seemed to be her closest friend.

Clark was unaware that he was the subject of an intense conversation among four girls from Harrison High who other students politely called loose or less politely sluts. They were all seniors and were perfectly normal in almost every way. They dressed nicely and got good grades. One was the vice president of their class council. The only thing different about them was that they really liked sex and were very open about it. The ringleader of the loose-girls, as they were often called, was Laurie, who really liked athletes and rough sex. Marie loved to deflower young virgins, the younger the better. Sally went for the teachers and their experience and automatic good grades. The other one, Toni, the least attractive and aggressive of the group, just picked up whomever she could.

Laurie was bored because Dwight had been grounded. But now there was a new star on the team, and Laurie collected stars. She had slept with anyone on any of the Harrison varsity teams who would do it. She had stayed away from Joey because of Marie who had had a crush on him since kindergarten. She had tried to get Ira earlier that evening, but he refused because of his religious conviction that he had to stay a virgin until he was married.

None of the loose-girls had any knowledge of whether Clark had ever dated anyone at school. Toni offered that he never even talked to a girl, but then Marie brought up the time, a week or so ago, when Julie Wells talked to him in the lunch room. They all agreed that that had been strange. Laurie had her own strong opinions about Julie, but she kept them to herself. Toni also mentioned that Clark always sat alone at the nerd table. Then Sally suggested that maybe he was a queer. That got a good laugh, but then some serious contemplation. All of this was augmented by the bottle of dark rum that Laurie had swiped from her parent's liquor cabinet. They had consumed most of the bottle, mixed with the cokes provided by Andy's parents.

"I'm going to find out," Laurie stated unequivocally. She stood up too quickly, lost her balanced, and grabbed Sally's hair to keep from falling down.

"Hey, bitch, that hurts," Sally yelled.

Laura gave her a pouty little kiss and headed off to find Clark. The other three looked around for their own targets for the night. As soon as they were on the move, the other girls at the party started looking for their boyfriends.

Clark had decided that Julie wasn't coming and that he would head home. He would walk to release some of the frustration that he felt. Suddenly a pair of female hands came from around his back and covered his eyes.

"Guess who?" asked a voice that was very distinctive, sort of raspy.

As much as he hoped it was her, he knew it wasn't Julie's voice. "I don't know."

"No guesses? You give up?"

He nodded and the hands left his eyes, found his shoulders, and turned him around to face her. Laurie could make a strong first impression, especially on an unsuspecting boy who had a few beers under his belt. Her eyes were sparkling blue, and her full red lips dominated a friendly, pretty, face. But her body was her best feature. She worked hard on it, and the results showed in all the right places: large firm breasts, a tiny waist, full hips, and very fit tanned legs (even in the winter). Clark had noticed her at school, but didn't know her name. He had to look at her breasts because they now pushed into his chest. When he quickly looked back up at her face, she smiled sweetly and seductively.

"Like what you see big boy?" She squeezed his upper arms. "Oh, strong arms - to be expected for a great pitcher. You were spectacular today, you know."

Clark stood speechless, and all he could muster in response was a weak smile.

"Let's go somewhere quiet where we can get to know each other." She practically purred as she pulled him toward a small bedroom that she knew from experience was through the door behind the pool table and next to the bathroom.

Clark felt like he was in a tractor beam, towed across the room by this irresistible force.

Bill noticed what was happening and nudged Joey. "Oh my God, look who Laurie has her hooks into. Should we warn him?"

Joey was still steamed at Clark. "No, I'm sure it's not his first time."

As Clark and Laurie approached the door, Marie appeared and was headed to the same place with Andy's little brother, who was in ninth grade and about to lose his virginity. Before they could argue over who would get to use the bedroom, Andy rushed over to rescue his brother. Marie shot him an angry look and her middle finger before she headed off for another potential conquest.

Laurie laughed and yelled after Marie, "That cherry doesn't even have a pit yet." She opened the door and pushed Clark inside. The room, meant for guests, was sparsely furnished with a bed and dresser. Laurie had had sex with Andy there and his father as well. It had taken months for Andy's father to finally get over her. Tonight she had noticed that Andy's mother was pregnant, and she took some pride in having ignited a dormant sex drive.

Clark looked around and felt a hot panic grow in his head and in his groin. But he was too overwhelmed by her to begin to get an erection.

Laurie moved around him as she ran her hands over his body, staying above the waist for now. She wasn't a quick action kind of girl. For that you went to a whore down on State Street near the state capitol building. She was also experienced enough to quickly realize that Clark was undoubtedly a virgin. Nothing made her happier. She prided herself on being the best, most caring, virgin-buster in town. Slow and easy and fun. Not some slam-bang quickie like Marie preferred. No, she considered herself a teacher, a guide to manhood, and here was her new pupil.

She noticed that there was no action in his pants yet. That wasn't normally what happened to the men she approached. Usually they were bursting at the seams. She had just undone one of the buttons on his shirt when the door flew open, and Joey came in.

"Clark, glad I found you man, Andy's dad wants to take a photo of all of us." He kept talking as he pulled Clark from Laurie's clutches and dragged him to the door.

"Fuck off Joey, just because you can't handle it doesn't mean that Clarkie here doesn't want it."

"Let's let him decide what he wants when he knows who he's getting into. So until then, back off Laurie." He almost smiled. He had known Laurie and Marie since elementary school and actually liked them, but just as friends.

"Fine, you two queer boys go play with your balls. See if I care," she shouted, as she pushed past them and out into the party.

Most of the crowd didn't pay much attention because Laurie was well known for her emotional outbursts. What many noticed was that Clark's face was pure white, and he seemed to need to lean on Joey for support. Some thought that he deserved to party hard after the day he had. Others wondered if Laurie had done both of them and thought that a threesome would be a first for her. They would have been very wrong about that, however.

Joey walked upstairs with Clark to the front hall.

"Thanks." Clark's voice almost failed him. He had never experienced anything like Laurie, and he was still shaking. He knew that he didn't want to have anything happen like that, not with her. But he had felt unable to do anything as she touched him. He wondered if it was like Jason and his Argonauts on Circe's Island. He had been under some sort of spell.

Joey was still angry but felt sorry for him. He just couldn't let him fall into Laurie's clutches like that. And he knew that if he was ever to have any chance with Clark's sister, letting him fall prey to Laurie wouldn't help his cause.

Finally, Clark got some color back in his face and was able to ask, "Who is she?"

"Her name's Laurie, and she's pretty infamous around here for her sexual appetite and prowess. She especially likes athletes and goes crazy over star athletes. So after today, you were dead center on her radar."

Clark shivered as he realized what might have happened. "She's intense. It was like I couldn't control myself."

"Yeah, well she's a legend. I've heard Dwight say that they did it all night, and she still wanted more."

Clark stiffened at the mention of Dwight and stammered, "So she and Dwight, have . . .? I, I thought he dated Julie."

"Oh man that's classic." Joey laughed. "She won't give it up for him, so he goes to Laurie. That happens with some other couples, but if the girl finds out, then it's over. Strange thing though, I'm pretty sure that Julie knows, but it doesn't seem to bother her."

Clark couldn't process anything else and had to leave. "Thanks again, I owe you," he mumbled to Joey, as he hurried out the front door.

Joey watched Clark leave.

Yeah, buddy boy, you owe me the truth about your pitching.

* * *

Rita had fallen asleep on the couch, but woke up when Clark came in and went immediately upstairs to his room. He was trailed by a strong odor of smoke and beer and that male smell of arousal. She wondered if this could have been his night.

Was it Julie?

Now able to go to bed, she couldn't fall asleep again and just tossed and turned for what seemed like hours. Then she felt the baby move inside her for the first time. She went very still and concentrated on that little thing in her womb.

What the bloody hell are you, and what are you going to do with my life?

The absence of a definitive answer wasn't surprising, but it allowed for all sorts of interpretations. Some good and some bad. The bad seemed to outweigh the good for a while, but then she imagined a life with Keith and the good struggled to make a comeback. It was an unfair fight because she couldn't believe that being with a musician would work for a family. And she now knew that she wanted more of a traditional family structure than she had grown up with.

When she finally fell asleep, she dreamed of a big stage with a rock band, and Keith singing to a crowd of screaming young women, many of them naked. A little toddler, a girl, wandered across the stage, through the band. No one noticed her or that she was in danger of getting trampled or electrocuted or worse. Rita tried to get the baby, but her body wouldn't respond, she couldn't move. She screamed out as the baby reached the edge of the stage. Keith paid her no attention as he gyrated to the music, and his leg accidentally struck the baby, propelling her off the stage and into the crowd of naked women.

Rita jerked awake, sweating and clutching her belly.

CHAPTER FIFTEEN

Clark woke up a little after nine and stumbled to the bathroom to find a couple of aspirin for his headache. Back in his room, he flopped down on his bed and stared at the ceiling. It had taken him almost thirty minutes to walk home, but he didn't remember much of it. His mind had been spinning around an image of Laurie and her red lips and the sensation of her breasts pushed up against him.

Thank God for Joey.

He felt bad about their argument, but he had just been telling the truth, as odd as it was. He finally drifted back to sleep and woke later to the sound of Sarah singing in the bathroom. He was really getting tired of those songs, particularly the one about how pretty she was. He went down to the kitchen to find something to eat. Rita sat at the table drinking her tea. She looked like she hadn't slept much, which she hadn't.

"Must have been some party," she remarked, as he foraged for food.

"Kinda," he answered, more to the box of cereal than to her. He brought it with a bowl and a bottle of milk to the table and tried to avoid eye contact.

"You know you might feel better if you shower first and get the smoke and beer smell out of your hair."

"Sarah's in there, and I was hungry." He finally looked over at her. "You look pretty tired yourself."

She nodded and they sat in silence, both comfortable with it.

* * *

Julie tightened the laces on the used pair of baseball cleats that she had found at the Goodwill Store in downtown Denver. They were old and a little big, but she hoped manageable enough that she wouldn't trip and make a fool of herself. She had an extra pair of socks in case she needed them. The glove that she had also found at Goodwill was even older and was for hardball, not softball. She had been trying to stretch and expand the pocket for the past days.

She had been one of the first to arrive at practice and had had to wait outside the field until Becky arrived with the key to the padlock on the gate. She noticed that Becky's greeting and smile seemed a little forced, not the same perky personality she had shown at tryouts. Julie knew that some coaches were all smiles when recruiting players and then tyrants after that. She hoped that Becky wasn't one of those.

One of the Cowgirl players collected the permission slips and their $25 fees. Julie was relieved that they didn't even look at the slips, not that they would know what her mother's signature really looked like. She noticed that most of the other girls had a check for the fee and only a few had cash as she did. She regretted sneaking the money from her parents' wallets, but there was no way she could ask for it. She had done it five dollars at a time, spread out over the past week, hoping that they wouldn't notice.

Practice began a few minutes after the scheduled time of 8:30, and Becky had a few caustic words for two girls who showed up late. She threatened to kick them off the team if it happened again. That was more than okay with Julie. She hated it when people were late and held up the others who had managed to arrive on time, especially those who had to take two buses and walk almost a mile to get there.

After twenty minutes of strenuous exercises and stretching, they broke up into position groups and worked on drills. Every forty-five minutes they changed groups. They didn't take their first real break until 10:30, and everyone was breathing hard. Julie noticed that she seemed to be in better shape than most of the other girls. A few of them didn't look too good, and one had gotten sick over by the right field fence.

They went back to more position groups and continued to rotate the rest of the morning. At noon Becky blew her whistle for the last time and called everyone together. "This was a really good first practice everyone," she began. "We're going to evaluate what we saw, and then next Sunday we'll put you into position groups that you'll concentrate on for the next weeks. Those won't be final, we might still switch people around, but we want you to begin to get some serious practice in your positions. Any questions?"

The girl who had been sick asked if the practices were all going to be like this one. Amid the snickers from the rest of the girls, one of the Cowgirl players responded, "No, they'll be harder." The broad smile that followed wasn't enough to prevent the sick girl from looking worse. Julie doubted whether that girl would return the next week.

As Julie packed her cleats and glove in her bag, she noticed that Becky and the Cowgirl players were engaged in an intense conversation. Becky was very animated, and not in a positive way. When they broke up, Becky came over and almost collapsed on the bench near where Julie sat.

"Are you okay?" Julie asked tentatively, not sure about the proper player-coach protocol.

"Oh, nothing that three thousand dollars won't solve."

Julie had no comment on that, other than to give her a quizzical look.

Then Becky laughed softly, and her body seemed to lose some of its tension. "We lost our primary sponsor yesterday afternoon, and I don't know where I'll find another one before the season begins. You know it just sucks with women's sports. The fucking men get everything they want, and we get shit. Pardon my French."

Julie had her own frustrations with the lack of women's sports in high school, and she nodded in agreement.

"Do you know that every woman in the last Olympics had to pay her own way to Rome? All their training? All on them. It just makes me so furious!" Becky tried to compose herself before she continued, "But you looked good today. I think you've got some real talent. I'm putting you with the pitchers."

Julie felt her smile consume her face.

* * *

As Rita waited for Coleen and John to home from Las Vegas, she tried to evaluate her role. She now felt like part of the family, and she wanted to act that way. Family members support each other, but sometimes they had to resort to tough love. She had had to do that with her mother in the last months of her life. It hadn't been easy for either of them, especially Rita at age sixteen. But at the end, they both acknowledged that it had been the right thing to do. Now she knew that John had to open his eyes and see what was happening with Clark before he slipped off the rails.

When Coleen and John finally got home, it was too late for Coleen to cook, and she didn't feel like it anyway. So they all went out for dinner to Luigi's, a local Italian restaurant that they liked.

During dinner everyone got caught up on the various events of the weekend. Clark's game and party were the big topics. He wasn't very expansive on the details so Rita filled in as many blanks as she could. Sarah seemed unusually quiet and offered that she was a little nervous about the play that would premier in about ten days. Rita mentioned feeling the baby move, and then babies dominated the conversation, primarily between Rita and Coleen. John mostly listened and watched as he struggled with a dawning realization that his kids were growing up fast and seemed like strangers in so many ways. He knew it was no one's fault but his own.

Later, back at the house, Rita stood in the doorway to the master bedroom and watched John as he packed for his trip the next day. "Where to this week?"

"Back to New York. Then a management conference and a workweek in DC. Unfortunately, I'll be gone a couple of weeks."

"Oh, really?"

"I know, but I can't help it. I have to go. I'm sorry."

She nodded, but no smile.

He stopped packing and faced her as he spoke, "I'm trying to clear my schedule for some time soon, in two or three weeks. Early June. I hope you'll still be here."

"I'm not the one you should be worrying about."

He struggled to stay positive. "Clark seemed really good. I'm so glad that you and Sarah were there."

"Oh, he's good for baseball now. He managed that brilliantly. On his own." Her emphasis on the last few words was not lost on him. "Do you know that he knows absolutely nothing about women or sex?"

That was probably the last place that John would have guessed this conversation was going. "What do you mean?"

"I mean that he's so clueless about women that he's unable to establish a real relationship with a girl, one who seems to like him. And sexually, when it happens, he's going to be in real trouble. He'll either muck it up so badly that he'll be scarred for life, or he'll get some girl preggers and ruin both their lives."

John, without thinking, looked down at Rita's protruding belly.

She noticed. "Yeah, well, I'm living proof that it can happen even when you probably know too bloody much about sex. But it's almost guaranteed if you don't know anything."

"What do you want me to do?" he asked, knowing that there had to be a purpose underlying this conversation.

"You need to have that parental father-son talk with him. You know, penises and vaginas and how they bloody work."

John looked away and stared at the window, searching for something out in the darkness.

Rita waited for him to return to the conversation, but he didn't. "I thought all dads had that conversation with their sons."

"No, mine didn't," he replied quietly.

"Then how did you learn?"

He gathered himself and turned back to face her. "Well, I don't remember exactly. Guys just talk about it."

"Well, I'm pretty sure that Clark's not having those kinds of conversations. He doesn't seem to have that kind of relationship with the other boys."

John had a moment of panic, and blurted out, "You don't think do you, that he's, you know, likes boys?"

Rita laughed as she realized where he was going. "Oh no, Clark's no botty boy."

John was visibly relieved but still uncomfortable. "Well, I'll talk to him when I get back."

She remembered the wild and distressed look on Clark's face when he had come home the night before, and she just knew that it had had something to do with sex. "I just hope that's not too late. Things are moving very quickly for him, and he's really in over his head."

* * *

Clark had just about reached the end of his proverbial rope, and school was barely half over for the day. He had not been at all prepared for the onslaught of students who wanted to talk to him and tell him that they had seen him pitch. It had been almost okay at the party, especially after the beers, but at school it really embarrassed him.

Julie had smiled at him as she came into English class first period, and then Mr. Smith had to practically yell to get everyone to take their seats. It had been even worse in the hallways between periods. And now in the lunchroom, they even approached the nerd table. Students who before would have given that table a wide berth, like it was the epicenter of all infectious diseases, marched right up to talk to him. Most of the comments were about the game, but sprinkled in were a few references to the party. No one said anything directly, but the inflections and inferences they put on their comments were open to several interpretations.

Through the ring of students that surrounded his table, Clark saw Sarah enter the lunchroom with Joey. He wondered what that was all about. It had become fairly obvious that Joey liked Sarah. But he wondered if it was possible that she liked him also.

Sara and a jock? That's Twilight Zone stuff.

As Clark tried to concentrate on eating his sandwich, Joey sat down next to him. "Hey," Joey said cautiously. "You got home okay, Saturday night?"

Clark didn't want to be rude and point out the obvious fact that he had. "Yeah, fine," he answered. "And thanks again for, you know, helping with that situation."

Joey laughed carefully. Not that it should have been funny, but Clark's look of terror, as he stood there with Laurie's hands all over him, had been a classic. "Sure, no problem." Joey glanced over at the table where Sarah sat with people from the play, her back to them. "Say, you know how I reacted to what you said at the party about it being, you know, your first game and all?"

Clark nodded and looked away.

"Well, I was really wrong and I'm sorry. Sarah told me about your moving and stuff, and I think it's totally amazing that you were able to teach yourself to pitch like that. It's just that it's kinda hard to believe."

Clark sharply turned back to him.

"Oh but I do, I do believe it. Anyway, I'm sorry, I was an ass," Joey added quickly.

"Thanks. I got frustrated, I'm sorry also."

"Why don't you come on over and sit with us?" Joey motioned to the baseball table.

Clark wasn't ready to abandon his nerd table, and besides Dwight was over there. "Thanks, but I'm almost done, and I want to go out for a little air."

Joey shrugged and headed for the baseball table, while Clark got up and quickly left the room, not acknowledging any more greetings from his new fans.

There was a small outdoor courtyard in the middle of the U-shaped high school building. It offered a place where students and teachers could go, sit on the concrete benches, and look at a pathetic assortment of wildflowers and a lot of weeds. It was often very hot out there because of the lack of air movement, but today it was pleasant with a little breeze.

The first person Clark saw was Julie. She sat alone on a bench, and he was almost paralyzed trying to decide whether or not to approach her. Her smile and a motion of her hand for him to sit, quickly made up his mind.

"Hi." "Hey." They said in unison.

"Had enough of your fans?" she asked, with a lot of sympathy and no judgment in her voice.

"I almost ditched school after second period."

"Yeah, I saw it in English. It was pretty intense, and you looked very uncomfortable." She watched him as he nodded and then looked down at his hands. "But you have to admit, it was a pretty amazing debut."

He laughed and began to relax. He really did like being around her.

"Don't worry, it'll pass quickly. Fame does that whether you want it to or not."

"I hope so. I really don't know what to say to them."

"How about just say thanks and give them a smile? I think that's really all you need."

"Thanks," he said, as he gave her a big smile.

She laughed and playfully punched his arm.

He noticed a stack of printed 8 1/2 x 11 sheets of paper next to her on the bench. He could see that they were announcements of the new Junior Cowgirls team and its schedule for the summer. It was obvious that no one had spent a lot of money printing them.

Julie saw him looking and handed him one. "It's a new softball team that I'm on, the Junior Cowgirls."

"That's cool."

Her excitement waned quickly, as she continued, "But now we've lost our sponsor and may have to fold."

"Bummer."

She smiled at his genuine concern. "Bummer is right. We'll probably find out this Sunday at practice whether or not we continue."

The bell rang to signal the end of lunch.

"Hang in there, it'll pass soon." She squeezed his arm and grabbed the flyers as they got up to leave.

He headed off to social studies. He knew that Dwight and his gang weren't going to be doing any of the big-fan stuff.

* * *

After school in the music room, Julie practiced her song with Clark's lyrics. The spring concert was just a little over a week away, and she felt pretty good about the song, which she now called *No Tears for Me*. Mrs. Rimaldi wanted her to do two songs for the show, and what Julie really wanted was a second song of her own to play and not to have to play Pete Seeger's *If I Had a Hammer*. She was determined that if she was going to do this, then she wanted to do it all on her own. She had the music for another song fairly well developed, but again no lyrics.

She had just finished *No Tears for Me* for the third time when she realized that Clark stood in the door, watching and listening.

Has he been there long enough to hear the song?

She pulled herself together. She had agonized over how and when to tell him. Now she was glad it was out in the open. She looked carefully at him and tried a warm smile and the direct approach. "Hi, Clark, how do you like our song?"

He had almost been out the door after school before he finally found the courage to head over to the music room and confront her about the song. He knew he had to clear it up. What he hadn't figured out was how to approach her, and that had weighed heavily on him as he got to the music room. Her simple question settled all of his turmoil, and he smiled. "I like it, a lot."

"I hope you're not mad that I used your poem. I had this music in my head and then it was like your words were written specifically for it. Kinda weird, huh?"

"Yeah. It sounds much better with the music," he offered, as he came into the room toward her.

"I should have asked first. I know that. I'm sorry."

"It's okay. I would have said yes." He smiled because he really would have.

"I call it *No Tears for Me* is that okay? I know that's not the title of your poem, but I thought that this is a new thing, part you and part me."

He considered for a moment. He did like the title, and he especially liked the part-you and part-me concept. "No, that's good, I like it."

"Thanks . . ." She paused, it was going well, so why not press ahead. "Do you have any others? I have this new music in my head, and I would really like another song to play for the concert."

"Oh, you're playing this for the concert, at school?"

"Oh, yeah, didn't I mention that?"

He shook his head, not really upset, maybe concerned. "No, but that's cool I guess."

Just cool I guess?

He immediately felt like a total dork. Julie Wells playing their song in front of the whole school was so much more than just cool. That was like saying that Paul Newman was just an okay actor.

"Oh, I've got a bunch more, but I don't know if they're any good, you know, as lyrics or anything." He knew he was stammering as he tried to recover.

"Maybe I could come over and see some. The thing is that the concert is next week and I could play this Pete Seeger song, but I'd really like to do my own."

"Which one?"

"Which one what?"

"Which Pete Seeger song? *Turn, Turn, Turn* or *Where Have all the Flowers Gone* or *If I Had a Hammer* or - "

"Hammer, wow, you know Pete Seeger, that's so cool."

"I was thinking more like sophisticated," he teased.

God, what a stupid thing to say!

He didn't want her to know that he had studied up on Pete Seeger, right after their previous conversation about him.

She laughed. "Very definitely, a worldly man of the arts. Anyway, what do you think? Can I come over?" She wondered why she was being so forward, but it felt natural with him.

"Um, sure, when?"

"How about now? You don't have practice today, and I'm feeling very desperate."

Her tone was so sexual, or at least it impacted him that way, that he felt his body tingle all over. "Uh sure, let's do it." He tried to sound nonchalant as he struggled to get comfortable with this astonishing turn of events.

* * *

Rita had just woken from a nap when she heard voices coming from downstairs. She recognized Clark's, but the other was female and not Sarah. Coleen was playing golf and not due home for an hour or more. Then the voices started up the stairs. Her curiosity quickly got the better of her, and she poked her head out of the guestroom door.

There was Julie looking like she was in complete control as usual, and then there was Clark who acted very peculiarly. For one thing, he was talking, and talking fast and not very coherently. The closer they got to his bedroom, the faster and less coherent he became.

No way they're going in there for sex.

Even if that was the intent, Rita knew that it could only be a disaster. Julie may or may not be a virgin, but she certainly knew what was what, and Clark didn't. Rita decided that she had to stop it, if that was indeed the plan.

"Hi, mates. Clark, I thought you had a practice today."

"Rita, you're home. Yes, yes, I thought so, but no, it's tomorrow and then the rest of the week. You remember Julie?"

Julie tried to assess the situation. She got good vibes from Rita, but wondered about her look of concern. She spoke cautiously, "Nice to see you again, Rita."

201

Rita's instinct was to hug the girl, but she resisted, waited so see what was going down.

"Julie has written a song using one of my poems as the lyrics, and I just found out, and she wants to write another and wanted to see my other poems." Clark blew the words out in a torrent. He hoped that Rita would not let on that he had actually heard the song a week ago but had been too chicken to talk to her.

Rita did catch his unspoken message. "Well, isn't that the dogs bollocks, I'd love to hear it. Maybe Julie can play it, sing it for me while you look for your poems?" She not very subtly steered Julie back toward the stairs. She felt for a moment more like a mother than a sister, but she knew that she had to protect Clark.

"Great," Julie said, as she preceded Rita downstairs.

Clark almost collapsed with relief. He hadn't wanted Julie to come to his room, not only because of his sexual fears and tension, but also because it was an absolute mess. But Julie had just kept on coming with him, even after he suggested that she would be more comfortable waiting in the den or the living room.

Downstairs in the den, Rita watched Julie unpack her old guitar and then sat transfixed as she listened to the song. Julie's voice was unpolished but very distinctive, and she emoted intense feelings with every note and word. Rita had read Clark's poem after he told her about Julie's song. She had liked it, but she wasn't prepared for the impact of the song. Her ears tingled, and her producer's mind buzzed. Her first thought was that this could be a hit song and perfect for Keith and his band. It spoke to men and women alike.

"That's totally the bees' knees. Wow! So you had the tune first and then added the lyrics, Clark's poem?"

Julie nodded.

"That's very unusual, you know, normally it works the other way or they get done together. And now you're trying to do another one?"

"For the school concert next week, I need two songs."

"How long have you been working on this one?"

"Oh, three, maybe four weeks total, I guess."

"So, do you think you have enough time to develop a new one? It would have to be awfully good to stand up next to this."

"I don't know, but I thought I'd try."

Just then Clark entered with a handful of papers and a very nervous grin. Rita suggested that Julie play the tune she was working on and then Clark should read some of his poems.

Julie's new song was similar to the other one in some ways but also different. The tone was more mature, the chord structure more elegant, and the beat more positive. Rita thought it had a lot of promise and hoped that Julie would let her help with it.

As he read the first of his poems Clark's voice was tentative and weak, but it grew stronger as he got positive feedback from Julie and Rita. The first two poems were very male centric, about baseball, and didn't fit the tune at all. However, as soon as he started the third one, both Julie and Rita stiffened in anticipation.

> Childhood things, toys and stuff
> Neat piles of hard decisions
> Mother's lament, not enough

It was again eerily perfect for Julie's tune. It was overall more hopeful than his other one but equally as mature in its symbolism and subtext. Clark must have felt it also because, as he reached the end, his voice had naturally taken on the rhythm of Julie's music.

Boyhood things, comics worn
Neat piles of hard decisions
Parting, bitter sweet, forlorn
Teenage things, kisses tasted
Messy unwanted decision
Moments of future wasted

Clark finished and looked down at his feet. Unable to contain herself, Julie rushed over and gave him a big hug.

Rita could see his face grow a bright red and his eyes go wide with excitement.

Oh good lord, this is going to be interesting.

Julie, Rita, and Clark were so intent on their work on the song that they didn't notice Coleen until she stood right next to them. In fact, she had been in the room for several minutes before they realized it. It was Julie who saw her first and stopped playing.

"Oh, hey Mom, we're, this is Julie my, a friend from school. She's writing, we're writing a song together, and Rita's helping us."

Clark would have kept babbling, but Julie stood up, approached Coleen and put out her hand. "Hello, Mrs. Westfield, I'm Julie Wells. It's very nice to meet you."

Coleen could tell from the smile on Rita's face that this was the girl she had mentioned. Coleen felt good about it but also apprehensive. This was not a young girl like Margaret had been. This was a young woman.

Clark could really get hurt here. I better get ahead of this one.

"I've got to go get dinner ready. Julie, would you like to stay for dinner?"

"Oh, thank you, but I should probably get going soon, I've got homework and it's a long walk home, the other side of the school."

Julie was torn. She would like to stay and didn't want to go home.

But this is moving a little too fast.

"Sure, okay, another time. Rita can take my car and drive you home. Clark, have you done your homework?"

"No, but I can take her home on my scooter."

"Not without a second helmet you can't." Coleen had chided him for months to get a second helmet so he could take someone on his scooter, but he had never before seen the need. Nor had he seen the need to rush out after his recent birthday and take his driving test for his license to be able to drive the car. Now he vowed to get both things taken care of in the next few days.

Julie enjoyed the comfortable silence in the car as Rita drove her home. As she drove, Rita occasionally looked over at Julie.

A talented, troubled, teenage cheerleader. Is that a strange mixture of clichés or what?

Except for the cheerleader part, Rita recognized some strong parallels to herself when she was that age.

And her talent has a lot more potential upside than mine did.

"Thank you so much for helping me, us, with the song." Julie wanted to speak her mind but didn't want to come across as too much of a sycophant. "You really do have a great ear."

Rita smiled, "It's what I do for work, help with musicians and look for new talent."

Julie smiled, envious. "That's my house there."

Rita stopped in front of the house, which was dark and looked empty. "Is anyone home? Are you okay?"

"I have a key, and I'm fine. People know that my dad's a cop so, you know, they wouldn't bother us. Thanks again for the ride. And remember, we drive on the right," she teased with a smile.

"Cheerio," Rita laughed.

Julie watched the car disappear around the corner. Part of her smiled at the good time she had had and part of her grimaced when she compared Clark's family to hers. Julie had just reached her front door when Suzie pulled up in her car. Julie immediately went on alert. Suzie always tried to avoid being anywhere near Julie's house and her mother.

Suzie jumped out of her car and rushed over. "I've got some big news about the party on Saturday. I told you we should have gone." She literally vibrated with excitement. "You'll never believe who was at the party and who Laurie tried to get her hooks into."

Julie couldn't imagine at first but then began to feel a dreadful premonition. "Who?"

"Clark."

"No, can't be. He's never gone to any party."

"Well, he did. Now that he's a big star, maybe he's changed. They all do, don't they?"

Julie knew that the boy she had spent the afternoon with had changed, but not in that way. "So what happened and according to whom?"

"Fran and Mindy were both there. They called us to come over, remember? Well, Clark was there and had a couple of beers with Joey and Andy and the others. Fran said he looked a bit tipsy."

"But what's this about Laurie?"

"Well, she got a hold of him and took him into that bedroom, you know, off the rec room."

"He went with her?"

"Fran did say that Laurie might have been dragging him, but he didn't put up a big fight or anything."

Julie sat down heavily on the front step, shocked and hurt to a degree that threatened to overwhelm her. "That's, that's it?"

"Oh no, the best part is that after a few minutes, Joey barges in there and there's all this shouting and then Clark runs out and totally disappears. Then Laurie comes out yelling at Joey to mind his own damn business. Is that classic or what?" Suzie paused. "Are you okay? You don't look so good."

CHAPTER SIXTEEN

The very last thing that Clark expected from Julie when he arrived at English class the next morning was what could only be described as a cold shoulder. Only the slightest nod of her head responded to his warm, "good morning." Then the bell rang, and he didn't have any time to react. But the forty-three-minute class gave him plenty of time to wonder what was going on. He was determined to ask her, but she scooted away as soon as the class ended.

He tried to find her during the rest of the school day but couldn't. She didn't come to lunch, and she wasn't in the music room after school. He couldn't wait around because he had to get to practice. He briefly thought of skipping it but knew that wouldn't be a good way to start things off. As it was, he was late getting to the locker room, and all the others had gone. He quickly changed into his practice shirt and pants. As he walked to the field he kept trying to figure out what was wrong. What had changed so dramatically since yesterday afternoon? He couldn't believe that Rita had said or done something to cause it while driving her home.

The two of them seemed to really get along.

The coach's loud yell caught his attention. "Westfield! You're late. I don't accept late. You're new, so this is a warning, don't let it happen again. Over there with the pitchers. Loosen up, easy throws."

Clark knew the basic practice routine from watching it for so many days from the hillside. He knew that a big part of what they did in practice was similar to what he normally did on his own. He found that practice was actually less strenuous because, with only two catchers and five pitchers, they had to take turns pitching.

The next game wasn't until Saturday, so they spent a lot of time stretching and working on conditioning. Clark noticed that he and Sebastian seemed to be the only ones who liked to run. They cruised along way ahead of the others. The two catchers brought up the rear.

"I hate running," Tommy complained loudly.

Joey pretended to kick him in the rear end to get him going faster. Clark noticed that Joey had a very easy relationship with all the players, even the seniors like Dwight and his buddies, Ed and Miguel.

Clark knew that pitchers had a reputation for being temperamental prima donnas and very superstitious about their routines. With the weeklong breaks between playoff games, Dwight would pitch all the games. If Sebastian was unhappy about it, he didn't show it. Clark found the other relief pitchers to be very loose, almost too loose. It didn't seem like they practiced very hard. Benji considered himself a jokester, always trying to get someone in trouble. Jason, who still nursed his tender hamstring, was a big talker and never seemed to stop to listen to anyone, not even the coach.

Clark was glad that Rory wasn't there. The word circulated that he was done for the season and not just because of the injury. Evidently Maggie's parents were both lawyers, and they had pressed charges against him. He hadn't been in school for a while. No one seemed to miss him except for Dwight because Rory was his main partner in crime.

As he worked out with the other pitchers on the practice field, Clark kept his eye on the main field and the action at home plate. He dreaded the part of practice that he had never done, that he couldn't do on his own in his backyard - batting practice.

From behind a screen that was set up in front of the pitcher's mound, Coach Jackson threw pitches for the players to hit. They didn't have an extra catcher so the balls clanged against the backstop if they weren't hit. Miguel, as Clark knew, was the best hitter and the others struggled to varying degrees. Coach Duncan would come by and offer encouragement or occasionally he would get frustrated at a player's lack of attention and yell at them. Clark knew it was coming soon - time for the pitchers to take batting practice.

Eventually Coach Jackson called the pitchers over. Clark positioned himself at the end of the short line that formed on the bench. Dwight went first, and Sebastian was in the on-deck circle. The comfort level of the pitchers in the batter's box started high with Dwight and then fell quickly, especially when it came to the relief pitchers who seldom had to bat.

If Clark had been watching from his old spot on the hillside, he would have found it comical as Benji swung wildly and managed to miss most of the balls thrown to him. Any solid contact with a pitch was more luck than skill. Clark didn't find it funny now because he knew that his turn was coming and that he would surely set a new standard for farcical. He stood in the on-deck circle and swung his bat, trying to mimic the motion used by Miguel and the good hitters he watched on television. Then it was Clark's turn. As the first pitch from Coach Jackson came at him, Clark instinctively closed his eyes and swung. His grip was too loose, and the bat flew out of his hands and tumbled halfway to the mound.

"Westfield, did you close your eyes?" Coach Duncan yelled from the bench area. "You got to watch the ball, and hang onto the bat."

Clark retrieved his bat and tried to ignore the snickers that came from some of the players who had stopped to watch. He distinctly heard Dwight say, "Jerk-off."

He planted his feet in the batter's box and waited. As Coach Jackson threw the next pitch, Clark struggled to keep his eye on the ball. He did, but he still missed and again lost the grip on his bat, which this time almost reached the coach.

Coach Duncan came over to Clark as he returned to the plate with his bat. "Son, you look like you've never done this before."

"I haven't," Clark replied.

The coach looked very skeptical. "It always feels that way after a long layoff, when was the last time you batted?"

Clark looked around and saw a lot of the team watching, including Joey. "I've never batted with live pitching," he replied softly.

The coach looked very confused until Joey came over to him and whispered something in his ear. After a moment's consideration, the coach called all the pitchers over to him and began a lesson in the proper technique for bunting. Then he had each of them practice.

Clark picked it up quickly and was soon bunting as well as any of them, including Dwight, who seemed to be very tentative about stepping in front of the pitch. Coach Duncan yelled twice at him to put his body out there and not reach with his arms.

Later as he got dressed in the locker room, Clark came to the conclusion that Dwight was a hot or cold kind of guy. Most of the time he was too self-absorbed to make trouble. It was only when he felt threatened, or maybe when he had too much time on his hands, that he found ways to get into trouble or looked for people to torment. He obviously had an issue with getting hit by a ball, and his quiet exit from the locker room seemed to indicate that he didn't want to draw attention to it.

Clark also realized that the reactions to his body hair were maybe a thing of the past. In a way it now seemed to be accepted as a macho kind of thing. He laughed to himself.

At least no one is going to accuse the hairy guy of being a homo.

* * *

Rita woke up Wednesday morning and felt a little better than she had when she had gone to bed early the previous evening. She knew that her dreams had been troubling, but she couldn't remember any specifics other than that they were about the baby. Not by nature a pessimistic person, Rita fought a feeling of anxiety that had taken hold of her the day before and wouldn't loosen its grip. It must have been obvious because Coleen had asked her several times if she was okay. Rita only vaguely remembered Clark talking at dinner about his baseball practice and Sarah's sudden interest in the team.

When Rita finally managed to force herself up and to the kitchen, Coleen was waiting for her. "I'm glad you're up. I have an appointment for you with an obstetrician at 11:30."

"Oh, well, thank you, but I really can't."

"Is your schedule too busy to take care of yourself and your baby?" Sarcasm came naturally to Coleen.

Rita really wanted to avoid the topic, but realized she couldn't. "No, it's just that at home I'm covered by National Health, but over here, well I can't afford it."

"Nonsense Rita, you're part of the family, we'll pay for it."

Rita could tell by the tone of Coleen's voice that there would be no argument, and, in fact, she was thrilled that Coleen had done it. She hadn't seen a doctor since right after learning of the pregnancy. She avoided doctors whenever she could, and she had been fortunate in her life so far that she had been able to do so. But in the last few days she had begun to accept that this baby was coming and that, after wishing for a long time that it hadn't happened, she had become very attached to it. She also knew that, after being with this odd but warm and accepting family, she didn't feel so alone in the world.

"This is a referral from a friend I play golf with who has had four kids and every one of them with this doctor," Coleen explained, as they drove downtown to a medical building. "I didn't want to take you to my doctor because he's too old and a bit of a fuddy-duddy about, you know, not being married and . . ."

"Oh, yeah, that's good. No fuddy-duddies," Rita laughed.

Dr. Ruth Silverman was a young-looking 41-year-old who was very pregnant. She waddled out into the crowded waiting room and greeted Rita and Coleen before taking them back to the examination room.

"Thank you so much for squeezing us in," Coleen said, as she settled on a chair while Rita sat on the examination table.

Dr. Silverman nodded and replied, "Seven and a half months. That's how far along I am. Everyone asks, so I get it out, right up front."

Rita took an instant liking to her and relaxed for the first time in several days. "Glad to see you practice what you preach."

Dr. Silverman smiled. "So, tell me about you, I'm guessing fourteen, fifteen weeks."

Rita proceeded to tell the doctor her history and how she got her bun in the oven. She felt no sense of judgment from the doctor and felt completely comfortable as she lay back for the examination. She was totally unprepared for the rush of excitement and emotion that flooded over her as she heard the baby's heartbeat from the speaker of the ultrasound machine. She couldn't keep the tears from seeping out of her eyes. When

Coleen handed her a tissue, Rita noticed that her eyes were moist also.

Later, they stopped for lunch.

"Tell your golf friend thanks, that was a great referral."

"I will." Coleen had grown very protective of her step-daughter and future grandchild. It had taken her a while to get there, but there she was.

"So Clark tells me that you're quite the golfer."

"Oh, I knock it around a bit. Have you ever played?"

"Oh, blimey no, that's a rich man's passion in England. The closest I ever got was when my mum's band played a gig in Scotland at St. Andrews during the championship week."

They ate for a while in silence. Then Coleen asked, "What do you know about Julie, Clark's uh friend?"

Rita considered with her response. She wanted to be positive but vague because it was unclear where that relationship was headed. And she didn't think that Coleen could step in and fulfill John's role by having the sex conversation with Clark. She couldn't imagine that any boy would want to have that talk with his mother. Fortunately, it seemed that vague proved to be good enough for Coleen.

As they rode home, Rita knew that she would never be the same again. No matter what happened with Keith, she would have and keep this baby, and she was determined to be a good mother. That concept, which had been so foreign to her just weeks ago, filled her with warmth and strength.

I can do this!

* * *

Clark spent Wednesday and Thursday feeling frustrated because he couldn't find a time or place to approach Julie and find out what was wrong. Thursday in English class he got sort of a half-smile when he waved at her, but that was all. At all other times, she was either surrounded by her friends, or they were both rushing to class or to their practices.

What he didn't know was that she felt just as frustrated because she couldn't think of a way to break the ice - the barrier that she acknowledged was her own doing. She hadn't been able to cope with the image of him and Laurie going into that bedroom. She told herself that it had to have been all Laurie's doing and that nothing had happened thanks to Joey. She convinced herself intellectually, but she was being ruled by her emotions these days.

Clark walked into the house after practice on Thursday and found Rita playing the piano in the living room. "I didn't know you played."

She smiled as she continued. "A little when I'm working out an idea. How does this sound?"

As he listened, Clark realized it was Julie's tune but with a slightly faster pace.

"Is Julie with you? Wasn't it today we were going to work some more on the song?"

He hadn't mentioned anything about Julie's behavior to Rita, hoping that it would resolve itself by now. "No, I don't think she's coming."

"Why not?" Rita questioned.

Before Clark could respond, the front doorbell rang. Clark opened the door to find Julie, who gave him that same half-smile.

"Hi."

"Hi," he replied and got stuck after that.

Rita rescued him. "Hiho Julie, come on in. I'm glad you came. Clark thought you weren't."

Julie felt glad that quiet people like Clark were normally also discrete. She grabbed and squeezed Clark's elbow as she came in and then followed Rita into the den.

"I've been doing some work on the tune," Rita and Julie each said, almost simultaneously.

They all laughed, relaxed, and got to work. After a couple of hours of intense collaboration, they all fell silent and reflected on what they now believed to be a pretty good song. During the process, the lingering tension between Julie and Clark had almost completely dissipated, but wasn't forgotten.

She caught him staring at her and whispered to him, "Clark, can we go somewhere and talk for a minute?"

He got up to take her out to the backyard while Rita watched with heightened interest.

"I'd love to go up on your arbor," Julie said, as they got outside.

They climbed up and settled down near each other, closer than he would have ventured just a week or so ago, but not touching. They watched the sun as it began to dip down beyond the mountain peaks, casting a beautiful warm light that poured into and over the clouds that seemed to always live on top of the Rockies.

"I'm sorry that I've been acting so weird the past few days," she started. She hadn't expected him to respond, and he didn't. "When I went home Monday after being here, I saw Suzie and . . . well, she told me about the party at Andy's and what happened with you and Laurie."

Clark struggled to contain his dismay. That had been what he'd been afraid of. "I can explain," he started haltingly.

"No, you don't need to explain. I know Laurie, and I think I'm beginning to know you. She came on to you, and she's pretty and very sexy." She forced out a laugh that was effective enough to break a little of the tension.

The image of Laurie's breasts, almost hanging out of her top, leapt across his mind.

"I mean, we're just friends and all," Julie continued. "So I don't really have any say in what you do with whom. But I, I just would hate to see you get mixed up with Laurie and her loose-girls."

Clark's spirits soared off the arbor when she said they were friends, and he believed that it seemed to include the possibility of more. "She kinda took me by surprise, but nothing at all happened. I'd gone there partly to, actually mainly to see if you were there," he added tentatively.

"Oh. Sorry, but I couldn't handle a party that night." She felt very happy that he had gone to see her and that he had given her space to be a bit of a bitch the past few days. The setting sun had now made the arbor a very romantic place, and she leaned over and kissed him firmly on the lips.

After his initial shock, he eagerly returned the kiss. Kissing was something that he knew how to do. He and Margaret had practiced a lot with different techniques that she had researched at the library. He still wasn't sure that kissing didn't somehow create babies. He had been too embarrassed to ask Margaret about it.

Kissing on the arbor proved to be awkward because they couldn't get their bodies in a good position without some body-part poking through the vines. As they tried again for a better position, Clark noticed out of his peripheral vision that Sarah had poked her head above the arbor. He paused his kiss and looked over to see a huge grin on her face.

"Sorry to interrupt you two love-birds, but Clark, Mom says you have to come in. We're going to the club for dinner." As she lowered her head down through the vines and climbed down, Sarah marveled at the changes that were happening to Clark.

Clark and Julie Wells, I'll be damned.

She had teased him about her, but she had never imagined that Julie would actually like him. She was one of the most popular girls in school and very sexy. Later during dinner, Sarah waited for the right moment, just when Clark put a bite of food in his mouth. "So Clark, have you asked Julie to the prom yet?"

Clark nearly choked. He turned a bright red as he realized that they were all staring at him. "No," he replied weakly.

* * *

Julie had been surprised to see her father's sheriff's car in the driveway when she got home from Clark's. As she had walked by the car, she had noticed that the engine was still warm, indicating that he hadn't been home very long. She entered the house cautiously and listened but didn't hear any disturbance. She found her parents sitting at the kitchen table staring silently at their cups of coffee. She assumed that Bea had a little kicker of something in hers. They barely acknowledged her as she said, "Hi," and then quickly went upstairs.

An hour or so later, Julie sat at her desk in her bedroom and tried to work on a paper for English class. She couldn't concentrate because most of her attention was directed downstairs to her mother and father. They weren't fighting, but the night was young. Finally, hunger got the best of her, and she returned to the kitchen. Frank and Bea had moved into the living room, where they talked with quiet but intense voices. She stained to hear what they were saying but couldn't make it out. She thought she heard her mother say, "You owe me that much."

Julie had almost finished eating some cereal when Bea suddenly entered the kitchen and threw Julie's gear bag on the table, knocking over the cereal bowl. "What the fuck," Julie cried, as she jumped back to avoid the milk that spilled over the edge of the table.

"What the hell is this," Bea snarled, as she pulled Julie's mitt and cleats from the bag. "I told you that I didn't want you to do this. And I know I didn't sign that permission slip. Did you Frank?" She turned her head toward Frank who stood quietly in the doorway.

"Permission for what?" he replied hesitantly.

"So little Miss Righteous here must've forged my signature. I'm gonna call them in the morning and tell them."

"No Bea, please don't. I'm sorry, but I really want to do it."

"You're a seventeen-year-old girl, and these are grown women, mostly queers."

"They're not, they're my age. And the coach, Becky, she knows Dad from high school."

Bea almost choked as she yelled, "Becky? Becky Arnson? That slut! That settles it, you're so not doing this!" She grabbed the gear bag and stormed out of the room.

Julie looked to her father for support, but he stared at the floor. "Dad?"

Frank looked up. On his face, a wistful smile struggled with a frown of guilt. Becky Arnson. For years now he'd thought what a terrible mistake he had made when he chose Bea over Becky. Flash over substance. Sexual desire trumped moral character. He'd been a fool, not unlike many boys that age.

"I really want to play, and there's nothing for a girl to do around here. I hate being a cheerleader and not a player. Do you realize how few opportunities there are for us?"

Frank had never thought of it. If he had, he would have assumed that there were plenty of teams for girls just like there were for the boys. He looked at Julie and felt so lucky that she wasn't like her mother. "I'll talk to her. Do you need me to sign something?"

"Thanks, but it probably doesn't matter anyway."

"Why not? Did you make the team?"

"I did, but the team lost its sponsor and unless it gets another one soon, it all falls apart. And that really sucks. This is important for a lot of women, not just the players."

CHAPTER SEVENTEEN

Friday flew by for Clark because he walked on a cloud like a Greek god, far above all those poor mortals who had not kissed Julie Wells. The only thing that nagged at him was whether he should or could ask her to the prom.

Coach Duncan yelled at him twice during practice, telling him to pay attention and get his head out of his butt. Joey thought he recognized the signs and prayed that it wasn't Laurie who had gotten to Clark. He knew that would end badly, at least for Clark. Then Saturday, on the bus to the game at Northern High, Joey saw Julie return Clark's look, and he knew.

Jesus, Clark, way to go.

But then Joey saw Dwight glare at Clark with a murderous look in his eyes, and he realized that could mean big trouble.

The trouble started the moment the game did. The Northern Owls had a pretty good pitcher who quickly and efficiently struck out the first three Harrison batters. Then Dwight took the mound and started to pitch like he wanted to hurt someone. A hit batter, a wild pitch, and then a four-pitch walk put men on first and third with no outs. Coach Duncan went to the mound with Joey and was met with an icy glare of silence from Dwight. The visit did succeed, however, in that Dwight found some focus and got a grounder to short for a nice double play. But the runner from third was able to score.

After a final out pop-up, the first inning ended, Owls 1 and Cougars 0.

Clark sat at the end of the bench, as far as he could from Dwight, but he could still feel the negativity radiating out from him like ripples in a pond, big ripples, waves. Clark didn't know for sure if he was the target or the cause of Dwight's anger, but he assumed he was.

The next three Harrison batters went down quietly, and then the team was back on the field. Dwight began to throw strikes, but Clark noticed something wrong with his delivery. He balked on just about every pitch. Clark debated whether to say something to the coach and wisely thought better of it. He noticed that the umpire seemed to be watching Dwight carefully. The balk rules were wide-open to interpretation, but what Clark saw Dwight doing was clearly balking, or at least he thought so.

Dwight managed to get out of the second inning without letting in any more runs. As Joey came to the bench, Clark moved next to him and told him about Dwight's delivery. That wasn't something that Joey had been looking for. Dwight's normally delivery motion was erratic and made it difficult enough for Joey to catch his pitches. Clark went back to the end of the bench and watched Joey go over and talk to Dwight.

Dwight erupted and yelled, "Who the fuck said that? I'll shove a balk down their fucking throat!"

Joey tried to calm him down and thankfully didn't look over at Clark. Ira then threaded a single between first and second so Dwight was up to bat with one on and two out. He beat his bat on home plate like it was an animal that he was determined to kill. He then swung at three straight bad pitches and threw his bat into the backstop. The umpire gave him and Coach Duncan a warning about behavior.

Already primed and warned, Dwight barely held it together when the umpire yelled, "Balk," on his first pitch of the third inning. Fortunately, the coach was able to get to him and calm things down so he could stay in the game. But Dwight was rattled and walked that batter and the next before giving up a bloop single to load the bases.

On the second pitch to the next batter, "Balk," yelled the umpire again, and waved all the runners to advance a base, including the runner from third, who scored.

This time Coach Duncan had no chance to reach Dwight before he got to the umpire, who calmly threw Dwight out of the game and told the coach that Dwight had to leave the field. Dwight was almost off the diamond when he saw Julie staring at him. That broke him completely, and he stormed back to the umpire to further argue his case. In the process, he bumped into him, sending the umpire sprawling to the dirt on his butt. Coach Jackson grabbed Dwight by the arms and forced him away, but the damage had been done. The umpire shouted at Coach Duncan that Dwight would be suspended for at least a game and more if he had anything to say about it.

The crowd, all Northern students and supporters, had watched in stunned silence as all this unfolded, but now broke into a frenzy of cheers and cat-calls and insults. Good sportsmanship didn't stand a chance in the face of such a spectacle.

The Harrison players couldn't believe what had just happened. Then the noise from the partisan crowd crashed over them like a tidal wave. They could have just given up, but they didn't. Joey called them all together in a huddle and exhorted them to put it out of their heads and concentrate on getting the win. "It's only two to nothing, we have four more innings to play, we can do this!"

Because of the ejection, Harrison was given time to get a new pitcher warmed up. Coach Duncan called on Sebastian, who immediately regretted his slacker approach to practice the past week. Clark took one look at Sebastian's final warm-up pitches and knew that it was soon going to be time for the relievers. As he predicted, Sebastian lasted an inning and a third before the coach put in Benji. Benji got into and then out of a jam in the fifth but was clearly tired.

The Harrison bats had been quiet all afternoon, but they began to come alive when Northern's starting pitcher pulled a muscle and was taken out. Clark wasn't surprised because he had noticed that the pitcher had a very awkward motion, which he thought had to put a lot of stress on his arm.

In the top of the sixth inning, the Cougars scored a run and then would have had a home run by Miguel, except for a spectacular catch by the Northern center fielder.

Clark warmed up and went in to pitch the bottom of the sixth. He knew he had to go the distance because there was no one else. He felt ready for it, and the noise from the Northern crowd just fueled his fire. Using his fastball and curve he swept through the top of the order with three straight strikeouts. That quieted the crowd. Between each pitch he made a quick glance to Julie. It didn't matter if she was looking or not, as long as she was there.

Slotted to bat fifth in the top of the seventh inning, Clark prayed for someone to hit a homer to at least tie the game before he came up to bat. But there was only one consistent home run threat on the team and that was Miguel, who had batted in the previous inning. He watched Andy, the first Cougar batter, walk. He then advanced to second on a balk by the Northern pitcher - maybe the umpire tried to be even-handed. Then Ralph laid down a bunt that they weren't expecting, and he reached first. First and third and no outs. Coach Duncan then had Ed sacrifice bunt to move Ralph to second but unfortunately it didn't score the runner from third. Second and third and one out. Joey came up next and tried to hit a home run but only managed a shallow popup that also failed to score the runner from third. So with men on second and third and two out, Clark came up to bat.

Clark had imagined many game-winning scenarios in his head as he practiced hour after hour in his back yard. But they had all involved him pitching, not batting. The only thing he had going for him was that the other team didn't know whether he could hit or not. No one had ever seen him play before. With that slim foundation of hope, he moved with purpose to the plate and tried to look like he knew what he was doing. He knew the look and the moves from watching so many professional players. He decided to adopt the mannerisms and the confidence of Mickey Mantle. His only unique addition was his glance at Julie.

He'd been watching this opposing pitcher for two innings and thought he had some tells to work with. He would test it. He saw the head bob that meant fastball, and there it came. Clark just stood and watched. The twisting of pitcher's hand in his glove meant curveball. Strike two.

Clark stepped back out of the batter's box and stretched his arms and bat high over his head. He didn't think of a big hit. He knew that a solid single would probably score two. He stepped back in and saw the head nod, fastball. It came in a little high and inside. Clark swung in anticipation and felt the solid contact between bat and ball. He watched as it sailed over the head of the second baseman and into right field.

"Run," yelled Joey.

If the right fielder had thrown to first, Clark would have been out and the inning over. But he tried to show off and get the ball to the plate before Ralph could score from second. Ralph was the fastest player on the team, and he slid in safely. Clark reached first.

The Harrison players went crazy, and Joey struggled to get them under control. The inning wasn't over yet. But it soon was, as Bill hit a grounder to short, which forced Clark out at second.

Three outs needed for a win, Clark went back to the mound for the bottom of the seventh. This was the scenario he had dreamed of. The only thing missing was a home crowd to go crazy and chant his name. But he had Julie and that was enough.

He had been watching the opposing batters all game, and they were completely predictable. He methodically struck out two and gave up a weak grounder for the third and final out. It was almost anticlimactic. He enjoyed the back pounding from his team and the "good job" from the coaches, but the best thing by far was the big smile from Julie.

That euphoria lasted only until they reached the bus. Dwight had been there for almost an hour, stewing. The moment he saw Clark, Dwight ran off the bus and jumped right up in his face. "You stay away from Julie, you hear me, you hairy freak," he growled, spit spewing from his mouth.

Clark struggled to maintain his control. "I can talk to whoever I want to, so get out of my face."

Dwight wasn't prepared for resistance and wasn't capable of verbal sparring, so he prepared to strike. He made such a big deal of his wind-up for a punch that Clark easily saw it coming and ducked out of the way. He had a great opportunity to smash his fist into Dwight's stomach as he stumbled past, but Clark resisted.

Miguel spotted Coach Jackson headed toward them, so he grabbed Dwight's arms and started to pull him away. Dwight tried to shake loose, but Miguel was too strong. Finally, Dwight managed to push Miguel away, venting his anger at his friend. Miguel watched Dwight storm off and shook his head. The rest of the team just stood around, not knowing what to do.

Dwight stomped into the bus and sat down in the last row, next to a window. Coach Jackson followed him in and sat next to him on the aisle, effectively blocking Dwight in. The rest of the team and then the cheerleaders slowly loaded onto the bus and filled the forward seats, leaving four or five empty rows between them and Dwight and Coach Jackson. No one spoke on the ride back to Harrison. They all felt cheated that they didn't get a chance to celebrate the win.

Julie hadn't seen the altercation but quickly got the story. She felt sorry for Dwight and thankful that Clark hadn't been hurt.

When they arrived back at school, the team got off the bus and headed for the locker room. They all kept their distance from both Clark and Dwight. Coach Jackson followed Dwight and stayed in the locker room while everyone quietly and quickly showered, dressed, and left.

Julie and Suzie had to leave immediately after the game to go on a Masters' family picnic in the foothills of the Rockies. Julie had hoped to have some time to talk to Clark, but that hadn't been possible. She felt more than a little responsibility for Dwight's attack. She hadn't been very careful to hide her growing feelings for Clark, and Dwight had obviously seen it and gotten jealous. She knew that she was going to have to deal with the situation, and it probably wouldn't be easy.

Suzie was the only person who knew about Julie's troubles at home. A few days earlier she had asked Julie if she wanted to stay at her house for a while. Julie spent a lot of time there as it was. They had been friends for almost twelve years and had never once hung-out at Julie's house.

Suzie's parents, George and Martha Masters, were incredibly supportive, and she felt safe with them. They knew Bea and were aware of her drinking problem. George had been a good friend of Frank's in high school, and they had stayed close as adults. So when Suzie had asked them if Julie could stay with them for a while, they had readily agreed, as long as it was okay with Frank. They hadn't tried to contact Bea.

Now as they sat around a fire pit and roasted marshmallows, Julie imagined who she would like to have there with her, and it was definitely Clark, not Dwight.

Later that night when they were getting ready for bed in Suzie's room, Suzie said, "I don't know why you're dragging this out. It's just going to get worse with that asshole."

Julie nodded. She and Dwight had been together for a long time, and she felt a responsibility to . . . well she didn't know what really. She assumed that it was to manage a smooth break-up. But in many ways it seemed like they were already broken up.

Dwight hadn't always been like this, she remembered. When they had first started dating he had been considerate and sensitive. But in the past couple of years, his personality had grown dark and troubled. She knew that part of it was caused by the pain of losing his mother and the incessant pressure from his father. Dwight wasn't as ambitious or as bright as his parents, but fortunately not as screwed up either. The only positive thing for him was his pitching, and now that was maybe in jeopardy.

"All I know," Suzie yawned, "is that if you don't snatch up Clark soon, someone else will, and I don't mean Laurie." Suzie paused for effect. "Could even be me. I could get used to the strong, silent type."

She ducked as a pillow came flying at her from Julie, but she pressed on. "He can be as silent as he wants while we do it. I can feel it now." She reached down and grabbed herself.

Julie struggled to keep from laughing and pushed that image out of her already jumbled brain. Suzie loved to talk a big game, but in reality she was just as much a virgin as Julie.

The difference being that Suzie seemed eager to change that status, while Julie was in no hurry.

The next morning Julie was up early and off to the Junior Cowgirl practice. She had to walk past her house to get to the first bus. The house seemed quiet, and there were no cars in the drive. She couldn't help but wonder.

Where the hell are you, Bea?

She imagined several tragic scenarios and the consequences until she realized that she had slowed down and was going to be late.

She arrived at the field just as practice was beginning, and she threw herself headlong into it. It proved a great diversion. They stretched and did calisthenics until they were warm and loose. Then they did some speed drills, sprinting from the left field fence to the first base line. Coach Becky took Julie and three other players to work on pitching drills. Julie had not had time to work on her technique during the past week, and she was clearly behind the other girls. But her competitive nature kicked in, and she pitched ball after ball until her arm felt like a dead weight.

Coach Becky called for a break, and they all headed to the benches for water and the orange slices that the coaches had provided. As Julie trotted over to the bench, she noticed someone sitting up in the stands and then realized that it was Clark. He smiled when he saw her recognize him. She continued to stare at him after she reached the bench.

Curious, Becky followed the direction of Julie's eyes and saw Clark. "Normally I would ask spectators to leave, but you seem to know him," she said to Julie with a slight edge of fun in her voice.

Julie nodded and then headed up into the stands.

"Hi," he said, as she reached him and sat down.

"Hi. What are you doing here?" she asked.

"I was curious. I wanted to see you play. You're really good."

"Thanks, but I'm just learning."

"Funny thing that you're a pitcher."

"Yeah," she laughed, "pretty strange. And my dad was a pitcher, he even almost made it to the big leagues."

"Almost? What happened?"

"He blew his arm out in spring training his rookie year. Surgery, and poof, no career."

"Ouch, that's tough, I'm sorry."

"Yeah, well, he was okay, I guess. But Bea, my mom, she never really got over not being the wife of the big star pitcher."

"So now she'll be the mother of a big star pitcher." He was ready to laugh with her but wasn't ready for the crestfallen, almost tearful, reaction. "Are you okay? Did, did I say something wrong?" He grasped for something else to say, but the words blew around in his head like they were in a tornado, and he couldn't grab one.

She struggled to pull herself together. She normally had better control over her emotions when it came to her mother. She grabbed his hand and squeezed. "No it's not you, I just . . ." she stopped, and hoped that he wouldn't press her on it. She also hoped that the team wasn't watching, so she glanced down at the bench. "Oh my God!"

"What?"

"That, that's my dad talking to Coach Becky. Sorry, I gotta go see what's going on." She jumped up, then paused when she noticed the odd look on his face. "Thanks for coming, really."

He watched her go and felt a heavy weight of failure settle down on him. His one big goal for the day, if he got to talk to her, had been to ask her to the prom, and he blew it.

Julie reached the bench area and approached her dad and Becky. It seemed like they were engaged in a very intense but pleasant conversation.

What the . . . they're flirting.

She had never seen her dad do it, but she certainly recognized flirting when she saw it. And with Becky it appeared even more obvious. Everything about her body, her voice, and her energy screamed flirt. They didn't realize it when Julie came right up next to them. Becky noticed first, despite that fact that Julie had grabbed her dad's upper arm and squeezed it.

"Hey Julie, I was just telling your dad how well you're doing, really picking it up super-fast. A natural just like him," she rambled on, clearly nervous.

"Hey, Dad. What are you doing here?" Julie asked someone for the second time in the last ten minutes.

"Hi. Did you know that Becky and I, we knew each other in high school? Small town, huh."

They all just stood and nodded for a moment.

"I need to talk to you for a minute, can we go over there?" Her father pointed to the parking lot where his sheriff's cruiser was parked. He led the way, and she followed. When they got there, he got right to the point. "When was the last time you saw your mother?"

"Is she okay?"

"She hasn't been home ever since you went to stay at Suzie's. No one's seen her at any of her usual places."

"I'm sure she's fine. She's been gone before." Julie remembered numerous times when she had stayed all alone for days while her mother had been on a bender and her father had been on 12-hours shifts.

"Yes, but I always knew where she was going. I think she's avoiding me because . . ." He paused and looked intently at Julie. "I've asked her for a divorce. She's basically agreed, and I have the papers."

Julie didn't know what to say or do. She had heard them arguing about it, but they had done that before, and he had never followed up on it. This seemed different. The way he looked was different.

Is it really going to happen?

She felt neither the joy she would have anticipated, nor fear. Just numb.

"I wanted you to know if, if you see her," he finished and kissed her cheek, which he seldom did, and then got in his car and left.

She slowly walked back to the field where the team had resumed practice. She looked up in the stands, hoping to see Clark, but he had gone. She knew from experience that having a dad show up in his sheriff's uniform had that effect on a guy.

Fortunately for Julie, the practice was about over because she found it hard to concentrate. Thoughts of her parents' impending divorce fought with thoughts of Clark and how she felt about him.

Becky blew her whistle to signal the end of practice and called all the players to the stands for a brief meeting. She told them it had been a good practice, but they needed to keep working hard. She wanted her decision on who to keep and who to cut to be a hard one to make. Then Becky added, "But I've got some very good news. We've found a new supporter who has agreed to sponsor the team this season. That means I can go ahead and finalize our schedule and then get uniforms when the team is set."

Julie and the others clapped and cheered. They really wanted to play, but it was hard to make a full commitment when you didn't know if it was going to work out. One of the girls asked Becky about the identity of the sponsor so they could thank them or support them, assuming that it was probably a local merchant.

"I'm sorry, but I can't tell you right now. They want to keep it anonymous for a little while. I should be able to announce it after we determine the final team lineup next week."

The prospect of being cut from the final team quieted everyone as they gathered their stuff and headed home.

* * *

Clark had been nervous enough just going to Julie's practice. But then when her father showed up, it had been too much, and he had split. He was angry with himself as he rode his scooter home.

She did seem happy to see me, so why the hell didn't I just ask her?

He knew why. He'd never asked a girl to a dance before, and this was the prom, not just an ordinary dance. For Clark, as a junior, this was the first prom he could go to. They were restricted to junior and senior boys. The girls, however, could go as sophomores or even freshmen if asked by a junior or senior boy. Many a freshman or sophomore girl had lost her virginity to a senior boy at a drunken after-prom party.

By the time he got home, Clark had fallen into a real funk about the prom, convinced that it was useless to even try. He figured that Julie was probably going with Dwight anyway. As he entered the house, he heard Sarah talking to their mom. That was the last thing he wanted - to have Sarah tease him some more. He moved quickly and quietly through the house, out to the backyard, where he began to pitch. This time he pitched lefty. He had been working on that for a few months now, and it forced him to concentrate more intensely. After thirty minutes or so, he stopped and sat down on the mound. That's when he noticed that Rita had come out and was sitting on one of the lawn chairs. She looked up from her book and at Clark.

"That side is getting almost as good as the other."

"Thanks." He nodded and almost smiled.

"Do you want to talk about it?"

"About what?"

"I've watched you enough to know that that was frustration pitching. Hard, no finesse."

His looked down at the ground.

"Something about Julie, I suppose?" she asked, then waited, knowing by now that he would respond in time if not pressed.

"She's trying out for a softball team, and I went to watch her practice," he began and then stopped. Just when Rita thought that maybe that was all, he continued, speaking very quickly. "I wanted to ask her to the prom, but I chickened out."

"Why? You know she likes you, right?"

"Yeah, I guess. But she's probably going with Dwight."

"Maybe, maybe not, but you'll never know unless you ask."

He nodded, and she waited because she had a sense that there was more. "And I don't know how to dance," he finally admitted.

She couldn't keep from laughing but stopped quickly when she saw his negative reaction. "I'm sorry. I'm not laughing at you. It's the situation, just so typical with boys. Do you think that girls really care about that, if they like someone?"

"They don't?"

Rita gave it a little more careful consideration. "Well, probably some do, but Julie doesn't strike me as one of those." She paused as she thought better of her impulse to try to just dismiss his fears. "It's certainly nice, though, if a bloke has a few moves to kick and prance. Would you like me to show you?"

They went inside to find some music and a place to dance. The place wasn't as hard to find as the music. Clark's collection of Kingston Trio records wasn't going to help. Sarah only had recordings from Broadway shows. So they relied on the small radio in Clark's bedroom and found KDNV, a local AM station that played top 40 hits. Little Eva sang *The Loco Motion*.

"So, what do you know?" she asked him, as he cleared some space in his room. He had been keeping his room much cleaner since that day Julie almost went in there.

"Mom made us take ballroom dancing lessons in New York, so I kinda remember those, the basics. But I don't think they'll be waltzing much at the prom."

"No, probably not." She laughed with him. "But there will be slow dances that are basically a shuffling three-step, box-step or fox trot or whatever you Yanks call it."

Tommy Roe's *Sheila* now played on the radio.

"All right, not great to dance to, but let's try. First you have to feel the beat. Ba Ba . . . Ba. Ba Ba . . . Ba." She swayed to the beat. "Try it. Close your eyes. Clear your mind. Just let your body relax and feel the music." She watched him struggle to relax. "Come on, you can do it. Don't over-think it. It's instinctual, primal animal instinct stuff."

Gradually he relaxed and managed to sway his body a little with the beat.

By then *Sheila* was over, and they had to wait through a minute of commercials before *Twisting the Night Away* by Sam Cooke came on.

"Oh shite, the fucking twist, I hate the twist. Let's wait for the next one."

Rita watched him shift awkwardly on his feet and remembered how well Keith moved when performing. He wasn't a professional dancer, but his whole body worked nicely in tune with his music. She really wanted to believe what he had said in his letter, that he wasn't screwing around.

Then she remembered the attraction that she had felt as a teen to the sensual motions of a good dancer. On more than one occasion she had fallen under the spell of a dancer and his moves and wound up in bed with him. It had always made her mother angry when Rita slept with a dancer because she thought they were too flaky, even by the standards of musicians. Rita had occasionally thought that her father might have been a dancer and that would explain her mother's negative attitude toward them. She laughed as she tried to picture John trying to dance. He would undoubtedly be much worse than what she saw with Clark.

The twist segued into the Surfaris' *Wipe Out*.

"Well, this isn't much better, but a good test. Now feel the energy of the music, and let it take over your body."

He tried, probably too hard, and his body didn't seem to be able to respond.

"Okay, try this. Don't think about it, just let your body go crazy trying to match the music, like this." She began to make exaggerated, very energetic motions to the beat of the music.

Clark stared, amused and amazed. Then he tried to mimic her. In his male way, he went even crazier.

She laughed. "Okay that's great, now begin to pull it in a little so you don't hurt yourself or your partner." She slowed her motions, and her body settled into a natural rhythm with the beat of the music.

Clark was almost there when the song ended and more commercials began. "But what are the steps?" he asked.

"There are no steps, you just move to the beat, whatever that is. Oh yeah, the stupid twist has steps and there are some other fancy things that dancers do, but trust me, as a guy, all you need to do is find the beat and move. And mostly your legs and hips, not so much with the arms and head. Let the woman do the fancy stuff. She's showing off for you, so enjoy it, appreciate it. And whatever you do, don't try to compete with her unless you're a real pro. And then you're probably a botty boy."

Clark's head was spinning too much to ask what a botty boy was, but he had a pretty good guess. He had watched American Bandstand on occasion with Margaret, and people at Andy's party had been dancing, and now it all made more sense. He had been trying to see patterns to the steps and now Rita was telling him that there mostly weren't any.

Heat Wave by Martha and the Vandellas came on, and he quickly found the beat.

"That's it, but not so exuberant," Rita cautioned, as she danced to the song, which she really liked. "Don't try to upstage me."

They danced and didn't notice Sarah, who stood in the hall watching them. She felt a mixture of emotions - amusement, tenderness and then jealousy - before she moved off to her room.

The next song was *Blue Velvet* by Bobby Vinton.

"Okay there will be these slow songs, and you need to take advantage of them to get close to her." Rita grabbed his hands and held his left hand in hers as she placed his right arm around her waist. "Start out like this. Close, but not too close. Then let it happen. You should be able to sense when you can pull her closer. Just be open to her body language."

She demonstrated with stiff arms holding him away, and then she softened and moved her body up against his and let her head fall against his shoulder. "Jesus, Clark, relax. I'm not going to bite. Just pretend I'm Julie."

Clark wasn't sure which felt more awkward, dancing close with Rita or dancing close with Rita trying to think of Julie.

"All right, that's much better. Now if I do this, that means you're, well it means she really likes you." Rita let go of his hand and put both arms around his waist and pulled him closer. "Now you put your arms around my shoulders. Okay too tight," she reacted, as he pulled her close and her sore breasts pressed against his chest. "Back off a bit. There that's better. Don't be too aggressive. Let her set the pace. Women like it to be acknowledged that we're in charge."

Coleen stood in the doorway to Clark's room. Her curiosity fought with her concern about the relationship between her son and her stepdaughter. She responded with a weak smile when she saw that Clark had noticed her.

Clark's body stiffened. "Hi, Mom." Just then the song ended, and he quickly stepped away from Rita. "Rita's teaching me how to dance."

"Okay. Well, wash up, dinner's almost ready."

CHAPTER EIGHTEEN

Clark had struggled with all the attention he'd received the week before, but he was totally unprepared for what he faced on Monday, as news of the game spread quickly through the school. The PA announcement during homeroom gave the score and mentioned that Clark was the winning pitcher. Julie came on and encouraged everyone to come to the game on Saturday at home against Red Rock High School, which had beaten the Cougars during the regular season. If they won that game, they would be in the finals for the county championship.

Clark tried to deflect most of the attention, but he had to admit that he found it a real high.

What a trip! This is how guys get big heads.

At lunch he still tried to sit alone at the nerd table, but Joey and a couple of other players joined him. That brought so much attention to the table that the nerds left to find a new one.

During the day he exchanged several quick smiles with Julie, but they were both always rushing somewhere or surrounded by other people and couldn't talk. The most he got from her was that she was coming to his house after cheerleader practice to work on the songs. That carried him through the rest of the day, even with the hostile reception from Dwight and his group in Social Studies class. Clark did notice that Tommy had changed his seat and didn't seem to be a part of the group anymore. Joey had told him that Tommy was an okay guy and couldn't understand why he hung out with Dwight.

Later at home, Clark had a hard time concentrating on his homework while he waited for Julie to arrive. His mind kept drifting back to the arbor and Julie's lips. She was a great kisser. When Julie finally arrived, Clark was unsure how to greet her. Should he hug her, kiss her, or just smile and be awkward, which is what he did. They got right into the new song, and that consumed them for the better part of two hours. Rita and Julie both had new ideas for the melody and some of the transitions between phrases. And Clark made a few modifications to the lyrics that helped them get over some rough spots. They worked really well together. Their personalities seemed to complement each other, and none of them had an outrageous ego that got in the way. A couple of times Rita played the producer and cajoled them into having another go at it, refusing to let them accept something that was just okay.

Coleen arrived home from her golf game during the rehearsal and was amazed at the dynamics of the trio. She didn't interrupt them and went immediately to the kitchen to start dinner. She still couldn't believe that the lyrics had come from her son.

By the time Sarah got home at seven o'clock, the song she heard was polished enough that she lingered out-of-sight in the front hall - transfixed and jealous. She sensed that the song would really resonate with people. Julie's voice reminded her of some of the folk singers who she told Clark she didn't like, but really did.

When they were done, Clark drove Julie to Suzie's on his scooter. He had gotten a second helmet, and he loved having her arms wrapped around him as much as he had imagined that he would. Standing outside Suzie's house, he was unable to decide whether he could or should try to kiss her. It had been hard for him to concentrate on the song when what he really wanted to do was to pull her to him and kiss her. She had been very friendly but hadn't given him any sign that she would be interested in that. Not that he would have recognized it if she had given him a sign.

Julie smiled and gave him a quick kiss on the cheek. As she walked off, he couldn't decide whether it had been the kiss of a friend or something else. He continued to mull that over hours later when he finally went to sleep.

The next day in school, Clark noticed posters on the hallway walls promoting the All School Talent Concert on Friday. They were next to the posters about the prom, which had been up for several weeks. He felt anxious about both of them - positive anxiety for the first and negative for the other. What he hadn't been anxious about was baseball practice that afternoon, but he should have been.

Dwight had spent all weekend trying to whip his gang, which had gotten smaller, into a frenzy of hate for Clark. He got varying degrees of response, from a total buy-in by Ed and Rory to the defection by Tommy. Miguel went along to get along, but his heart wasn't really in it. He wanted to win and saw Dwight's vendetta as a threat to that goal.

At the beginning of practice Coach Duncan told them that the county athletic commission had initially suspended Dwight for two games but then reduced it to one because it was during the tournament. He added that he had also suspended Dwight for one game for fighting but it would be the same game that fulfilled the county's ruling. So Sebastian would start the game this Saturday with Benji, Jason and Clark in relief. Dwight would not be allowed to practice with the team and could not suit up for the game.

Everyone heard Dwight mutter obscenities about the stupid ref and the assholes at the league office. The coach heard, but he chose to ignore it.

Joey led the team through warm-ups, and then they broke into position groups for drills. Dwight started out to the mound, but the coach stopped him. That escalated Dwight's pissy mood, and he glared at Clark as he trudged off and sat on the bench.

Clark tried to ignore him, but he couldn't manage it entirely and it affected his concentration. He had no focal point to use because neither Julie nor Rita was around. After Clark threw a series of bad pitches, and Dwight made increasingly negative comments from the sidelines, the coach stormed over. "Dwight, get your butt off my field. If you can't be positive and supportive, I don't want you around." Dwight started to protest, but Coach Duncan shut him down, "I don't want to hear a word, just go!"

Everything stopped. The players were stunned that the coach would banish the star pitcher and co-captain from the field. But no one, not even Ed or Miguel, blamed Clark. Dwight and his negativity were hurting the team. Clark felt a solid level of support from the coach and others, and that helped him settle down and find his pitching groove.

* * *

Looking out the living room window, Julie saw Dwight's car but didn't answer the door when he rang the bell. She had come home to wash some clothes and have some time alone. She loved the Masters, but they were all very chatty, and it got pretty loud when they all tried to talk at the same time. It made Julie realize how much she liked the quiet that came with being an only child, especially one with an absentee mother.

"Julie, please, I know you're in there, I can hear the music. I just, I need to talk."

Dwight's voice sounded full of an emotion that she hadn't heard from him in a long time. She opened the door, quickly stepped out, and closed it behind her. She sat down on the front steps and waited for him to follow, which he soon did.

"Are you okay? You look like, well, not too good actually." She tried to keep it light, and it almost worked.

He managed a very weak laugh, and they sat in silence for a minute or so.

She couldn't point to a specific time when they had started dating and were no longer just friends, but the friendship had been a good basis for a relationship. It had happened naturally and had been good for a time, before Dwight wanted more. Two years ago, when he started high school, the seniors on the baseball team had gotten into his head and convinced him that he was a baseball star and that baseball stars weren't virgins. Julie hadn't agreed. She had plenty of reasons, but the main one had been that she didn't know if she really loved him in that way. She felt that they were soul mates on many levels, but not necessarily sex-mates. And now she knew that he was jealous of Clark.

"Talk to me, Dwight," she urged. "Like we used to."

"Yeah, the good ole days," he replied sarcastically. Then his tone softened. "It used to be so much easier. We could, I could count on you to listen, to understand, but now . . ."

"I'm listening, and I'm trying to understand. But you're making it hard because . . ."

"Because what?"

She stared out at the street as she replied, "Because it's like sometimes I just don't know you anymore. You've changed. We used to be able to tell each other everything until, well until sex got in the way."

"I'm a man, and I have things that I want and that includes sex with my girlfriend."

"A man knows the difference between what he wants and what he really needs. Do you?"

"Oh, Christ. My stepmom has me going to this butt-hole shrink every week and that's the way he talks. Wants. Needs. What's the fucking difference?" He managed to pull his anger back, get it under control.

"I know about Laurie," she interjected softly.

He considered lying, but then just nodded.

"I'm not really that upset. You're ready for something like that, and I'm not."

"Or not with me, at least."

"What do you mean by that?"

"You know damn well what I mean. Clark fucking Westfield," he spat it out.

"I'm not planning on having sex with Clark or anyone. We're friends. Just like you and I are friends. That's what we've always been, and always will be, I hope."

"I want us to be much more than friends and I'm done with Laurie. Can you please give us another chance? If I don't have you, I'm thinking of following my mother's . . ."

"Don't you dare pull that shit on me, Dwight Dunn! That's fucking blackmail. If I ever do have sex with you it certainly won't be because you threaten to kill yourself. It'll be because I rediscover the nice sensitive guy that I used to know."

"I can be that guy again, I swear."

She took his hand, and they sat quietly. She wasn't sure that she believed him. And there was a part of her, maybe a big part, that didn't necessarily want him to be right.

* * *

It was lunchtime Thursday, and everyone who was in the talent show on Friday had gathered in the auditorium for a rehearsal.

Joey stood center stage and looked very nervous as he began to sing the version of *Oh Shenandoah* that the Kingston

Trio had recorded as *Across the Wide Missouri*. But by the end of the song, he seemed to be almost comfortable. The polite applause bolstered his growing confidence that he could step out of his comfort zone and take a chance to do something that he had always wanted to do - sing in front of an audience. Clark had been his role model for that. And he hoped that it might impress Sarah, which it did.

Mrs. Sanchez, the choral music teacher, then called for Julie, who was next on the program.

Sarah heard one of the chorus geek girls make a snide comment.

"Oh, this should be good, a cheerleader with a guitar."

Sarah couldn't help but smile. Whatever the feelings were that she experienced when she was around Clark and Julie, jealousy maybe, Sarah did appreciate talent, and Julie had it. And she had somehow managed to bring something out in Clark that no one had seen before. And Rita seemed to be the catalyst for all of it.

It always comes back to her.

Sarah really enjoyed watching the faces in the crowd as they listened to Julie. She saw their dawning realization that here was a person they had completely misjudged. The expression on the face of the chorus geek girl was priceless. Her attention then went back to Joey, and when she turned to look at him, she saw him staring at her. Caught, he gave her a nice, embarrassed smile before he turned back around to watch Julie. Sarah could no longer deny to herself that she liked him and probably as more than just a friend.

When Julie finished there was a moment of silence as the students' brains caught up with their emotions, and then they broke into spontaneous applause. Julie tried to take it in stride. She had been nervous because she knew that this could be a tough crowd to impress. They were all talented in their own ways, and often just as cliquey and insular as the jocks or nerds or any other group in the school.

Sarah then took center stage. She was on the program to promote the play, and she suddenly felt self-conscious about singing her song, *I Feel Pretty*, in front of Joey.

Strange, I've never felt that before.

She began slightly off-key, not so much that most people would notice, but she knew it. As she struggled to maintain her composure, she glanced over at Joey - quickly but long enough to see that he was totally into it, into her. Her smile broadened, her body strengthened, and her confidence soared.

* * *

Rita slowed down as she approached the house, pleased that she wasn't nearly as winded as she had been a few weeks ago when she started exercising. It wasn't a big workout, just a fast walk for a few miles, but it was a few miles more than she had ever done at home.

She had her mother's figure and metabolism. She wasn't a pin-up centerfold, but she did turn a few heads when she dressed in a way that showed off her nice proportions of chest, waist and hips. And like her mother, she could eat anything she wanted and not worry too much about gaining weight. But the pregnancy had brought more changes to her body than just the embryo growing inside her. She knew that it was normal and necessary for women to gain weight when they were pregnant, but she was determined to keep it manageable. Today she had even managed to jog almost a mile of her route around the neighborhood.

In the bathroom she stripped off her clothes and went right into the shower. Julie was coming soon to work on the songs. Clark would be at baseball practice, and it would just be the two of them. She was looking forward to it. She had just finished dressing when she heard the doorbell.

"How did the rehearsal go," she asked Julie as she let her in.

The smile on Julie's face gave her the answer. "I was so nervous."

"But you perform in front of people all the time."

"Oh, that's different. I'm part of a group, and most people aren't really paying attention. And those that are, the boys mostly, they're just staring at our boobs and panties."

Rita smiled.

Maybe not just the boys.

They discussed and dissected and rehearsed the songs for over an hour until Rita realized that they had reached that point of diminishing returns that Terry, her boss, called the dragon's lair. Nothing good ever came from going any further into it. Were they perfect? No. But nothing ever was, and that was what made it so exciting and so frustrating to create music. She was explaining this to Julie when Clark got home.

The energy in the room shifted dramatically, and Rita smiled as she watched Clark and Julie do a little dance around each other. Their feelings for each other were clear to her, but they weren't yet ready to reveal them to each other. She knew it would probably be up to Julie to take the lead on that because Clark was seriously handicapped. And they both seemed to be under a lot of pressure.

Clark asked Julie how the rehearsal for the show had gone, and said he was sorry to have missed it, but he'd had the opportunity to retake a math quiz, which was not something that Mrs. Menke did very often, and he was worried about his grade.

They tried to concentrate on the songs for a little while, but then they all agreed that they were deep in the dragon's lair. Both Clark and Julie liked that analogy and could see how it also applied to other aspects of their lives.

Clark drove Julie home on his scooter and couldn't completely enjoy the feeling of her arms wrapped tightly around his waist because he was too nervous about asking her to the prom. They stood in front of Suzie's house, and Clark realized that it was now or never, so he rushed right into it.

"I was wondering if you wanted to, if you would like to go to the prom with me."

Julie had anticipated that this might happen but had been unable to figure out a way to head it off, to let him know that it was only one night. At least she had rehearsed her response, which she said carefully. "Clark, thank you, I would love to, but I'm going with Dwight. He asked me months ago."

Clark wasn't surprised. He knew that Julie and Dwight had been a couple long before he arrived in town. But he had allowed himself to hope, to dream, and the rejection hit him hard. His face fell along with his composure. Julie tried to give him a sympathetic smile and even touched his arm. That didn't help. The touch sent a bolt of electricity searing through his brain, knocked out all common sense.

He almost yelled, "How can you go with that guy, he's, he's such a jerk."

She wasn't prepared for that outburst and felt automatically defensive. "I know you don't like him, but I've known him for a long time, and well, he has some good qualities. He's going through some rough stuff right now."

Clark didn't hear any of that. He was consumed with jealousy and anger at himself for putting himself in this position. "But he's, he's . . ."

"He's what?"

"He's also seeing that Laurie and making a fool out of you."

That hurt. "It's good to know what you really think of me, but this fool is going home!" She stormed off and into the house before he could respond.

He didn't have anything else to say anyway.

Stupid girls. Who needs 'em?

Much later, Clark's anger set with the sun as it disappeared over the Rockies. He told Rita that he wasn't hungry when she came to his arbor to call him for dinner. He was glad that she didn't pry. He had already begun to realize that he'd been a jerk and had no right to be angry at Julie. He kept seeing the look of hurt in her eyes and really felt shitty.

When he finally came inside it was dark. He forced himself to eat a little of the leftovers his mother had put in the refrigerator for him. Afterward, he waited in his room for Coleen and Sarah to go to bed, and then he found Rita alone in the den. He told her what had happened. "What should I do?" he asked her, hoping for a miracle cure or at least some absolution.

"Well, it wasn't your finest moment, that's for sure." There went the absolution. He waited for a possible cure. "But I doubt it's irreparable. I do think she likes you, and if you make a really sincere apology, I think she'd accept." Rita let that sink in and then continued, "And then you should ask someone else to the dance, so it isn't awkward for either of you."

"But I don't want to go with anyone else." And more to the point, he added, "I don't know anyone else to ask."

The next day proved to be long and hard for Clark. The intense wall of ice surrounding Julie stopped him in his tracks and totally thwarted his plan to apologize before English class. She didn't come to lunch because there a final walk-through rehearsal for the concert, which was later that afternoon. He briefly contemplated going to the optional study hall for those who didn't want to go to the concert. But his mother and Rita were coming, and he knew he had to be there.

Clark found a seat in the back of the auditorium and gave a little wave to his mother and Rita who sat in the area in front that had been reserved for parents. He looked in the printed program and saw that his name had been listed as the lyricist for the songs Julie was going to sing. Seeing that made him feel proud, but it also twisted the knife of guilt and remorse that pierced his heart. He knew that he really valued their creative relationship and wanted that to continue even if there wasn't going to be anything more than that.

"Hey." Tommy poked him on the shoulder as he plopped down next to him. "Come to see ole Joey sing? Pretty strange huh, who knew?"

"Joey? Really?" Clark looked again at the program and now saw Joey's name, which was right before Julie's.

Tommy looked at his program. "Hey, you're in here too. Jesus, I feel left out. What's a lyricist?"

Tommy's stream of blather made Clark relax a little and brought a slight smile as he responded, "Julie wrote the music, and I wrote the words."

"That's so cool. Okay, so then what's an arranger and who's Rita McDonald? Is she a student? I never heard of her."

"No, actually that's my older sister, and she helped us put the song together, blend the music and the lyrics." As he spoke, Clark looked around to see if Dwight or any of the other baseball players were there, but he didn't see anyone. He felt his anger rise again that she would date a guy who didn't even come to her concert. He then put that aside because he realized that he was actually thrilled that Dwight wasn't there. This was his and Julie's thing.

As soon as the bell rang, Mrs. Sanchez got the show going with some announcements and a plug for people to come to the play the next week. The show began with the chorus and then alternated between solo performances and the whole chorus. Joey, Julie, and Sarah were all scheduled toward the end.

When it came time for Joey's solo, Clark could tell that he was nervous. Joey shifted his weight from one foot to the other and stared hard at the floor. His voice started soft, barely audible from where Clark sat. Then after a few careful looks up at the audience, he began to pull himself together, raised his vocal level, and finished strong.

Clark clapped. But Tommy jumped to his feet and cheered loudly, like he would for a home run. Joey looked to see where the cheer came from, and then laughed and pointed when he saw Tommy.

Julie was the next solo. She took a deep breath, picked up her guitar, and headed to the microphone. She glanced around the audience, absorbed the fact that they were there, and then dealt with it. She paused ever so slightly when she came to Clark. He noticed.

"I'm going to sing two songs that I wrote with my friend, Clark Westfield, and with the help of his sister, Rita." She hoped that Clark picked up on the emphasis she put on friend. She had not slept very well because she was so upset about their fight. She knew that her reaction, her anger had been justified. But she also knew that she could have handled it much differently. Of course, so could he, but he was a boy and clearly clueless about that kind of stuff. Now as she began to play, she looked directly at him and saw him smile.

Oh good!

She had sung the songs easily a hundred times by now, but she didn't know that they hadn't yet reached their full potential for her. Something about performing in front of the audience, and the lingering emotions from their fight, took her to a different level, a new place that was full of energy and passion and an unbelievable high. When she finished the second song, the audience sat dead silent for a moment, then broke into wild applause, many of them jumping to their feet and cheering.

Clark was on his feet.

Unbelievable!

His feelings soared and crashed simultaneously.

Rita clapped and laughed.

Sarah applauded.

Shit, I have to follow that?

Mrs. Sanchez must have seen something on Sarah's face because she stepped up to the microphone after Julie took her seat on the stage. She made some impromptu remarks about the play coming up next week. That succeeded in giving Sarah enough time to calm herself and then use the energy left in the room from Julie's performance to raise the level of her own. She felt really good about it at the end and so did the audience, which responded to her as enthusiastically as they had to Julie. Thus ended a concert that the students and the teachers would talk about for weeks, which was a long time in the attention span of high school.

Julie and Sarah gave each other genuine but cautious smiles as they both headed for the stairs that led from the stage to the audience where Rita and Coleen waited. They each thought the other had been really good and wondered what that meant - would it lead to friendship, a rivalry, or what?

Julie noticed Clark approach the front of the auditorium to join them. She knew what she had to do. This wouldn't have been possible without him. She first reached Rita and gave her a big hug and whispered, "Thank you," in her ear. Then there was an awkward little half-hug with Coleen who had just finished a big hug with Sarah. It took a while for things to calm down because so many students wanted to congratulate them. Julie noticed that Joey had managed to get next to Sarah. She saw that Clark had his own little group of admirers, and he looked as uneasy with that as always. The end-of-school bell rang, and the remaining students instinctively headed off for their lockers.

Julie knew that Clark had practice, so she had to act quickly. She moved over to him, grabbed his arm and steered him to the side of the auditorium. She tried to read the expression on his face: surprised, annoyed, hopeful? "Clark, I know you have to go to practice, but I need to talk to you. I'm really sorry that we argued yesterday, and I want you to know that I really really want us to be friends. But that's all I can handle in my life right now, and I would be incredibly sad if, if that can't happen."

Clark stood stone-faced, unable to utter a word, not knowing what words to say.

Before he could manage a response, Joey appeared. "Hey, we've got to go, coach is as nervous as a squirrel on a four-lane highway."

Clark felt frozen in place, unable to move, torn between the two.

Julie solved the dilemma for him with a nervous smile and a gentle push toward the door. "Go. I'll talk to you later."

* * *

Coach Duncan was indeed nervous, and practice turned out to be a disaster. Everyone on the team picked up on the coach's vibes. They thought too much about every move, and most moves turned out like shit. No one, not even Dwight, dared to step out of line, and Clark had his first practice with no taunts or teasing. This carried over into the locker room, where they could feel the presence of the coach lurking nearby.

At dinner, Coleen couldn't stop praising Sarah, Clark and Rita. They tried to change the subject several times, but Coleen kept coming back to how proud she was. They fought over who would do the dishes because they all wanted to get away from the table. In the end, they did it together, and they agreed that it was nice that Coleen was so proud and happy.

Later in his room, Clark finally had a chance to carefully reflect on what Julie had said after the concert. He thought he could be okay with it, if that was what she really wanted. He felt disappointed, but he wasn't absolutely sure what he wanted otherwise. After all, The Question was coming, and they would soon be moving away. He knew that he had strong feelings for her. And maybe what he felt like was love, but he didn't really know. And that mixed with a still undefined sexual yearning that was growing extremely powerful. He wanted to be back up on the arbor kissing her. And he knew, he felt, that there was much more, but it was vague. He also wanted that high he felt when they were working on the songs or talking in the halls about school or just being on the same field together during a game. He had never had a friend like that, not even Margaret. He fell asleep determined to do whatever she wanted.

If it's just friends, then so be it.

CHAPTER NINETEEN

Clark's resolve lasted only until the next morning when he saw Julie at the game talking and laughing with Dwight. Jealousy grabbed him and thrashed him around like a monster from a Japanese B-movie. He couldn't bear to look at them.

Before they started their semifinal tournament game against Red Rock High, Coach Duncan tried hard to motivate the team, but it was his anxiety that rubbed off on them. Their play was erratic, overly aggressive and sloppy. Two fielding errors and a home run given up by Sebastian led to a 3 to 0 deficit by the end of the third inning. It didn't help that Dwight sat in the stands yelling critical comments.

In the bottom of the fourth inning, a home run by Miguel with Billy on base brought them closer, three to two. The runs, however, just amped up the pressure from the coach and the home crowd. Sebastian was tired, and another infield error put Red Rock men on first and third with one out. Benji was called in and gave up another run before they managed to get out of the inning. It was now 4 to 2 in favor of Red Rock.

After a scoreless bottom of the fifth, Jason went in for Benji to start the sixth. Major league nerves had Jason sweating before his first pitch. His pitching was erratic but some good defense backed him up, and they escaped the top of the sixth without giving up another run. Then the Cougars managed to push across another run in the bottom of the inning, helped in part by the growing pressure on the Red Rock team as they began to taste a victory. An overly aggressive throw to third sailed over the head of the Red Rock third baseman and allowed Ed to score. The sixth inning ended with the score 4 to 3 in favor of Red Rock.

Now it was Clark's turn, and he had to keep them from scoring so the Cougars would have a chance to tie or win in the bottom of the seventh. He felt the pressure as he walked to the pitcher's mound. He desperately wanted to look at Julie, but he couldn't. That point of focus didn't come from seeing her only as a friend. There needed to be the potential for more, but now there wasn't. In addition, Rita wasn't out in her normal spot. She had come with his mother, and they sat in the stands. Clark tried to force himself back to the moment. He looked at the batter and all the scouting information that he had gathered during the game disappeared. Joey called for a fastball.

Sure, why not?

The why-not was that the Red Rock batter hit it for a solid double. Clark tried to ignore the collective groan from the home crowd and the cheers from the visitor stands. He stared at the next batter and managed to recall his assessment of the batter's weaknesses. He threw four good pitches all grazing the plate. But the ump didn't see them that way and called four straight balls. The batter walked. Clark was furious at the ump and almost lost it, but Joey quickly ran to the mound and tried to calm him down.

"The ump's a blind jerk, those were crazy good pitches. Don't let it get to you."

Coach Duncan now arrived and offered his standard advice, "Okay, no problem, just trust in your defense. Don't try to do too much."

Clark was happy to trust the defense, but it didn't happen that way. Three easy ground balls and two Cougar errors led to an out, a run, and bases loaded. Five to three in favor of Red Rock. He struck out the next batter for the second out. But the subsequent batter worked the count to full - three balls and two strikes.

"Go, Clark, you can do it!"

Julie's voice cut through the noise of the crowd. He had been able to put her out of his mind, which had been maybe good or maybe bad. But whichever it was, it was no more. He forced himself to not look over at her before he threw the next pitch. But he lost his release point, and the ball flew over Joey's outstretched arm, hitting the backstop. One run scored. The only reason that two runs didn't score was that the ball bounced back toward Joey, and he tagged out the runner from second who had raced toward home. Inning over, but the damage had been done. The Cougars were now behind six to three.

As he trudged to the bench, Clark felt like it had been entirely his fault even though there was plenty of blame for the whole team to shoulder. Eight errors and lackluster hitting wouldn't win tournament games, no matter who pitched.

Joey did his best to keep them up and focused on their at-bats. They still had three outs to catch up. But the defeat had already been psychologically accepted. They managed only one weak single before the game was mercifully over.

No one spoke as the team trudged off the field and into the locker room. It was a tomb of silence as they quickly showered, dressed, and left. Clark was one of the last to leave, and he froze when he saw Dwight standing in the doorway. He steeled himself for an onslaught. The way he felt, he would happily pummel the jerk. He wouldn't hold back this time. But Dwight just stared, and then abruptly turned and left.

As he emerged from the school, Clark saw Rita and Coleen talking to Julie, and he started to turn around, but someone grabbed his arm.

"Tough game, but you pitched really well, that ump was terrible," bubbled Suzie as she stepped in front of him.

"Uh, thanks, Suzie."

"I'm having a party tonight and I would really like for you to come. It's mostly just the team and us cheerleaders and some others, and it's not open to the crazies like, well, like at some parties." She hoped that he got her reference to Laurie and the loose-girls at Andy's party.

He did. He cringed, then tried to smile while he replied, "Oh sure, I'll try to, thanks."

With that, Suzie bounced over to Julie, who she grabbed and pulled away toward home and the party preparations. As they were leaving, Julie glanced back at Clark and gave him a shy wave. He didn't respond, so she wasn't sure whether he had seen her or not. The situation was confusing and tense, and she hated it.

Clark sat on his arbor and tried to decide which bothered him more, his pitching or the thought of Julie as just a friend. He heard voices below and recognized Sarah and . . .

Is that Joey?

Then he heard someone climbing up and turned to see Joey's head emerge through the vines.

"Hey," Joey said.

"Hey." A typical exchange of pleasantries for guys.

"Man, this is so groovy up here." Joey stepped cautiously on the vine floor. "Is it safe?"

"Yeah, you just have to watch where you step - on the vines not the holes."

"Oh, yeah, very good, funny." He sat next to Clark. "How are you doing?"

Clark paused, there were so many different levels to that question, and all of them had different answers. He went with the obvious. "Bummed, I really stunk the place up."

"Jesus, Clark, it was everyone. Christ, we had eight errors, eight! Yeah, you had a couple of bad throws. One really bad." He forced a laugh. "But you were much better than Benji or Jason or Sebastian. Everyone saw that."

"Thanks." Clark really wanted that to be the end of the discussion, and it seemed like Joey did as well. They both lay back and began to relax in the sun.

Joey gathered up his courage. "Say, do you know if your sister really likes the guy she's going out with?"

"I don't know. He's some guy who's in the play with her. They spend a lot of time together, although . . ."

"Although what?"

"Well, lately she doesn't talk about him except to complain. But she -" he stopped because he didn't really want to disparage his sister. "Why?"

"Oh, I don't know, she seems nice and all, and we seem to be able to talk."

"Really? She's always telling me how limited jocks are, no appreciation for the arts. But then you were really good in the concert, so maybe."

"Well, I was just wondering, no problem. I gotta go help my parents at the store. Hey, are you going to Suzie's party tonight? It should be cool, not like the last one."

"I don't know. I may drop by."

* * *

Julie kept busy helping Suzie get ready for the party, but her heart wasn't in it, and her mind wandered. She kept thinking about the devastated look on Clark's face at the end of the game. They were all bummed out, but he looked like he was taking it harder than the rest.

Maybe that's the nature of a pitcher. Am I going to be like that?

That was one more reason that she didn't want to have a party. She didn't want to be tired for practice the next day. She had seen the impact on the guys when they were tired, and it had to be the same for girls. Unfortunately, Suzie was determined and counted her as a co-host since she was staying at Suzie's house. At least this party wouldn't get out of control because Suzie's parents were going to be there. She would tell Dwight that she had a headache or something so she could get to bed at a reasonable hour. He had been sweet the past days, almost like the Dwight of old. On a couple of occasions, she had seen him go out of his way to avoid Laurie, but maybe it was because he knew that she was watching. She wasn't sure that she could ever really trust him again.

"Do you think Clark will show? I asked him very sweetly." Suzie batted her eyelashes in a risqué pose that made Julie laugh in spite of the topic. "I told him that Laurie and the loose-girls wouldn't be here. I thought that might make a difference after, you know."

Julie nodded and tried to get engrossed in the 45-rpm single records that she was sorting for a music selection. Suzie had an amazing collection thanks to her substantial five-dollar a week allowance and the fact that she often skipped lunch and saved her lunch money. Suzie had a terrible singing voice, but nevertheless she loved to sing along, loudly, with all the pop hits. She particularly loved the Beach Boys.

"Are you really serious about this friend-thing with him?" Suzie probed.

"Yes, definitely," Julie answered quickly, maybe too quick-ly because Suzie looked skeptical.

"Well, if you really are, I might take a shot, you know, sort of keep it in the family. As long as you don't mind of course."

"Oh no, I don't mind. Why would I? He's a nice guy, just don't . . ."

"Don't what?" Suzie was instantly on alert. "Are you afraid I'll come on too strong? I won't, I can be very subtle, you know."

"No, nothing like that. I just meant don't get your hopes up for any action sex-wise."

"Hey, that's not all I think about you know." She considered it for a moment. "You don't think he'll like me? Will he think my breasts are too small?"

"No," Julie laughed. "He'll like you, you're pretty and fun and . . ."

"And sexy?"

"Yes, very sexy, probably too sexy. I have a strong sense that he's not very experienced."

"Whoa, a hunky virgin, now that's really a turn-on. I can be his spiritual sexual guide. Take his hand and guide him right down to the Promised Land. And then two virgins, wham-bang, history." She finished with an exaggerated thrust of her hips.

They broke up laughing, and then got back to their preparations. Suzie didn't notice Julie's anguished expression, and she probably couldn't have interpreted it anyway. Julie couldn't completely explain it herself. She had so many different vague and unformed feelings that fought with each other. The only feeling she fully recognized was jealousy, and she tried hard to hold that one down.

We're just friends. We're just friends.

CHAPTER TWENTY

Clark hadn't intended to go to Suzie's party. He was still traumatized from his experience at Andy's. Joey had been pretty sure that Dwight was going, and Clark didn't want to see Julie there with him. But his mother, Sarah, and Rita had gone out for dinner. They had asked him to go with them, but he had sensed that they were only being polite, so he declined. He moped around the empty house for an hour or so and then realized that he needed to get out.

He aimlessly drove around the neighborhood on his scooter for a while, and eventually found himself cruising by Suzie's house. He was leaving when Tommy and his girlfriend Mindy, another one of the cheerleaders, saw him and convinced him to go inside with them. He didn't put up a lot of resistance.

The party was far less chaotic than the one at Andy's. The Masters' basement had a paneled recreation room that opened out onto a large patio. People were dancing in the rec room and talking on the patio, and no one seemed to be drunk. Clark glanced around and didn't see Laurie or any of the loose-girls. Most of the players on the team were there and most of them seemed to have girlfriends or at least dates. He started to relax a little, until he saw Julie dancing with Dwight. His first instinct was to flee. But before he could, Suzie grabbed him and pulled him into the area where everyone was dancing.

They exchanged greetings, but it was too loud to hear much. Suzie began to dance very energetically, and he hesitated for a moment as he tried to remember Rita's instructions. He listened for the underlying beat of the song, and his body began to move with the beat. He kept it under control as Rita advised. He let Suzie do the fancy stuff, and he watched and began to smile. She looked very pretty, and he realized that he had never paid too much attention to that. She wasn't as tall nor as curvy as Julie, but her short light brown hair framed an attractive face that seemed surprisingly mature. And her bright hazel eyes sparkled with energy.

One fast song quickly changed to another and everyone danced and sweated in the room, which was had gotten hot despite the open door and windows. He almost forgot about Julie as he relaxed with Suzie, who seemed to really enjoy herself. Then the song changed again, but this time to a slow dance. Suzie immediately put her hands on his shoulders and pulled him toward her. He hesitated a moment but then put his arms around her waist and squeezed a little. He felt her body relax against his as she laid her cheek on his chest. They moved around slowly, swaying to the music. Then her hands moved up and encircled his neck. She began to rub her fingers through his hair. This was happening too quickly for him, and his body stiffened slightly. She didn't seem to notice and began to massage his neck. That felt good, and gradually he relaxed. The song ended, and he didn't know what to do.

Should I let go of her?

She didn't let go of him and actually hugged him a little tighter. He wished half-heartedly for a fast song, but he wasn't terribly disappointed when another slow song came on.

Julie knew she had told Suzie that it was okay for her to pursue Clark. She knew she had told him that she only wanted to be friends. She also knew that she was really upset to see them dancing like that. She could tell that Suzie was rubbing her body against his, and he was probably responding. What guy wouldn't. Suzie looked very sexy in her halter-top and short shorts. Julie felt comfortable in Dwight's arms but not terribly happy. She realized that she wanted to be with Clark, but she was stuck.

God, this is really fucked up.

She told Dwight that it was too hot and pulled him outside to the patio.

Clark was in uncharted territory here. He felt strongly drawn to Julie, but she was with Dwight, and Suzie appeared to be clearly interested in him. He enjoyed the feeling of her body pressed against his and was bummed when the slow song ended and Suzie let go of him and started to gyrate around the floor. He noticed that her top was damp with perspiration and clung to her breasts, which seemed to be unencumbered by a bra.

She saw him stare at her breasts, and she smiled, happy with the positive attention. It had taken a while, but she had felt his body finally respond during the slow dance.

This is progress.

Suzie looked around to see if Julie had noticed, but she wasn't in the room. She hoped that Julie was being honest about her feelings toward Clark because she thought this could finally be her moment.

Where should we do it? Bedroom? Difficult. Mom and Dad. My car? Big back seat. Yuck, such a teenage sex cliché.

She saw his eyes move from her breasts and begin to survey the room. She grabbed his hand and yelled in his ear, "Let's get something to drink, I'm parched." She pulled him out to the patio where people congregated as couples or groups of couples. Most of them were talking, but some were in heavy make-out mode. Julie and Dwight were talking to Tommy and Mindy. There were a few singles like Joey who hung out at the table of snacks and soft drinks. There was no beer because the Masters didn't believe in providing alcohol of any kind to the kids.

Suzie pulled Clark over to the drinks/snacks table and started to pour a soda. Joey smiled at Clark and tried to give him a wink, but he couldn't do it very well and looked like he was drunk, which he wasn't. Joey had hoped that Sarah would be there, but she obviously wasn't. Before he could ask Clark about her, Suzie had poured two cups and pulled Clark over to a quiet corner of the patio. "Cheers," she said and touched her cup to his before taking a long drink.

He realized that she had done all of that, including pouring the drinks, without ever letting go of his hand. She began a steady stream of conversation. Well, not exactly conversation because he didn't have much chance to respond even if he had wanted to. But he was happy to let her ramble on. Several people came over to them and told her what a great party it was. She always managed to keep him close and involved. He had more genuine personal interactions with different classmates in that hour then he had had the entire year at school.

* * *

It had started Friday when John had called to say that he wasn't coming home as planned and would be another week in New York. Sarah and Rita had noticed that Coleen was disappointed but not eager to talk about it. Then Saturday afternoon Rita had suggested that they go out to dinner, a girls' night out. Coleen had felt compelled to ask Clark if he wanted to join them, but she hadn't been surprised or disappointed when he declined.

They had finished dinner and felt no urgency to leave. Their conversation had been interesting, but they had carefully avoided mention of any men until Rita told a story about an old boyfriend and then made a comment about the unreliability of men in general. That opened the floodgates to an increasingly intimate exchange. Sarah and Coleen had at first treaded carefully around each other, but with Rita's encouragement, they both opened up.

Coleen wasn't a big drinker, and three wine spritzers had given her the courage to finally ask Sarah a question that had weighed on her mind for a long time. "Sarah, I'm sorry, but I just have to know, so I'll just ask . . . are you still a virgin?"

Sarah had actually anticipated the question given the way the conversation had shifted toward relationships with men and their many issues with women. But it was still a bit of a shock to actually have her mother ask it. She smiled and answered quickly to not give any false impressions of reluctance or less than complete truthfulness. "Yes Mom, I am."

Coleen was visibly relieved; and Rita smiled as it confirmed her assumption.

"Did you really think that I wasn't?" Sarah asked her mother, more curious than accusing.

Coleen faced it head-on. "Well, you have been spending a lot of time with that older boy from the play, and I know that girls your age are exploring these things, and we just don't talk very much anymore." She finished with a little rueful smile and a slight shrug of her shoulders.

Sarah felt a little ashamed and admitted that she understood how her mother could have maybe feared or assumed otherwise. It could have been a conversation-stopper, but Coleen didn't want to let the door close when it had been so hard to get it open. "I was still a virgin when I married your father."

Sarah looked at her mother and then at Rita before she quipped, "Well, we know Dad wasn't."

They all laughed. Rita started to add that her mother had also been a virgin when she first met John, but then stopped. It now seemed less like they were mother and daughter and stepdaughter and more like they were just three women. Rita liked where it was going, so she tried to move the conversation further along by describing how her mother had lived a very open sex life. It was the music scene, and there weren't many secrets.

Coleen then added that she and her four brothers and sisters knew all about her parents' sex life because they all lived in a very small house in Georgia with paper-thin walls. Sarah kept silent with nothing to add. And Coleen then realized that she and John had kept all of their sexual activity hidden from the kids.

Oh, my God, is that bad?

Rita noticed the sudden quiet and detected a look of concern from Coleen as she looked at Sarah. She didn't want the momentum to lag, so she changed topics. "I think it's so interesting that so many men are basically repressed about their sexuality because that's how they were raised. They only come alive with the encouragement of a strong and open female."

Coleen nodded in agreement, clearly thinking of her husband.

"We're talking about Clark here also," Sarah offered, not as a criticism, but as an astute observation.

They all nodded their heads, and thought the same thing thing.

Poor Clark.

* * *

Suzie's party shifted into a quieter mood as more couples began to make out and the music was more consistently slow. All of the single people, including Joey, had gone.

Suzie and Clark had danced some more, and now she pulled him over to a chaise lounge on the patio, and they sat down. She waited for a moment for him to kiss her, but when he didn't, she kissed him. His response wasn't as strong as she would have liked it, but it was enough for her to push her tongue forward and into his mouth.

Julie was so absorbed watching Clark and Suzie that she didn't realize that Dwight had his hands all over her.

Clark noticed because he had been paying more attention to her than to Suzie. Motivated by hormones and jealousy, he turned his attention back to Suzie. His hand moved cautiously up to the side of her breast, and she twisted her body so that his hand fully cupped her breast. He squeezed gently and felt her body respond.

She whispered in his ear, "Come on, let's get out of here."

"But it's your party."

"Nobody will notice, and Julie's here, it's her party also." Suzie pull him toward the house and into the rec room. As they passed through the rec room and up the stairs, Clark saw Julie standing at the record player with her back toward them. At the top of the stairs Suzie paused and put her finger to her lips, signaling for quiet. Satisfied that her parents weren't going to see them, she pulled Clark up the stairs, into her bedroom and locked the door behind them.

Suzie turned off the light and the room darkened, lit only by the streetlight outside the open window. They stood and looked at each other. He tried not to show how nervous he was. This was unknown and dangerous territory for him. She came over to him and gave him a long sensual kiss, which he eagerly returned. Then she stepped back, and he watched as she pulled her halter top off over her head and casually dropped it to the floor. Her breasts glistened in the soft light.

"You like my breasts?"

The only thing he could do was nod.

"You don't think that they're, you know, too small?"

Clark barely managed say, "No, I think they're wonderful." He was on the verge of panic. His rational mind was totally blocked by desire and fear and confusion.

Oh my God, oh my God.

Suzie glanced at his crotch and was disappointed to see no sign of an erection. But she pushed on, sure that she could fix that. She began to unbutton his shirt. As she exposed his chest, she marveled at the thick hair that covered it. She had heard rumors, but this was truly impressive. It created a very tactile and sensual reaction in her that was mostly positive, and she quickly suppressed any negative reaction. She ran her fingers through it and touched his nipples, which instantly hardened. Her nipples were now hard also and brushed against his chest as she worked his shirt over his shoulders. He stood there almost catatonic, unable to stop her, not wanting to stop her. She continued to rub his chest, felt his tense muscles, and spoke quietly, "Clark, I really like you."

"I like you too," he was barely able to whisper.

"And you know what?"

"What?"

"I'm tired of being a virgin," she confessed, as she reached down and felt for his penis underneath his pants. Still not much happening, but she pressed on. "Do you have any protection?"

"What do you mean?"

She now got a little exasperated.

Christ, do I have to do everything?

"You know protection, a condom, rubber."

"Uh, no," he stammered, just as someone tried to get into the room.

"Suzie? Are you in there? Your mom is looking for you. Someone's sick."

"Oh, damn! Damn! Damn!" Suzie swore, and then yelled at the door. "Julie, tell her I'll be right down."

The moment Clark heard Julie's voice he felt such an urgent need to get away that he contemplated jumping out the window. Then Julie's voice, her image, and Suzie's almost naked body finally propelled his penis into some action. Suzie noticed his growing erection as she reached down to pick up her top.

Oh, great, now he gets excited.

Julie had felt bad when she lied to Mrs. Masters about the person getting sick so she could get Suzie's mom involved. She told herself that it was to save Clark, and she tried not to admit to herself that it was a lot more selfish than that. She loved her friend, but if Suzie had sex with Clark she would immediately be madly in love with him and cling to him like a barnacle to a boat. That would be a disaster for both of them. Julie told herself that she was being a good friend to save them from it.

She could see the stairway from the kitchen and saw Clark race down the stairs and out the front door. Suzie followed shortly after, frustrated, mad, and disheveled.

I'm so sorry, Suzie. I'm such a shitty friend.

Clark didn't go right home but drove around without a clear destination or a sense of what to do. Yes, he liked Julie, but Suzie was very pretty, and she had stood there almost naked, and she wanted to have sex. He had no idea what to do, and even if he did, he didn't know if he could have done it.

Is there something wrong with me?

By the time Clark reached home his breathing and blood pressure had returned to normal, but his anxiety was still out of control. He thought Rita might be in the living room or den and he felt a strong impulse to talk to her, but he resisted and went up to his room. Everything was dark in the upstairs hall except for the light coming from Rita's room.

Rita had been reading in her room when she heard Clark come in, stomp up the stairs and almost slam his door shut. She glanced at her watch. It was only twelve-thirty, which she figured was too early for a good party to be over.

Something must have happened again. Poor Clark.

She heard him open his door and then close it, quietly this time. The sound of music came from his room. She sat there for a minute trying to decide what to do. The best thing she thought was probably to leave him alone and go to bed. But her curiosity and compassion got the better of her, and she went over and knocked gently on his door.

"Clark? Are you okay?"

"I'm fine. Go away," he answered, his voice choked with emotion.

She hesitated but then moved back toward her room. She was just about to shut her door when she heard his door open. He stood there and looked at her, then moved back into his room, but didn't close the door. She entered his room and sat next to him on his bed. A small lamp on his desk provided the only illumination. They sat there for a while without speaking.

"There was this girl at the party, it was her party actually, and she wanted . . . she wanted to have sex with me."

Rita looked at him but didn't respond.

"I, I couldn't do it. She was standing there naked almost, and I froze."

"Well, I'm glad you did."

"Why?"

"Because you're not ready, that's why."

He felt partly hurt and partly relieved.

"Do you like this girl?"

"I don't really know her that well. She's pretty and sexy, and a cheerleader."

"With Julie?"

He nodded, "And her best friend."

She waited.

This is bloody complicated for sure.

"I had no idea what to do and I didn't feel that, you know, that excited. Is there something wrong with me? I don't want to be a homo."

She had to suppress her laugh, as she answered, "Oh no, I don't think you're a bender. I do think, however, that there are a couple of other plausible explanations."

That got his interest. "Like what?"

"Well, for one thing, if she really is Julie's best friend and if Julie was around, then I think you didn't want to have sex with this girl because you really like Julie and would probably prefer to have sex with her." She paused and saw a look of acknowledgement on his face. "And secondly, I think that even if it was Julie standing naked in front of you, that you would freeze because . . ." she paused, and then pushed on, having decided not to worry about being tactful. "Because I don't think you know very much about your body, and nothing about a woman's body or sex."

He started to protest but stopped, then nodded, accepting the truth of her statement.

"I don't think that's your fault," she added quickly. "You Americans don't talk about it, and your father hasn't done his fatherly thing to educate you. In Europe we teach it in school for God's sake. Here it seems like you, boys mostly, have to learn it on the streets or by trial and error in the back seat of a car."

He nodded again and stared out the window.

"Listen, even when we know how stuff works, we can still muck it up - witness yours truly." She pointed to her baby bump. "But if you start out totally ignorant it's like guaranteed to fail or to mess up your life and hers."

He now felt quite lost, defeated and overwhelmed.

She sighed and made up her mind what she had to do, half-brother or not, or maybe because of that. She got up and closed the door, then turned to face him.

"All right, Clark, look at me. What do you see?"

"Is that a trick question?" he joked, trying to get out of his depression.

She smiled and shook her head.

"I see you."

"And I'm a woman right? Not a trick question."

"Sure."

"And what are these?" she asked, as she touched her breasts.

"Uh, breasts."

"Right, breasts, boobies, knockers, baps, jubblies, strawberry creams. And all women have them, correct?"

He nodded and then watched in shock as she took off her shirt and bra. Not sexually, but very perfunctory, like she was getting undressed for bed.

What the hell?

"They're mammary glands that have a very specific purpose. You know for what, I hope."

He struggled to speak, "Yeah, to feed babies with milk, breast milk."

"Okay, that's a start." She tried to keep it light. "But they are also very sensitive and an erogenous zone for women. A light touch to the nipple with fingers or lips feels really good. Soft sucking goes to another level, even very light biting. Here try it." She sat down next to him.

He looked at her and anticipated the moment, any time now, when she would laugh at him for falling for the joke. But she looked very serious. She shifted closer to him on the bed and took his right hand, which she placed on her left breast.

"It won't break. Have you ever touched a breast?"

"A couple of times, tonight and with Margaret, this girl in Boston, but they both had their shirts on."

She sighed as she realized the depth of the problem.

Christ, Clark, you're seventeen.

"Well, that doesn't count, so go ahead and really feel them."

He was still very tentative, so she grabbed his other hand, put it on her right breast, and held both hands there until he slowly began to massage her enough to get her nipples erect.

"Okay that's working, see my nipples, they want to give milk so they need a little sucking. Now put your mouth on it and suck."

He was still not relaxed, but he was no longer paralyzed with anxiety. He cautiously put his mouth on her nipple and sucked hard.

"Okay, big boy, that's too much, too hard, there's no milk there, so go easy. Okay that's better. Now try using your tongue to sort of tickle the nipple. Oh, yeah, you got that first try."

Now he moved his mouth to the other breast and worked on that one. He didn't look at Rita who realized that she had started to enjoy this too much. She pulled herself back and lifted his head from her breast.

"Now this is very important. Most guys think that sex is just shagging, and they wonder why they can't keep a woman's interest. This stuff with the breasts is called foreplay and if you do that right she's yours forever. Well, not really, but she'll definitely come back for more. It's the variety of sex that leads to a satisfying intimate experience between two people, what people refer to as making love." Rita paused to let that sink in. She couldn't help but feel sorry for him. But on the other hand, she didn't feel awkward at all. She felt like some kind of love doctor on the telly. "But foreplay doesn't end with the breasts."

Dramatically, she stood up and pulled down her shorts and panties.

After Rita left, Clark just sat there and stared at the door.

Did that really happen?

He couldn't believe what he hadn't known and how surely he would have made a tragic mess of it with Suzie or Julie or anyone. Rita had saved his life for sure. But he knew that he could never tell anyone. No one would understand or believe it, even though they hadn't really done much other than talk and look. It had all been weirdly educational. Sure he had gotten an erection, and she had told him how to masturbate, but it had been very technical, and she hadn't touched him.

It had been Julie he thought of when he had kissed Rita's breasts and used his finger in her vagina as she had instructed. And it was Julie he now thought of as he closed his eyes and finally managed to masturbate for the first time. Overwhelmed by the intensity of his orgasm, he collapsed on his bed and immediately fell asleep.

CHAPTER TWENTY-ONE

When Clark woke late the next morning, he felt hopeful and empowered. He knew he'd been let in on some secrets, a secret fraternity or sorority or something like that. He quickly showered and got dressed. His father wasn't home, so there would be no church or chores to worry about.

After a quick breakfast he got his scooter and rode downtown to the softball field to watch Julie practice. But this time he didn't go into the stands because he didn't want her to know he was there. He just wanted to see her and not risk running into Suzie.

Julie struggled to keep her focus as she pitched in the inter-squad game at the end of practice. She knew it was a big deal that she had started the game because Coach Becky had mixed the players up to get two competitive teams.

Does that mean I'm one of the two best pitchers?

But when she sat on the bench her thoughts keep going back to the party and what had happened between Clark and Suzie. When the girls had finally gone to bed, Suzie kept analyzing all the details of her evening with Clark. Julie hadn't responded or encouraged her or asked questions or anything, but Suzie had been on autopilot. Julie had cringed when recounted how she took her shirt off and felt Clark's chest hair. Julie had noticed it the first time she met Clark and wondered how it would feel. It seemed like it was something that Suzie was valiantly trying to convince herself that she liked. Julie's only positive reaction was when Suzie quietly confessed that he hadn't gotten very aroused.

Either he's a homo or he's not into her that much.

She hoped it was the later and was pretty sure that it wasn't the former.

Julie had been relieved that Suzie was still asleep in the morning when she got up and ready to leave for practice. But she dreaded having to go back and listen to another blow-by-blow retelling of Suzie's failed seduction of Clark.

Suddenly it was very quiet, and she noticed that Barb, the catcher, stood in front of her.

"Hey, Julie, are you okay?" Barb inquired.

"Oh, yeah, sure, sorry I just spaced for a moment."

"Okay, no problem, let's go get some outs."

They were playing a three-inning game, and the score was tied, two to two. Julie got two quick outs in the bottom of the second inning. Then the next batter popped up to short center field. The center fielder missed the ball, and Coach Rhonda went out to use it as a teaching moment. The lull in the action gave Julie time to let her mind wander again.

A shout from Barb brought Julie's attention back to the batter at the plate, and she proceeded to throw three nice curve balls for three swinging strikes and the third out. As she jogged to the bench, Julie thought she saw Clark lurking near the small concession stand along the first base side of the field. By the time she stopped and then backpedaled to check it out, there was no one there.

Great, now I'm seeing things.

Coach Becky pulled her aside and talked about technique and concentration. And Julie forgot about Clark for the rest of the game.

The game ended in a tie. Julie was one of the girls who argued to keep playing to settle it, but Coach Becky said that they had to relinquish the field to the next team promptly at noon, and it was already 11:45. She reconfirmed that they were going to have a season, thanks to their anonymous sponsor. "But the bad news is that we can only keep sixteen girls because of the tight budget. The roster's posted on the board in the-" Coach Becky stopped because everyone had jumped up and raced to the dugout to see the list.

Julie didn't push to the front but held her breath as space cleared. It was easy to tell who had made it and who hadn't by their reactions as they read the list. It was sad to see the disappointment, and it made her mad that there wasn't a way to keep all these great girls on the team.

Coach Becky had indicated that they would carry three or four pitchers and she had been one of the two starters in the game, so Julie was cautiously optimistic as she got to the list. But she still held her breath until she saw her name as the number two pitcher. In softball that meant she would be mostly a reliever because the first pitcher would start the games, which were once a week.

That was just fine with Julie. She knew firsthand from Dwight what kind of pressure came with being the starter.

I'm a reliever just like Clark.

The thought popped uninvited into her head, and she tried to shake it out. She literally shook her head, and Coach Becky approached her.

"Are you all right, Julie? You've seemed kind of distracted today."

"I'm fine, coach, thanks." She turned to go back to the bench and change her shoes.

Becky walked with her. "I wanted to tell you that, well now that the team is set, I can tell you who our sponsor is. I thought you should know."

Julie stopped, confused.

"When your dad came by last week, he told me that he had some money in his campaign fund and that he felt like this would be a good image for him as he, you know, runs for sheriff."

Julie processed this. She was surprised at first, then a little upset that he hadn't told her, and finally anxious about the reaction of the girls. She almost didn't hear Becky continue.

"He didn't want to announce it earlier because he didn't want anyone to think that you made the team because of, you know, because of that. And you didn't, I can tell you that for sure. And I told him last week that this would have no influence on me one way or the other."

Julie tried a complex grin of pride and worry.

Easy for you to say, I have to face them.

"I know that's easy for me to say, but I know these women will understand, they've seen how good you are," Becky continued. "And I think everyone knows I'm a straight shooter."

For a cowgirl.

Julie couldn't help but smile.

"And they'll know that I don't play games like that. And Frank said he knew you could handle it just fine."

Julie noticed that Becky smiled and maybe blushed ever so slightly as she talked about Julie's father.

Now that would really give them something to talk about.

* * *

Clark longed for his old anonymity at school. He could almost manage the attention from the students, but he was totally unprepared to handle the force-of-nature named Suzie. She was a relentless but cute and sexy stalker. They only had one class together, but she would just appear everywhere. His old silent tricks didn't work on her because she talked enough for both of them. And her hands were on him from the moment she appeared to the moment she left.

Guys on the team kept giving him knowing looks. Word of Suzie's party had spread like a wildfire in the dry foothills, and they all knew that he had disappeared with her.

As much as he wanted to avoid Suzie, he wanted to talk to Julie. But she was always just out of reach, or as soon as he was close to her, along came Suzie, sliding between them and pulling him away. He knew that Julie noticed, but he couldn't tell what she thought about it. He wondered if Suzie had told her about what happened in her bedroom.

She shouldn't care if we're just friends.

Julie felt sorry for Clark as she watched him try to deal with Suzie. She loved her friend, but Suzie could be extremely pushy, especially when she was unsure of herself, as she was now. Suzie had talked of nothing but Clark all Sunday afternoon and evening. Did he like her? Did he want to have sex? What would have happened if it hadn't been for that stupid sick person who left before she could find them? Was Clark going to ask her to prom? Should she ask him?

Julie had just nodded and let her ramble on. The only input she had given was that Suzie should not ask him to prom. "That's the boy's responsibility, and you don't want to seem desperate."

"But I am desperate," Suzie had whined. "I don't have a date. He doesn't have a date. What's so hard about that? Who says it always has to be the boy asking? What about that Sadie Hawkins person?"

"She's a bimbo from a comic strip. It's a joke," Julie replied, and then laughed to cover her discomfort.

Why don't I want her to ask him?

Julie had no answer for that, at least not one that she would admit to. She did, however, appreciate it that Clark was being really nice to Suzie. Even though obviously uncomfortable, he smiled and tried to laugh at her jokes. And he didn't seem to mind her hands all over him. Julie liked to see him come out of his shell, but she also liked him the old way.

But as friends, of course.

Clark was thrilled to have practice after school. He liked practice, but it also gave him a good excuse not to hang out with Suzie. He had, in a moment of weakness, promised her that he would come over to her house to study on Wednesday after school. He had no doubt that what she had on her mind was something very different from studying. On Wednesday morning, he planned to develop some excuse not to go. After that there would be practice again on Thursday and Friday, and he would be safe.

Clark had feared that Coach Duncan would review the disaster from Saturday and dissect everyone's failings. Instead, he just said that he knew they could all do better and that it was history. They would focus on the future, which was the consolation game a week from Saturday against Denver Central. They were over halfway through practice before Clark realized that he had not received one negative comment, look, or anything else from Dwight or any of his friends. In fact, except for Dwight, they all seemed to have accepted him. And Dwight wasn't being overtly hostile, just silent. Clark could handle silent.

During a water-break Joey approached Clark with a question. "What summer team are you thinking about joining?"

Clark paused. Any mention or thought of summer immediately brought The Question to mind. But he didn't want to think about that or discuss it. "I don't have any plans for the summer."

"Well you should consider my team, the Mustangs." Joey was eager because he believed that Clark was a better pitcher than anyone they had, and he really wanted to win the state tournament that had eluded them the past summer. He tried to understand Clark's less than positive reaction to his suggestion. He wondered if Clark knew that Dwight was on the same team and if that would explain it.

When they started practice again, Clark said to Joey, "You know, I've also got a change-up that I'd like to work on."

"Jesus, Clark, a change, why didn't you tell me before?"

"I don't think it's as good as my other pitches, especially for a game."

"But even an average change-up will wreak havoc with these yokels," Joey joked.

Clark threw his first couple of change-ups. They were good, and Joey just shook his head. This confirmed his opinion that Clark had the stuff to be a starter, and a very good one. He would ask his summer coach to come to the game and see Clark pitch.

Clark saw Dwight watching him pitch the change-ups, but he couldn't interpret Dwight's reaction. It became obvious a little later, however, when Coach Jackson decided to have the pitchers face live pitching from each other for batting practice.

Clark had begun to feel more comfortable in the batter's box. He stood in and waited for the pitch from Dwight. The fastball caught him squarely on his left shoulder. It seemed like the whole team saw it and stopped to wait for his reaction. Clark's first instinct was to charge the mound and pummel Dwight. But he didn't have to look around him to know that all eyes were on him and that his reaction would be critical to his continued acceptance as one-of-the-guys. So he glared at Dwight for just a second and then stepped back into the box.

On instinct he twisted his body, and the next fastball caught him on his back and not his shoulder.

"Dunn!" Coach Duncan and Coach Jackson yelled simultaneously. They had both seen these kind of mano-e-mano battles before and they were usually detrimental for the chemistry of the team. But as coaches they couldn't be seen as taking a side. Coach Duncan continued, "If your control isn't better on the next pitch, you're not starting Saturday."

Clark stood still while Dwight threw two curveballs away and too low to be strikes. He could see Coach Duncan get more agitated. Anticipating a fast ball, Clark swung and connected on a hard line-drive right back at Dwight, who flinched so hard to get out of the way that he tumbled awkwardly to the ground. He didn't make even a feeble attempt to catch the ball. The coach took that as a perfect opportunity to call off the pissing match, and he yelled for Benji to step up to bat and for Jason to pitch.

In the locker room after practice, Clark noticed that Dwight didn't shower or change but grabbed his clothes and left. He stood at the mirror and looked at the bruises that were developing on his shoulder and back. They were both sore to the touch.

I guess I should work on batting lefty.

At lunch the next day, Clark sat with the team, but at the end of the table away from Dwight. He had begun sitting there on Monday. He had hated to abandon his nerd table, but he was safer at the team table. Suzie didn't hesitate to join him at the nerd table, but she wouldn't sit at the team table. Some sort of professional courtesy between team and cheerleaders, he surmised.

He stopped by the cheerleader table and told Suzie that he had to do something for his mom that afternoon and couldn't come to her house after school. She seemed really unhappy, and he felt bad about the lie. His resolve weakened, and he asked her if she wanted to catch a movie on Saturday. The eager expression that lit up her face was enough to make him look forward to it.

Suzie really wanted an invitation to the prom not a movie, but she reasoned that it was a good step in the right direction.

* * *

Sarah entered the house frustrated and angry after a difficult dress rehearsal. Her mother saw Sarah's mood and quickly put a plate of leftovers on the table and fled to her bedroom to read. Coleen knew from experience that she didn't have the words or tools to deal with Sarah when she was in that kind of a mood.

Rita, who had very little experience with Sarah's moods, came into the kitchen and was surprised to see her. "How was the rehearsal? You're home early."

"Stupid Sanchez thought we had . . . well, I don't know what she thought, but we sucked and she didn't seem to notice, or care."

Rita knew better than to tell her not to worry, that it was only a high school production. That might be true for most of the kids, but Rita had had plenty of experience with temperamental musicians and other artists, and she knew that it meant a lot to Sarah. Rita admired her passion.

"I could run through it with you, if you'd like."

Sarah started to dismiss the idea out-of-hand, but then realized that it might help her settle down and maybe get some sleep, which she normally found hard to do the night before a performance. "If you don't mind, that would be great. Thanks."

They decided to work in the basement rec room so they wouldn't bother Clark or Coleen in their bedrooms. There was a record player there, and Sarah brought her soundtrack album from the *West Side Story* film. She didn't want to compete with the voice of Marni Nixon, who had sung for Natalie Wood in the film, but the orchestration would get her on the right note and mood to start.

They worked through the play, and Rita took the parts of the characters that appeared and sang with Maria. She had a decent voice and could carry a tune, but it was clearly outclassed by Sarah's strong alto voice.

Sarah's enthusiasm was infectious as she sang *I Feel Pretty*. It got Rita to not only believe it about Sarah, but also about herself.

The last song, *A Boy Like That*, didn't mean as much to Sarah as it did to Rita. Sarah had not yet had such a meaningful relationship with a boy, but Rita was absorbed with her conflicted feelings for Keith. Sure there were problems to be faced, but she realized that she did love him and needed to go home soon.

One more chance for some time with John, and then I'll leave.

She felt the baby kick in agreement, and she automatically stopped and stared at her belly, which was partially exposed under her short t-shirt.

Sarah followed Rita's eyes to the baby bump and paused. "You okay?"

"I felt her move, kick."

"Do you know it's a girl?"

"Well, the ultrasound wasn't clear, but I'm pretty sure she's a girl. I want it to be a girl. Don't get me wrong," Rita continued, "I really love men, but I don't want to raise one. They should put all boys on an island until they're twenty or so and then let them into society."

"Remember what happens in *Lord of the Flies*?" Sarah added excitedly, and then laughed and Rita joined her. "Oh, and I read that the movie of that is coming out this summer."

Sarah looked again at the baby bump and cautiously asked, "Can I touch it?"

"Sure," Rita replied, and raised her t-shirt up to fully expose her belly.

Sarah gently placed her right hand on Rita's belly. "Is she still moving?"

"A little."

"I can't feel it," Sarah said, disappointed.

"Try both hands and press harder, you won't hurt it, her. Wait a moment though, I've got to sit down."

Rita plopped down on the couch and leaned back, which brought her belly up front and center. Sarah knelt on the floor in front of her and placed both hands firmly on Rita's belly. She concentrated, and then began to move her hands around the bump. She was clearly getting excited, even without feeling the baby move. Then she did feel some movement, but didn't say anything because she wanted to continue to have her hands on Rita. Sarah struggled with her confused feelings. In the past few weeks she had begun to experience unusually strong feelings toward Joey, and now she was ready to have a go at it with a woman, and her half-sister to boot. She forced herself up and again sat on the couch.

"Can you tell me about your, uh, friend, roommate?"

"Eva? Well we're very close, mostly as friends and sometimes as lovers."

"And your boyfriend is okay with that?"

"Oh, I think he probably suspects but doesn't want to acknowledge it. For most guys there would be an immediate impulse to go for a threesome." Rita laughed as she wondered if Eva would ever go for that . . . maybe. But she wasn't sure how she would feel about it. Normally she was pretty open to new things, but now with the baby she felt herself changing. She didn't have any guilt for her past, and she no longer felt particularly anxious about the changes happening to her. It was all hormones, and they too would pass.

"How did you know that you, uh, liked girls in that way?"

Rita paused and studied Sarah for a moment before she replied, "We'd been friends for some time and just very close and comfortable with each other. Never shy about walking around naked or anything. Eva had been in a relationship when we met, but it wasn't healthy for her. They fought constantly and her friend was exceptionally jealous. She kept accusing Eva of cheating on her with me. At first I found that funny, but I guess it got me thinking, subconsciously at first. Then Eva broke up with Autumn and needed some consoling, and one thing led to another as they say."

They sat in silence for a while. Sarah desperately wanted to ask more, but she was afraid of her own confused feelings. When she began to feel unable to resist pursuing the subject, she said she was tired and needed to go to bed.

In her room Sarah lay in bed and tried to image herself with a boy. She started to imagine Joey in a sexual way and realized that she didn't have a good frame of reference. She knew about the different girl's and boy's parts and theoretically how sex worked, but she had only seen one naked guy and his penis. That had been Clark when they were twelve and she had accidently on purpose walked into the bathroom as he got out of the shower.

Sarah imagined that down there most boys were a lot alike in the same way that most girls were much the same. For the first time she felt a strong twinge of desire to see what a boy, Joey specifically, looked like. Surprisingly, that helped her finally fall asleep.

* * *

The next morning, Clark was happy to have a dentist appointment and delay going to school. As the dentist filled a cavity, Clark reflected on his old routines and his old walls, which in the past had very successfully protected him from most stress and heartache. He hadn't needed anyone, and other people hadn't bothered him. The exception, of course, had been Margaret.

And that didn't end so great.

But as he thought about maybe going back to his old ways, he realized that he couldn't, and then it struck him that he didn't really want to. Most guys would love to have any kind of relationship with Julie and would kill to have a hot cheerleader like Suzie pursuing them. So what if he wanted it to be the other way around? He told himself that he should accept the reality of it and just go with the flow. The problem was that every time he tried to imagine himself with Suzie, Julie magically appeared and took her place.

* * *

Julie sat in the lunchroom and watched Suzie stare at Clark, who ate at the baseball team table. He didn't appear to say much, but he was clearly engaged with the others. She marveled at the changes in him over the past weeks. She wondered if she liked all of them, but only as a concerned friend, of course.

"I'm sure he'll ask me on Saturday." Suzie tried to be confident. "He asked me what movie I wanted to see, and I don't know. What do you think? *Cleopatra, Irma la Douce* or *8 1/2*?"

There was a moment of silence before Julie realized that Suzie had been talking to her. She turned to face her friend. "What did you say?"

"Oh nothing. I think *8 1/2*. It'll be less crowded, more intimate. And it's Italian so it has to be sexy, right?"

Julie nodded and added, "But don't you hate subtitles?"

"Oh, I don't plan on watching much of the movie, if you get what I mean," Suzie grinned.

Julie grimaced.
Oh, poor Clark.

* * *

The capacity of the high school auditorium was three hundred and fifty people, and it was a little over one-half full for Thursday evening's opening performance of *West Side Story*. Almost all of the crowd were family and friends. Despite the drama club's best efforts at promotion, most students in the school were not that interested. But there would be better crowds Friday and Saturday evenings. There was a matinee scheduled for Saturday afternoon, and that was always a crapshoot in terms of getting an audience. The advance ticket sales didn't look that strong.

For an opening night, the performance went well. A few flubbed lines and missed cues as were to be expected. Sarah's fear of a disaster, based on the last dress rehearsal, proved to be unfounded. Paul had continued to act like a jerk because she had again refused to have sex with him. But he had done a good job as Tony, and she noticed that he was being particularly attentive to Marybeth, her understudy.

It was during the curtain call that Sarah finally looked out to the audience to acknowledge her family and then saw Joey applauding wildly.

Will he wait around?

Backstage in the dressing room, Sarah rushed to remove her make-up and get dressed. She had felt a particularly strong connection to Joey as she sang *I Feel Pretty*. But she also remembered the feeling she had had the night before when she sang it with Rita.

Joey did wait, and he stood by patiently as Sarah hugged her mother, then Rita, and finally Clark before she turned to him.

"You were so good," Joey gushed with a big genuine grin on his face.

"Surprised?" she teased him without thinking about it. She thought she saw him turn a little red. "Oh God no, you have an amazing voice. And I really believed you were Maria. I almost cried for you at the end."

"You did cry dude," Clark interjected.

But Joey didn't deny it, and Sarah looked at him in a new light.

What boy admits that?

* * *

Julie had thought that the week would never end. She was so tired of keeping up a happy facade while Suzie obsessed over Clark and why he hadn't asked her to prom. But she reached her limit Friday night when her friend suggested that maybe Julie should tell Clark to ask her.

"You know, since we're all friends and all," Suzie had implored.

Julie was pretty sure that Suzie was not being sarcastic or snarky because that wasn't her nature. She was an uncomplicated, tell-it-like-I-see-it kind of girl. But that didn't mean that Julie wanted to hear it. It got so annoying that she considered going home even with the possibility of facing her mother. She hadn't thought about her mother in several days and wondered what was happening. She had tried to call her father, but the sergeant on duty said he was out on patrol.

I wonder if he's patrolling Becky's house.

On Saturday morning she walked by her house, and when she didn't see any sign of her mother, she went in. It was immediately clear that Bea had been there and was now gone, maybe gone for good. Her mother's closet had been emptied out as had the drawers of her dresser, which were all left open. She checked the cookie jar where Bea kept her rainy day booze money and all the cash was gone.

Money in the cookie jar, what a cliché you are, Bea.

She found the wedding photo of her mother and father on the living room floor, thrown there with enough force to bend the frame and shatter the glass. What she didn't see was any evidence that her father had been there recently. She knew he had been spending nights at the Sheriff's barracks because he had talked to the Masters and asked if Julie could continue to stay with them for a while.

Like she was on autopilot, Julie began to straighten things up, beginning with the wedding photo. The house had a lot of ghosts, but she could imagine herself living there with just her dad.

I wonder if he really is patrolling Becky's house.

The Junior Cowgirls had a game the next day, and maybe he'd be there. As the sponsor he should be if it was going to help his election efforts. Eventually the scope of the task overwhelmed her, and she left to go back to Suzie's. She had promised to help her get ready for the movie date with Clark.

We're just friends. We're just friends.

She repeated her mantra over and over, but she still felt awful because no matter what she did she still felt jealous.

"Where have you been? I need help with my nails. You promised." Suzie assaulted Julie as soon as she walked in the front door of the Masters' house.

"Chill, Sooz," Julie replied, purposefully using the nickname Suzie didn't like. "It's only three pm. Clark's not coming until six." She had never seen her friend in this state before, except for once when her dad had gotten her tickets for a Beach

Boys concert. But never for a boy. Julie knew that this was bad on so many levels that it made her brain hurt.

"I can't decide whether I want to ride on his scooter or drive my car."

Julie just nodded. She knew Clark was a safe driver from the couple of times she had ridden with him. Her arms tensed as they remembered being wrapped around his waist. She shook them out to stop the feeling.

"Are you okay?" Suzie asked. "You've really been acting kinda weird lately, you know."

"Oh, yeah, I'm okay. Just a lot on my mind. Sorry. So what did you decide?"

"Oh, I think his scouter. It gets us much closer that being in my car. You know, I wish you'd call Dwight and then double with us. It would be so much fun."

"That's a terrible idea. You know they don't like each other. Why would you want to spoil your night with a stupid testosterone fight? And besides, I have my first game tomorrow, and I can't be out late, or at all. I'm tired. It's been a long week."

"Wow, that's a lot of excuses. But if you're asleep when I come home, how am I gonna tell you everything that happened?"

Julie forced a smile because she didn't want to know what happened. "We've got all day on Sunday after my game."

CHAPTER TWENTY-TWO

Clark paced around his room and tried to calm his nerves.

You'd think I'd never been on a date before.

Then he realized that he hadn't been on very many. It almost didn't count with Margaret because it seemed like they had always been just hanging out, and he couldn't remember many real dates with her. And, more importantly, she had never said that she wanted to have sex with him.

Clark wouldn't be accused of being particularly fastidious about how he looked, but he wasn't a slob either. Most definitely not the male peacock type, he dressed to blend in and not bring attention to himself. He knew that his suit for church wasn't appropriate for a movie date, so he dressed like he was going to school.

Someone knocked on his door. "We're leaving, Clark. Have a good time," his mother called.

She was on her way with Rita to Sarah's play. Rita had been there for all the performances, but two was all that Coleen could manage.

Clark made sure that the extra helmet was secure on the back of the scooter. He imagined arms wrapped around his waist, but they were Julie's and not Suzie's. As he approached Suzie's front door and the inevitable meeting of her parents, his nervousness threatened to overwhelm him. Had they seen him flee their house last Saturday night? Did they have any idea what had been about to happen in Suzie's bedroom? To make matters worse, he knew that Julie was living there.

I wonder if she's here or out with Dwight?

He tried to convince himself that it didn't matter because, after all, they were just friends.

Suzie's parents acted perfectly normal, and even their questions about his safety record on the scooter were not obnoxious. Julie didn't seem to be there. But Suzie was, and she looked . . .

Wow!

Suzie gave him a big hug right in front of her parents. He smiled and tentatively hugged her back as he wondered what kind of hug was appropriate in front of parents you'd just met.

As he helped her with the strap on her helmet, she gave him a big kiss. "I just had to do that, I'm so happy we're going out."

"Yeah, me too," he replied honestly, as she wrapped her arms tightly around his waist. She proceeded to chatter nervously all the way to the movie theater. She had never ridden on a scooter before and was actually terrified of them, but she was determined to be brave.

I will not be one of those wimpy, scaredy-cat girls.

Federico Fellini's film *8 1/2* screened in a small art-house theater near the campus of the University of Denver. There were only a few people in line at the box office and at the concession stand.

Clark glanced around the small auditorium as they entered. He saw a number of older couples and some younger college-age couples with long hair and all black clothing. From the back it was hard to tell who was a man or a woman. He didn't notice anyone he knew or who looked like they were in high school. Suzie pulled him into an empty row near the back. Everyone else was scattered around in the middle of the theater.

Clark had read a review of the film in the newspaper that called it 'Fellini's existential self-examination of the tortured mind of a film director'. He found that initially he liked it as much as he had anticipated. The black and white cinematography of Italy looked beautiful. And he quickly figured out that there were many levels to the story as it moved back and forth between the director's current reality, his imagination, and memories of his childhood. The film, however, demanded complete attention to follow what was going on. But complete attention to the film meant not paying attention to Suzie, and that proved to be unacceptable to her.

Her first complaint was about the subtitles. "I hoped it would be, you know, dubbed like those Japanese monster horror movies." Then, because her mind was more on Clark then the film, she got lost in the shifting realities of the story. She perked up when it appeared that there was finally going to be some sex. That soon disappointed her also. "Is that it? It's a foreign film. They should be showing more of the sex," she whispered to Clark, who felt the same.

As Suzie lost interest in the film, she grew more aggressive with Clark. Despite the armrest between them, she moved herself so close to him that he feared that her next move would be to jump on his lap. She took his face in her hands and pulled him to her for a kiss - a long kiss. He struggled to keep up with the film out of the corner of his eye, while also responding to her probing tongue. Finally, he gave up and let himself enjoy her attention, especially when she took his hand and placed it on her breast. He massaged them both and got a thrill from her reaction. He kept his hand on top of her blouse even though she had unbuttoned it. He felt too self-conscious because they were in a movie theater.

It wasn't too long before they were both horribly uncomfortable in the seats, their lips were tired, and they realized that the film was nowhere near over.

"Do you want to go?" he asked, and she jumped to her feet in response.

The night still young, so they decided to go to The Mountain, a local soda shop where kids from Harrison High like to hang out. It was quiet at first, and they sat in a booth and talked about school and the game next Saturday. Safe, innocuous stuff that Clark was comfortable with. She asked him where he was from and enjoyed hearing about his nomadic past. She had been born and raised in Denver, and she admitted that she never thought much about other places, except Paris - she was obsessed with Paris. He found a level of comfort talking to her that was new and enjoyable. He thought that this must be what it was like to have a friend who happened to be a girl. The kissing and petting part made it complicated, but such was his life.

Gradually, as other movies got out and the play at Harrison High finished, the soda shop started to get crowded. Suzie and Clark were soon part of a large boisterous crowd of teens. He noticed that while Suzie enjoyed being the center of attention, she didn't need to be.

Clark was surprised, but not completely shocked, to see his sister and Joey enter The Mountain. Joey had increasingly been asking little questions about Sarah, while trying not to seem too interested, but in a he-doth-protest-too-much Shakespearian kind of way. Clark was glad that Sarah looked so happy because she clearly hadn't been that for the past few months. The play was over so that would explain some of it, but not all of it.

Sarah and a jock, crazy.

"Clark, isn't that your sister with Joey?" Suzie asked, and then waved at them and motioned for them to join them.

Mindy and Tommy, who were in the booth with Clark and Suzie, shifted over to make room. Sarah sat next to Clark while Joey sat across the table next to Tommy. Joey would have preferred to be squeezed tight against Sarah, but they were together and that was perfect.

The conversation bounced around between movies (Tommy and Mindy had seen *Cleopatra*), the play (Joey admitted that he had been to every performance), and the game next week. At one point Suzie complained that the Fellini film didn't have any great sex scenes, and Clark felt Sarah playfully poke her elbow in his side. He didn't look at her, but he smiled. Then Mindy started talking about her prom dress and asked Suzie and Sarah what they were wearing. The silence from both girls became awkward and uncomfortable for everyone. Tommy, in a moment of sensitivity, quickly changed the subject to how few days there were left until school got out for the summer.

"Like only fifteen, isn't that insane," Joey added.

Clark glanced at Sarah and could tell that she was thinking about the same thing he was - The Question. It had to be coming sometime soon and then no more Joey, Suzie or Julie.

"You know I'm really exhausted from the performances. Joey can you please take me home?" Sarah asked.

She started a chain reaction as others realized that it was almost midnight and curfew time for most of them. Suzie's parents had told her to be home no later than 12:30.

On Clark's scooter, Suzie wrapped her arms tightly around his waist. This time, however, her hands rubbed his chest and moved down very close to his crotch. It took a supreme effort for him to keep his mind on the road and on his driving. Fortunately, it wasn't far to Suzie's house, which was mostly dark except for the front porch light and a lamp in the living room.

"Do you want to come in?" she entreated Clark, as she got off the scooter.

He felt hopelessly conflicted. His body had responded very positively to Suzie's hands and the feeling of her breasts pushed against his back. He wondered where that would go and whether he was ready for it. He worried that her parents would catch them doing . . . whatever. And Julie might be there. Earlier, Suzie had casually mentioned that Julie was out with Dwight but hadn't expected a late night because of her game, which they had already decided to go to the next day. Suzie strained to keep from grabbing his hand and pulling him inside.

Clark finally responded, "Yeah, sure."

The house was quiet. It seemed like everyone was asleep as she pulled him down the stairs to the rec room. The only light in the room came from the stairway.

"I'd put on some music, but I don't want to disturb my parents," she whispered, as she pulled him down to sit next to her on the couch.

She immediately moved her leg over him and sat straddling him. The woman in the film had taken this position, and Suzie thought it looked hot. She immediately started kissing him and could feel him begin to relax and respond. Her panties rubbed against his crotch, and she could feel him harden.

Yeah, it's working.

Clark tried to push thoughts of her parents and of Julie from his mind and enjoy the moment.

After one long passionate kiss, Suzie came up for air and stared at him. He had surprised her by being friendly, talkative and attentive to her all night. Not what she had expected. She had thought it would be a lot of work to get him to talk and engage, but that it would be worth it to get to this point. Now she realized that she had had a good time all night, despite that drag of a movie. She returned his shy little grin and began to unbutton her blouse. She tried to go slowly, sexy and watched his eyes widen as he followed her fingers and saw her lacy beige bra. She pulled her blouse off and then reached behind her back and unclasped her bra. She waited for him to pull it off her breasts, but he just stared at her. She couldn't wait, so she did it herself.

Like most boys who were in the process of becoming men, Clark had a constant fascination, often obsession, with female breasts. Clark had been too terrified the previous weekend to really appreciate Suzie's set of jubblies, as Rita called them. But now, thanks to Rita, he was confident that he knew what to do with them - and this wasn't an educational exercise.

He carefully touched them and felt her entire body stiffen. Then he leaned in and put his mouth gently on one nipple. He gave it a few licks with his tongue and then softly began to suck at it. Her body responded instantly to every action. His own excitement spread through his body and then centered in his groin. He paused as her groans of pleasure grew louder and louder.

Can her parents hear that?

He pulled back to try to listen, but she immediately grabbed his head and yanked it back to her other nipple. Instinctively she began to move her hips and rub against the bulge in his pants.

"Oh, God, that feels so good," she cried with little attempt to be quiet.

Clark grew steadily more apprehensive that the growing, pulsing sensation in his now very stiff penis meant that it was going to erupt and embarrass him. He tried to focus completely on her breasts, her nipples. After several minutes, she scooted back along his legs and reached down to his pants. He almost yelled in anticipation.

Just as her hand touched the bulge in his pants, they heard footsteps above them. Heavy steps, fatherly-type steps, that made no attempt to be quiet, as they came down the upper level stairs and into the kitchen.

They both froze for a second. Then Suzie quickly jumped up, grabbed her blouse and put it on. Clark stood and surreptitiously tried to move his erection around in his pants so it didn't stick out so much. Then they stood quietly and listened as her father rummaged through the refrigerator and cupboards in the kitchen. Suzie couldn't believe what was happening.

A midnight snack, Dad? Really?

After several minutes of fighting off panic, they heard the footsteps head back up the stairs and both of them started to breathe normally again. The threat seemed to have passed. She embraced him and hoped to feel his excitement return, but his body was stiff - all except for the part she wanted. It was late and the moment had passed. They made awkward small talk as they went upstairs and then kissed before she let him out the front door.

As Clark got on his scooter, he didn't know whether he felt disappointed or relieved. It had been a lot of fun and very exciting, but most of the time he had wished that it had been Julie sitting on his lap.

On his way home, Clark rode through Creekside Park, a local make-out spot. He almost fell off his scooter when he saw Dwight's car in parking lot, with Dwight and a girl standing next to it. The girl sat on the hood of the car and Dwight stood in front of her. The fact that Dwight's pants were down around his ankles caused Clark to take his eyes off the road and hit the gravel shoulder. He barely managed to regain control and avoid a serious fall. He shut the scooter off and quietly snuck back toward Dwight's car.

No, not Julie, please God, not Julie.

He barely kept it together as he tried to get close enough to see who it was. He was behind Dwight and saw his white ass thrusting hard toward the girl who had her legs wrapped around his waist, her arms wrapped around his neck, and her head pressed down against his shoulder.

You can do it standing up?

Clark knew he had probably gotten too close, but he had to find out.

They were reaching a moment of climax when the girl suddenly lifted her head and screamed, "Oh, yes, Dwight fuck me harder!" Laurie. Her eyes were wild with passion.

Clark almost collapsed in relief. But he must have made a noise because Laurie suddenly looked over toward him. He froze. She stared for a moment, but couldn't see anything in the darkness and soon went back to enjoying the sex.

Clark slowly and quietly crept away and retrieved his scooter. He walked it down the road for a while before he turned it on and rode home.

* * *

Julie had been in Creekside Park in Dwight's car earlier in the evening. They had gone out for pizza, and she had tried earnestly to picture them having sex, but it hadn't worked. As they sat in his car after dinner, he had kissed her and rubbed her breasts, and she had responded a little, but her heart just hadn't been in it.

She stopped his hands as they had started to work on her buttons and told him she was tired and had a big game the next day. She had half-heartedly said she hoped he would come, but his answer had been muddled by his sexual frustration. Barely civil, he had dropped her off and then sped away. She had been positive that she knew where he was going.

Julie was in bed, almost asleep, when she heard Suzie and Clark come in and go down to the rec room. At first she tried to ignore what she was sure was happening down there. That didn't work, so she opened the bedroom door and listened. Faint sounds of Suzie's moans and groans floated up. She moved to the top of the stairs that led from the bedrooms down to the first floor and sat where she could hear better.

As Suzie's groans of pleasure grew louder and louder, Julie knew she had to do something. So she walked heavily, as Mr. Masters' might, down the stairs and into the kitchen. She opened the refrigerator door, rummaged around, and closed it loudly. Then she opened a cupboard and ran water in the sink. The sounds from the rec room had stopped. Mission accomplished, she thumped back upstairs.

She had started the evening determined to do nothing to ruin things for her friend. She really did want Suzie to be happy and even get laid by a nice guy like Clark.

But just not Clark.

She knew she was being a terrible selfish friend, but she couldn't help it.

* * *

When Clark arrived home, he sat in the backyard, too full of nervous energy to go to bed. Images of Suzie, Julie, Rita, and Laurie cycled through his head like a crazy kaleidoscope twisted into motion by sexual desire and frustration.

He finally went up to bed and only managed to sleep after he masturbated. The images of Suzie, Julie, and Rita excited him to the point of climax, but it was Laurie calling out, "fuck me harder", with that wild passion in her eyes that put him over the top. It was a great new skill that he had Rita to thank for.

Sunday morning, Clark ate breakfast with Rita and his mother. Sarah came in and flashed them a sly little smile as she poured milk on her cereal.

"How's Joey?" he teased her, but was disappointed to get no immediate response.

Sarah kept them hanging, controlling the dramatic moment. "Oh, you mean Joey my prom date?"

Rita and Coleen were thrilled. They both liked Joey and had disliked Paul.

Clark groaned. He wasn't unhappy for his sister and his friend, but it reminded him of the not very subtle pressure from Suzie for him to ask her to the prom. Rita was the only one who noticed his reaction. Coleen and Sarah were immersed in a discussion of prom dresses and shoes.

Clark had to stop and put some gas in his scooter, and he arrived at the softball park just as the starting teams were being announced. He first looked to find Julie, and then he looked for a seat behind the Junior Cowgirl dugout along the first base side. It wasn't very crowded. There would be more people there for the regular Cowgirl game that started later.

"Clark!"

He heard Suzie shout and looked to see her waving at him. As he worked his way across the bleachers to her, he glanced around to see if Dwight was there. He didn't see him, which was very good. The image of what he had seen in Creekside Park the night before was still fresh in his mind.

Clark sat down next to Suzie, and she immediately grabbed his arm and pulled him closer to her. She tried to kiss him but missed his lips because he had turned to see the first pitch. Even though uncomfortable with the public display of affection, he was happy to see her. He couldn't help but stare at her breasts, which were partially exposed under her low-cut halter-top, and remember how nice they felt. She noticed and smiled.

The loud thwack of a bat hitting the softball brought his attention back to the field in time to see the Junior Cowgirls' second basewoman make a nice play on a ground ball and throw to first for the first out.

"Is it me or is that field smaller than what you play on?" Suzie commented.

"It sure looks like it. But that big ball doesn't go as far and it's not as hard."

"Right, that's why it's call softball, silly," she teased him.

Enough action happened on the field to keep Clark and Suzie focused on that and not so much on each other. Every time after they clapped for a good play, Suzie would immediately grab his hand again and give it a little squeeze. Clark didn't mind, and he couldn't see Julie in the dugout, so he didn't feel terribly conflicted.

During warm-ups before the game, Julie had seen Suzie arrive. Earlier she had still been asleep when Julie left the house. Mrs. Masters had offered to drive her to the park, but Julie had planned for enough time for the buses and didn't mind the trip.

As the players stood for the national anthem, Julie had looked around again and hadn't seen anyone else she knew except for her father, who sat in the first row right next to the dugout. He looked happy as he gave her a big smile and a thumbs-up sign. She had noticed him earlier up in the stands where he talked to people and handed out buttons that read 'Wells for Sheriff'. Normally quiet and reserved, this was a side of her father that she hadn't seen before.

As they announced the starting lineup, she was sure she heard Suzie call out Clark's name. She really wanted to peek out of the dugout and see if he was there, but she didn't want to see any displays of affection between the two of them. As the game went on, she was sure that she heard both of them cheering. It wasn't that big of a crowd. She wondered if Dwight was there. If he were, he obviously wouldn't be with Suzie and Clark. But she didn't hear him cheering, at least not loud enough for her to notice.

The Junior Cowgirls' center fielder hit a home run for the first score of the game in the third inning. The whole team went out to home plate to congratulate her. As Julie walked back to the dugout she scanned the stands. Suzie was so close to Clark that they seemed like one body as they applauded enthusiastically. No Dwight in sight.

My friends get here but not my so-called boyfriend - what's up with that?

By the top of the sixth inning, the Junior Cowgirls were safely ahead seven to one. Coach Becky decided to make some substitutions in the field to give more girls some game experience. She turned to Julie.

"Julie, warm up, you're in. Have fun."

Julie struggled to keep her composure as she warmed up. She had worked hard for this and felt ready, but it was in front of all these people, particularly her dad, Suzie, and Clark. She could hear Suzie screaming her name as she went to the mound, and she had to smile despite wanting to maintain her game-face.

Her final few warm-up pitches were not very good, and she had to work to calm herself. Her mind flashed back to that first game when Clark had pitched, and she now completely understood what he had gone through.

He did it, and so can I.

As luck would have it, the first batter she faced was their best hitter. It forced her to really concentrate. She didn't like to take a lot of time between pitches. So she got the sign from the catcher and went right into her motion, not giving herself any time to think, to worry. Her first pitch was a strike, and the crowd reaction felt great. That adrenalin rush powered her to plow quickly through the first two batters. The third batter hit a solid grounder back to her, which she fielded cleanly and threw to first for the third out and the game.

Wow! So that's how it feels. No wonder the guys get so pumped.

As the entire team gathered, hugged each other and celebrated at home plate, Julie looked over to her dad, who was beaming. Then she looked to see Suzie and Clark applaud and then hug each other. She had to turn away from that before it totally bummed her out.

It took a while for the team to calm down and then listen to Coach Becky congratulate them. She had a positive comment for each player. She reminded them about the game the next Sunday. They couldn't afford to hire the field for a mid-week practice, so they would practice for an hour before the game.

By the time she was free, Julie saw only Suzie and her father left in the stands. She had expected her father to stay, and she had hoped that Clark would also.

Suzie gave her a big spontaneous hug. "That was so cool, you were amazing, congratulations," she gushed. "Clark wanted to stay, but he had to go home and help his father," she continued and missed Julie's look of disappointment.

Julie then stiffened as someone's arms suddenly wrapped around her waist and squeezed. She spun around and faced her dad, who gave her a big hug. Frank chatted with Suzie for a few minutes before she had to leave. He then took Julie out for a late lunch. They chatted casually about the game and school and the tournament game on Saturday. Frank remembered when he had been the starting pitcher in the championship game of that same tournament. They ate in silence for a while before he finally got around to what they both wanted to talk about.

"I see that you were at the house, so you know about your mom." He continued after she just nodded. "She says she's not going to fight a divorce. And evidently she intends to move to Alaska. Can you imagine that?"

Alaska, Julie repeated to herself.

That just might be far enough.

"I'm moving back into the house next week, and you can too if you like. But unfortunately, I won't be home very much what with work and the campaign. I talked to George and Martha, and they're happy to have you stay there until the end of school, if you want to."

"Yeah, I'll probably do that."

"I'm so sorry. I know this has been very hard on you. You deserve so much better." He was really emotional, not normal for him.

Julie leaned over and hugged him, not normal for her either.

* * *

Clark didn't have to help his father because his father was still away. It had been an excuse to avoid being with both girls. He just knew that he would really want to hug Julie and tell her how proud, how happy he was for her. Of all people, he knew how hard it had been to do what she had done. But with Suzie right there, hanging on to him, he figured it was better to leave.

He picked up another ball and threw it left-handed into his backstop. He had been working on that almost exclusively when at home, while using his right hand at practice. He had also been studying Jason, who was left-handed, and had seen a couple of things that had improved his throwing motion. For the fun of it, he tried to mimic the underhand throwing motion that the softball pitchers used. His first attempt sent the ball sailing over the backstop, out of the yard and into the woods. With the next one he over-compensated, and it hit the dirt, three feet in front of him.

Wow, that's harder than I thought.

He wanted to find Rita and talk to her about his crazy situation. How he had gone from not having any interest in, or relationship with, any girl to having two of them, and they were best friends. He hesitated because he wasn't sure how she would react. And also because he wasn't entirely sure himself whether he was doing the right thing. He sensed that his rationale might prove thin.

Suzie clearly likes me. And Julie says she just wants us to be friends.

* * *

Julie knew she had made a mistake, and now she was stuck with it. If she hadn't been so convincing about just wanting to be friends with Clark, then Suzie wouldn't have gotten involved with him. Now she had to grin and bear it while she listened to her best friend as she paced around her bedroom and gushed over her date with Clark.

"I give him a B+ for kissing, but oh my God, what he did to my boobs was just unbelievable. I was so hot and wet. If only my dad hadn't picked that time for a midnight snack . . ."

Julie didn't want to hear any more details, but she had already been almost rude in her efforts to avoid Suzie. Now she had to just sit there and pretend to be happy for her friend. And on one level, she really was. Suzie was a wonderful person and deserved a nice guy - just not her nice guy.

"I know it's just because he's, you know, kinda shy that he hasn't asked, but I'm sure he will soon. I mean he has to, right? Oh my God, do you think he just doesn't want to go? Could he be anti-prom? Maybe I have to ask him? What do you think?"

It took Julie a moment to realize that there had been a question to her in the stream of words that poured out of Suzie. It reminded her of the poem *Howl* by Ginsburg that she liked but didn't understand. Words and words flowing past without any punctuation or pauses.

"I don't know."

"No, I don't either," Suzie admitted, dejected, as she plopped down on the bed next to Julie. "I guess it wouldn't be the end of the world to not go to prom. There's always next year," Suzie unsuccessfully tried to convince herself.

Julie just nodded, conflicted. She was going but didn't want to anymore.

CHAPTER TWENTY-THREE

During the final weeks of the baseball tournament, the Denver County High School Athletic Commission relaxed its rules about practice, and Coach Duncan had called for daily practices the week before the last game. That pleased Clark for several reasons: he knew the team needed the work, and it would give him a good and consistent excuse to avoid spending the afternoons with Suzie.

It wasn't that he didn't like the constant kissing and the occasional petting, he did. He had finally come to terms with the thrill of his new celebrity status. But the public displays of affection that Suzie was comfortable with were far beyond his comfort level. He was cool with holding hands and a quick kiss on the cheek or even on the mouth. But Suzie's propensity to drape herself all over him caused him to cringe and search for the closest exit or pray for the bell to ring.

The other, and much more complicated, problem for Clark was that he knew he should have asked Suzie to the prom by now, but he just couldn't bring himself to do it. He tried to convince himself that he wasn't a prom kind of guy. But then he had already asked Julie. So it always came back to her. He knew it would probably be fun with Suzie, and there would be an excellent chance to have sex. She had already mentioned, several times, that Mindy was having an after-prom party/sleepover at her house. And Mindy's parties had a reputation for sexual activity that he found difficult to fathom.

Monday afternoon he left the school and was headed for the practice field when he heard Julie call his name. He hadn't had a chance to talk to her all day, and he congratulated her on her game the day before.

"It was really nice that you came with Suzie." She continued before he could correct her that he had come on his own and only met up with Suzie once he was there. A small point, but important to him.

"I know this is awkward and all, but she's my best friend and you're, you're my friend, and . . ." she paused, struggled, then rushed ahead. "Well, you should ask her to the prom."

"That's okay with you?"

"Of course, why wouldn't it be?"

"No reason really. But you're right, I'm sorry."

"Don't apologize to me, just ask her already." She tried valiantly to smile and make things light, but her heart wasn't in it. She hurried off to cheerleader practice before it got any worse.

Clark stared after her and momentarily forgot practice until Tommy ran by and yelled at him that he was going to be late. Once he got to practice, Clark didn't have a second to think of Julie or Suzie or prom. Coach Duncan seemed determined to make up for the relaxed atmosphere of the previous week and push them extra hard this week. One set of twenty-five push-ups became two sets; thirty sit-ups became sixty; and five sprints across the outfield became ten. As co-captains, Joey and Dwight led the warm-ups and exercises. Joey seemed like he could do even more, while Dwight was obviously one of the more out-of-shape players on the team. The nervous energy from Clark's conversation with Julie propelled him through it all, strong but tired.

Clark had been working hard on his change-up, and the coach was pleased with his progress. "Clark, you're my long reliever on Saturday, so I want you to go hard today and tomorrow and then taper off."

Long reliever had been Benji's role, and Clark looked over to gauge his reaction. Benji just nodded slowly. He had known it would happen as he had watched Clark come on strong the last few weeks. He and the rest of the team, including Dwight, had come to the realization that Clark had the stuff to be a starter.

As he walked back to the locker room at the end of practice, Clark noticed that Julie and Suzie and the other cheerleaders were putting up posters around the school promoting the game on Saturday. He resolved that if Suzie was still around when he came back out of the locker room, he would ask her.

Suzie delayed going home by volunteering to put up the rest of the posters, and then placed herself in a position where Clark couldn't miss seeing her when he emerged from the locker room. He offered her a ride home and she readily accepted, not mentioning to him that she had her car in the parking lot. On the way he mentally rehearsed his invitation.

Why is this so hard? Just ask her.

As soon as he parked and shut off the scooter, he turned to her. "You know Suzie, I was wondering if you would like to go to the prom with me."

She flung her arms around his neck and kissed him hard in response. "Hell yes! Christ, what took you so long?"

"Well, um, I've never been to one and-"

She stopped him from further embarrassment by kissing him again. "Come in for a bit, okay? My parents won't be home for hours." Then she added very seductively, "We can pick up where we were the other night before we were so rudely interrupted."

He was torn between his urge to again get up close and personal with her breasts and his budding sense that this was all a big mistake. "I'd love to, but I've got a ton of homework and a test in math tomorrow." He jumped back on his scooter before she could try to convince him, because he wasn't sure he could resist for very long. He left her standing there on the sidewalk.

For Suzie, the relief of finally getting the prom thing settled compensated for her disappointment over what she imagined would have been a very sexually exciting time in the rec room. She raced into the house, eager to tell Julie the good news.

Julie had already figured it out. She had been walking to Suzie's and stopped down the block when she saw Clark and Suzie standing in front of the house. It became clear from Suzie's actions that he had asked her, and that was good.

But why do I feel so shitty?

She didn't know what she would do if they went in the house. She knew that that Suzie's parents wouldn't be home for hours and that Suzie was eager to get Clark back into the basement. But then she saw him get on his scooter and drive away. He passed by her and gave her an awkward little wave.

Julie took a deep breath and walked on. She hoped she could stand to listen to Suzie obsess over the prom twenty-four hours a day for the next five days. At least it wasn't more. She realized that that was one good thing about Clark's procrastination. She tried to convince herself that looking for dresses would be fun.

* * *

The next day at school, as Suzie's prom-euphoria brought more aggressive public displays of affection, Clark's level of anxiety increased. He knew that he should be happy to be going out with such a pretty and popular girl. That should have been enough to make anyone, any red-blooded American boy happy. But it wasn't working for him. And he didn't have to look very hard for the reason. Even with Suzie draped all over him in the lunchroom, he felt like he'd been punched in the stomach when he saw Dwight put his arm possessively around Julie's shoulders. It hurt again the next morning after English, when he walked out of the class with Julie, and she mentioned that she would like to find time to work on more songs together.

He felt ready to explode from the tension when he got home after practice Wednesday afternoon. He had snuck away to avoid Suzie, who he knew would have found some new excuse to be there when he left the locker room. His frustrations pushed him to the pitching mound, but he couldn't pitch because the coach wanted him to taper off for Saturday.

Rita sat in the sun wearing one of Sarah's skimpy bikini bathing suits. "Whatever's going on in there you need to get it out," Rita offered without looking directly at him. "Seems like you're about to have a bloody heart attack."

He sat down heavily on the mound and wrapped his arms around his knees. "I think I made a really big mistake."

She kept sunning herself and gave no reaction other than to slightly raise her eyebrows. That was a family trait she shared with John and Sarah. She waited for him to continue.

"I asked Suzie to the prom. I wasn't sure that I wanted to, but I did."

"Why?"

"Pressure. We're dating and she kept talking about it, and well, Julie said I should."

That got Rita to sit up and turn toward him. "She's still going with that other guy?"

"Dwight. Yeah."

"Did she want you to, you know, go together, dual-date kind of thing?"

"Oh no, not that!" He stopped and she didn't press.

Finally, she asked, "So what's the problem? Suzie seems nice. She's very energetic and cute."

"Oh yeah, she's very nice, and she seems to really like me and I'm pretty sure she wants to, you know, have sex after." This was hard for him. "The problem is, I'm really not eager to do that with her or even go to the prom at all."

Rita waited. It was hard but she knew she had to be patient with him.

"I just really want to go with Julie."

She knew it. "So what have you been doing with Suzie? You must have done something to make her so eager to go with you."

"Oh, I guess. We made-out at her party. And we went to the movies and then kissed and stuff."

"Stuff? Like what stuff?"

"Well, I did some of what, you know, you showed me, some foreplay with her breasts. She really liked that."

Now Rita got angry. "Listen Clark, it sounds to me like you've been giving off some stonking false signals. I didn't teach you so you can abuse some poor unsuspecting girl when you're really hot for someone else."

"Well, Julie says she just wants to be friends and I thought-"

She cut him off. "You were thinking with your bloody knob is what you were doing. That's what most guys do, but I thought, I hoped, that you would be different." Rita jumped up and went inside before he could answer and before she said anything else that she might regret later. She hated speaking to Clark that way, but she was really pissed at him. Then, as she sat on the bed in her room, she began to realize that her anger was partially based on guilt.

Maybe I shouldn't have told him, shown him, all that stuff.

Her overall opinion of boys, young men, wasn't that positive to begin with. They were all testosterone and hormones wrapped around a fulltime obsession with sex. She had hoped that she could give Clark some tools to raise above all that, but maybe she had just given him ammunition to be really destructive. She knew that you couldn't teach common sense to someone. They had to learn it on their own, if they ever did. But she knew that the learning process could be a real bitch. And she wondered why the bloody hell their parents didn't deal with this stuff? Or more to the point, the dads were the problem because they weren't teaching the boys. But then the dads didn't seem to know much themselves, John being a good case in point.

And would the boys listen if the Dads tried? Probably not.

Her thoughts drifted to Keith. He had always seemed more mature than most guys his age. That was a big part of why she had been attracted to him. He seemed to handle the developing celebrity thing better than most, and he was a very considerate love partner.

Hell, even Eva likes him, and that's saying something.

She debated whether she should go back and talk to Clark, but when she looked out her window at the backyard, he wasn't there. She assumed that he would be up in his arbor, but she didn't feel like climbing up there.

Clark was indeed up on his arbor, feeling sorry for himself. He had initially been upset with Rita for getting angry with him. But soon after she left, he began to realize that she was right. He had been, and was still being, selfish and inconsiderate. And that wasn't something that he could rationalize away as he normally did by blaming it on his frequent moves and lack of experience with normal relationships between boys and girls. By the time he watched the sun drop down behind the mountains, Clark had decided to talk to Suzie and come clean. He would tell her that he liked her but not enough to go to prom with her and certainly not enough to have sex. He hoped that she would understand.

She didn't!

But, of course, he could have approached it better. Much better. His first mistake was to procrastinate until Friday, the day before prom. Then he did it in the lunchroom. And he was so nervous that he just jumped to it with no preamble or warm-up. But the reality was that no matter when, how, or where he had done it, she was going to explode. The fact that it was so sudden and public, so humiliating, caused her to lash out even more.

"You fucking asshole," Suzie screamed and then repeated it several times despite the presence of several teachers. Suzie's language alerted her friends that this was a true crisis because she seldom used any of the serious swear words. Tears then flowed. They were followed by a sharp slap across his face as other words failed her and her body had to do something to defend itself.

He kept repeating, "I'm so sorry. I'm so sorry."

But understandably she didn't hear it or process it or believe it.

Julie interceded and led Suzie off to the girls' bathroom, leaving Clark with an entirely new type of notoriety.

Julie and Suzie stayed in the bathroom during the transition to sixth period and then went back into the lunchroom, which was now empty except for the custodian. By the time seventh period started, Suzie was okay to go to class, and they agreed to meet and go home together right after school. Cheerleading practice would be canceled. Julie felt terrible for her friend. But she also felt relieved, and that then caused her to feel guilty as well.

Later as Suzie drove them home, her feelings swung wildly between hurt and anger. "That rotten SOB, who the hell does he think he is?"

Julie listened quietly, gamely trying to support her friend.

"Dumped the day before prom, how will I ever live that down? I'm an f'ing laughing stock."

Gradually, subtly, and without thinking about it, Julie began to come to Clark's defense. "Maybe that's why he hadn't, you know, asked you before Monday."

Suzie slowly began to think that while Julie was being supper supportive, she was maybe also . . . Then it hit her, reality, like a bolt of lightning.

That just-friends thing is a load of crap.

She suddenly parked the car and looked directly at Julie. "Tell me the truth, are you in love with him?"

Julie struggled to answer. She knew the answer, but she didn't want to admit it. She also knew that this wasn't the time to discuss it with Suzie. "No, no, we're friends, that's all," she finally replied, but not very convincingly.

Suzie, in her current state, couldn't feel anything except absolute betrayal by her best friend. So she wanted to make her pay for it, feel the same kind of hurt. "Well, your so-called friend didn't hesitate to screw me, did he?" She enjoyed the stunned look on Julie's face. "That's right, last Saturday in my basement."

Julie wasn't sure she believed it. She certainly didn't want to believe it. "That's not what, what you said before."

"No, cause it was a wham-bam-thank-you-ma'am thing right after my dad went back to bed. We had been almost there, so he just pushed on in. Completely unsatisfactory. I thought that if I didn't mention it then it wouldn't officially count. But I guess it did for him. Conquest made, move on to the next virgin. Fucking asshole."

Suzie watched the signs of anguish and hurt cross Julie's face. But she didn't feel any better. She felt worse. They had been best friends for many years. But they had never liked the same boy before. This was a completely different ball game. "I think you should get your stuff and move back home."

Later, as Julie lugged her suitcase home, she still couldn't believe that Clark would have done that. But she knew that her friend wouldn't lie about something that important.

* * *

The rest of the day hadn't gotten any better for Clark. Sarah yelled at him that he was stupid and insensitive. Most of the team, including Joey, gave him a lot of space. It seemed like they thought he might be contagious, and they didn't want any of the bad karma to rub off on them, not the day before prom. He was pretty sure that it was Dwight who muttered, "Way to go Romeo."

When he got home he wanted to tell Rita that he had come clean with Suzie, but she was distracted and distant all evening. His mother reported that Rita had received a telephone call late in the afternoon and had been like that ever since. Coleen had asked her if it was bad news, and Rita's cryptic reply had been, "I don't think so, we'll see".

CHAPTER TWENTY-FOUR

Clark didn't know what time he had finally gotten to sleep, but he felt exhausted as he struggled through his breakfast Saturday morning. He then retreated to his room to rest until it was time to leave for the one o'clock game.

The consolation game for third place in the Denver Regional High School baseball tournament should be played at the home field of the team with the best record. But Harrison High and Denver Central High had identical records, so a coin toss had settled it. Harrison won the right to home field, and the team had, of course, seen that as a good omen.

Coach Duncan approached the game primarily as a foundation for the next year because many of the starters, including Joey and Clark, were juniors. Like most competitive athletes and coaches, he viewed third place trophies as motivational tools and nothing more.

Clark was doing some additional pre-game stretching when Joey came up to him. "Say Clark, did you notice that the ump today is the same one that called those balks on Dwight?"

Clark shook his head, he hadn't noticed.

"You had that pegged last time, can you tell me what you saw?"

Clark tried to give Joey as simple a description as he could of how Dwight's pitching motions conflicted with the very subjective rule. "Dwight's got a slow pickoff move, maybe because he thinks about it too much. I don't think he's trying to fake it, but it could be interpreted that way."

"And this ump seems to do that."

"Yeah, and I would guess that he's really gonna be on top of it after, you know, what happened the last time."

Joey nodded and then trotted over to Dwight and began to talk to him.

It was a beautiful sunny day, and there was a very good crowd, mostly Harrison supporters, but a lot of Denver Central students and parents were there as well. The stands were packed, and people lined the hillside along the third base / left field line.

Clark had a hard time finding Coleen and Sarah in the stands, and then he didn't see Rita with them.

Where is she? She's never missed a game.

Then he saw someone sit down next to his mother.

Holy shit, Dad!?

His father hadn't arrived home by the time Clark had left for the game, and no one seemed to know his schedule. It wasn't even clear if he would be home at all for the third weekend in a row. Clark was happy to see him, but he was mostly worried about Rita.

Julie wanted to scream. She was fed up with everyone. Her mother for being a shitty parent. Dwight for being a shitty friend, boyfriend. Clark for being such a jerk with Suzie. And Suzie for screwing Clark. She had seriously debated whether or not to come to the game. But Julie wasn't a person who hid from her problems. So there she stood, a very uncheerful cheerleader.

She wouldn't have been surprised if Suzie had bailed on the game. But a large boisterous crowd was every cheerleader's dream, and they all wanted to be there. That didn't mean, however, that the tension wasn't thick and obvious between the two friends. The other girls gave them both a lot of space, and eventually they shifted their focus from themselves and their troubles to the enthusiastic crowd.

Julie could see that Dwight had his game-face on. She knew that he wouldn't look over at her or acknowledge the cheers from the home crowd or the boos that came from the Denver Central fans. She noticed Clark staring into the stands, and she saw his mother and sister but not Rita.

When the game finally started, it was soon clear to everyone that all the players on both teams were nervous and tight. The first two innings were full of errors and long at-bats as pitchers and hitters on both teams struggled to relax and not be overly aggressive on every pitch, every play.

As Clark watched the game, his frustration grew. Joey seemed to be calling a game that made sense, but Dwight kept shaking him off. He knew that they were lucky to still be in a scoreless tie as they came to the end of the top of the fourth inning. He wasn't exactly sure, but Clark knew that Dwight had thrown a lot of pitches and was possibly nearing the pitch count that meant a mandatory pull. He anticipated Dwight's reaction to being taken out of the game.

That won't be pretty.

During the bottom of the fourth inning, he watched a short but intense conference between Dwight, Joey and Coach Duncan. Dwight didn't look at all pleased.

Whatever the Coach said seemed to work for a while during the top of the fifth inning because Dwight seemed to follow Joey's calls and retired the first two batters fairly easily. Then the Denver Central first baseman came to bat. He was a lefty and bigger than any player on the field. In the first inning he had hit a ball further than Clark had ever seen in a high school game. Fortunately, it had been foul. Clark felt some admiration for Dwight as he battled the big guy to a full count and then beyond. He counted sixteen pitches before Dwight made a small mistake, and the Denver Central batter sent the ball flying a mile over Ira's head and over the fence in center field.

Clark saw the effect on Dwight and was not surprised when the coach told him to get warmed up - quickly. Dwight was tired, and he had reached the maximum number of pitches allowed by the state high school athletic commission. Unfortunately, while Clark warmed-up, Dwight allowed the next two batters to reach base - one on a single and the other on an eight-pitch walk.

It was the bottom of the fifth inning, two out and two on base and behind one to nothing - not the ideal time to enter a game, but it wasn't all that unusual for a reliever. As Clark passed Dwight on his way to the mound, he heard him mutter, "Don't fuck this up, butthead." Clark had to laugh.

An asshole to the very end.

Clark didn't need to look around to know that all eyes were on him. He was okay with that. After the past few weeks, and especially the past few days, this was a calm place at the center of the storm, the eye of the hurricane. He wanted to throw strikes, but more importantly, he needed quick outs.

He had talked with Joey between every inning about what they saw with the Denver Central batters, and he anticipated Joey's signal before he made it. Fastball in. Late swing, soft grounder to first, easy out. One pitch and the inning over.

Julie had watched Clark take the mound and react with that little smile at whatever it was that Dwight had said to him. She knew it wouldn't have been words of encouragement. Then she watched as Clark stood tall and seemed to bask in the crowd noise. This was not that shy boy who had run away from that first disastrous tryout just a few weeks ago. She looked around, and, except for Suzie, everyone was yelling his name. She felt her pride for him smash up against her anger and hurt.

How could I have been so wrong about him?

She would have bet her life that he would never have sex with Suzie and then dump her like that. She felt terrible for her friend, and she felt a real sense of loss for herself. Plus, she knew that she was not blameless in the whole affair. She had had some instinct, or hope, that even if she took the just-friends stance that he would remain hers.

Shit, I was just manipulating him. And then Suzie . . .

She felt terrible for poor Suzie, who had gotten caught in the crossfire. Then she realized that the crowd was yelling, and she refocused on the game just in time to see Bill slide into home and score for the Cougars.

How the hell did I miss all that?

She quickly joined the other cheerleaders and worked to maintain the crowds' suddenly revived enthusiasm.

Not that he needed to be any more pumped up, but when Bill scored to tie the game, Clark knew that it was now his game to win or lose. He could go the last two innings. He felt strong enough to go all seven. He would have loved to have a lead, but he felt good as he went out to pitch the sixth inning with the score tied one to one.

Clark and Joey proceeded to operate as a well-oiled machine. None of the batters had faced Clark, but he knew all of them, having studied each of them for three at-bats. He proceeded to efficiently strike out two batters and forced a shallow fly ball to Ralph playing deep at shortstop. He felt more than heard the roar of the crowd as it grew with each out.

As he sat on the bench, he kept within himself, and the team left him alone. He allowed himself only a quick glance to the stands to see his family. His dad smiled, but Rita was still not there. He quickly suppressed any concern that he felt, and he carefully avoided looking over at the cheerleaders.

Joey was up third in the inning. As he got up to go to the on deck circle, Clark told him, "Put one out of here and we'll close it out."

Joey smiled. He hadn't hit a home run all season.

"He normally goes fastball away after the slider," Clark reminded him.

Sure enough, on the third pitch, right after a slider, the Denver Central pitcher threw a fastball away. Joey hit it hard and far. Home run and a two to one lead.

Andy was up next, but he had to wait while the Denver Central coach pulled his starting pitcher for a left-handed reliever. Clark was on deck. He watched Andy as he fouled off four straight pitches before sending a high fastball into the gap between right and center for a double. Clark came to the plate with an opportunity to really help himself if he could just get a single and score Andy from second. The Denver Central relief pitcher was the most erratic that Clark had seen in a long time. He hadn't been able to figure out any reliable tells because of his seemingly ever-changing motions.

As he stood in the batter's box, he kept reminding himself to just keep his eye on the ball. He read the first two pitches as curve balls and took them both, one for a ball and the other for a questionable strike. He fought off his impulse to argue with the ump. He knew that would be a mistake because he wanted the ump on his side, or at least neutral. Maybe he would get the same call when he went out there next inning. Clark then barely missed connecting with an inside fastball that dribbled weakly foul down the first base line. The next pitch was the same, but he was on top of it and hit it down into the side of his right foot. He dropped his bat and hopped around on his left foot. He took a tentative step with his right foot. He needed that foot to push off on his pitches. It hurt, but he was sure nothing was broken, and he was determined to stay in the game. So he willed himself not to show the pain he felt and tried to walk as normally as possible.

Coach Duncan was halfway out to him when Clark forced a smile and yelled, "I'm okay." He almost made himself believe it as he stepped back into the batter's box. The pain forced him to concentrate, and he hit the next pitch, a line drive toward short that he knew was a single. The Denver Central shortstop, however, made a major-league leap and hit the ball with the very tip of his glove sending it straight up in the air and then down for an easy catch.

So the score stood at two to one in favor of the Cougars when Clark and the team took the field for the top of the seventh inning. They were three outs from a win, but the top of the Denver Central batting order was up. Clark really wanted to get the first three batters out because he knew that the lefty Denver Central first baseman was due up fourth, and he hadn't shown any weaknesses to any pitches that Dwight had thrown.

As he tossed a couple of warm-up pitches, Clark felt the throbbing pain in his right foot and knew it was going to hinder his push on his fastball. Fortunately, the first Denver Central batter was overly eager and swung at the first pitch, sending the fastball weakly back toward Clark, who tossed it to Bill at first. One out.

The second batter showed more patience and forced Clark to throw ten pitches, working the count full. Joey called time and came out to Clark to see why he kept shaking off his call for a fastball.

"Are you okay?"

"My right foot hurts like a bitch when I push on the fastball."

"Should I call coach?"

"No! I'm good. Let's get this done."

Joey nodded and went back to the plate just as the ump was about to head out and break up their conference. Joey called for a slider down and away. Clark delivered and was rewarded with a swinging strike on a pitch that would have been ball four. Two out.

He wasn't so lucky on the next batter, however. He threw a decent pitch, but the batter got most of it and sent it high toward Ira in center. Ira unfortunately misjudged it, and by the time he realized his mistake, he could only watch it drift over his head. He recovered quickly, but the damage was done, and the batter made it easily to second base. That brought the big lefty to the plate.

Clark stood there and stared at the batter. He hadn't really acknowledged this idea, but it had been lurking in the back of his head ever since he hit his foot. And then it had started to come front and center as the inning progressed. He called Joey to the mound. "I haven't seen any weakness with this guy, have you?"

Joey shook his head. "None."

"I have a plan, but you're gonna think it's crazy."

Joey smiled and replied, "You got another pitch you haven't told me about?"

"No something crazier."

"What?"

"I'm going to switch to southpaw."

Joey thought he had misheard. "You're what?"

"I can pitch lefty almost as good as righty, and my left foot doesn't hurt to push off. I really want this out."

Joey slowly replied, "Okay, let's do it. What can I call?"

"Fastball or curve. Slider doesn't work too well lefty."

"Jesus Clark, anything else I should know about?"

Clark just smiled and shook his head. He switched his glove to his right hand and swung his body around to take a southpaw stance. He tried not to, but couldn't help but notice the dead quiet that immediately settled over the entire ballpark.

Coach Duncan stood frozen for a moment, then quickly called time and went out to the mound. Joey scrambled back out there to join them. "Son, what the hell are you doing?"

"I'm going to get this guy out."

"He says his left is almost as good as his right," Joey added for support.

"Well, I'll be damned." The coach had briefly thought of going to Jason, a left-hander, for this situation, but had decided that Clark was much stronger, the better option.

Damn crazy luck.

"Are you sure?"

"Yeah, I got this."

By now the Denver Central coach had had time to react, and he approached the umpire with a complaint that Clark couldn't just switch sides. The umpire didn't know of any rule against it, but called in the two other refs to make sure they didn't know of something. They all agreed that as long as Clark took a side and stayed with it for all pitches to the same batter, then it was okay. The umpire told the Denver Central coach that he was always able to put in a pinch hitter, a right-handed hitter if he wanted. They wouldn't allow Clark to then switch back to his right side. The Denver Central coach considered that but only briefly. This was by far his best hitter, and he assumed that there was no way this kid could be any good lefty. No one could do that. It had to be a stunt, a diversion.

"Play ball!" the umpire yelled at everyone.

Clark settled in and gave the hitter a long hard stare before going into his windup. He wished he could have thrown a couple of warm-ups lefty. His first fastball was way inside, and only the quick reflexes of the hitter kept him from getting drilled on his right arm.

Clark felt he could push off better now on his left foot and sent the next fastball screaming past the hitter, who had no chance to catch up with it. He was a little more prepared for the next fastball, but still only managed a weak foul into the third base stands. Strike two.

Joey called for another fastball, but Clark shook it off and agreed to the curveball sign. He paused a little longer than he normally did. Through the crowd noise, he even heard Suzie yell his name. He looked up at the batter, and instead of a hard stare, gave him a little grin. Joey saw it and almost laughed out loud.

Clark threw the curve, and the batter, anticipating another fastball, swung wildly and missed by a mile. Strike Three. Game over. Harrison won by a final score of two to one. All the Cougars rushed the mound and mobbed Clark. They slapped each other's hands, butt-patted and even hugged each other. It was only third place, but it still felt great.

Joey grabbed Clark by the arms and said, "Man, you are a beast!"

Then the crowd rushed out from the stands and joined the celebration. Julie headed toward Clark intending to give him a big hug. But Dwight saw her and jumped in front of her, twisting her away. Clark pretended not to notice, but he had a hard time keeping his anger in check. The strong emotions of the moment could have turned from positive to negative in a flash. Fortunately, at that moment his dad arrived and pulled him into a big man-hug. Clark was stunned. His father had never done that before.

Then after dealing with teammates, the crowd, and family, Clark thought about Rita. "Where's Rita?" he asked his mother.

"She got another telephone call this morning, just as we were getting ready to come over here. She asked to borrow the car and then ran out of the house, barely saying a word."

"She hasn't missed a game. I hope she's okay," Clark said.

* * *

Rita was much more than okay. She was ecstatic, but also more than a little nervous. The call the night before had been from Keith, telling her that he had just landed at New York's Kennedy International Airport and was on his way to see her. He would call her the next day when he got into Denver. Her emotional response had been so strong that it made the baby kick harder than it ever had.

I hope that's a good sign.

The baby again kicked hard and Rita's heart raced as she saw Keith standing with his bag outside the baggage claim area. She started to jump out of the car before she realized that it wasn't in parking gear. Flustered, she finally got out and stood in front of him. It took only an instant of looking in each other's eyes for them to realize how happy they were. They grabbed each other in a tight hug. After a minute, Keith realized he had felt the baby bump and pulled back to examine it. He cautiously put his hand on it and moved it gently around the protrusion. In response, the baby kicked, and Keith's hand jerked back.

Rita smiled.

She knows her daddy.

"So we got a wee footballer here, huh," Keith laughed. "Are you doing okay, love?"

"Never better."

She grabbed his arm and led him to the car. As they drove they felt like kids on a first date but with someone they were already intimate with. Small talk about the scenery and the weather occasionally punctuated the quiet anticipation that they both felt. They stopped at a coffee house near the campus of the University of Denver, where they found a quiet, seclude table.

"So how did you get Eva to tell you and to give you my address?"

"I told her that I would camp outside the door of your flat every night until she told me what the hell was going on. It took almost a fortnight to break her."

"But what about your tour?"

"Well, I've given that up actually. I figured that if I'm to be a family man I can't be on the road all the time. We both know what that life is like."

"What do you mean family man?"

He looked intensely at her for long enough that she began to get nervous. Then he reached into the pocket of his coat and pulled out a ring box and opened it to reveal a simple ring with a small diamond.

"Rita McDonald, would you make me the happiest bloke in the world and marry me?"

* * *

Julie had stood outside the school and waited for Dwight. She hadn't been able to get the image out of her mind of Laurie rushing up after the game and giving Dwight a quick but aggressive hug and a kiss on the cheek. Dwight had shrugged it off, but Julie knew he was pleased by it.

Now they were in his car, and she realized that they seemed to be headed for his house. "I thought we were going to The Mountain to join the others?"

"No, I thought we could celebrate ourselves, my stepmom is gone all day."

A sinking feeling seized her stomach. "I'd really like to go with the others."

"Come on babe, we never spend any time alone anymore. This way we can, you know, relax before tonight."

Julie knew all too well what he meant by relax, and she wanted no part of it or the battle to avoid it. "Dwight! Stop the car now. Right here."

He considered ignoring her, but realized from the tone of her voice that she was serious. "Okay, okay," he said, as he pulled to the curb and stopped. "What?"

She turned in her seat to face him directly. "I know what you want, and I want to tell you that it's not going to happen, not now, not tonight . . ." she paused.

"Not ever?" he finished her sentence for her and struggled to keep control. He had anticipated this, but the rejection still hurt. "You've been teasing me long enough. If you won't do it with me now, then we're finished. I don't need to put up with this shit."

In response, she opened the door and got out of the car. "Fine. Go get Laurie. I'm sure she'd be happy to fuck you before and after the stupid prom," she yelled, then slammed the door and walked away. Her body tensed, afraid that he might follow her, but she relaxed when she heard his car pull away and speed off. The walk to her house was almost a mile, but her step felt incredibly light.

I should have done this long ago.

CHAPTER TWENTY-FIVE

Clark sat on top of his arbor and basked in the late afternoon sun and the memory of the game. Echoes of the cheers, the adulation, the thrill, swirled around in the cool breeze. Even his ankle had responded positively and barely hurt at all. He also struggled to keep the dark clouds of worry about Rita and Julie and Suzie far off on the horizon. That became more and more difficult as time passed.

He heard someone climb up the vines and turned to see Rita.

"Clark, congratulations on the game! I'm so sorry I missed it, but I hear that you were bloody brilliant." She got a big smile of pride and of relief from Clark. "Can you come down? I've got someone I really want you to meet."

Extremely curious, Clark followed her down and into the house. He heard a lot of voices in the living room and entered to find his parents, Sarah, and Keith all talking excitedly. He stopped, but Rita pulled him forward.

"Clark, this is my, my fiancé Keith, from London," she gushed, as she held up her left hand and showed off the ring on her finger. "We're getting married."

"You missed it," Sarah exclaimed. "It was so dramatic. They walked in and the first thing Keith did was ask Dad for his permission to marry her. So very proper." She finished with a good British accent.

Keith moved to Clark and shook his hand. "I was so bloody nervous. I thought he was going to say no."

"Hah, you should have been more worried about me." Rita grabbed Keith's arm as she turned to the others and continued. "When he asked me, I admit I wasn't sure. Not about my feelings for him, but about my fears of raising a kid in a musician's lifestyle."

"But I told her that I'm willing to give that up," Keith continued. "I've snagged a job as the musical director for Eaton Public School, my alma mater, starting in the fall. A right proper job."

"And he'll do some gigs with his band on weekends, just no touring. He addressed all of my fears, so I had to say yes." Rita laughed and gave him a big hug and a passionate kiss.

Clark was really happy for them. The first person he thought to tell about it was Julie. And that brought him crashing down as he remembered seeing her leave the game with Dwight's arm wrapped possessively around her waist.

* * *

Julie knocked tentatively on Suzie's bedroom door. Suzie's mother had assured her that Suzie was in there. But the door was locked, and there was no answer.

"I know you're in there Suzie. Please, I just need to get my last few things and then I'll get out of your hair."

After almost a minute of silence, she was just about to give up when the doorknob turned and unlocked. The door didn't open, but that was enough of an invitation for Julie to enter cautiously. She saw Suzie lying on her stomach on the bed. She looked intently at a book, a science textbook, which meant that she was probably faking interest in it.

Julie went quietly to the closet and began to pull out a few items.

"Cool game," Suzie said quietly to the book.

Julie paused but didn't look over at her friend. "Yeah, very cool."

"Ambidextrous. That was a surprise."

"For sure. The looks on that batter and their coach were fucking hilarious."

They both laughed, and the tension relaxed slightly. Julie paused and then continued to take things from the closet, the last of which was the dress she had planned to wear to the prom. She didn't notice that Suzie had sat up and now watched her.

"You'll look great in that tonight," Suzie commented, without being the least bit snarky.

"Thanks, but I'm not going. Dwight and I broke up. I wouldn't be surprised if he goes with Laurie."

Suzie straightened up. "I'm so sorry," she said automatically, but then her protective feelings for her friend came out strong. "No actually I'm not, I'm glad you finally dumped him. Piece of shit."

"Say, why don't we hang out, our own little non-prom party?" Julie offered hopefully.

Suzie looked like she was considering it. "No, I think you should put that dress on and go. You should ask Clark." Julie started to protest, but Suzie cut her short. "No bullshit, Julie, I know you like him, and he obviously likes you. So don't insult me by trying to deny it."

"That doesn't really matter does it, not after what he did to you. I hate him for that."

Suzie stared at her toenails, which she noticed needed painting. "I um, well . . . I lied about that actually." Now that she had started, she hurried to finish, "I was so angry, so humiliated, so stupid. He never touched me. Well, not other than that thing he did with my boobs, which really incredible. But I did thrust them right in his face." She made an exaggerated motion with her body to demonstrate, which

Julie had to laugh at. "Julie, I'm so sorry," Suzie said, as she began to cry.

Julie sat and put her arm around her friend. Her sense of relief combined with a feeling of compassion. Their friendship was strong enough to deal with this. They sat quietly as the possibilities raced through Julie's head. "But what about you, I don't want to leave you alone."

"That's cool, I'm okay. It's just a stupid dance."

Julie suddenly had an idea but knew it was crazy. "I know this will sound bat-shit insane . . . but what if we got Clark to take us both?"

Suzie laughed so hard she could barely respond. "That poor boy would have a massive heart attack with the two of us." She got herself under control. "But I don't want to ruin it for you."

"Well, like you said, it's just a stupid dance. And I don't know exactly what it is between us. I do really like him, but it's just so hard to tell what going on in that head of his."

"Yeah, tell me about it."

* * *

Clark lay on his bed, exhausted from dealing with the whiplash of mood swings. Euphoria, depression, concern, longing, and heartache all marched across his psyche like little armies, each trying its hardest to control him.

It's so much better to just not get involved.

"Clark, can I come in?" Rita asked through his closed door.

He hesitated for a moment before answering, "Yeah."

She came in and sat on his bed near his feet. As usual the silence was not uncomfortable for either of them. Finally, she said, "Joey said to say hi."

"That's cool."

"Keith and I might catch a cinema, do you want to come with us?"

"No, that's okay, but thanks. He seems like a really nice guy."

She couldn't help but beam. "Yeah, he is."

"So I guess you'll be leaving soon."

She hadn't really thought about that yet. "Yes, probably so. I've been here a long time, wearing out my welcome," she teased to minimize the sadness.

A moment later Coleen called up the stairs, "Clark, someone is here to see you."

As he entered the living room, Clark was astonished to see Julie, who stood there talking about the game with his parents. She looked great in her shorts and tank top. But he wondered why she wasn't dressed for, going to the prom.

She gave him a warm but cautious smile when she saw him. "Hi."

"Hi," he responded, unable to process any more.

"Can we talk for a minute?" she asked, clearly meaning anywhere but there with the very curious audience.

He led her out to the back yard. "Do you feel like going up?" He indicated the arbor. "Looks like it might be a nice sunset."

She smiled, "That would be great, perfect."

They reached the top of the arbor and got settled just in time to see the start of a spectacular sunset. The sun had just disappeared over the top of the mountains and now cast the first strong splashes of red, orange and purple light on the surrounding cumulus clouds. They sat and watched in silence.

Finally, it was too much for him. "Aren't you, you know, shouldn't you be getting ready for prom?"

"I'm not going."

"Oh." That was all he could manage through the sudden onslaught of happiness. He didn't press for more.

As if on a cue, they both reached for the other's hand at the same time. They continued to sit in silence as the clouds now glowed darker shades of color.

"Actually that's not totally true," she began, and his heart started to sink. "I was thinking that maybe we could go together, if you still wanted to go with me that is." She looked at him and smiled.

He did the only thing he could think of. He kissed her, and she eagerly joined in.

"I take it that's a yes," she laughed, when the kiss finally ended.

"Yes!"

"Great. Now there's one more thing, and it's kinda far out there, but it could be fun. What would you say to taking Suzie with us?"

The expression on his face sent her into a spasm of laughter.

Julie liked having Clark's arm around her as they walked back into his house. She was anxious to get home and tell Suzie. They wouldn't have time to do the pre-prom dinner thing. They would barely have time to shower and get their makeup on. Clark had expressed his concern that he didn't have a tux, but she assured him that not having one would be fine. His good Sunday suit would be perfect. The three of them would make an incredibly odd sight anyway.

She had a hard time keeping her grin under control as Clark announced their plans and Rita almost leapt for joy. John and Coleen were stunned, but they handled it well.

"Keith, Julie and Clark wrote these songs that I would love for you to hear. I think they're really quite good," Rita said, as she looked at Julie, who was obviously anxious to get home and get ready for the big dance. "Maybe tomorrow we can get together?" Rita proposed to Clark and Julie, who both eagerly agreed.

As she drove back in Suzie's car, Julie vacillated between hoping that Suzie would still want to go and that she wouldn't. She did love her friend, but a big part of her wanted Clark to herself. She was more than a little surprised that he had agreed to it. It would certainly not be a low profile date. But she reasoned that there was so much drama surrounding all of them already that this wouldn't seem so big.

But, if she's decided not to go, I won't try to convince her.

Suzie was up for the adventure and the attention. And if she had to share a date with anyone, who better than Julie, who looked incredibly sexy in her dress. Suzie also looked great as they stood in front of her parents, ready to leave.

The Masters weren't sure what to think about the arrangement, but they decided to trust that their daughter and her friend knew what they were doing. They wouldn't see Clark because the girls were picking him up in Suzie's car. They obviously couldn't all go to the prom on Clark's scooter.

* * *

Clark looked out the bathroom window, watching for Suzie's car. Not seeing it, he turned back and for the tenth time adjusted his tie in the mirror over the sink. He was glad to not wear a tux, but he also felt self-conscious that he would be the only boy not wearing one. A month ago that would have definitely kept him from going, but now his various bouts with notoriety had prepared him to believe that he could deal with it.

At least I won't look like a waiter like everyone else.

He checked the street again. He knew he shouldn't be surprised that it was taking them so long to get ready. Sarah had spent the entire afternoon preparing. He kept coming back to the central issue of this crazy decision.

How am I going to face Suzie?

Clark hoped that when the girls finally arrived he could escape without everyone coming out, but he feared that that wouldn't be possible. Sure enough, as soon as Suzie's car pulled up and he opened the front door, his parents and Rita all rushed out with him. The girls got out of the car and stood on either side of Clark. Clark got a big silly grin on his face as he tried to process what was happening. Both looked beautiful - overwhelmingly so. Julie's dress was very mature, strapless and cut just above her knees. It fit her upper body like a glove but had plenty of room below the waist to allow for serious dancing. Suzie's dress had straps, which allowed for a very revealing cleavage cut that showed a lot of her breasts. Whereas Julie's dress asked you to imagine what was there, Suzie's let you know right up front. Clark had to suppress the memory of stroking and sucking those breasts only days earlier.

"Oh my God," Rita said quietly to Keith, who had joined her.

"Blimey, he's quite the lad isn't he," Keith mused admiringly.

Coleen and John were transfixed by the change in their son. They would have bet the house that he would never in a million years go to a prom, let alone go with two beautiful girls as dates. That, plus the memory of him as the winning pitcher of the game earlier that day, combined to rock their world. But it was a good thing, and they smiled.

Suzie tossed her keys to Clark and got into the back while Julie rode shotgun. Clark drove a couple of blocks, and then he pulled over and stopped.

"Why are you stopping?" Julie asked, as Clark turned around in his seat to face Suzie.

"Suzie, before we go any further, I want to apologize for the way I acted. I was a total jerk, and you're right to hate me. I'm so very sorry, and I hope you can eventually forgive me."

Suzie couldn't answer right away. She hadn't expected this, but it really felt good. She had agreed to this arrangement because she loved parties and had dreamed all year of going to the prom with Julie and her date, which she had assumed would be Dwight. She had figured that she could hide her anger at Clark and still have a good time. All of her friends would be there. This, however, changed the equation in a super positive way. "Apology accepted, but don't think that this is going to get you some ménage a trois action, buddy." Suzie tried to keep a straight face and mostly failed.

Clark was confused because he wasn't familiar with that term or with the concept of a sexual threesome.

It surprised Julie that Suzie could have even thought of that. It had certainly never entered her mind.

After an awkward moment of uncertainty, Clark and Julie joined Suzie in mostly embarrassed laughter.

CHAPTER TWENTY-SIX

The theme for the prom was Under the Sea. The gym had been transformed into an underwater paradise, and everyone paused when they entered to take it all in. The inspiration had come from the recent television show *Sea Hunt* and the Disney film *20,000 Leagues Under the Sea*, which all of them had seen as young kids. It proved to be even more exotic because most of them had never been to an ocean.

The retractable bleachers were pulled back and covered with blue and green paper that had been painted to look like a coral reef. Blue, green and white crepe paper streamers hung down from the ceiling and slowly twisted to create a shimmering effect. Two spotlights had been moved from the theater and one placed on the top of each bank of bleachers. Tenth grade theater-tech boys swung the spotlights around the gym, constantly rotating the blue and green gels that colored the light. Small tables were set up around the dance floor with play-toy buckets of seashells as centerpieces. A DJ sat in one corner with his two turntables and a big bin of 45s. His big speakers blasted the music to all parts of the gym.

Julie and Suzie had heard people discuss the decorations for the prom, but they hadn't paid too much attention to it because Julie hadn't been that excited about going and Suzie had been worried about not going. The gym was already crowded, the party in full swing by the time they entered. Only a few people noticed the threesome at first, but the news quickly spread.

Joey and Sarah were dancing when he spotted the trio and whispered to her, "Oh my God, look, it's Clark with Julie and Suzie." They immediately stopped dancing and rushed over to them. Clark and the girls were relieved to get some friendly attention and gladly accepted Sarah's invitation to join them at their little table.

Julie felt like everyone was staring at them, and when she glanced around she saw that it wasn't just her imagination. She got a big smile from Fran and then saw Mindy silently mouth "wow'" as they passed by. Mindy must have said something to Tommy, because he immediately swung his head around to look at them. Julie glanced at Clark to see if he noticed, but he stared straight ahead, not overwhelmed, but not comfortable either.

The table was fairly close to the speakers, and Julie was happy that the loud music gave them all an excuse not to force a conversation or have to answer awkward questions. After a few minutes, Joey grabbed Sarah's hand and pulled her back to the dance floor. Julie sat with Clark and Suzie, not knowing what to do.

He needs to ask one of us to dance.

Clark knew that he should ask one of them to dance. If he asked Julie, then Suzie would be left sitting alone - awkward. He remembered from the ballroom dancing lessons that it was impolite to leave a girl sitting alone. He looked around at the dance floor, and it was really hard to tell who was dancing with whom. It looked like Joey and Sarah were actually dancing with other people as they all moved around to the music.

Would it be too crazy for us to all dance together?

It was Suzie who finally spoke up, "Why don't we all dance together?"

It must have been on Julie's mind too because she jumped up quickly, grabbed both their hands and pulled them to the dance floor. As he began to dance, Clark tried to send a mental plea to the DJ to not change to a slow song.

Sarah felt relieved when Clark and the girls came out and began to dance. It had been painful to watch the three of them sit so nervously at the table. She wondered how she could help Clark and tried to think if she knew any boys who were just friends with their dates or if there was a couple that had recently stopped dating but had come to the prom together anyway. She assumed that almost any guy would like to spend time with Suzie, certainly one of the best looking girls there and very sexy in her dress.

Julie surveyed the crowd with the same idea that Sarah had. She was prepared to share Clark all evening if necessary, but she still hoped that she could get him to herself. She realized that they needed a bigger group, a bigger table, to give them the opportunity to always have someone there with Suzie, if Julie was dancing with Clark. But it also made her very happy to see that Suzie looked like she was having fun. And she noticed that Clark seemed to have danced much of the tension out of his body and smiled more often. She knew how awkward this must be for him. She was so proud of him for making such a big show of his apology to Suzie. He could have easily tried to skate over it, as most boys would have done. She looked up at him and caught him staring at her. She rewarded him with a very warm smile.

The DJ had played the fourth fast song in a row, and Julie figured that there would probably be a slow one soon. Sure enough, Martha and the Vandellas' *Heat Wave* segued into *La Vie En Rose* by Louis Armstrong. Julie watched Clark shift nervously on his feet, so she grabbed his hand and was headed back to the table when Suzie grabbed her arm and pushed her up against Clark. "Dance!" Suzie ordered them, and then headed off across the dance floor toward the refreshment table.

They didn't dance as much as they hugged and shuffled their feet a little. An emotional hug, born of weeks of frustration, misunderstanding, and pent-up desire. Neither of them felt the need to talk for the entire song. Then they both breathed a sigh of relief when the next song was *Blue Velvet* by Bobby Vinton, and there was no need to break apart.

Julie pulled her head off his shoulder and smiled at him. "Hi."

"Hi," came his simple response. It was quickly followed by a long passionate kiss. Apropos to the theme for the dance, Clark felt like he was floating. At some point they stopped moving altogether, but neither noticed.

Sarah and most of the crowd on the dance floor did notice, however. A few were put off by the public display of affection, some were jealous, but most were motived to follow suit and kiss their dates. As most of the motion on the dance floor slowed or even stopped, Sarah noticed Dwight and Laurie staring at Clark and Julie. She giggled when she saw Laurie grab Dwight's head, yank it back toward her and pull him into an aggressive kiss.

They really deserve each other.

She turned back to look at Joey and saw desire in his eyes. She slowly tilted her head up toward him and pressed her lips to his. She enjoyed their first real kiss, and it seemed like he did as well.

The start of *The Loco Motion* by Little Eva caused lips to unlock all over the dance floor. Some moved into the new beat, while others headed for the tables or the refreshment area. Clark and Julie walked arm-in-arm over to get some of the fruit punch. Clark noticed Tommy standing with Benji and Ralph and a couple of the football jocks near one of the large punch bowls. They smiled odd little smiles as Clark and Julie approached.

"Try this, this is the good stuff," Benji said conspiratorially to Clark and Julie, as he handed them paper cups of punch.

Clark was very thirsty and downed it all at once. He then noticed the silly smiles on the guys' faces. "What?" he asked.

"If you're thirsty use those," Benji replied with a smirk, and indicated the other two punch bowls. "But for other purposes, this is the right stuff."

Clark still didn't get it, but Julie held her cup and smelled it, then tasted a bit of the punch. "Did you guys spike this?" she asked, with a one-of-the-guys grin.

Benji, who had been the chief instigator and taster, nodded enthusiastically, "Vodka. No one will know."

Suzie stood close by, talking to the dates of all the guys at the spiked punch bowl. Clark felt Julie pull him toward them. "Ask Suzie to dance," she whispered to him, as they approached the gaggle of girls.

Suzie was thrilled to dance, and Clark played the perfect foil to her dance moves. She had had a couple of cups of the spiked punch and was a little manic as she tried to follow the beat of the music. Her motions accentuated her cleavage and occasionally brought her dress flowing up to expose her great legs. Clark wasn't the only boy to notice and appreciate it. When the music switched to a slow dance, he hesitated. But Suzie moved quickly into his arms, a comfortable but not passionate embrace.

"Thank you," she whispered in his ear and then kissed him on the cheek.

"For what?"

"For just being a good guy and not making this weird."

Pleased, but embarrassed, he replied, "Um, thanks, I'm glad you're having fun."

"But if you hurt Julie, I will cut your balls off," she added, with a big smile that didn't hide her intense seriousness.

Clark instinctively looked over to where Julie talked and laughed with the group of girls and then turned back to Suzie. "I won't, I promise."

As long as moving to New York doesn't count.

The impact of The Question had been lurking in the back of his consciousness. He then tried to get it out of his head by concentrating on the music and on Suzie's boobs.

She noticed his look. "You can look but no more touching," she teased, but didn't pull her chest away from his. She wondered if it would be okay for a friend, ex-boyfriend, to caress your boobs the way he had in her rec room, but then she tried to ignore that thought.

The music changed to *Twist and Shout* by the Isley Brothers, and Clark was happy when Suzie said she didn't like to twist, so they moved off the dance floor.

* * *

John and Coleen had taken Rita and Keith to Luigi's Italian restaurant for dinner. There had been too much going on all day for Coleen to have a minute to think of making dinner. And besides, there were many things to celebrate.

Rita could tell that Keith felt comfortable with Coleen and John. He kept up a steady flow of questions about their history together. Then he segued into questions to John about his time in England with Rita's mother, who Keith had never met. Keith was comfortable asking John questions that she hadn't been able to ask. He had none of the personal baggage to get hung up on. It also seemed like John felt more at ease explaining things to Keith, who wasn't part of the family. Not yet. So Rita learned more about her parents' relationship in that couple of hours than she had ever learned from her mother in her lifetime or from her father in the previous month.

She also learned that Keith was extremely articulate and a very bright conversationalist. She knew he had an easy way with her and with his mates in the band, but she had never had an occasion to see him with people outside of that world. It showed her a different level of maturity and intelligence, and it made her very happy.

Coleen leaned over and whispered in her ear, "He's a wonderful young man. I'm so happy for you."

They made it an early evening. Sarah and Clark were probably both going to an after-prom party and weren't expected home until very late that night or probably the next morning. Both couples were eager to get home and into bed.

As the only one of the four who had ever gone to a prom, John felt more than a little apprehensive about his kids and what he had heard went on at those after-prom parties.

And, my God, Clark is with two very sexy girls.

He suddenly felt very guilty that he hadn't had that difficult talk with his son. Rita had seen this coming and had been right to press him. John kept all that to himself, however, to not bother Coleen and ruin their evening.

Rita and Keith had been apart for a long time. Once in the guest bedroom, she pulled him over and sat him down on the bed. She then got undressed, slowly and not overly sexually. She wanted him to see that she was the same but also very different. She still wanted sex but as mature lovers, parents-to-be, and not just passionate, impulsive kids.

She moved to him and took his hands and placed them on her baby bump. She saw the look of wonderment in his eyes, and she almost cried. He touched her so gently. She finally pushed his hands lower. "It's okay, it'll be a bit different, but I really want you inside me."

That was all he needed. He quickly removed his clothes, and they got into bed. The first time proved to be awkward, fumbling around to find the right positioning for their bodies. But by the third time, hours later, they did it like old pros.

In between, they heard sounds of aggressive sex coming from Coleen's and John's bedroom. Not having the kids around allowed them to let it all out. Rita smiled to herself.

I didn't take Coleen for a screamer.

* * *

Julie, not by nature a pessimistic person, was sufficiently cynical to think that it had been going too good to last. She noticed the girls who had begun to rush around the gym handing out freshly mimeographed half-sheets of paper to everyone. When she had one shoved in her hand with a quick, "good luck", her curiosity turned to shock. Everyone was to vote for the couple that would be crowned the King and Queen of the Sea. Julie and Clark were listed as a couple. But someone with a wicked sense of humor had also listed Clark with Suzie.

"What's that?" Clark asked, as he peered over her shoulder. He stood behind her and put his arms around her. Two months ago he would have panicked to see his name on something like that. Two months ago he would never have believed that he would be paired with Julie on anything. Two months ago he would never have believed that he would be at the prom. But now he just laughed and squeezed her. "That's a hoot. Why can't I just have two Queens?"

Julie twisted her body and punched him playfully on the shoulder. "Don't you wish, big boy."

Suzie now joined them with a ballot in her hand. "Hey, I'll vote for you guys if you vote for us," she said while taking Clark's arm and pulling him close.

"Deal," Julie laughed, "we'll cancel each other out. Anyone got a pen?"

Clark looked again at the ballot and saw that Sarah and Joey were on there as well. "Wait, no, I'm voting for my sister. She's the drama queen," he added affectionately.

Julie and Suzie latched onto that idea as the perfect diversion and left to campaign for Sarah and Joey. For the next forty-five minutes everyone danced in a big group for the fast songs and then switched up for the slow songs. Julie watched as Clark fast-danced with several different girls including Mindy and Fran. She was strangely pleased to notice that he still seemed to be a little uncomfortable with the other girls. She felt relieved that he hadn't changed completely from that shy quiet boy she met at orientation so many months ago. Then, when they slow-danced together, no words were necessary as they held each other tight.

The music stopped, and the voice of June Schwartz, the prom committee chairwoman, blared out from the speakers. "Can I have your attention please, citizens of the sea? I have the honor to introduce your king and queen. It was a very close ballot. Could all the couples that were nominated please come over here? The couples not chosen will be the royal court to the king and queen." She paused while the couples made their way toward her.

Julie nodded at Suzie and they each took one of Clark's arms and walked over together. They both hoped it wouldn't be them, which was ironic since in a different situation they would both have loved to be elected.

"And the King and Queen of the Sea are . . . Sarah Westfield and Joey Benton. Congratulations, your majesties."

Clark exhaled, happy for his sister that she won and for himself that he lost. That was one extra bit of notoriety that he could do without.

Julie could have done without the promenade around the gym by the King and Queen and their court. A look at Suzie and Clark confirmed that they felt the same. She tried to ignore the jeers that came from the loose-girls as they passed them. She could feel the intensity of Dwight's glare.

After the coronation, the energy started to slip away from the dance like low tide on the beach. It had gotten pretty hot in the gym, and most of the guys had taken off their jackets. Many of the girls felt their bare shoulders glisten with a sheen of perspiration as they danced. People talked about the after-prom parties and how to get around their curfews.

Julie tried not to focus on it too much, but the question of what would happen with Suzie after the dance kept coming back to her. If they went to June's party, it would be fine for the three of them to go. June was the original straight-arrow, and the party would be fun, with no alcohol and definitely no sexual extracurricular activity. That would be safe. But she really wanted to get Clark alone, and while not sure exactly what she wanted to happen, she did want to explore a little. She recalled Suzie's description of what Clark had done with her breasts.

That sounds nice.

But that meant going to Mindy's party and that left Suzie out. Julie listened to hear what the others were saying about parties to try to judge who was going where. Having watched them all night, she wasn't surprised to hear that Sarah and Joey were going to Mindy's. She hoped that it wouldn't be too awkward for Clark to have his sister there. Then she realized that she had an entire empty house to go to for some real privacy, but quickly discarded that as a bad idea.

"Hey Suzie, what do you want to do? We could all go to June's party," Julie asked.

Suzie had already considered it and decided. "No, I've had a great time, but I'm done being a third wheel. I want you to drop me at home, and then you can take my car and go to Mindy's." Julie started to protest, but Suzie cut her off. "Julie,

I'm fine. Really I am. As long as I get all the gory details later, promise?"

Julie smiled at her friend and nodded, confident that Suzie knew that she would never talk about intimate details. That was one big difference between them.

When he heard the proposed plan, Clark tried to hide his excitement. He offered that it would be great for the three of them to go to June's party. He even tried to be a little nonchalant as he responded to the idea of Mindy's party with just Julie. He hoped that Julie would understand that he was trying to be polite to Suzie and was, in fact, very eager to go with her to Mindy's.

CHAPTER TWENTY-SEVEN

Clark was exhausted. The game, the nervous tension, the drama, the dancing, had all taken their toll. He fantasized about curling up on a comfy couch with Julie in his arms and just relaxing. He was too tired to fantasize about anything sexual as he drove to Suzie's house. It felt strange to drop Suzie off and then take her car to continue the evening. But Suzie seemed to be genuinely happy, and as they drove away from her house, he stopped worrying about it. Then he looked at Julie and felt a stirring of new energy, mostly fueled by hormones.

Julie had gone through a similar progression of feelings from worry to guilt to acceptance to excitement. By the time they parked outside Mindy's house, she focused completely on Clark and what might happen next.

Mindy Pruett was a senior with a well-earned reputation for her open attitude toward sex. It had been fostered by her parents who were sociology professors at the University of Denver. Their area of research was sexuality and the development of cultural identity. Her party wasn't a big one because she had only invited real couples, no casual dates, no singles. It didn't surprise her when she saw Julie arrive with Clark. She had sensed the sexual tension between them for some time. Her instincts told her that Clark was still a virgin, and Julie probably also, but she couldn't tell for sure.

Mindy's parents collected all car keys at the front door. They had some beer and alcohol around and available for the kids, but they monitored it very closely. And they planned to feed everyone a hot breakfast in the morning.

Clark had heard a few of Tommy's stories about his sexual experimentation with Mindy, but he had a hard time reconciling that with the cute, petite, dark-haired cheerleader who looked like the classic girl-next-door. He knew that Julie had originally been invited when her date was Dwight, and he cringed at that thought. But she had wanted to come with him, and that was all that really mattered. Clark wasn't prepared, but should have been, to see Sarah and Joey walk in a few minutes after them. From the look on Sarah's face he could sense that she felt the same awkwardness. He didn't know what he would do if she was with someone he didn't like.

"Are you okay?" Julie asked, as she felt the strong sexual vibe that permeated the entire house. It almost overwhelmed her, and she hoped it wasn't too much for him.

Before Clark could respond, Mindy bounced over to them, grabbed Julie and pulled her aside to whisper to her, "I've saved my bedroom for you two if you need it, want it. It has groovy good karma, and I thought that you might want, you know, a little privacy if it's going to be a special night."

Julie forced a smile, pleased that her friend thought of it and terrified of what it meant. If she were a drinker this would require a drink. She didn't know about Clark, but when she asked him, he responded that a beer would be good.

The large basement recreation room was filled with couches and love seats. The air was warm and tingled with energy, sexual energy. A record player played a slow song with more records stacked on the spindle. A few couples danced in the middle of the room. Most couples, however, were seated, either talking in low voices or making out. All of them had changed from their tuxes and dresses into more casual clothes that they had brought with them. In their rush to get ready, neither Clark nor Julie had thought of that.

He took off his jacket and tie and drank his beer, while she sipped on a very weak vodka and tonic. They chatted casually about the dance. She felt nervous, and she was positive that he felt the same. "Do you want to dance?" she asked, and he readily agreed.

They moved to the middle of the room, and as their arms wrapped around each other, their bodies started to relax and move slowly to the music. Julie buried her face on his shoulder and hugged him tight. Halfway through the song, she felt his body stiffen slightly and she looked over to see Sarah and Joey on a love seat, kissing and moving their hands all over each other. She looked up at Clark, and they gave each other wary, nervous little smiles. Then he kissed her gently on her mouth, then her cheeks, her eyes, and back to her mouth. She felt her body respond with desire and it seemed like they floated, untethered toward . . .

Oh my God, could this really be going to happen?

Julie had certainly had opportunities to get beyond the virgin thing. She had always resisted. It hadn't been because she felt that she should save it for marriage, and it was not because she was waiting for the perfect guy. She knew that was a fantasy. She had tried to explain it to Suzie, but it always came down to her belief that she would just know somehow when it was the right time and the right guy.

Pretty much like what I feel right now.

Clark began to caress her hair and gently rub her head. He loved the smell of her hair. He felt her body respond to his touch and that empowered him to explore further. He rubbed and then kissed her ear lobes, then her neck. As he gently massaged her shoulders, he wondered if she felt what was happening in his pants.

"I'm tired of this dress," she whispered in his ear. "Mindy said I could borrow some of her clothes to change." She took his hand and pulled him with her toward the stairs.

Upstairs, as Clark followed Julie down the main hall, he glanced into the living room where a few couples stood and talked with Mrs. Pruett. Mindy and Tommy were there talking to a couple that Clark didn't know. Mr. Pruett was in the front hall guarding the keys. As they passed him and began to go upstairs, he came over to Clark and pressed two condoms into his hand.

"Uh, thanks," Clark barely managed to say through his surprise and embarrassment. He quickly stuffed them in his pocket.

Julie paused at the door to Mindy's room and waited for Clark to catch up.

Did Mr. Pruett say something to him?

She found Mindy's parents so interesting and so absolutely different from any others she knew. One night the past summer she had slept over at Mindy's house for the first time. Mrs. Pruett had come in to Mindy's room to say good night, wearing just her panties. When Julie turned around, Mindy had taken off all of her clothes and was ready to climb into bed. Julie's first reaction had been to think about how she could get out of there, fast.

"Come on silly, you've seen me naked in the locker room before," Mindy had teased her. "And I've seen you, so no big deal. I just hate to sleep with anything on."

Julie had taken that as a dare, so she had removed her bra and panties and quickly slid into the bed, under the sheet, which she made sure covered her breasts. Soon she felt Mindy's hand touch her shoulder. She had tried not to look but couldn't help notice that Mindy had propped herself up on her elbow, with the sheet resting just over her hips, her top half naked and exposed.

"You really do have the most beautiful body in school, you know," Mindy had crooned, as she rubbed lower on Julie's shoulder. "Have you ever fooled around a little with another girl?"

Julie had wanted to meet this head on and quickly replied, "No, and I really don't have any interest in that."

Mindy had laughed, "Well, I'm not a lesbian or anything, but I really love a woman's body. You do masturbate, don't you?"

Julie had nodded.

"It's just like that, except more fun when someone else does it for you." Mindy had then moved her hand over to Julie's breast. "Just relax and let yourself enjoy it."

Julie had tried to go with the pleasure, and it had worked until Mindy's fingers had begun to tease her pubic hairs. She involuntarily tensed. And when Mindy started to move beyond that, she had had enough. She had turned away and yanked the sheet up over her. Julie had been anxious that Mindy would be upset by the rejection, but she had just laughed.

"Okay, that was an excellent start, we'll get further next time."

Julie hadn't told her that, as far as she was concerned, there would never be a next time. And there hadn't been. Now as she and Clark entered Mindy's room, Julie flashed back to that night and thought of the girls she knew who regularly slept over at Mindy's.

Are they all doing that?

Clark watched Julie close the door to the bedroom and felt his chest tighten and wondered if that was the sign of a heart attack.

Hell of a way to go.

He almost laughed as he watched Julie turn on Mindy's desk lamp and then turn off the overhead light. She kissed him and asked, "Can you please help me undo the clasp." She pointed to the back of her dress.

His fingers felt like large sausages as he fumbled with the tiny clasp. The dress was tight across her back, and he pulled it tighter to get some play in the clasp and heard her gasp. "Sorry," he mumbled, and finally managed to get it undone. He stood and looked at her, unsure of what to do next.

"You can unzip it for me," she smiled at him, touched by his nervousness.

Dwight would have ripped it to shreds by now.

She pushed any thought of Dwight from her mind as Clark carefully pulled the zipper down, exposing her bra strap. She turned to face him and slowly pulled her dress off, revealing her fancy black bra and panties.

Clark wondered whether he should then try to undo her bra, but she did it herself. He watched as it dropped to the floor, leaving her breasts exposed, her nipples eagerly anticipating some attention. He knew what to do, and this time he was doing it for much more than the physical pleasure. He bent over and gently kissed them while his hands carefully massaged them. Then he took a nipple in his mouth and sucked on it. Her groans of pleasure energized him, and he gently bit down on it.

"Oh, that feels so good." She carefully worked her hands around his arms so she could unbutton his shirt and not stop him from doing what he was doing with her breasts. Once she had his shirt unbuttoned, she saw his chest hair.

Oh my God, it's amazing.

She pulled his shirt off him, and then pulled him toward her. They both sank down on the bed. Clark lay on top of her, resting on his elbows so as not to crush her. He looked down at her for what seemed like a long time. He drank in every tiny detail of her face. Her sparkling blue eyes, cute nose and wonderful sensuous mouth. It struck him that her right ear seemed to be slightly larger than her left.

DaVinci says that no work of art can achieve perfection.

He smiled, almost laughed.

"What's so funny?" she asked with a smile. She had been studying his face also.

"I just can't believe that I'm, that we're here, doing this."

"And what are we doing?" she teased. Then she quickly relented when she saw the look of panic capture his face. "Whatever it is, don't stop now."

Clark relaxed, kissed her and then moved back to her breasts. She rubbed his hair and his face. He would have been very happy to do that forever, but she began to put pressure on the top of his head, and he allowed her to push him down to her panties. Going on instinct, he gently pushed her panties down. He looked up her naked body to see her staring at him. There was an intensity to her look that almost caused him to worry, but instead it spurred him to proceed, using the things he had learned from Rita. From the way that her body responded, he could tell that they seemed to be working.

Julie knew she could let it go on and that she would soon have an orgasm and be happy. But that wasn't what she wanted, and Clark didn't seem inclined to take the next step. She pushed Clark's head away from her. She began to sit up, and he got off her and stood at the foot of the bed, facing her.

Clark had tried to ignore his erection as Rita had told him. He was unsure of the next step and was relieved when Julie made the move.

As she undid the belt on his pants and pulled them down, she took his boxer shorts with them and immediately exposed his erect penis. "Oh, Clark," she said softly, as she took him in her hands.

Will that fit inside me?

She knew there was only one way to find out. Just as she began to pull him back on to the bed, she remembered. "Do you have a condom?"

Clark barely heard her as he struggled to keep from losing control. He tried the trick that Rita mentioned, thinking of something very un-sexy like getting a cavity filled or a polio shot.

"Clark?"

"Oh, yeah, sorry, Mr. Pruett gave me some," he muttered, as he bent down and fumbled with his pants until he got the condoms from his pocket.

"He gave you two? Jesus," she laughed.

Clark fumbled with the condom. He'd never seen one before and had no idea how to open it. It was vacuum sealed and didn't have an Open-Here marking. He struggled with it, quickly getting very frustrated.

"Here let me try, I've got fingernails." Julie took the package, and after a struggle, tore open the wrapper, pulled out the condom and held it up. "Do you know how to do it, how it works?" she asked, and laughed at the silly looking round piece of wet, rubbery material.

"No," he mumbled, as she gave it to him. Clark tried to pull it on, but he had it backwards, and it wouldn't unroll. He turned it around and got it started but he was having a hard time unrolling it.

"Can I help?" She reached over and took his penis in her hands and began to rub the edge of the condom down its length.

Clark looked down at her naked body. He felt her hands on him and imagined what would happen next. All thoughts that were way too powerful, uncontrollable, and unable to stop it, he felt his body shake violently as he erupted into the condom. He barely stayed upright with the release of so much sexual pleasure and tension.

"Oh, no," he moaned.

Julie could only sit there and watch.

Well, that's not how it's supposed to work.

She was much more fascinated than frustrated. She enjoyed the look on Clark's face. Then, as his body started to wobble, she grabbed him and pulled him down on the bed next to her. She put one leg over his hips and kissed him for a long time until she felt his body begin to relax.

"I'm so sorry," he began, but she put her finger to his lips.

He felt her body down the length of his. It felt great except for the wet mess hanging from his limp penis. He wondered how long it would take for it to be ready again. He had never tried that. He felt like a total failure, but Julie didn't look upset. If anything, she looked really happy.

Julie was happy. She had been ready to go all the way and would have been fine with it. But now her feelings told her that maybe she wasn't entirely ready yet. She felt certain that it would be with Clark, and it would be soon, but this was enough for right now. After all it was their first date.

That condom thing is a real downer. No wonder people don't use 'em and get into trouble.

They were both exhausted and suddenly cold. She pulled a cover over them, and they promptly fell asleep.

When Julie woke, she saw through the window that it was almost dawn. She hadn't wanted to spend all night in Mindy's room, but there they were. She listened carefully and didn't hear any sounds of life in the house. She remembered that Mindy's parents were heavy sleepers and didn't get up very early. She doubted that any of the people at the party, those who had stayed anyway, would be up yet.

She felt Clark stir in his sleep. Neither of them had moved, but his body seemed tense and uneasy, his eyelids fluttered, like he was having a bad dream. She replayed the evening in her head and chuckled as she remembered the look on his face as he came into that silly condom. The memory of his kissing and exploring of her body was so strong that she felt herself get aroused again. Then, as if he could sense her, she felt a stirring in his penis, which was pressed against her thigh. She carefully reached down, pulled off the gross condom, and tossed it on the rug.

Wow, even in sleep that thing works.

She marveled at that and tried a little experiment by stroking it gently. Sure enough, it soon stood straight out. She rolled over on top of him and put it between her thighs, then squeezed gently. She felt her body respond, wet, eager.

Clark's eyes suddenly sprang open. He looked confused as to where he was and what was going on. The sight and feeling of Julie lying on top of him sent a wave of emotion coursing through his body. He felt his erection and the pressure of her legs on it.

"Good morning sleepy head," she said softly and kissed him. She knew that this was a very dangerous moment. It would be so easy to let him thrust inside of her. He was obviously ready, and she felt a strong desire to do it, get it over with. But that would mean no condom.

Am I okay with that?

She didn't have to answer that question because he suddenly rolled his body and hers so they were lying on their sides.

Clark's instinct was the same as hers. They could do it now, the hell with the condom. He wanted it, and the look in her eyes and the strength of her kiss told him that she did also.

But I can't!

Clark had woken from a dream that had begun great but had quickly turned into a nightmare. He had been having sex with Julie for the first time, no condom, but this time they were in his bedroom. Just as she began to climax, Clark's father had come into the room and sat down on the bed as if there was nothing unusual happening. "Clark, what do you know about Los Angeles?" his father asked. The classic Question -

just as he was about to have sex with Julie. He had screamed and jumped up. Rita had come rushing into the room, which was now Mindy's rec room, pulling Sarah behind her. Rita had been naked, and Sarah was in her underwear. He heard someone call his name from a bed that had appeared on the prom dance floor, and he had looked around, expecting to see Julie but instead saw Suzie. She had her hands under her breasts and pushed them out toward him as she made sucking motions with her mouth. Julie, now with Margaret, stood next to his father and the girls screamed at him, "You bastard, how could you fuck me and then move away!" "It'll be fine, Clark, you guys always adapt so easily," his father said, spouting the familiar family platitude. Clark had spun around, searching for Julie, but everyone was gone.

As he had burst out of sleep, Julie had come into focus, and he convinced himself that she wasn't a dream. He felt an instinctual urge to thrust himself into her, but as much as he wanted her, he knew that he couldn't live with the guilt when The Question came. And it was certainly coming soon. So he had rolled over.

After he moved and they were lying next to each other, he felt so demoralized and sad that his erection quickly subsided. He saw Julie's look of confusion and knew he had to explain it and quickly. "I'm so sorry about that, but we have to talk." His tone was far too serious for the moment because she pulled away from him and lifted the sheet up to cover herself.

Julie couldn't imagine what had caused him to react like that and then to want to talk. So she covered up for protection and fought an impulse to jump out of bed. But she stayed because of curiosity and a strong sense that he really did want her. The look in his eyes after she pulled away from him was so sad that she felt like crying. She waited patiently while he tried to find his voice.

Haltingly, Clark reminded her of his family's normal pattern of move, new school and move again, at the end of every school year. She had believed him when he had told her that that was the reason he never went out for teams and didn't get involved with people. He mentioned a girl, Margaret, from his last school and talked about how awful they had both felt. And they had only kissed, with a little friendly petting. She noticed that he turned a little red as he described that.

My God, here we are naked in bed, and he's embarrassed about feeling some girl's boobs through her shirt.

She would have laughed if he hadn't looked so tormented.

"So The Question," he explained, "is due any day. And our, my time in Denver is coming to an end." He paused to catch his breath. "As much as I really want to have sex with you, I don't want to do it without you knowing about this. I . . . I don't think it would be good or fair for either of us."

Grateful for his honesty and compassion, astonished at his self-control, she hugged him but kept the sheet around her. The passionate part of her argued to throw caution to the wind and do it anyway. The sensible part of her responded that she should be grateful for difficult condoms. All-in-all, she was relieved that she, that they, hadn't made a big mistake last night. She pulled herself up to sit on the edge of the bed, still keeping the sheet around her.

"Can we still, you know, go out?" he asked cautiously.

She looked at his sad face and struggled with an impulse to jump back into his arms. "Yes, of course, silly," she whispering to him. "You've seen me naked, touched me places . . . we spent the night together. You're not getting away that easily." She knew she could do with a good healthy relationship, even if it was only for a few more weeks.

A knock on the door startled them both.

"Hey in there, are you decent?" Mindy hoped they weren't and didn't wait for an answer, as she opened the door and came in. She saw Julie with the sheet and quickly looked to find Clark. He didn't have anything to wrap up in so he jumped up to grab his pants, keeping his body faced away from her.

Mindy turned to Julie and told her that breakfast was ready. She reminded her that she had some clothes that might fit her if she didn't want to put her dress back on. As she spoke, Mindy moved toward her dresser and tried to get a better look at Clark. But he kept turning away, and then he quickly reached down and grabbed his underwear. Then she noticed the used condom on the floor and smiled.

Good for you guys.

"Come on down when you're ready, or if you're ready for something else, don't worry, have fun." She laughed as she left the room and closed the door behind her.

Julie also laughed, partly at Mindy's brazen personality and partly at the little dance that Clark had done to hide himself from her prying eyes. She then accepted his offer to finish dressing and get out, giving her some privacy. But she was disappointed that he continued to keep his back to her as he put on his pants. Then she realized that she still had the sheet wrapped around her and didn't feel compelled to drop it.

Is everyone this conflicted about their bodies? I just slept naked with this guy and now I'm hiding in a sheet?

To test things, she dropped the sheet while he was buttoning up his shirt. He froze, and she giggled.

Wow, that's interesting. What will he do?

Clark just stared at her for a long time. He mostly looked at her face, but his eyes did wander hungrily up and down her naked body a few times. It seemed like all the air had gone out of the room. His mouth moved, but he couldn't get any words out.

Julie saw his erection begin to push up in his pants. It was then that she realized that she was teasing him, and that was cruel. She walked over to him and gave him a very meaningful kiss. "To be continued," she said, and meant it as a statement, not a question.

It succeeded to bring some life, some color, back to his face. She then pushed him out of the room so she could get dressed.

Clark stood in the hall and tried to steady himself. The ground under his feet seemed soft, pliable, like sand on the beach. The image of Julie's naked body, the smell of her wet arousal, the feeling of her skin and firm muscles, the power of his orgasm - all combined to overwhelm his senses, sap his strength. He fought off tears of frustrations, powered by his sexual desire and his hatred of The Question. He couldn't imagine seeing or talking to anyone, so he leaned against the wall for support and waited for her.

CHAPTER TWENTY-EIGHT

Rita woke before Keith and spent a few minutes admiring her ring before she got up to take a shower. On her way to the bathroom, she noticed that both Sarah's and Clark's bedrooms were empty.

Must have been a good night all around.

Later, when she walked into the kitchen, Rita saw that Coleen and John were all over each other like newlyweds. They all exchanged sly smiles as Rita poured some coffee. She recalled the doctor's warning about too much caffeine.

This is going to be a hard habit to break. Good thing Keith is a tea drinker.

Keith entered a few minutes later and immediately went to the coffee pot. "Ah coffee, great! I really need that."

Rita listened as Coleen, John, and Keith chatted casually about the weather. She knew it was going to be traumatic, but she had agreed to leave with Keith and return home on Tuesday. It was time, and she now finally felt a connection with her father. She didn't understand him completely, but she had come to accept his limitations. He could be an open book with a stranger like Keith, but he got stiff and protective with Clark or Sarah or her.

It's like he's afraid to hurt us somehow.

Sarah got home first, exchanged a few pleasantries and went right upstairs to shower and go to bed. Rita got the sense that she had had a very good time with Joey, but her instinct said no sex. She knew that if she could see Joey, she could tell for sure.

Men are so transparent about sex.

A little later Clark dragged in, and Rita gasped.

Oh my god, he looks terrible.

He was already an emotional basket case, and then each person in the room elicited a different strong emotional feeling. He knew he couldn't begin to face any of that in his current condition. He was barely coherent, but he managed to communicate that he was going to pick up Julie at three o'clock and bring her over. He heard Sarah come out of the bathroom, and he headed upstairs.

"That must have been quite a night," Coleen offered, a little confused about how to interpret her kids' behavior.

John, as usual, took it all at face value and asked, "What's happening at three o'clock?" Rita explained, and he complained he was the last to know about Clark and Julie and their songs. Coleen assured him that she had told him, but regardless, it hadn't registered. A star pitcher, prom dates with two hot girls, a songwriter. John's head hurt as he tried to reconcile all of that with his image of Clark as a quiet, sullen teen who never wanted to help with chores.

Rita decided that her announcement about leaving should wait.

* * *

Despite an almost four-hour nap, Clark still felt exhausted as he drove his scooter to Julie's house. He couldn't stop agonizing over whether he had done the right thing last night.

Have I blown my one chance to have sex with her? God damn Question.

He tried to reconcile his sexual frustration with his conscience. He remembered how upset Margaret had been, and there was absolutely no comparison between her and Julie in terms of intimacy. Images, moments from his dream, danced through his head and pivoted around his memory of Julie, naked on top of him. The loud blare of a car horn jerked him back to the present. He had been sitting still at a stop sign, blocking traffic.

He had never been to Julie's house, but he recognized it immediately because of the sheriff's car parked in the driveway. As he pulled up in front, he realized that Suzie's car wasn't there. He hesitated but then went to the front door and rang the bell.

The door opened and Frank stood there in his full uniform, ready to go to work. He took a moment to look Clark over, and then stepped out on the porch and offered his hand. "Clark, I'm Frank Wells, Julie's dad. She went to return Suzie's car and will be right back. Julie told me that you guys had a good time last night."

"Oh, yes sir, it was great."

Frank could tell that Clark was nervous, but he couldn't tell if it was only because he was meeting a girl's father for the first time.

A father who wears a uniform and a gun.

All that really mattered, he decided, was that Julie had come home safe and happy. And he was thrilled that she had finally dumped Dwight, who he had never trusted.

Clark shifted nervously on his feet and wondered what he should do or say next. He was really glad to hear Julie's voice.

"Hey Clark. Sorry, I had to take Suzie's car back to her." Julie bounced up and gave him a quick kiss on the cheek. She looked like she'd had a full night's sleep and was ready to go cheer on the team. Her energy made him feel even more tired by comparison.

"Dad, this is my boyfriend, Clark."

"We met," Frank answered, and smiled as he realized that this was the first time she had ever said that about a boy. "You two have fun, and drive carefully." The last part was very serious and directed at Clark. Frank had seen plenty of scooter accidents, and they were never a pretty sight.

Julie buckled the strap on the helmet and hopped on the scooter behind him. Her guitar case was strapped across her back. "I hope my dad didn't try to interrogate you. He was more than a little surprised that I hadn't been out with you know who."

"Oh it was fine, no problem," he replied happily, as he felt her arms tighten around his waist.

She introduced me as her boyfriend!

"Was Suzie okay?"

Julie laughed. "Yeah, but she's pretty insistent to hear all the details from last night." She felt his body tense up. "Oh, don't worry, I don't kiss and tell - not about everything anyway." Then she couldn't help tease him, "And besides she's already familiar with some of your moves."

Clark had to struggle to maintain his concentration on the road as he wrestled with that concept. He hoped that the extra squeeze she gave him meant that she was teasing. After they stopped in his driveway and got off the scooter, they stood awkwardly for a moment. Then they finally hugged each other. Clark felt his body relax and knew that he could stay like that forever. But the front door opened, and he turned his head to see Rita and Sarah standing there, smiling at them.

After some friendly banter in the living room, Julie got out her guitar, and Rita sat at the piano. As Julie sang the first song, she felt a new connection to the lyrics now that she knew Clark more intimately. She didn't realize how much it affected her performance until she finished and looked over at Rita. The changes were subtle, but to Rita they made the song grow from very good to fantastic. She jumped up, hugged Julie and whispered in her ear, "That was incredible."

Julie gathered herself and started the second song, which she now also understood on a new level. The pain of leaving expressed in the lyrics hit her in her gut, her soul. She looked over at Clark and felt her eyes tear up. She managed to hold back her tears until she finished and then tried to hide them behind exaggerated bows made to the applause from the group.

Rita hugged her again. "That must have been some night."

Julie responded quietly, "You have no idea."

Rita did, in fact, have a pretty good idea as she looked over to ascertain Keith's reaction to the songs. "I assume, love, that you're going to sign them up because I'd love to record these with the band," he said, as Rita came over to stand next to him. "I was thinking we could all go as partners on this, keep it in the family," she answered and looked around the room. "The extended family."

John approached Clark and Julie and put a hand on Clark's shoulder. "I really like your songs," he said softly, and then done, he turned and faced the room.

Rita took Clark and Julie by the hand. "I would love to be your agent and sign you both to a record deal to produce your songs as soon as I get back to London. And Keith would like to record them with his band. What do you think?"

Clark's first reaction was to be upset that she had confirmed his fears. "When are you leaving?" he asked weakly.

Rita heard the pain in his voice and gave him a quick sisterly hug. "Day after tomorrow. But I'm going to work on John to have you all come and visit. You too," she added, as she grabbed Julie's hand.

They spent the next few hours in the backyard discussing Rita's departure and her wedding plans, the possibility that the songs would be recorded, and the last two weeks of school and exams. Coleen went out and picked-up some Chinese food for an early dinner. After dinner, John expressed his regret that he had to leave in the morning for New York. And then he and Rita went inside to talk privately.

Sarah was deeply engaged in a conversation with Keith about theater in London, and Clark saw his opportunity. "Would you like to go up and watch the sunset?" he asked Julie.

It was a beautiful night, and they lay down on the arbor and held each other. Neither of them spoke, and it was perfect.

* * *

Rita knew John well enough now to be warmly accepting of his feeble efforts to express his feelings. She knew he still had a hard time accepting the fact that he had made a baby all those years ago in London, when he barely knew where babies came from.

At dinner the night before, she had felt his fatherly instinct to be protective, as he had pressed Keith on his work plans and his overall commitment to being a husband and a father. And now as she sat on the bed and watched him pack, she accepted that he was genuinely regretful that he hadn't been able to spend much time with her. She assured him that she had been very happy with their time together and really loved getting to know Coleen, Sarah, and Clark.

John acknowledged to himself that Rita knew his kids better than he did. He hoped that he could change that. He asked her how she was doing financially and if she needed any money. That was one form of support that he could understand and provide.

She smiled and touched his arm. "No thanks, Dad, I'm fine."

It came out very naturally, and she loved the happy look on his face when he realized what she had called him. Then he sat down next to her for a few more minutes before they went back to join the others in the backyard.

* * *

Julie stood in front of Suzie's house and waved to Clark as he rode off on his scooter. She turned and could see the light on in Suzie's room. She took a deep breath and went inside.

Suzie tried to act casual, but Julie could tell that she was dying to get all the juicy details about Mindy's party. Actually, Suzie's interest was specifically about Julie's night with Clark. She had already received a rundown on the overall party and who had been there from other sources. "Well?" Suzie finally demanded.

"Well, what?" Julie parried, trying to keep a straight face.

"I know that you two didn't just sit around and talk all night, especially after you disappeared into Mindy's bedroom. So I want all the details. Did he, you know, do that thing with your boobs?"

Julie laughed at her friend's fixation on breasts. "Yes."

"I knew it. Wasn't it totally awesome?" Without realizing it, she began to caress her breasts.

"Yes, yes it was," Julie admitted, as she continued to get undressed. She felt her body warm as she remembered Clark's mouth sucking on her nipples. She then could almost feel his tongue in her vagina, but she quickly tried to get that out of her head. This wasn't the time for that.

But Suzie sensed something. "Julie Wells, did it happen? Are you no longer, you know . . ."

The question hung in the air, a spark floating in the updraft from a campfire. Julie was glad that she didn't have to lie to her friend. "No, I'm still virginal, if that's what you mean," she teased, knowing perfectly well that that was indeed what Suzie meant.

Suzie felt both disappointed and happy. She wouldn't admit it to herself, but she wanted to be the first of them to lose her virginity. Having watched Julie and Clark at the dance, she had thought that it was very likely going to happen at Mindy's. She relaxed because she knew that Julie wouldn't provide any intimate details about her night. But her most important question had been answered.

Clark would have been flabbergasted to know that both Suzie and Julie fell asleep thinking of him as the guy that they would like to lose their virginity with.

CHAPTER TWENTY-NINE

All day on Monday the school buzzed with stories about the prom and the after-prom parties. Everyone wanted to know what happened at Mindy's. But those who had been there were all being discrete.

Sarah didn't tell anyone that she had even been there, and no one would have imagined that she would have been invited. But eventually word got out, and that raised her to an exalted level in the hierarchy of students in the school. No longer just the theater geek, she was now the girlfriend of a jock and a friend of Mindy's, which meant she played in the incredibly fascinating world of sexual experimentation. She couldn't help but laugh as she felt the significant change in many people's attitude toward her.

It also didn't take long for the rumors about Clark and Julie to flood the school. Some reports had them dating and others had them eloping to Las Vegas right after school was out. The rumor mill was further churned up with the talk of how Laurie had been draped all over Dwight at the prom. It was great theater and a welcome distraction from the final exams that were scheduled to start on Thursday.

Clark floated through the day. It seemed like a month had gone by since Friday. So much had happened. So much had changed. He and Julie didn't get to spend any meaningful time together. But they were around each other and often exchanged smiles that were full of intimate meaning and secret messages.

Suzie joined Clark and Julie at lunch, acting like they were all best buddies. The Suzie thing really threw Clark. Yes, they had all had a good time together at the prom. And he really appreciated it that she had made it easy for them to go alone to Mindy's. But he hadn't anticipated having her as the close friend that she seemed to want to be. He wasn't sure he could ever look at her and not remember kissing her naked breasts. He wondered whether Julie had any misgivings, but she acted as if it was all perfectly normal.

Girls are so strange sometimes.

Dinner at the Westfield house that night was a bittersweet celebration. Clark felt very happy to see Rita and Keith so much in love and excited about becoming parents. But he was almost devastated to have her leave. The only thing that tempered his sense of loss was the promise that his father had made that they would all visit them in London after the baby, his grandchild, was born. Clark looked at Sarah several times and could see that she felt the same way. His mother also looked conflicted, alternating between smiles and watery eyes.

Rita shared their dichotomy of feelings. She had journeyed to America to look for her father and had found a whole family. Like one of those rare days when a violent thunderstorm is chased by sunshine, clear sky and a rainbow. All these things existed in the same sky, just as did the smiles and tears, hopes and fears, in her heart. She squeezed Keith's hand and felt confident for the future: hers, his, and theirs. She was sorry that Julie wasn't there, but she understood Coleen's decision that it was a dinner just for family. Clark hadn't insisted, and Rita thought that had been very mature of him.

Later, as Rita finished packing, both kids came in separately to talk. The difference between them was so pronounced. Sarah just started talking, while Clark sat quietly on the bed for many minutes before saying a word. But they were both embarking on new relationships that were uncharted territory for them.

Sarah's confidence contrasted with Clark's doubts. But they were both consumed by the same fear of what they called The Question, which meant that they would soon be moving, leaving Denver. They both described, Sarah in more graphic detail than Clark, how it had impacted their actions on Saturday night at the party.

Rita carefully considered how to respond to Sarah, who had come in first. She was happy that Sarah was mature enough to be able to delay such an important thing as her first sex. Later, she was amazed, shocked even, that Clark had done so also.

Most boys wouldn't have been able to do that.

But Rita was afraid that this constant moving was going to warp their ability to have normal relationships or to understand what such relationships meant on a day-to-day, month-to-month, year-to-year basis. It seemed like the annual upheaval created, or could easily create, a tendency to quickly commit to someone, but only on a very surface level.

And be just about sex.

That mirrored her lifestyle growing up through her teens, and it had taken a lot of soul-searching, and more than a little luck, to bring her to where she was now with Keith. She knew that it could have easily gone a much different, bloody-awful way.

She told Sarah to confide more in her mother, that she was a very savvy woman with excellent bullshit radar. Sarah almost fell off the bed laughing at that, but then admitted that it was true.

Rita didn't tell Clark the same about his father. Unfortunately, she had learned that John was going to be of little help to Clark as he navigated these rough, uncharted, waters. She felt Julie was just right for him now. But what would happen when they moved and he tried to establish a relationship with another girl. There were far too few Julies in the world, and like most boys, he would be at the mercy of a perky personality and a hot body.

She told both of them to play-it-cool. Not to tease, but not to smother either. Don't try to force things, but let them happen naturally. "Sex is for the moment, but love is for life," her mother had told her, and she passed it on to Sarah and Clark. Rita knew that she hadn't understood this maxim at seventeen. But, probably like her mother before her, she felt good for at least having said it to them.

For Clark, she added her own philosophy that being friends was the key to being in love. She believed that this came naturally to girls but always proved a difficult concept for boys. And it left them susceptible to being led around by a manipulative girl. She remembered poor Huey the bass player and felt bad that she had once been guilty of doing just that.

When she had had a last hug with Clark and finally gotten into bed with Keith, it was almost midnight, and she was exhausted. She felt sad to leave, but she was very eager to begin the next phase of her life. As if in agreement, the baby gave its biggest kick ever.

* * *

Clark was surprised the next day to see Joey without Sarah. He had quickly gotten used to always seeing them together.

"Clark, I've been looking for you," Joey said, unusually earnest. Before Clark could respond, he pressed on, "I heard from Coach Wilson that he would really like you to try out on Saturday for the Mustangs, our summer league team. He saw you pitch last Saturday and thinks you could be a starter. Isn't that cool?"

Clark was thrilled and then immediately crushed.

God damn Question!

Joey noticed the wild mood swing and asked, "Is there something wrong?"

Clark hesitated, unsure how to proceed. "Yeah, that's cool really, but you know that I won't be here this summer."

Joey immediately felt terrible because he realized that if Clark moved then so did Sarah. "Oh shit, I keep forgetting that about you two." Joey, however, was a glass half-full kind of guy, and continued, "but anyway it wouldn't hurt to try out. Who knows you might not make it," he teased, and then got hopeful. "And well maybe it won't happen this summer."

Clark tried to mimic his friend's optimism, but he had little hope that he would ever spend a summer doing anything except moving. However, he did think it would be fun to try out and see if this coach thought he could be a starter, which had always been his dream.

* * *

Julie couldn't decide if this was okay or a really bad idea. She and Clark had decided to study together for exams after school - probably at his house because she didn't think her dad would like them being alone in her house. And if she was honest with herself, she wasn't sure how much studying they would do in that situation. But then Suzie had reminded her that they had also agreed to study together. Unwilling to not be with Clark, Julie had suggested that maybe they could all do it together, and Suzie had quickly and eagerly agreed.

Clark didn't say anything at first when he heard the news. But he wasn't silent long enough for Julie to get nervous. He smiled. "What the heck, sure why not. She knows the periodic table a lot better than I do."

When the three of them pulled into the driveway at Clark's house in Suzie's car, Julie noticed that Joey's car was parked in front. She looked at Clark and assumed that he had seen it also. "The more the merrier?" she offered hopefully.

Clark's first thought was that Rita would really get a kick out of seeing the five of them studying together in the backyard. His second thought . . .

Shit, she's gone.

What Clark had feared might be somewhat awkward turned out to be nothing like that at all. They each had a course or two in common with someone else in the group, and that led to natural study groups. Other than some long looks and occasional brushing of hands or a light squeeze of the shoulder, no one made any big displays of affection that might make anyone else uncomfortable. They did that primarily for Suzie's benefit, but as it turned out, Suzie was totally cool with it and even found it funny.

"Just kiss her already and then get back to science," she teased Clark when she again caught him gazing over at Julie, who reviewed math with Sarah.

Coleen returned from the airport, and she quickly forgot her sadness over Rita's departure when she saw the group in the backyard. She prepared some lemonade and took it out to them. Really happy that her kids had such a nice group of friends, she didn't spend much time worrying about what they might be in addition to being friends.

About six o'clock, they decided to call it quits and agreed that they should do it every day before and during finals. As he got ready to leave, Joey suggested to Clark that they should get together on the practice field right after school and let him throw some pitches to be ready for Saturday's tryouts. Clark had planned to use his backyard but was happy to have a real catcher on a real field. Julie chimed in that she would like to work out with them. After Clark brought Joey up to speed on Julie's Junior Cowgirl's team, they all agreed to practice together the next afternoon.

That night, Clark had a hard time falling asleep as he contemplated whether he was a new Clark who could accept pain as the price for being happy and ignore the inevitability of The Question. He didn't know. These were unexplored waters for him. He felt the calm of a captain with a solid sailing ship beneath him. But he also felt the apprehension of that captain as he stared at a violent storm looming on the horizon, right in the path of a course that he could not change. More than enough to make anyone seasick.

The next day was the last day of regular school before exams. For Clark, the day seemed like a whirlpool of different but familiar emotions. He watched as his classmates talked about their summer plans for camps and family trips and college-hunting trips. And most of them looked ahead to the fall and the start of their senior year together. As always, Clark felt like an outsider to all of that. Normally he had the answer to The Question by now, and he would have begun to try to imagine a new city and a new school. But this year he felt stuck in a strange and awful state of limbo. Then he saw Julie or Suzie or Joey and it proved enough to pull him back to the present. Most of the time he could concentrate on that and be happy.

After school it felt good to be out on the field stretching and pitching. Julie joined them, and Clark smiled as he watched Joey quickly become impressed with Julie's skill. When they arrived at Clark's house to study, Sarah and Suzie were already deep into reviewing their vocabulary for their French exam. Julie and Joey started working on their Spanish. And they all teased Clark that his study of Latin was a total waste of time on a dead and useless language. He knew he had had a good reason for choosing it, but he struggled to remember what it was.

Oh right, I didn't want to have to speak in front of the class.

* * *

That night Julie tossed and turned in bed. She always had a hard time sleeping before exams. But she knew that this was different as she lay in bed and listened to Suzie's shallow, rhythmic breathing. All day she had wanted to ask Clark about moving, this thing he and Sarah called The Question. The uncertainty was killing her, and she wondered how the two of them lived with it all year, year after year. She had overheard Clark and Sarah talk about an audition for a summer stock theater that Sarah had been invited to and about Clark's tryout for the Mustangs. They both angrily referred to The Question like it was the foulest of swear words.

She had begun to appreciate on a whole new level how difficult it must have been for Clark the other night at Mindy's to have stopped what they likely would have done. She knew that for most boys it would have been an almost ideal situation - to be able to fuck and then leave. No commitment, no messy relationship stuff to deal with. But Clark was different and that made her happy, and also extremely sad.

Is he special enough that I want to have sex anyway, to have him be my first?

That question remained unanswered as she finally drifted off to sleep.

* * *

The next couple of days were a blur of exams, workouts and study groups. Clark didn't mind exams and normally did well on them. His technique was to focus and study hard up until bedtime the night before and then not worry about them at all the next day, exam day.

Joey, as it turned out, was a last minute crammer and worrier. So Clark had to apologize and walk away from him as they waited outside the room for their math exam. Joey was cool with it and went to find someone else.

The next day Suzie was not so easily avoided as they waited for their science exam to begin. It was an advanced placement course and had been a real stretch for both of them, him more than her. Clark had actually anticipated her approach and was okay with it. He had grown increasingly fond of her over the past days. She was intensely loyal to her friends, and he was glad that he was one of them. He had even gotten comfortable with her sexual jokes and teasing about their brief relationship.

Clark, Julie, and Joey worked out each afternoon before study group. Clark followed a pre-game routine so he would be fresh for the tryout on Saturday. He found that he was excited to do it even though ultimately it would be a futile endeavor. He debated whether or not to tell the coach beforehand about his situation, but then decided that he would do it straight and see what happened.

I probably won't even make the team, so it's no big deal.

What continued to drive him crazy was Julie - she was just so damn perfect. Affectionate in just the right amount to let him know that she liked him, she didn't go so far as to get him, or them, too excited and then frustrated. A great friend who unfailingly supported his efforts to get ready for the tryout, she never let it rise to the level of an obsession.

And he realized that she was very smart. He had gotten only a sense of that in their English class, which was advanced placement level, but she had never flaunted it like some others. She hadn't done that as a sexy cheerleader either, but that was her only image to most people in the school. He relished the recognition of Julie's intellect that he saw happen to Sarah as they all studied together. She had not had a class with Julie and had only viewed her through the sexy cheerleader lens, subsequently augmented by her musical talent. And now it was clear that she appreciated Julie's intellectual side as well.

* * *

Clark had a lot of spectators for a non-spectator event. Both Julie and Suzie were in the stands trying to remain as inconspicuous as two pretty girls could be. They hadn't asked if he wanted them to come because they assumed that he would say no, and then they would have come anyway. Julie looked around for Dwight. She didn't see him and was glad, but wondered why he wasn't there.

The Mustangs were one of five amateur teams in the Denver area for boys sixteen to nineteen. For a high school player, a successful season or two with the Mustangs almost guaranteed a full scholarship to a good baseball school such as Arizona State, UCLA, or Texas A&M, or even to a powerhouse baseball school like Texas or Florida.

Coach Wilson called them together to lay down the rules and go over the schedule. Clark didn't know what to make of this coach. There was a strong, no bullshit, factor to him. He had already reamed-out one boy for clowning around with a buddy. He had this intense, icy stare that demanded respect. Yet, Joey had said he was approachable and very supportive once you were on the team.

After some warm-up calisthenics, the players were broken up into position groups, and each one worked with a coach. Coach Wilson took the catchers and pitchers while his assistants took the others, one infield and one outfield. They would all rotate through batting practice with a third assistant.

Clark felt his warmup pitches were working pretty well and wondered what would happen next. That was soon answered when Coach Wilson asked his batting coach to send over his two best hitters from last summer and have them go live against Clark and another pitcher. The first batter was six feet four inches tall, the biggest and seemingly strongest guy Clark had ever faced.

Joey knew the batters from last summer, and Clark had to rely on him for the right calls. After a quick glance at his cheering section, he took a deep breath and threw a fastball. Crack. The sound from the bat told Clark that the ball was long gone.

Shit, not a great start.

He heard Joey call out to him and brought his focus back to his mechanics. He normally liked to work quickly but he slowed it down just a little to improve his focus. The next fastball was hit, but foul, and the one after that blew by the batter for a swinging strike. The batter dug in and pounded the plate with his bat, expecting another fastball to challenge him. But Joey called for a slider, and the batter's wild swing spun him around almost 360 degrees.

In the stands, Julie and Suzie struggled to keep from cheering. They kept tugging at each other to stay seated. The last thing they wanted was to embarrass or distract Clark. They also felt a little self-conscious being the only spectators in the stands.

After a few more pitches, most of which Clark won, Coach Wilson called for the other batter, who was left-handed. The coach then said to his assistant, "Now watch this." He walked over and spoke to Joey, who then walked out to Clark. Clark switched to his left hand and threw two strikes before the batter was able to connect on a curve ball that hung up over the middle of the plate.

"Son of a bitch, never seen that before," the assistant muttered, as he shook his head.

At the end of two hours of pitching and batting, Clark felt pretty good. And Joey was very high on Clark's chances to make the team. He knew Coach Wilson well enough to be able to read some positive signs behind his tough exterior. Those who made the team would get a phone call and then a letter in the next week that would outline the schedule for the summer. Those who didn't make it would eventually get a thank-you letter.

* * *

Julie was happy that they had all agreed to make it an early night on Saturday. She and Clark had gone to see *Cleopatra* with Joey and Sarah. Now they sat quietly in The Mountain before realizing that they were really tired. Julie had a Junior Cowgirls' game the next morning, and they all planned to go to cheer.

Clark kissed her on the Masters' front porch while Joey and Sarah waited in Joey's car. A big part of her just wanted to pull him inside and fall into bed together, just to sleep. But she knew that would be a little much to expect Suzie to be okay with. As she drifted off to sleep she wondered if she could be such a friend if the roles were reversed.

Not if it involved Clark, I think I clearly proved that.

Sunday was overcast and unusually hot and humid for Denver. All the Junior Cowgirls felt hot and sticky, and the ones who normally sweated were miserable. The fans in the stands, including Clark, Suzie, Sarah, and Joey, all suffered, especially because the team played poorly through the first five innings.

Sarah was the first to notice that Julie had gotten up and begun to warm up. She poked the others, verbally and physically. Clark watched Julie and tried to be objective but couldn't. He was worried.

Is this how she feels watching me?

Julie hadn't slept well, and she struggled to concentrate as she took the mound for the top of the sixth inning with the Junior Cowgirls trailing five to two. With the heart of the Cowgirls' lineup scheduled to bat in the bottom of the inning, it was critical that she keep the score from getting worse. But the first batter she faced sent a hanging curve ball over the left field fence. Six to two.

Coach Becky called time and came out to calm Julie down. Julie listened, but was distracted by her father, who stood behind the dugout clapping encouragement. She nodded when Coach Becky asked her, "Are you good-to-go?" She found Clark in the stands, and he gave her a wave and a big smile.

Aided by a solid defense, she got the next three batters out and retreated to the dugout. The Junior Cowgirls battled back and by the end of the inning had narrowed the deficit to six to five. Coach Becky sent in Ruthie, their closer, who barely managed to hold that score and give them a chance in the bottom of the seventh, the last inning. Unfortunately, the other team's closer was better and got the third and final out with a Junior Cowgirl stranded on second base.

Coach Becky encouraged her players, "You did good today, ladies. We'll get another chance at them toward the end of the season."

"Hey, kid, you were great," Frank told Julie, as he took her shoulders and pulled her into a hug.

What the hell?

Julie couldn't remember the last time her father had hugged her like that. It was like his terrible marriage had sucked him dry of any interest in physical contact. Out of the corner of her eye, she noticed Becky looking over at them with this strange look on her face.

Oh, my God.

She pulled out of the hug, looked intently at her father, and asked, "Dad is there something you want to tell me?" She waited, but he looked up at the sky. "You know, about Coach Becky."

He then looked at Julie and smiled.

"Your dad and the cowgirl!" Suzie shouted, when Julie told them the news.

They all sat in Baron's Ice Cream Parlor and ate ice cream or drank milk shakes.

"Are you, you know, okay with that?" Clark asked.

Julie smiled. She really was okay with it. She hadn't seen a look like that on her father since, well, she couldn't remember ever seeing one. "I'm really glad he's happy, he deserves it." She had told Clark some, but not nearly all, of her family history and certainly not the depth of the awfulness. She didn't want to dwell on it anymore. That was now the past, and she was all for looking toward the future, whatever it might be.

Later, while they all studied for the next day's exams, she took a moment to try to visualize a life with Becky and her father. It would only be a year before she left for college and beyond. But it sure could make a positive difference for how she managed senior year. Then she looked at Clark.

Except for him.

She marveled at how Clark and Sarah could handle the uncertainty in their lives. But she realized that for them there was already a strange, perverse, kind of certainty if it happened every year.

CHAPTER THIRTY

Sarah didn't have an afternoon exam, so she walked home after her morning French exam. Clark sat in the backyard and called her over. She immediately noticed the strange look on his face.

"Are you okay?" she asked.

He smiled, but not a good smile. "Good news and bad news."

"Good first, of course."

"You got a call-back from the Red Rocks audition. Saturday morning, congratulations."

She had hoped for this and was very happy, but . . . "Okay, bad news."

"Dad's coming home Wednesday and wants to talk."

She sank down to sit heavily on the grass.

It's just so God damn unfair!

"Yeah," he agreed, as if he had read her mind.

* * *

Julie could tell immediately that something was wrong with Sarah and Clark. It didn't take any of them very long to figure it out. It had been hanging over all their heads, like the blade of a guillotine, for over a week. She was glad to see that Joey seemed to have figured it out as well because he took Sarah off to talk.

Julie took Clark's hand and led him out to the arbor. The heat of the day had begun to dissipate, but it was still very warm up there. They sat with their backs to the sun in the west and looked out at the flat eastern horizon as it touched the brilliant blue sky. Finally, she had to ask. "Do you know when, where?"

He shook his head. "No, we'll find out Wednesday night at dinner. There's this big stupid production that my father goes through. I hate it. I hate him."

Julie squeezed his hand but didn't argue. She knew that he didn't hate his father, but they didn't seem to have a very close relationship. She put her arm around him and held on.

They sat there for almost an hour before coming down to join the others. They all had their last exam the next morning, but studying wasn't on anyone's mind. Sarah had obviously been crying, and Joey seemed to be on the verge of it.

Julie could feel Clark pulling away, and she didn't know what to do about what was obviously a defense mechanism. And on one level she didn't blame him, but on a personal level, she felt herself becoming angry. "Well, whatever the hell happens, I don't want to ruin what time we have together," she said to the group. "I say we study for an hour and then all go to Pepi's for pizza and whatever." The whatever she referred to was the fact that on a slow night during the week you could get a beer at Pepi's Pizza Parlor with no ID check. Joey and Suzie joined her in a little impromptu pep rally, and gradually Clark and Sarah came around.

Later, Julie and Suzie lay in bed not able to sleep. They were both a little high from the two beers at Pepi's. It had been a very subdued evening.

"I can't imagine how they go through that every year," Suzie said quietly. "They've really lived in a lot of places. Most of them pretty cool places. The only other place I've ever been to was Dallas, and that was so boring."

"You were only six."

"Yeah true, I guess it might be different if I went now. I'd love to see New Orleans, especially at Mardi Gras. Or Los Angeles, Disneyland and the beach. Surfer dudes."

Julie laughed, thankful for her friend and her ability to babble on. She knew that if she felt this bad now, it would have been really awful if she and Clark had actually had sex. She realized that he had anticipated those feelings, and it almost made her want to do it anyway. She fell asleep still wrestling with that decision.

* * *

Exams were over, and there was no study group. There was no school the next day because it was Senior Day. Julie had agreed to help her dad with campaign stuff in the afternoon and evening.

Clark could tell that she would have canceled that if he asked her, but he didn't. He fought against his walls that instinctively wanted to come up. He kept telling himself that this time it was different, that Julie was different. But the pain was the same. No, the pain was worse because the feeling, the connection, was greater, much greater. He found himself thinking of Rita.

If only she were here, she'd know what to do.

He found Sarah sitting by herself in the living room. He joined her and they sat in silence for a long time. Sarah appreciated Clark's attempts at support. They had never felt as close as they had the past week or so. They had their odd pattern of being very close for two or three months during the summer while they moved, and then they went their separate ways during the school year. Their personalities and interests naturally pulled them apart.

At dinner, Coleen realized that she had never seen them act this way. She was concerned enough to try to reach John, but he was traveling to Chicago for a quick meeting before flying home the next afternoon. She wished that she could offer some sympathy to the kids. But she knew that they saw her as part of the problem, even though this time she didn't know any more than they did.

After dinner Clark went up and sat on his arbor until it got dark, very dark on a moonless night. He finally came down when his mother's calls got frantic with worry.

* * *

It was late when Julie got to Suzie's house because the campaign rally for her father had been more successful than expected. Julie had enjoyed the work, and her cheerleader instincts and experience made her a natural campaigner. She had a little time alone with her father between events, and he had made a point to tell her that he wanted them to work to establish some sort of normal family life over the summer and next year. One that would likely include Becky. Julie was fine with that.

The other good thing about the day and evening was that she had been so busy that she hadn't had much time to think of Clark. But now she did, and it threatened to overwhelm her. She felt incredibly torn between the desire to consummate their relationship and the fear of the consequences for both of them. A big part of her believed that the pleasure of the sex would outweigh the pain of the separation. But that was for her, and she wasn't so sure about him. And maybe he did know best, after all he had been through it before.

But women are just stronger than men.

She remembered her mother yelling at her father that he would never really know pain until he pushed a seven-pound baby through his vagina. Julie seldom smiled when she thought about her mother, but she did now because that had been one of Bea's classic strategies, a punch with no possibility of a retort.

What the hell does a guy say to that shit?

She had to admit, however, that her mother had been right about that. Women had to be strong to keep from being run over by men. It was very hard to keep a long-term perspective and not give in to short-term pleasure.

Yet I was ready, and he stopped it.

* * *

Clark had a fitful night with a mishmash of images held together in dreams that reflected the turmoil he felt. The strangest one that he could remember had been where Julie and Suzie and Margaret all sat along the side of a swimming pool and giggled at him as he treaded water out in the middle. Sometimes they had on two-piece bikini bathing suits, and sometimes they had their tops off and their breasts exposed. He was naked and felt his penis rise and fall repeatedly as he saw the girls and then felt the cold water on his naked body. He had tried to swim to them at the edge, but he couldn't reach them. No matter how hard he swam, they had remained the same distance from him.

He looked at the clock and saw that it was after nine and he had slept in, which was good.

If only I could sleep right through it and make it all a dream, a bad dream.

He heard the telephone ring in his parents' room and downstairs. He hoped that it was his dad calling to say that he wasn't coming home. But he heard his mother call, "Clark, you have a phone call, a Coach Wilson." He couldn't believe that he had actually made the Mustangs and now had to move. Reluctantly he got up and headed into his parents' bedroom.

As anticipated, Coach Wilson offered Clark a spot on the team as the third starting pitcher/relief pitcher. Clark had intended to decline and explain, but he instead allowed himself to enjoy the moment and the attention. He thanked the coach and hung up. He turned to see Sarah standing in the doorway in her pajamas, a knowing smile on her face.

"It feels good for a moment doesn't it? I did the same thing with my call-back."

"Yeah, but it also sucks big time." He watched her nod and head back to her bedroom to get dressed. He really wanted to call Julie and tell her, but that only made him feel worse.

At breakfast he tried again to get some information from his mother. Normally she was a vault and wouldn't reveal a thing, which always made him mad that she participated in this farce. But this time he believed her when she said she didn't know anything.

It's strange. I wonder why not.

Time fell into a jar of molasses for the remainder of the day. It didn't help that he had to constantly battle his desire to race over to Julie's. He would never get his old walls up, and he didn't really want to do that anymore. But there was no sense in sticking his head in the fire. He didn't know what kind of relationship they would be able to have during their last days, but he knew he was going to remember this as the worst day of his life. Well, the worst until the actual day of the move, the last time he would see her.

He knew Sarah was around, but she stayed to herself. There was little they could do to help each other now. He was pretty sure that she hadn't had sex with Joey, so they were in much the same boat.

Love sucks!

He then realized that he'd used the L word for the first time. That realization made him want to hold Julie even more.

Finally, late afternoon, the front door opened, and his father waltzed in grinning like he'd won the trifecta at the racetrack. Clark was so upset that he couldn't look at him. He would have been out on his arbor, but it was a brutally hot day.

John took Coleen and they went into their bedroom and stayed there for a while. Sarah listened for sounds of sex, but it was just whispers of conversation. When Coleen came out to finish getting dinner on the table, she had a hard time suppressing a smile. Clark watched her and wanted to sarcastically ask her if she was enjoying this, but he knew better.

It was a typical kind of dinner for The Question - formal and in the dining room. It was only a roasted chicken, but it seemed more like a Thanksgiving spread. They all took their places, and there was no conversation. John asked about school, and Clark had to bite his tongue.

Christ, he doesn't even know that school is over!

It wasn't evident, but Sarah had gotten her dramatic impulses from her father. It seldom surfaced when he was around the family, but it was part of what made him such a good presenter at his business meetings. He didn't remember how it started, but this routine for revealing a new move now seemed like a good old performance-chestnut. Unfortunately, he hadn't realized that what had worked for the kids when they were young didn't work for them as young adults.

"So," John began with a flourish once the dessert, cherry pie and ice cream, was on the table, "What do you guys know about Bar Harbor, Maine?"

Clark and Sarah turned to each other in shock.

What the hell? Maine?

Sarah found her voice first and asked, "What happened to New York?"

"New York? What do you mean?" John responded, seemingly genuinely confused.

"Aren't we moving back to New York? Isn't that what this is all about?" Sarah almost yelled.

"No, we're not moving anywhere. I just got promoted to head of Mountain States. So now we can take a vacation, and I thought we'd go to Maine and then do some college tours around the northeast." He made it sound so natural, normal like it happened all the time. "I know Clark has interest in Harvard and Dartmouth, and I think you'd like Boston University, they have a great theater program."

Clark struggled to understand what was happening, whether it was real. But he was mostly angry, really angry. "Do you think this is a God damn joke?"

Both his parents stiffened. "Clark," his mother started a reprimand.

He overrode her. "I will not apologize for my language, I'm really upset. Do you have any idea how screwed up this is? You play this routine like you always do when we're moving, but . . ." He paused only a moment to control his anger. "Do you have any idea the hell we've been through the past month, waiting for the big Question, and it's a, a damn vacation!"

He jumped up from the table before his father could respond. Sarah was right behind him. They had important people to tell the news.

As he raced out the front door for his scooter, his anger completely fell away, and reality took hold. He thought he would explode with joy.

What a great summer this is going to be!

Acknowledgements

I would like to thank my family for all their support. First there's my Mom, so steadfast and generous, who always encouraged me to read and write. And, of course, I couldn't have done it without Perky, my amazing wife and best friend. And finally my three lovely daughters: Michelle, Carolyn, and Claudia.

I would also like to thank my beta readers, Susan Hughes and Nori Horvitz, who were a great help when I was so uncertain at the beginning. And Kimberly Johnson who did a very professional proofreading edit.

Coming . . .

The *Education of Clark Westfield* is a trilogy about a young man coming of age and maturity in the late 1960s, early 1970s - a time when relationships were up-close and personal, not electronic. *Lovely Rita* is the first book, and I hope you will continue to follow Clark in the next book, *Curse of the Nice Guy*. He spends his junior year of college in London and has a traumatic, formative adventure in Turkey. That book will be out in the summer of 2017. The third book in the trilogy, *Clark's Choice*, is underway with plans to be available in the summer of 2018.

Thank you for reading *Lovely Rita* and supporting independent fiction. If you enjoyed it, please review it and tell your friends because word-of-mouth is critically important for all authors. And I'd love to hear from you at blairfilms@hotmail.com